Into the Shade
First published in 2022 by Mellester Press

ISBN 978-0-473-61576-5 Soft Cover
ISBN 978-0-473-61577-2 Hard Cover
ISBN 978-0-473-61578-9 epub
ISBN 978-0-473-61579-6 Kindle

Published in New Zealand
A catalogue record of this book is available from the
National Library of New Zealand.
Kei te pātengi raraunga o Te Puna Mātauranga
o Aotearoa te whakarārangi o tēnei pukapuka

With heartfelt thanks.
Edited by Walter Matthews
Cover by Mea

http://www.paulwfeenstra.com/
Into the Shade © 2022 Paul W. Feenstra

Published by
Mellester Press

Other Books by

Paul W. Feenstra

Published by Mellester Press

INTO THE
SHADE

by

Paul W. Feenstra

Published by
Mellester Press

ACKNOWLEDGEMENTS

Accurately portraying the past always presents challenges for a writer of historical fiction. My novels wouldn't exist without the in-depth knowledge of subject matter specialists who allow me to repeatedly hound them and field my endless questions. For that privilege, you have my gratitude and thanks.

I would like to acknowledge Father David Gruschow, Saint Joseph's Church, Levin, New Zealand. Pastor Terence Neil Hanson for balance and perspective. Robbie Wallace, California, USA, for his unsurpassed nautical insights. Gordon West, California, USA, for his encyclopaedic knowledge of radio. Commander Michael L. Mercer, USN retired, internationally recognized authority in Naval Mine Warfare. Jim Wallace, California, USA, for his expertise on marine engines. Ex MI6 operative and author Matthew Dunn, *I promise not to tell a soul*. Erik Berzins – Naval Architect, *you walk a thin line*. Natalie Cambrea. Jeff Hathcock for his encouragement and for buying me endless cups of coffee. Scott M. Dickson, where friendship and support surpass sailing virtuosity. To Jane Petersen, whose attention to detail and encouragement keep me honest and on my toes. And finally to Warwick Hill, thank you.

Weltpolitik

'Weltpolitik' (world policy) was a word created by Kaiser Wilhelm II to signify Germany's new approach to foreign policy. In the years spanning 1890–1914 and spearheaded by the Kaiser, Germany adopted aggressive foreign policies that would strengthen its identity, boost industrial expansion, develop a large navy, and transform the country into a global power.

Historians believe the origins of the 'Weltpolitik' concept originated from a Reichstag debate in 1897, where German Foreign Secretary, Bernhard von Bülow, stated –

*"We wish to throw no one **into the shade**, but we demand our own place in the sun."*

INTO THE SHADE

by

Paul W. Feenstra

PROLOGUE

London, England, February 1913

The morning began with promise. Sunlight streamed through patchy clouds and provided some much-needed warmth, but it didn't last. By 9:30 a.m., a cold northerly blasted in. Spawned in the north Atlantic, dark, ominous clouds soon followed and rolled in, and with them, Londoners knew, rain was sure to follow.

Oblivious to the changing weather, statues worthy of remembrance stood resolute and offered some protection from the bone-chilling wind. Few people took advantage of the meagre shelter, as most in this part of Whitehall were needed elsewhere and cared not to loiter and expose themselves to the elements during what would be another dismal day.

One exception was the military officer who casually strolled onto the manicured lawn that blanketed the peaceful park known as Whitehall Garden. Seeking shelter from the biting wind, he paused behind the statue of William Tynedale, looked up at the innocuous building that peeked from above the trees, and then carefully unfolded a grimy scrap of paper. For the umpteenth time, he checked to see if he was at the correct address. *#2 Whitehall Court.* He shrugged, folded the paper and tucked it back in his trousers, and faced the building again, wondering why he had been summoned.

William Tynedale, the Protestant reformer who looked down, remained moderately unhelpful as a windbreak. The lieutenant turned his gaze away from the building and gave the statue a sympathetic glance. He knew the poor fellow had been sentenced to death for heresy in 1596 - an irony lost on many, as William Tynedale was best remembered for translating the Bible into English.

Behind the officer, only a dozen yards away, flowed the Thames, and on his left, a little more distant was Downing Street. Other people passed him by, most of them dressed in military uniforms, and he felt a little self-conscious. He was considerably older than the average youthful-looking lieutenant he encountered, but then again, he had voluntarily joined the military on the advice and urging of his late uncle when in his late twenties and not as a teenager as most tended to do.

The War Office was located on the other side of Whitehall Court, on Horse Guards Avenue, which explained the presence of so many high-ranking officers. Representing all Britain's military branches, they ambled by in ones and twos or small groups, most of them engrossed in conversation. Many ignored him, not sparing him a second glance, while a few cast him disparaging looks. They undoubtedly recognised the red vertical sword formation badge he wore on his upper arm that identified him as belonging to the volunteer infantry regiment known as the Territorials.

The Territorials were a reserve force and weren't expected to fulfil the same role as regular army, nor obliged to serve overseas, hence their name, 'Territorial'. Regular soldiers felt that the Territorials were 'Saturday night soldiers' or 'part-timers' and couldn't tell their arses from their elbows; however, few regular army types knew Lieutenant Kaha Peterson.

He tried to remember if there was a reason, or for any breach of regulations that warranted his summons here. For a fleeting moment, he thought of the captain he encountered behind the officer's mess a month or so ago and felt his stomach twist. There was always the slim possibility the officer may have reported the altercation. No, he decided, the captain would've kept his mouth shut, as doing otherwise would only raise questions and draw attention to the reason why he'd received a good thrashing in the first place. It was unlikely the depraved little man wanted it recorded in his personnel file that he'd been inappropriately meddling with young girls from the village. The captain deserved it, and regardless of rank or social status, Kaha had no qualms about dishing out a little punishment when deserved. He grimaced. In any case, no matter why he'd been told to report here, he just hoped it wouldn't interfere with his plans. In six months, he would marry, and he wasn't going to allow anything to stand in the way of that.

With his hands buried deep in his pockets, Kaha turned his back to the stoic William Tynedale and made his way across the lawn towards the Thames and watched a tug lethargically tow a couple of barges upriver. The water looked uninviting and dirty, and for a fleeting moment, he thought of his home in New Zealand and the land where he was born, where the rivers were unspoiled and still clear and pristine. He missed the country where he grew up and hoped to return home one day, but for now, he would remain living in London, where overall, he was reasonably content and happy.

On his right, a short distance away, he saw Big Ben and could tell he was a few minutes early for his meeting but thought he might as well get it over with. To ease his anxiety, he inhaled deeply, held his breath for a moment, and slowly exhaled. Feeling more relaxed, he squared his shoulders and moved away from the path that paralleled the river, walked back through Whitehall Gardens, around the building onto the footpath of Whitehall Court, and looked for the entrance to number two.

Surprisingly, he was required to show his identification papers numerous times, and on each occasion, he was led by an uncommunicative orderly through a labyrinth of institutionally bland corridors and dreary offices. With military precision, the sound of his boots clacked loudly on the linoleum as he passed dull clerks immersed in hushed conversations. Yet to his astonishment, other than the guards, no one he saw wore a military uniform. Although a very stylish, attractive young woman carrying a heavy leather satchel gave him a long curious look, then clip-clopped away. Kaha wasn't interested, but the orderly was and turned, sparing her a long yearning look.

Eventually, he was led to a nondescript, unmarked office suite when it dawned on him that there weren't any posted signs that identified who these people were and what they did. *This was a peculiar place*, thought.

The young orderly escorting Kaha knocked once on the door and entered the suite, and with a wave of his hand, suggested the lieutenant should follow. Once inside, the orderly shut the door, leaving Kaha alone with an officious woman who openly appraised him from her position of absolute authority behind the dominion of her desk.

"Lieutenant Peterson, please have a seat. The director will be with you shortly."

He shouldn't have been surprised she knew who he was, after all, he had an appointment, but all the same, he found her astuteness a little unsettling. He smiled at her as he removed his peaked dress service cap, nervously took a seat on a chair against the far wall and waited.

"What is this place?" he asked the secretary after a minute or two of awkward silence.

She looked up from her work, smiled at him and said nothing.

"Looks like it might rain."

Again, she looked at him and smiled politely. Kaha decided the secretary wasn't delightful company and resigned himself to waiting in silence and wondering what was in store for him.

A minute or two later, the interior office door opened, and a harried middle-aged man quickly walked out clutching a sheath of papers and didn't spare Kaha a second glance.

On cue, the secretary rose and walked to the open doorway, said a few words to whoever was inside the office, then turned back to look at him. "This way, Lieutenant," she said, giving him the same smile he'd already seen twice before.

Kaha rose, self-consciously straightened his tunic, tucked his service cap under his arm and walked towards the open doorway as the secretary stood aside. He could smell her perfume.

"Lieutenant Peterson to see you, sir."

Kaha heard the reply. "Thank you, Marge."

The first thing Kaha noticed when he stepped into the room was the beautiful mahogany desk and then the man who presided over it. With a solid *thunk*, the door was closed firmly behind him.

"Impressive, isn't it?" said the man as he rose from his chair, extending a welcoming hand. "This desk belonged to Admiral Nelson."

"Lieutenant Peterson, sir," said Kaha, shaking the man's hand. "Yes, it's, uh, beautiful."

Naturally observant, Kaha glanced around the room at ornaments, some gadgets and other personal mementoes. Glancing again at the desk, he decided the man was probably a naval officer. On the wall behind, a large framed photograph of King George V stared benignly down at him.

"Sit," instructed the man with practised command, confirming Kaha's belief that he was indeed of senior rank, although he still hadn't introduced himself.

As ordered, Kaha sat and waited. The man returned to his seat, twisted slightly, causing his chair to squeak, and then folded one of his legs over the other. He repositioned the monocle he wore and looked at the lieutenant with bemusement.

Kaha kept his expression neutral and, in return, studied the man who sat behind the desk, wondering what it was about him that was so perplexing.

After a moment or two of silence, the man spoke. "I assume you wonder why you were ordered here today."

"It has crossed my mind." Kaha didn't address the man with a respectful, sir. If the man didn't identify himself, then he saw no reason to.

The man twisted in his chair, again causing it to squeak, and reached behind to a credenza, from where he picked up a newspaper. Kaha saw it was *The Weekly News*. The man tossed the paper onto his desk in front of Kaha.

"They're offering a ten pound reward for information leading to the capture of any German spy."

In response, Kaha inclined his head. He'd seen the notice of reward offer in the paper. It was a substantial amount of money.

"The threat is genuine, and we find ourselves in a rather perilous situation, considering we are having an arms race with Germany. Ten pounds is a healthy incentive, is it not? Doesn't that, uh, tempt you to find a mole?"

"Money isn't the motivating factor for me. If I found a spy or a mole, I would turn him into the authorities regardless, no matter if the reward was one hundred pounds, ten pounds or nothing," replied Kaha earnestly.

The man nodded. "Yes, money isn't a problem for you, is it? I believe you have more than enough to see you live comfortably without want for many lifetimes."

Kaha tensed. Not many knew of his recent inheritance. He'd taken steps to ensure the details of his fortune were not made public, and solicitors were paid unreasonable fees to keep his finances private. Obviously, they'd failed, and he'd have another quiet word with them. He decided not to respond to the comment.

The man laughed. "Please don't be offended, it's our job to thoroughly vet and know all about those who work for us."

"Work for you? Perhaps you've mistaken me for someone else," stated Kaha, doing his best to control himself.

Sensing Kaha's growing agitation, the man held up a hand to appease him. "Let's talk about your work, shall we? You're an instructor and train people in a variety of skills, unarmed combat, firearms, explosives, covert surveillance, navigation - shall I go on, lieutenant?"

Kaha's anger dissipated to puzzlement. His work was designated top-secret, and few people knew of what he did. But neither was he easily intimidated. He responded tersely: "I'm not allowed to comment on the nature of my work. Perhaps you could explain to me who you are, what you are after and why I am here?"

Ignoring the abruptness of his guest, the man smiled and continued. "For the last two years, lieutenant, you've been seconded from the 1st London Division, Territorials, and been working for me, or rather, for the Secret Service Bureau."

"The Secret Service... I'd heard rumours, but..."

"I hope they were less than rumours, or we haven't been doing our job well, have we?" The man gave Kaha another friendly grin. "I am Captain Mansfield Smith–Cumming, presently the Director of the Secret Service Bureau. Although there is currently a restructuring going on, and we'll soon be known as the Directorate of Military Intelligence, Section 6."

"Well, that answers many questions I had," replied Kaha, shaking his head in surprise. "But why am I here, sir?"

"Ah, yes." Smith-Cumming unfolded his legs and leaned forward across the desk. "We are somewhat concerned about the build-up of Germany's military, just as they are curious about ours." The director stabbed his finger on top of the newspaper and the German mole article. "We've taken some steps to ensure we know what those buggers are up to. And you've been a huge help in training most of the people who are now doing this for us. However, the present state of tension in Europe has forced our hand a little. We need to dig somewhat deeper and increase our clandestine presence in those, uh ... areas, and continue to keep a watchful eye on the Hun and her allies." Appropriately, Mr Smith-Cumming repositioned his monocle.

"I see, and where do I fit into this?" asked Kaha. "Increase the level of training, quicken the process?"

Director Smith-Cumming raised his head. "Marge!" Moments later, his secretary opened the door and gave her boss a questioning look.

"Show her in," ordered Smith-Cumming.

Almost at once, the secretary reappeared, leading a woman into the room. Kaha recognised her immediately and stood quickly, his chair scraping loudly on the wooden
floor.

"Pam, what are you doing here?" He was stunned.

The woman, equally surprised, looked with uncertainty from him to the Director.

"Be a good girl and fetch that chair for Miss Tulley, Marge." The director turned his attention back to his two guests. He was enjoying the moment, and it showed. "I see the two of you know each other," he added dryly.

"Miss Tulley is my fiancée," stated Kaha defensively as Marge slid a chair over for Pam.

"I apologise for dragging you away from your work, Miss Tulley."

Kaha returned to his seat after Pam sat down. She still looked shocked and turned from Kaha to look at the director.

Smith-Cumming looked closely at the couple and studied their reactions. The man before him may have been of Mediterranean descent, but a closer inspection would reveal his skin was a little darker in colour, his lips fuller, and his nose a little rounder. His hair was black, and a slight premature greying at his temples added a distinguished look. He was tall at six foot–one–inch and had a deep, muscular chest and broad shoulders that suggested power and strength. But he wasn't Italian, Spanish or Greek; Kaha Peterson was a Māori, a race of indigenous people native to *Aotearoa*, or as Europeans called the country, New Zealand. Kaha's mother was Māori, and his father was English. Pam, was also a New Zealander, or as they preferred to be called, *Kiwi*'s, but both her parents were immigrants of European descent.

"It's quite alright, sir. I'm not that busy at the moment, but why is Kaha here? Have we done something wrong?"

"You work for the Secret Service Bureau, Pam? You never said anything to me. You told me you worked at the Post Office," interrupted Kaha.

Pam was unsure how to respond.

"Miss Tulley does not work for me, lieutenant. As she truthfully told you, she works at the Post Office, but for Military Intelligence, Section 8, which is based there. As you might know, her unique talent as a linguist and skills as a wireless operator has made her incredibly useful." The director paused briefly, then continued. "But no, Miss Tulley, you've done nothing wrong. However, recently the Germans have begun using other secure forms of communication such as wireless telegraph and telephone, and we've seen a downturn from the more traditional forms of communication they've used in the past."

"I'm sorry, Kaha. I didn't lie to you, I just never told you the entire truth. I was never allowed to talk to you about the work I did," Pam reached for his hand across the small gap that separated them.

This is turning into quite a day, thought Kaha. He wasn't angry at Pam; he was precluded from sharing details of his work with her, so he understood. It just came as a surprise. He looked into her eyes and smiled reassuringly, then took her proffered hand and squeezed it gently.

"Good, now that is over with," stated Smith–Cumming, "I'd like to explain why I've brought you both over here."

Both Lieutenant Kaha Peterson and Miss Pamela Tulley looked at him expectantly.

"We are very interested in the activities of the Imperial German Government," began the director. "As I told you earlier, lieutenant, the Germans have been increasing the size of their military, especially their navy, and we want to know the extent of this expansion and how it is impacting other areas such as resources, new technology and ultimately mobilisation – should we be concerned? We need eyes-on, reliable human intelligence, or what we call 'humint', through highly skilled covert operatives, or agents, that can remain undetected." The director stopped to take a sip of water from a glass before he continued. "We've had our eye on both of you for some time."

Kaha and Pam exchanged another look.

"We have decided that together, you have all the required skills to work as a highly specialised team. Miss Tulley is fluent in English, French, Italian and German and is capable and very experienced with wireless telegraphy, while you, Lieutenant, have other skills, different but equally important that complement each other. You are resourceful and expert in surveillance, close-quarter combat with or without weapons, and your seafaring skills are unquestioned. You are both New Zealanders, and although our countries share close ties, neither of you would be an obvious choice as an operative for British military intelligence. Thus, you can function without attracting undue attention or arousing suspicion."

Kaha was shaking his head. "How exactly do you expect this idea to work?"

"Miss Tulley put in a request for an extended leave of absence for her honeymoon. We support that," Smith-Cumming offered his best fatherly smile, "and would like to see you both marry and go on your honeymoon as planned."

"We're going on a honeymoon on a seventy-three-foot sailboat to Sardinia, sir, not prowling railway stations looking for German moles," interrupted Kaha testily.

"Quite, lieutenant," nodded the director. "In fact, we would prefer you continue your honeymoon indefinitely and sail to various ports around the Mediterranean and Italy as a wealthy couple enjoying life's pleasures, and then report directly to us at the directorate through coded wireless messages or alternately, dead-letter mailboxes. The only other change would be the announcement of your inheritance; this must become public knowledge to justify your travelling and torpid lifestyle. Of course, you will be reimbursed for your expenses," offered Mansfield Smith-Cumming with another smile.

"We aren't equipped or trained to be operatives, sir," stated

Pam.

Director Smith-Cumming looked to Kaha for his opinion.

"I have to agree with, Pam, er, Miss Tulley, sir. I mean, we don't know what to look for or even recognise what is considered useful information," added Kaha.

"We intend to begin an intensive training regimen immediately. You'll learn to identify relevant intelligence; essentially, you'll be trained to know exactly what to look for. We'll teach you about tradecraft, codes and hone your respective skills in surveillance and wireless communications. More importantly, and as part of your role, you'll recruit foreign nationals and acquire skills to extract reliable information from them."

"As a married couple?" stated Kaha.

"Yes, that's what we had in mind. Obviously, you're not going to spend all your time sunning yourselves and drinking gin," added the director with a laugh. "An important part of your work will be in cultivating relationships and recruitment. You will manipulate people and extract information we need from them. Naturally, you will do this under cover of your real identities and some background we'll create for you. Does that bother either of you?" he looked from one to the other in question.

Kaha turned to Pam and exchanged a look. "I'm not sure, we need to discuss..."

Mansfield Smith-Cumming inclined his head.

Kaha realised the director required a definitive and immediate answer. He cleared his throat. "No, sir. It doesn't bother me, but Pam–"

"–Miss Tulley?" asked the director interrupting Kaha's protestation.

Pam turned back to Kaha, then looked to the director and shook her head and swallowed, "I, uh. No, sir," she stated.

"And we will do all this from *Mana*, our boat?" Kaha asked.

Smith-Cumming nodded in affirmation. "We would need to add a few refinements to it, of course."

"Refinements?"

"Yes, a small weapons cache and a powerful experimental radio transmitter-receiver will be hidden aboard the yacht. It wouldn't look good to have such equipment in full public view, now, would it?"

"Will we be in danger?" asked Pam. "If we are to carry weapons...."

"Ultimately, your function will be to observe, listen and report. If you are identified as being foreign military intelligence operatives—"

"Spies!" interrupted Kaha. "We'll be spies, will we not?"

The director looked at Kaha, then at Pam. "Indeed, if compromised, you will likely be classified as unregistered agents or spies. Yes, there is always a serious element of endangerment, but your identity as a wealthy, newly married New Zealand couple will hold up under the closest scrutiny because, uh, it's true. The weapons are purely for defensive purposes."

Lieutenant Peterson sat back on his chair and scratched his head.

Mansfield Smith-Cumming looked from Pam to Kaha, and they saw the corners of his mouth twitch in a suggestion of a smile.

All heads turned to the door as Marge knocked once and entered. "Excuse me, sir, your eleven o'clock in Whitehall," reminded the secretary.

CHAPTER ONE

Saturday evening, June 27th, 1914, Sarajevo.

A barking dog signalled the presence of a stranger, an intrusion into the mundane domestic life and territory of a bored animal. Seconds later, another joined in and was quickly followed by a third. Had the stranger been of a mind to curse, he would have. Instead, he glanced anxiously over his shoulder, awkwardly repositioned the dirty canvas bag he carried and quickened his step. Anyone closely watching may have observed the man also clutched a relic, a small wooden cross, stained and scarred with age.

Doors remained closed, and curious children were ushered away from windows lest they see something they shouldn't. It was best this way, the least anyone knew, the better and safer it was for everyone.

The dogs eventually lost interest and ceased their incessant baying, but not before alerting others of the approaching man. From the obscurity of a nondescript and neglected two-storied suburban house, two pairs of eyes scanned the darkened street and searched for a threat or a sign of something amiss. With relief, the lookouts recognised the form of the approaching man and then looked further and beyond, praying he wasn't followed.

The man paused in the middle of the street, gently lowered the heavy bag to the ground and began rummaging in his pockets. After a moment, he extracted a small tin, nimbly flicked open the lid, pulled out a pre-rolled cigarette and placed it in the side of his mouth and lit it. The sputtering flame illuminated his face and confirmed to the two watchers that the man was Father Stevan Belić, the man they expected. The lit match was a signal and verified to the watchers that all was well. If his appearance in the neighbourhood concerned its residents, they didn't show it. Curtains remain closed, and no one questioned his presence.

From a window on the upper story of number fourteen, an answering match was struck and then quickly extinguished. Father Stevan didn't acknowledge the prearranged return signal indicating it was safe to proceed; instead, he picked up the heavy bag, hoisted it to his other shoulder and quickly turned toward the dilapidated gate of number fourteen.

He slowed and casually glanced down at the brick gate post. It was difficult to see, even by the generous light from the moon, but it was there – another precaution. He saw a simple horizontal chalk line, barely discernible but in stark contrast to the aged, red brick. He quietly exhaled with relief – it was another prearranged signal, an indication it was safe to proceed.

The old and recently oiled gate swung noiselessly open as the priest nudged his way through. Ahead, an overgrown path wound through an untended garden and ended in the approximate vicinity of a high concrete step and a heavy wooden door. Still aided by moonlight from a cloudless sky, Belić navigated along the winding path, and as he approached the two-storied house, the door opened. He dropped his cigarette, ground it into the dirt, and looked behind one last time before stepping inside.

The house interior was musty and smelled of mould and tobacco. Not even the warm weather of a Sarajevo summer could altogether remove the dampness of a harsh and cold winter. Wordlessly, the man who opened the door trudged up the stairs, and Father Stevan followed closely behind, his bag clunking against the wall announcing his expected and much-anticipated arrival.

Light spilt from an open door at the top of the stairs and revealed a wall lined with yellowed wallpaper that may once have been floral. In places, darker patches hinted at a long-forgotten water leak. No one presently inside the house cared; according to the authorities, this place was abandoned and ideally suited the needs of the secretive nationalistic Black Hand organisation who used number fourteen as a place of refuge – it was a safehouse.

As the priest creaked up the stairs, he could hear subdued and muffled voices coming from the room above. The man leading the way stepped to the side, and with a respectful nod, allowed the priest to enter the large room before he went back downstairs to resume his watchful position at the door.

All conversation subsided. Eight men of varying ages were in the smoke-filled room, most of them familiar to Father Stevan, but the three young Bosnians sitting together on a threadbare sofa were all strangers. He'd never seen them before, but he knew each of their names and was acutely familiar with their backgrounds and circumstances.

He recognised the emaciated young man seated on the sofa's left as Nedeljko Cabrinović, a graphic worker from the outskirts of Sarajevo and the product of an abusive family. In the middle sat the violent Trifko Grabez, ironically the son of a Serbian Orthodox priest. On the right, was the son of a postman, nineteen-year-old Gavrilo Princip, a printer. The three young men eyed the priest warily and offered no greeting.

Large black cloth curtains were nailed to the window frames and prevented light from leaking outside, which could alert the authorities the abandoned house was being used for nefarious purposes. The only armchair in the room was occupied by the oldest man in the group, Major Vojislav Tankosić, by day an officer in the Serbian army, and by night a leader of the secret Black Hand organisation. He dropped his cigarette into a chipped cup that sat on the dirty wooden floor beside his chair, eased himself upright and greeted the priest with a warm smile. "Hello, Father."

Father Belić acknowledged the major and quickly glanced around the room towards the other faces, men he knew and trusted, and nodded to each in turn before pocketing the talisman he carried and unslung the canvas bag from his shoulder. Everyone in the room watched as the bag dropped to the floor with a metallic clunk.

Immediately Danilo Ilić rose from the rickety kitchen chair he sat upon and walked towards the bag; one eye was partially closed from irritant smoke that wafted from the ever-present cigarette that dangled from the side of his mouth. He undid the bag's clasps and enthusiastically began pulling out its contents one by one, arranging them neatly on the floor beside where he kneeled.

"We expected you earlier. We were worried, Father," casually offered the major without looking at him. He was watching Danilo as he began to inspect the assortment of goods from the bag.

"The dutiful work of a priest doesn't end when the sun goes down."

"Was it the bishop? Was he asking questions again?" The major lifted his head in concern and turned to look at Belić.

The priest shook his head. "No, worse ... a father brought his son to me and asked me to explain to the boy why he shouldn't use his fists to solve a problem."

Trifko Grabez, one of the young radicalised Bosnians on the sofa, snickered.

"And?" questioned the Major with a raised eyebrow.

All the men in the room turned their attention to the priest and waited for his response. The irony of his duplicitous role wasn't lost on anyone.

Belić dug a hand into the folds of his cassock and pulled out his tobacco tin. With a flick of his finger, he opened the lid, pulled out another pre-rolled cigarette and placed it in his mouth. The Major graciously lit a match, and Belić lowered his head briefly, dragged heavily, and blew a stream of smoke upwards.

"Perhaps if you all came to Mass more frequently, you would know what I told the boy," admonished Father Stevan with a lightness of tone.

The Major smiled and flicked his eyes towards Muhamed Mehmedbasic, who sat on the floor with his knees drawn to his chin.

Seeing the major glance at the only Moslem in the room, Belić quipped with a smile, "You too could learn something from a good Christian sermon, Muhamed."

In silent response, Muhamed lifted his head from his knees and looked at the priest with interest.

"Oh, and what would you have told the boy?" continued the priest.

Muhamed's eyes sparkled in amusement and bored into the priest's. "Allah commands justice, the doing of good, and liberality to kith and kin, and He forbids all shameful deeds and injustice and rebellion. He instructs you that ye may receive admonition," said Muhamed, quoting from Islamic scripture without pause.

Father Stevan laughed. "Perhaps I should have the father and the boy come to see you?"

"I've heard your endless sermons as you preached to my brothers here. You do quite well without me," answered Muhamed with a laugh of his own.

Gavrilo Princip scoffed from the sofa. "And what of us, and will you preach to me too? We are here to do a job, not listen to religious babble from a priest."

The major opened his mouth to reprimand the youth, but the priest placed a restraining hand on his arm. He turned to the nineteen-year-old with a measure of pity and appraised him. He knew the three newest recruits of the Black Hand were all terminally ill with tuberculosis and were bitter - their radicalisation had them primed. He paused a moment to collect his thoughts, as what he would say to the young man was an essential cornerstone of his core beliefs, both as a priest and an activist. "Committing a moral sin to achieve a righteous and just end *is* acceptable. Even at the expense of trust." Before the young man could respond, the priest continued. "Are you here only to satisfy your thirst for violence, or is there a greater cause worthy of your life?"

Princip took the bait, stood defiantly with chest thrust out and began to recite propaganda. "I am a Yugoslav nationalist, aiming for the unification of all Yugoslavs; I do not care in which form of state, but it must be free from Austria." He glared at the priest with a sneer as he completed his rehearsed ideology. "And who are you? Are you here to preach righteousness and gospel or do what is best for our people and help unify our country?"

The young conspirator Trifko Grabez, seated on the sofa, leaned forward in tacit support of his young Black Hand brother. Nedeljko Cabrinović just stared blankly and didn't appear to have been listening.

Danilo paused and looked up at the priest, as did everyone else in the room. Gavrilo Princip obstinately remained standing, challenging with youthful insolence. The room was deathly quiet.

The arrogant young man surprised the priest with his retort. Father Stevan considered his words carefully, as only this morning he'd asked himself the very same question. He nodded.

"I am foremost a warrior, a soldier, and I proclaim to you and everyone else here that Austria is our first and greatest enemy." The priest slowly swivelled his head, speaking to everyone, not just Princip. "Just as the Turks once attacked us from the south, so Austria attacks us today from the north. I preach the necessity of fighting Austria and keeping Serbia free from Austrian imperial oppression, and I preach the sacred truth of our national position." The priest turned his attention back to Gavrilo Princip and met his challenging glare with his own. "For the sake of bread and land, for the sake of the fundamental essentials of culture and trade. Yes, my brothers, the freeing of the conquered territories and their union with Serbia is necessary to gentlemen, tradesmen, peasants, and even you, young man." Belić paused a moment to drag on his cigarette before continuing, "And to religious men alike. Those who rule should avail themselves of the laws and institutions of our country. And yes, our masters and wealthy owners must be mindful of their duty, too." He took two steps towards Princip and placed a reassuring hand on his shoulder. "Rest easy, my friend, we are all here for the same purpose."

Against the far wall sat Cvetcko Popović. "Well said, Father, spoken like a true man of God." He clapped his hands in appreciation as Princip returned to his seat, scowling. Even Muhamed was smiling because anyone familiar with Father Stevan Belić knew a little of his murky past and experience, but his commitment and sacrifice to their cause were without question.

The major turned to Danilo, who had the bag unloaded. "Is everything there?"

Danilo nodded, spilling cigarette ash in the process.

"Pass out the weapons as we discussed," ordered the major.

All attention again turned to Danilo and the armament laid out before him.

Father Stevan sat on the chair vacated by Danilo. He wouldn't be receiving any weapons;

he'd completed his role, and his work was done. But he still listened attentively as the major and Danilo went over the plan, again and again, leaving no room for misunderstanding and errors. It wasn't that he would involve himself in tomorrow's attack; he'd made secretive arrangements and planned to be far away by the time the Austrians were licking their wounds inflicted by his Black Hand brothers.

The three newest recruits, Nedeljko Cabrinović, Trifko Grabez and Gavrilo Princip, had no previous experience in the use of firearms and bombs. In the preceding weeks, and under the patient tutelage of Major Vojislav Tankosić, were taught how to toss grenades and to use the Browning FN, model 1910, automatic .380 calibre pistol they would each be given. The three young men would join Danilo Ilić and his cell of three additional insurgents, bringing their attacking force to seven.

Each man received a Browning pistol, a hand grenade, some cash, and contact information of local sympathisers who could aid with their escape. In the unlikely event they were captured, the major decided each man would also carry a phial of potassium cyanide. Death would be quick and painless, they were each assured.

The heightened tension in the room, so prevalent earlier, dissipated into a sombre mood of self-reflection and a little anxiety as each conspirator considered their part, much like an actor in a play.

Deciding it was time to leave, as he still had a long night ahead of him, Father Stevan Belić rose from his chair, took a single step and paused. Major Tankosić was discussing the mechanism of the Browning pistol with Nedeljko Cabrinović and looked up. Muhamed and Vasco Cubrilović were quietly reviewing their escape route. They stopped their chatter and also turned to the priest. The others, silent and brooding, shifted their attention to the figure standing uncomfortably in the centre of the room.

With all the attention focused on him, Father Stevan looked down at the cross he was fidgeting with and compulsively flipped it over in his hands while he collected his thoughts. He raised his head and took a big breath. "We must offer forgiveness to those who will be sacrificed, but their sins will be absolved before God, as will ours. The people of this great nation are also God's children, and so we act in the name of God." The priest turned to Muhamed, who listened attentively. "Let us rejoice in the dignity and freedom we bestow on our people, our families – and let God forgive us for our sins." He opened his mouth to say more but decided against it. "Amen," he whispered.

"Amen," a few randomly responded.

"*Allah Akbar*, God is great," replied Muhamed.

Father Belić knew he'd probably never see his fellow conspirators again, and with a heavy heart, he crossed himself, nodded to the group and, without another word, quietly left the room.

CHAPTER TWO

Railway Station, Sunday, June 28th, 1914, Sarajevo.

The distant sound of a chugging locomotive caused Sarajevo's Governor, General Oskar Potiorek, to reach into his pocket and flick open the cover on his watch. It was almost nine-thirty, and the train was perfectly on time - he expected nothing less. He flipped the lid closed, placed the watch back in his pocket and looked towards the source of the sound.

A trickle of sweat ran down the back of his neck and he silently cursed the dress uniform protocol demanded he wore, but at least the weather obliged for the occasion. Sarajevo turned out a splendid day, although a bit warmer than he preferred. Around him other dignitaries, alerted by the sound of the approaching train, stopped their idle chatter and shuffled their feet nervously. Children honoured to partake in the official welcome were shepherded to the appropriate place on the platform and waited anxiously, if not too noisily for some disdainful luminaries. General Potiorek looked over his shoulder and gave a final glance towards the automobiles that waited to transport their honoured guests. Everything was at it should be.

Smoke belched from the gleaming locomotive as it slowed to a rumbling crawl. The train hadn't travelled far, only a few miles from the outlying municipality of Ilidza, a resort town famous for its spas and thermal hot springs. The general hoped the locomotive's driver stopped the train at the required place on the platform and not fifty metres from where they all gathered.

With a screech and a cloud of steam, the locomotive's driver applied the brakes and the train with its luxury carriages ground to a halt exactly where it should. Somewhat relieved, General Potiorek dabbed at his face and neck with a handkerchief, then straightened his tunic and took a step forward.

Curious onlookers kept at a respectable safe distance shuffled a step closer in anticipation, and the leader of the Black Hand, Major Tankosić, who'd situated himself at a suitable place to observe, was unceremoniously jostled forward. He had no desire to be recognised or draw attention to himself, so he carefully threaded his way back to the rear of the crowd where he could blend in and leave quickly if the need arose.

An attendant, dressed in his finest livery rushed up and opened the carriage door with a flourish and the fifty-one-year-old heir to the Austro-Hungarian empire, Crown Prince Archduke Franz Ferdinand of Austria, appeared in the doorway with his wife, Sophie, the Duchess of Hohenberg. The prince gave his nervous wife a reassuring look of support and encouragement, affirming all would be well.

Not everyone had been ecstatic about the marriage of the royal couple, in particular the Austrian emperor, Franz Joseph, who was not satisfied with the pedigree of Sophie's royal lineage. Finally conceding to the marriage request, the emperor allowed the smitten couple to marry, but only on the condition that their children would not have succession rights to the throne. In addition, Sophie would not share her husband's rank, title or privileges, and was not permitted to appear in public, ride in the royal carriage or sit in the royal box with him.

For this official visit, a special concession was granted because the prince was here as a military leader and not fulfilling his imperial duties as Crown Prince, and so Sophie was graciously permitted to be at her husband's side. She wanted to create a good impression, not only for the emperor and her husband, but for the throngs of people who came to cheer and wave. Understandably, she was anxious.

Around the time Prince Ferdinand and the Duchess of Hohenberg were arriving in Sarajevo, Kaha and Pam were sunning themselves on the deck of *Mana,* anchored in a beautiful bay in Corfu. Green translucent waters lapped against the hull, and bush-covered hills rose around them, providing a truly romantic and beautiful setting.

Pam rolled over and looked over the rim of her sunglasses at her husband. "I feel guilty doing this, the government is paying us to do a job, and here we are sunbathing on the deck of a sailboat in Corfu. It doesn't seem right."

Kaha closed the book he was reading, looked over at her, and grinned. "Would you rather be in dismal grey London?"

She laughed. "You know what I mean."

"Regardless of our assignment, we need to appear to be affluent travellers without a care in the world. People expect to see us doing this, and so we should."

With her finger, Pam absentmindedly traced along the woodgrain patterns of the teak deck. "I'm unsettled, Kaha, something doesn't feel right."

He sat up, and his expression turned serious. "What do you feel? Is it me, our marriage?"

"No, silly." She sat up and scooted beside him and leaned her head on his shoulder. "I think it's our job, it's like...."

"Like?" he echoed.

"It's like we aren't taking this role seriously, that something is going to happen, something horrid."

Kaha exhaled loudly and wrapped an arm around his new bride. "We should never take this job for granted, we will always be at risk, especially in another country, but we should also learn to adapt and not let it interfere with our relationship."

She pushed herself away so she could look at his face. "Then you feel it too?"

He leaned forward, kissed her, pulled away, and cupped her face with both hands and kissed her again. "Do you know what I feel?"

She shook her head.

Kaha eased himself to his feet. "I feel like a swim." Without another word, he dove over the safety lines and into the pristine warm waters of Paleokastritsa.

The prince stepped from the doorway and onto the platform amid a smattering of friendly applause, placed his cavalry helmet securely on his head and proudly waited for Sophie to alight the carriage before turning with a smile to greet the welcoming party.

The Duchess of Hohenberg looked positively regal in a long white silk dress, tied at the waist by a red sash and complimented by a white wide-brimmed hat and veil. An ermine stole completed her ensemble and all the women, and even some men in attendance, appreciated her sense of style and grace.

People cheered at the sight of the beautiful duchess when she alighted from the train. Of course, the crown prince chose his wardrobe carefully too, and to befit the occasion, decided to wear the uniform of a Cavalry General. He wore a blue tunic with three silver stars attached to a high gold collar and black trousers with a red stripe down the leg. With flair, green peacock feathers adorned his helmet. The prince and the duchess were a striking couple and their love for each other was well known and documented.

After much handshaking and bowing, the prince beamed delightedly when children handed Sophie a beautiful bouquet of red roses, they were his favourite, and under the watchful eye and protection of an assigned personal bodyguard, Lieutenant Colonel Count Franz von Harrach, the royal couple was escorted to the waiting motor vehicles.

The Prince and Duchess were designated to travel in the prized 1910 Graef & Stift Type Double Phaeton open tourer automobile, owned by Count von Harrach, who, as you'd expect, rode with them, and of course, was accompanied by the governor, General Potiorek.

With a tight schedule to maintain, the motorcade departed the railway station and headed towards the military barracks, where the crown prince was scheduled to inspect the troops before heading to the town hall to deliver a speech. The first motorcar contained three police officers and the chief of special security. Sarajevo's mayor and the Chief of Police rode in the second vehicle, while the beautiful forest green coloured Graef & Stift tourer conveying the honoured royal guests was third. Three other official automobiles followed closely behind.

"See, all is well, m'dear. You look positively radiant and the people love you – as they should," remarked the prince once the procession was underway.

She returned his thoughtful words with a loving smile and by giving his hand a squeeze.

At about the same time as the motorcade departed the railway station, Father Stevan Belić was walking quickly down towards the docks in the coastal town of Ragusa[1] on the Adriatic Sea. After

1   Ragusa – Modern day Dubrovnik.

hurriedly leaving the safehouse the previous evening, the priest returned to the rectory of his church, changed into civilian clothes and with a single suitcase, walked quickly to the railway station. Careful to ensure he encountered no familiar faces, he purchased a single trip ticket to the historic town of Ragusa, about two-hundred-and forty-kilometres south-west of Sarajevo.

He spent an uncomfortable night aboard the train. A combination of nerves, anxiety and the jittery ride over the narrow-gauge railway tracks kept him from sleeping. Other than the conductor, who gave him a curious second glance, the journey was uneventful and he encountered no one he knew. He spoke only sparingly in polite greeting to the odd stranger who met his apprehensive gaze.

Now, in Ragusa, his main objective was to find the familiar fishing boat that waited for him. Belić wore a black peaked cap pulled down over his eyes and kept his face tilted down. The last thing he wanted was to be recognised and have to explain his presence and disguise to a curious parishioner or acquaintance. In his left hand, he carried his suitcase and in his right, he clutched the old wooden cross. He appeared casual and relaxed and kept his eyes focused on the docks just ahead.

Only a couple of boats were tied to the pier as the bulk of the *Falkuša*[2] fishing fleet departed some days earlier, and only boats that were unable to put to sea remained behind. Feigning a problem with his rigging, the skipper of the *Kralj Mora*, Boris Marković, who was an old and trusted family friend, waited for the priest to arrive.

In the letter Father Stevan Belić received in response from his

---

2   Falkusa – Typical Croatian fishing boat.

friend, Boris clearly stated that he was to wait near the fishmarket and under no circumstances approach the boat. Given the most unusual situation of his hurried departure, Boris was concerned a stranger might observe Belić boarding his vessel. Tongue wagging was a national pastime that fishwives practised with zeal, and, as instructed, Father Stevan Obediently waited.

Typical of a seaside town, the market was busy, and the man with the black cap and suitcase attracted no unwanted attention. Belić browsed the various stalls and spoke kindly to merchants and fishmongers as he perused their wares and loitered. It came as some surprise when he felt someone tug his sleeve. He looked down to discover a familiar face staring up at him.

"Zoran? Is it truly you? Oh, how you've grown since I saw you last," smiled Belić to the upturned face.

The boy looked at him with a serious expression. "Welcome, Father Stevan. Papa asked that I bring you to the *Kralj Mora*. Please follow me," Boris's son instructed with stiff formality.

Belić affectionately patted Zoran's shoulder. "Very well, lead the way."

A loud cry disturbed the peacefulness of the market and all heads turned curiously towards two young men who began loudly arguing. This was the planned distraction that young Zoran had been waiting for. He set off, pushing past gawkers and headed towards the docks with Belić following close behind.

Just as Boris anticipated, everyone kept their attention focused on the disturbance and Belić and the boy were largely ignored as they made their way towards the fishing boat. On board the nine-metre-long *Falkuša* type fishing boat, *Kralj Mora,* Boris Marković watched his son and old friend run down the wharf. Led by Zoran, Father Stevan stepped aboard and was quickly hidden away from prying eyes.

At 10.00 a.m., Crown Prince Ferdinand and Sophie left the military barracks by motorcade and travelled along Appel Quay, which ran parallel to the Miljacka River, towards Sarajevo's town hall. With their route publicised ahead of time, admirers and well-wishers excitedly lined the streets to catch a glimpse of the royal couple as they drove past.

Major Tankosić and Danilo Ilić strategically placed their small force of six insurgents at various positions along the Appel Quay route and confirmed that the crown prince and his wife would be travelling inside the third motor vehicle in the procession.

Standing in front of the Mostar Café garden, Muhamed Mehmedbasić was first to see the cavalcade as it slowly approached. Armed with a grenade and a Browning pistol, Muhamed was perfectly positioned; however, at the last second, a policeman appeared, Muhamed lost his nerve, and the motorcade safely passed him by. Vasco Čubrilović, who was standing near Muhamed, also failed to act and missed his opportunity.

Further down the quay, Nedeljko Cabrinović, the first of the three new young Bosnian recruits, anxiously waited. With weapons ready, he positioned himself on the other side of the street, adjacent to the river and watched the cavalcade draw nearer. A thousand thoughts raced through his mind and, for a fleeting moment, considered turning and walking quietly away. But his musings turned to shame. He was not a coward, he was courageous, principled, and by his actions and those of his Black Hand brothers, Nedeljko believed he alone could weaken Austria's hold over his country. His nation - his people - they needed him. It was his moment to shine in glory and become a celebrated hero, a revolutionary worthy of recognition and remembrance, and with renewed commitment, he prepared. As the Graef & Stift motorcar with the prince and duchess inside, approached, he tapped the small hand-held bomb against the wall to arm it.

Nedeljko Cabrinović was well-schooled and successfully radicalised, and the Black Hand had selected and trained their recruits with skilful zeal. While the spectators focused their attention on the approaching royal couple, no one saw the fused bomb in the hand of the young terrorist. Without a thought to the victims, the damage it would cause, or of the consequences, Nedeljko tossed the small hand-held bomb. Riveted, he watched with heightened senses as the grenade arced directly towards the target.

Prince Ferdinand immediately saw the incoming missile and, in reflex, raised an arm to ward it off. The grenade glanced off his outstretched arm, hit the folded down top of the tourer, bounced behind and rolled beneath the oncoming, fourth vehicle in the motorcade where it detonated. Even though it was a small explosive device, the blast was enormous, and hundreds of metal fragments scythed up through the vehicle's underside, instantly disabling it. Continuing outwards, the shrapnel indiscriminately hurtled into twenty royal watchers, who only moments ago were cheering in excitement.

Severely injured, the driver of the fourth motorcar slumped over the steering wheel, while his passenger, Governor Potiorek's aid, Eric von Merrizz, was also severely wounded. As a result of the violent blast, Sophie suffered a small cut to her cheek, while the blood-splattered prince was fortunately unharmed.

Prince Ferdinand was bewildered and shocked; the thought that he and Sophie had come so close to death had just dawned on him, that it was a miracle they both survived. In growing anger, he dabbed at Sophie's cheek with his handkerchief and then looked behind at the carnage created by the powerful explosion.

"I'm unhurt, Franz, but those people ... many are injured," stated Sophie trying to sound strong. She put on a brave face and hid her fear, but she was frightened.

The prince tried to remain calm and control his temper. "They'll be taken care of, but we can't stay... we must get away to safety."

The first three cars drove away at high speed, leaving the damaged vehicle behind, and headed directly to the town hall. Sophie took the handkerchief and, as best she could, wiped blood from her husband's face. In the front, beside the driver, the governor, still in shock, was also unharmed, as was the bodyguard riding on the vehicle's running board.

The assassination attempt on the lives of the Crown Prince and his wife was a total failure, and Nedeljko knew it. He'd let his brothers in the Black Hand down, and it was improbable another opportunity would present itself. The shame was too much to bear.

Immediately he reached into his pocket for the cyanide phial, swallowed its lethal contents, and in growing panic, leapt over the handrail into the Miljacka River, only to land in a place where the water was thirty centimetres deep. The cyanide failed to act, and splashing in the shallow water did little more than further dampen his spirits. Not only was his mission a failure, but he was unable even to kill himself. Spectators followed him into the river and quickly set upon and beaten. Nedeljko Cabrinović was arrested and taken into custody when the police arrived soon after.

Other members of the Black Hand who waited along Appel Quay

heard the explosion and, unsure of the outcome, were surprised to see three official motorcars, including the Graef & Stift carrying the royal couple, speed down the quay towards the town hall. The vehicles were traveling too fast for them to launch a second attack and subsequently all lost their nerve.

Gavrilo Princip left his assigned position and sought shelter inside Moritz Schiller's Café and Delicatessen, on Franz Joseph Strasse until things calmed down and he could slip safely away.

The stiffening breeze came from the north and propelled the nine-metre fishing boat beyond the protection of land. The *Kralj Mora* responded accordingly and heeled over; her distinctive lateen rigging hummed as the water hissed by.

"I forgot how fast these boats are!" yelled Belić, his broad smile an indication of the pleasure he felt at being at sea again.

Once clear from port, Boris allowed him to leave the cramped storage space at the stern and sit at the rail. Boris stood aft, legs splayed on the canted deck with one hand on the tiller. With skill, he expertly navigated them from port, safely manoeuvred around other vessels and could now relax a little as the expanse of open sea lay before them. His head moved constantly, looking for danger and changing conditions with the experience inherited from generations of fishermen before him.

Designed to sail long distances to catch prized sardines, the *Falkuša* was well equipped to handle rough weather in the open ocean. Made from tough cypress wood grown on the volcanic Croatian island of Svetac, the *Falkuša* could reach an astonishing speed of 12 knots. One of the most innovative features of this durable boat was its removable sides. Sections of the sides could easily be raised and removed which allowed fishermen to haul their nets aboard without having to lift heavy loads over a high gunwale. It was a very useful and convenient feature.

Without the weight of 8 tonnes of cargo, and with 121 square meters of sail hoisted, the *Kralj Mora,* under Boris's remarkable sailing skill, was now approaching her top speed. Boris estimated that if the wind held, they would make landfall during late afternoon the following day.

"You too could have fished, Stevan," Boris stated.

The priest looked up at his oldest friend and grinned. This was a conversation they'd had many a time. He didn't reply; words weren't needed, Boris knew what he would say.

"Will they come for you?" This time Boris spared a second to look down and meet Stevan's gaze.

Belić gave the matter some thought before he replied. "I expect they will."

Boris lifted his head and looked ahead. He could predict the wind shifts with almost uncanny ability. With precise adjustments on the tiller, he lifted the bow into increasing pressure. When the wind eased, he slightly altered and lowered his course, always keeping the boat sailing as fast as possible.

"I don't know, is too early to tell." Stevan's reflective words were lost to the wind.

"What?"

"We'll know soon enough!" Stevan yelled.

Boris nodded and looked thoughtful. "Where will you go once you're in Italy, do you know yet?"

Stevan reached for the gunwale for support and stood up carefully. He took a step closer to his friend. "I can't tell you where I'm going. If you don't know, then you can't tell anyone."

Boris turned to look at the crew who were sorting through nets on the slanted deck, young

Zoran amongst them. "We thought that when you became a priest, you would end your rebellious ways. Look at you now, on the run from something." Boris shook his head and laughed. He knew the authorities had been searching for his boyhood friend for years and failed. "And they won't find you this time, will they?"

Stevan turned away from his friend and stared over the bow. "I do wonder."

Sarajevo's mayor, Fehim Curcić, was extremely anxious and stood at the steps of the town hall and awkwardly delivered his welcoming speech to a visibly stressed and upset Prince Ferdinand and his wife Sophie. Others assembled dignitaries and guests felt the mayor's unease when the prince angrily stepped up to him.

"Mr. Mayor, I came here on a visit and I am greeted with bombs. It is outrageous!"

Seeing her husband in such a state, Sophie pulled him gently aside before his anger made him say something he would later regret. She leaned closer to him. "Franz," she whispered, "We are fortunate, others were not. We must have compassion for the injured and do what we can; the people need you to be strong at this time."

After a few moments, the prince responded to her comforting, supportive words and noticeably calmed down. He met her gaze and nodded, then took a step away from the mayor and allowed him to complete his official welcome.

After the speeches, it was decided that the prince and duchess would abandon their planned schedule, and instead visit those injured by the bomb blast at nearby Sarajevo Hospital. The duty of informing the drivers and personnel of a change in plans was normally the responsibility of the governor's aid, Eric von Merrizzi. However, he'd been in the bombed vehicle and was now receiving medical care in the hospital and unable to fulfil that task. Thus, the drivers of the motorcade were not informed of the change in schedule and the new destination.

With much apprehension, the prince's motorcade departed the town hall at 10:45 a.m. and headed back along Appel Quay, which was also the route to Sarajevo Hospital. However, the drivers intended to turn right from Appel Quay onto Franz Joseph Strasse, which would take them to the National Museum as originally scheduled. They were unaware that the young Bosnian radical, Gavrilo Princip of the Black Hand was waiting at the café near the corner of Appel Quay and Franz Joseph Strasse.

Lieutenant Colonel Count Franz von Harrach, the prince's bodyguard, was standing on the running board of the Graef & Stift automobile and fully expected another assassination attempt. He dutifully kept a watchful eye for anyone who roused his suspicion as the motorcade travelled down Appel Quay. Much to his and General Potiorek's astonishment and outrage, the vehicle made an unexpected, sharp right-hand turn to Franz Joseph Strasse.

"Where are you going?" the general immediately shouted to the driver.

"To the museum, as planned, sir," came the reply.

Franz Ferdinand and Sophie exchanged looks of bewilderment, and she reached for his hand. "Franz?" she questioned.

The prince leaned closer to his wife. "All is well, m'dear, just a little confusion, I expect."

Surprised by the unexpected turn, Count von Harrach was momentarily distracted and failed to identify the threatening figure of Gavrilo Princip, who was equally astounded to see the motorcade slow to a stop outside the café where he stood. Princip couldn't believe his good fortune and decided he wouldn't allow another opportunity to slip by.

The Black Hand believed the Austro-Hungarian Empire would invade Serbia, and by killing the Crown Prince and the Duchess, the world would know that Serbia wouldn't just sit passively back and allow it to happen. They were making an important statement to Austria and the world. The people of Bosnia and Herzegovina suffered under the Empire's rule, and it wouldn't continue. Princip had no doubts about the enormity of his task. He'd rehearsed the event for weeks, and the thought of running away was incomprehensible. The targets were only a step or two away, and now the onus to complete the mission was his. It was his duty and a responsibility he took seriously. Like the others, the Black Hand had trained him well.

"No, no! Turn around, we are going to Sarajevo Hospital, go back along Appel Quay," insisted the governor, waving his arm in frustration.

The driver stopped the heavy motorcar and set about reversing the vehicle through a complicated assortment of levers that changed pulleys. It took time, and Gavrilo Princip seized the moment. Within seconds he stepped forward, simultaneously pulling his Browning automatic pistol from his pocket and aimed at the two occupants sitting in the rear seat, whom he hated with a passion.

Princip only had one thought in mind. Obsessed with executing his mission, he fired. The .380 calibre bullet ripped through the door and struck Sophie in the abdomen. Again, the pistol bucked in his hand - the second bullet hit Prince Ferdinand in the neck.

"For heaven's sake! What happened to you?" cried Sophie, ignoring her injury when she saw a stream of blood erupt from her husband's mouth.

Lieutenant Colonel von Harrach on the running board watched

in horror as Sophie, now mortally injured, collapsed across her husband. Both he and General Potiorek incorrectly assumed she'd fainted.

Prince Ferdinand was the only one aware his beloved wife had been shot. "Sophie, Sophie, don't die, stay alive for our children," he managed to utter. His cavalry helmet tumbled from his head when his head lolled forward, and he slumped over his dead wife.

Von Harrach leapt over the door and immediately went to the assistance of the prince. He lifted his head upright, hoping to stem the flow of blood. "Is Your Imperial Highness suffering very badly?"

"It is nothing," said the Archduke weakly, "it is nothing."

Urged by the general to take them to his official residence, the driver managed to speed away. The heir to the Austro-Hungarian empire, Crown Prince Archduke Franz Ferdinand of Austria, died a short time later.

Realising the enormity of what he had just done, Gavrilo Princip raised the Browning pistol to his head only to have it struck from his grasp. He reached for the cyanide, and that too was swiped away. The stunned spectators reacted in anger and attacked the defenceless assassin and knocked him to the ground and repeatedly punched and kicked. As with his co-conspirator, the arrival of police saved him from certain death.

CHAPTER THREE

The door to the conference room was thrust open, and Mansfield Smith Cumming strode in, followed closely by his secretary, Marge, who placed some files on the desk and then took a seat near the door against the wall. Those in attendance looked up with a feeling of expectancy. It was late, and they should all have been home with their families.

The director of the Secret Service Bureau looked harrowed and weary; it had been a long day and most likely be a long night. With a heavy sigh, he sat down on his chair and re-arranged the placement of the files as he formulated his thoughts. The room was silent other than the sound of Michael Sykes sucking on his pipe.

"The assassination of Prince Ferdinand has caused a bit of a ruckus upstairs." The director paused and slowly looked at the small group assembled around the table.

"Why?" came a voice, "Who cares, a lowly Austrian prince is killed, why should it bother us?"

The director nodded. "Because there are some who feel that we have a commitment to protect France." He raised a hand to forestall any further interruptions. "As you are all aware, France and Russia are bound by treaties to protect Serbia. The Foreign Secretary has made it quite clear that he believes that Germany's Kaiser will support the Austro-Hungarians and our Prime Minister is, er, somewhat reluctant to act. However, other Liberals within the party are threatening to quit if we do not assist France–"

"–and that means our Liberal party cannot govern alone, a coalition government?" Michael Sykes asked.

"Exactly," replied Smith-Cumming. "It becomes political, and I'm pleased to see you've been paying attention."

"But, sir, we cannot go to war just because the French are crying for help, or because we feel like it," Sykes added.

"And that is what I said to the Foreign Secretary, Michael. What we are unaware of is the fact that England signed a treaty, called… uh," he began opening files on the table until Marge rose from her seat and pointed out the one he needed. "Thank you, dear. Ah, yes, the 1839 Treaty of London. It means that England is obliged to come to the aid of Belgium if they're invaded, and this gives our Government a legitimate reason to enter into any hostilities – and protect France as well."

People began talking at once. This news was dramatic, and they all were astute enough to realise that Britain could go to war.

"The Royal Navy is the largest in the world, sir, and I can't see much of an issue locally," Captain Leech, the navy's liaison officer, proudly stated.

"Yes, agreed, but don't forget our army is small, and we need useable intelligence and lots of it. The Adriatic is of some concern, and the admiralty has recommended that the Royal Navy, in conjunction with the French, set up a blockade to prevent the Austrians and Germans from escaping the Adriatic and running rampant in the Mediterranean."

Captain Leech nodded in support of the navy's plan.

"Then we are going to war?" asked Peter Bething

"I expect we shall," said the director with a sorrowful shake of his head.

"This creates a rather sticky situation," interrupted Allan Reed, before anyone could react to the directors statement. "How can we gather intelligence in the Adriatic when the navy has blocked all access? If they do that, then we can't just go steaming up there without creating a fuss. They'll sink our ships, unless..." Reed paused and began toying with a lock of hair.

Mansfield Smith-Cumming looked on. "Yes, Allan, you were about to say."

He released his hair and leaned forward. "Sir, I suggest that we send Anchor and Chain into the Adriatic before the blockade is in place, let them be our eyes and ears, I believe they're fully equipped."

The director turned to Peter Bething, their technical wizard.

"I don't see a problem, sir. They've got all they need, and everything is working perfectly."

"That new radio isn't causing problems?" asked the director.

Bething shook his head. "It's working a dream, and we've been receiving regular reports from them without issue."

Director Mansfield Smith-Cumming leaned back in his chair and rubbed his chin.

Kaha leaned back against a pillow, and with a shoeless foot, made a slight correction on the wheel of the Mana to bring her back on course. They'd departed Corfu the previous day and were now en route to Venice. Almost twenty-four hours ago they'd received a brief message from London alerting them of a change of plan and were instructed to sail directly to Venice *with best speed*, and to standby for further instructions. Later that evening, they received another radio message outlining their new directive, which informed them that they were to pay particular attention to naval activity in the Adriatic, specifically the Austro-Hungarian and the German navies. Further, their instructions detailed they should exercise particular caution with their radio transmissions and strictly adhere to safety protocols. Radio Detection Finding ships with the ability to detect radio broadcasts were seen near Italy's coast, which represented considerable danger to them. These small ships could triangulate and determine the location of a transmission by taking multiple readings from different places to isolate the location of the broadcast.

Pam appeared on deck carrying a tray of sandwiches. "Are you still thinking about those messages from London?"

Kaha removed his foot from the wheel, sat up, and looked around. A few small boats plied their way here or there, no one was anywhere near them, and he didn't see any commercial vessels or warships. "I think this has to do with the shooting in Sarajevo. We know tensions are high, and in response, I believe London wants us north in the Adriatic to be their eyes and ears."

"Will England become involved?" Pam asked while handing him a sandwich.

"Good question," he shook his head and took a bite. Automatically his eyes drifted up towards the big mainsail and checked the trim. Satisfied, he turned back to Pam. "I really don't know, Sarajevo is a long way away from England... but it's the other countries who become involved that could force England's hand."

She took a bite of her sandwich. "And these RDF trawlers?"

Kaha laughed. "I'm not worried. Even if London is correct and they are out here, we move soon as we broadcast, and they can't get a bearing on us. We're fine." He reached over and grabbed another sandwich.

Pam looked thoughtful. We need to re-charge the batteries before tonight, the radio uses a lot of power, and I think we should keep them topped up and not let them drain."

Kaha nodded in agreement. "I'll do that after lunch." Again, and as any competent sailor, he scanned the horizon and made sure he knew where other boats were located.

The wind was light, and they were sailing at a moderate eight knots. *Mara* loved these conditions, and even if the wind stiffened, she could still sail quickly and smoothly. Kaha stood, and automatically checked the sail trim again. "Take the wheel, I'll go below and start the engine."

Pam slid over as Kaha disappeared below. Within moments she heard their diesel engine cranking over, but it didn't fire. She heard him curse, and again he tried with no luck. The Bolinder-Munktell diesel engine wouldn't start. Pam grimaced; this wasn't a good time to experience a problem.

Again, she heard the engine turn over, then finally it coughed, spluttered, almost died, then spluttered again and with a cloud of black smoke, caught and began running irregularly.

Kaha reappeared, wiping his hands on a rag. "I think we have a problem."

Father Stevan Belić sat amidships, just behind the mast, where he could sit quietly and still let the crew of six go about their duties without being in the way. Ahead he could faintly see the brown smudge of the Italian coastline, and if the wind held, they would make landfall in the fishing township of Pescara within a few hours.

"Here, I brought you a coffee," said Boris Marković, handing the priest a steaming mug. "Were you praying?"

Father Stevan took the proffered mug and nodded.

"And who or what were you praying for? That our catch would be bountiful, and we would return safely home with barrels full of fish to happy and uncomplaining wives?" Boris grinned, his white teeth stark in contrast to his full, pitch-black beard.

"I prayed that our sins would be forgiven ... that the horrific acts of violence committed against the Austro-Hungarian empire will be seen for what they really are," replied Father Stevan. "That our people would be free from the oppressors, from the tyranny of Austro- Hungarian rule."

Boris sat down on a barrel beside the priest. "Oh, in the eyes of God, murder and killing can be forgiven?"

"Yes, absolutely."

Boris looked at his friend with sadness and raised his eyebrows in unspoken question.

"You want me to quote you scripture? Is that what you want?"

"I think you need to justify to yourself the actions you have taken before you can turn to God for forgiveness," replied the fisherman.

Father Stevan sighed, looked away and stared out across the wave tops. "You should have come with me, Boris. You would have made a fine priest."

"And deny myself all the pleasures of life?" Boris laughed. "I am better off as a fisherman. This way, I can administer sound advice to people in need and at the same time live life to the fullest. While you live your pious life, wallow in guilt and torment yourself by trying to justify your conflicting beliefs. Not to mention, staying out of gaol."

"What we did, what I have done, it was the right thing to do, Boris. I know this within my heart."

"Then leave the rationalisations for your time of judgment and concentrate on staying alive." Boris paused for a moment as he sipped his coffee. "They will come for you, and this time, they will find you; you know this, don't you?"

"I do."

Boris placed a hand on his friend's shoulder. "I know you are in a hurry to get ashore, but I have decided that we will not go to Pescara until just before sunset. Once it is fully dark, and only then, will it be possible for you to leave the safety of this boat."

Father Stevan knew it was pointless to argue. "Very well."

Night fell over the Italian town of Pescara, and Boris Marković executed their arrival perfectly. Not only had the wind died down, but they slowly sailed behind the seawall and into Porto di Pescara d'Inverno as the sun, in a fiery orange ball, signalled the end of another day and slowly dipped beneath the shimmering horizon.

Crew members immediately secured the *Kralj Mora* to the dock and waited for the appearance of Antonio Conti. He was not only the *Capitaneria di Porto* but the *Funzionario Doganale* as well. With impeccable timing, the Harbour Master, who was also the Customs official, strode down the dock and was greeted by Boris with a slap on the back and a broad smile.

Boris knew Antonio only too well, and so as custom required, he discreetly slipped a few lire into the pocket of the official's jacket. No questions were asked which would prompt the *Kralj Mora*'s skipper to alter the truth significantly, although a brief lapse in memory caused Boris to amend the total number of crewmen aboard his fine vessel by one. *Capitaneria di Porto* Conti was more concerned with other important details, such as arriving home on time for dinner and felt there was no reason to board and search the *Kralj Mora*. Thus satisfied with the execution of his official duties, he quickly hurried away.

The crewmen were released to spend an evening ashore while Zoran, with the glow of a lamp, was in his favourite place near the bow studying.

"I've left some money for you," said Father Stevan as he stood on deck with his suitcase.

"I don't want your money; take it back," replied Boris gruffly with a shake of his head.

"Then use it for Zoran, buy him some books and get him a good education."

"He's getting that now."

Both men remained silent. Their verbal sparring only delayed the inevitable. Each knew they might not see each other again, and neither wanted to discuss it.

Finally, Boris stepped forward, wrapped his arms around his friend and hugged him close. Still, neither spoke. Words weren't needed; they each knew how the other felt, and with a final squeeze and a pat on the back, Boris released the priest. Stevan stepped to the dock, raised a hand in farewell and strode off. He buried his hand in his pocket, grabbed the old cross and clutched it tightly as he walked away in the darkness. Boris Marković stood on deck, lost to his thoughts, long after the priest disappeared.

Only twenty metres away, tied to one of the guest slips of the marina, sat the seventy-three-foot yawl, *Mana*. In the stern of the sleek yacht, a couple sat enjoying the evening and the waning breeze. The sound of their laughter drifted across the water, an unkind reminder of the lifestyle the affluent enjoyed.

Kaha and Pam Peterson arrived in Pescara the previous day to perform some necessary unscheduled repairs on *Mana*'s motor, and while in port, re-provision. After a busy day cleaning the boat, they were now on the deck, relaxing and enjoying each other's company.

Kaha saw the fishing boat, *Kralj Mora,* enter the inner harbour and immediately pointed it out to Pam. Sailing into an enclosed harbour with light and fickle winds was always challenging, and he admired the skill of her skipper as the fishing boat came about, doused her massive expanse of sail and drifted to the dock with nary a bump.

It was unusual to see this type of boat on the Italian side of the Adriatic, and Kaha was naturally curious to the reason. They both watched as the fishing boat was met by *Capitaneria di Porto* Conti, who typically seemed to be in a rush to leave. His official duties took less than two minutes, and he departed very quickly.

It was Pam who spotted the shadowy figure carrying a suitcase leaving the boat shortly afterwards. They made a mental note to watch the fishing boat the following day and then retired below for an early night.

Thirty minutes after stepping ashore, a workman wearing a black cap arrived at Pescara Railway Station carrying a battered suitcase. He walked to the ticket window and, speaking fluent Italian, purchased a single one-way ticket to Naples from the surly clerk. He placed the ticket in his pocket, found an empty bench, well away from the nearest gas lamp and wearily took a seat. With his back to the light, to keep his face in shadow, he sat quietly and rested while waiting for his train to arrive.

A conversation beside him made him open his eyes and sit a little straighter. He shifted slightly, hoping to learn more and clearly heard every word. The two men standing near the bench where the priest sat were talking about the assassination. Belić felt his heart rate increase; the Black Hand had succeeded; Prince Ferdinand and his wife were dead.

One man spoke of his outrage at the senseless murders committed by the terrorists and went on to say that most of the Black Hand gang were now caught and in custody. The other man, obviously older and with a healthy memory, expressed no love for the Austro-Hungarian Empire and recounted to his friend with some passion how the Austrian *bastardi* invaded Italy some years earlier.

"Let the *cazzo* suffer!" The old man spat to emphasise his point.

Father Stevan saw flecks of spittle land on his boots and determined the elderly Italian was referring to the grieving emperor, Franz Joseph.

The conductor announced that passengers could now board, and the two men walked away. Belić fully expected the next day's newspapers would report the assassination details, and he would soon learn what happened. He sat for a moment longer and looked down reflectively at the old cross he compulsively fidgeted with. With a sigh, he closed his eyes and mouthed a silent prayer before crossing himself. He rose, picked up his suitcase and walked towards the nearest carriage. To assure that he wasn't observed, he casually glanced around before stepping aboard.

The rail journey to the busy city of Naples from the coastal town of Pescara involves a complex series of transfers and covers a distance of more than two-hundred-and-fifty kilometres. But Father Stevan Belić's plans didn't include completing the entire journey, and he hoped anyone pursuing him would lose his trail.

Most passengers aboard the train removed their coats, stowed their possessions and settled in, but Belić kept his jacket on. His case lay at his feet, and his workman's cap was still pulled low over his face. In a few minutes, the train would make its first stop in Chieti, only fourteen kilometres inland from Pescara.

The warning shriek of the whistle alerted passengers and crew that the train was making its first scheduled stop. One or two passengers rose and began making their way to the carriage door while Belić feigned sleep. Once the train pulled into the station and departing passengers stepped off, Belić unobtrusively eased from his seat near the door and was the last person to leave the train. He attracted no curious glances, and no one appeared to have noticed his departure.

The conductor blew his whistle, and in a thick cloud of smoke and steam, the last train of the day departed Chieti. In preparation for closing the station for the day, a lone caretaker conscientiously swept the platform and emptied rubbish tins. While the caretaker seemed focused on his job and uninterested in his surroundings, Belić took no chances and avoided the man. He walked around the corner, then ducked inside the station and entered the public urinal.

Father Stevan Belić planned meticulously. He had weeks to think, revise and adapt. He knew that when they came searching for him, they would discover he'd abandoned the traditional garb of a Catholic priest and instead chose to wear the clothes of an ordinary workman - a labourer, and that's who they'd be looking for. Resorting to looking like a priest again would be the last thing they might expect. In Italy, Roman Catholic priests were more or less invisible, or so he hoped.

Belić quickly changed clothes in the privacy of a stall and donned the traditional black cassock he was usually accustomed to wearing. He pulled one last item from his case, smoothed the wrinkles, and with care placed the *cappello romano*, the wide-brimmed round hat worn by priests, on his head. At once, he felt a sense of calm descend upon him. Feeling more confident, Father Stevan Belić walked out into the night, clutching his case in his left hand and the worn old cross in his right.

CHAPTER FOUR

Deep in the bowels of the building that housed the *Imperial and Royal Ministry of War*, on Wien's famed *Ringstrasse*, or Ring Road as it was frequently known, lay another small but overworked department known as the *Evidenzbureau*. This was Austria's military intelligence organisation. The Direktor of the *Evidenzbureau*, Oskar von Czvetassin, was not partial to getting his hands dirty with routine investigations, and with the skill and enthusiasm of a seasoned bureaucrat, he delegated with zeal. *Herr* Czvetassin used his administrative skills adroitly to keep his superiors at the Imperial and Royal Foreign Ministry updated and pacified while others did the actual work. The recipient of the *Evidenzbureaus'* most important high-profile assignments always went to Major Maximillian Richter, a highly competent and most resourceful investigator who'd been urgently tasked with investigating the assassinations of the royal couple.

Major Richter stood in the centre of the cramped and overcrowded *Evidenzbureau* operations centre and distractedly rubbed his chin as he stared at a collection of photographs pinned to a cork board. "Where is this man?" The major pointed to a photo.

"*Herr* Major, that man, Muhamed Mehmedbasić, has presently slipped our grasp," answered a subordinate.

The Major raised his eyebrows, "And where do you think he has gone? He can't be far away." He reached for a file on Mehmedbasić, one of many that lay on a desk and quickly scanned its contents.

"Local Bosnian Police believe he is seeking shelter with

sympathisers, sir."

"Yes, perhaps ... but not in Bosnia."

This time it was the subordinate's turn to look surprised.

"No one has seen him since June twenty-eighth. If he was still hanging around, then word would have spread, and we would know. I believe he's gone elsewhere." The major continued to read the file on the wayward insurgent while his subordinates kept respectfully silent until he'd finished.

Richter threw the file back on the desk and took a step closer to study a map on the wall. "If I were he, then this is where I would go." The Major thrust a manicured finger at the map.

All heads craned to look where the Major indicated.

"Montenegro?"

"Yes, he has a history there. I want you to go down and work with the local *gendarmes.* Find him; I want him in custody."

"Yes, sir. I will go immediately, *Herr* Major."

The Major turned again to look at the photographs and study another face. "Who is this man

and why hasn't he been arrested?"

Ignored until now, *Oberleutenant* Hans Koell quickly stood and handed another file to Major

Richter. "This is Father Stevan Belić, sir."

"Is he the man who stored, hid and delivered the weapons?"

"According to the statement made by Gavrilo Princip, he claims Belić is a Catholic priest, and we have confirmed, he did, in fact, obtain, store and deliver the weapons the previous evening to the Black Hand at their safehouse," informed the *Oberleutenant.*

"And where is he now because I happen to know he's not locked up in a cell in Sarajevo?"

The *Oberleutenant* stood a little straighter. "That is correct, *Herr* Major. We thoroughly interrogated the parish priest where

Belić worked, and he confirms that Belić disappeared on the evening of Saturday twenty-seventh and has not been seen since. We think he is in hiding close by and have instructed local police to visit every church– "

"You won't find him in a church," interrupted the Major testily. "Do you believe that a man who has the foresight to make good his escape before the assassination will hide in a local church?"

"It seemed logical to explore all possibilities, *Herr* Major."

"He's flown the coop!" Major Richter had a gift, an intuitive talent for solving complex problems, and he found it easy to second-guess fugitives' whereabouts. On the other hand, social interaction was much more challenging, and both colleagues and superiors frequently found him to be emotionless and highly abrasive.

His gut feeling on Father Stevan Belić told him the man had meticulously planned his escape. Why else would he have fled before the assassination? The priest was astute enough to know the killers would be caught regardless of whether they succeeded in their objective or not, and so he prepared well in advance. The Major gave the matter a few moments of considered thought and turned to the *Oberleutnant*. "Take him with you," he pointed to *Stabswachtmeister* Deiter Wollf, a hulking brute of a man seated near where the *Oberleutnant* stood, "and go to Sarajevo and find this priest."

"Very well, sir. And what about searching the churches?"

Richter looked at the officer coldly. "Let the local police continue with that task."

"He may have gone north, sir," volunteered *Oberleutnant* Koell. "If he has fled, the logical route would be to go to Belgrade, and from there, he can take the Orient Express to anywhere in Europe."

"Or Asia," replied Richter, "and if he has, someone at the

railway station will have seen him."

Oberleutenant Koell gave *Stabswachtmeister* Wollf a quick look and faced his superior. "With your permission, we shall leave now, sir."

The major nodded; he was already focusing on another matter. "I want to interrogate Vojislav Tankosić and Danilo Ilić, have them ready for when I arrive in Sarajevo.

"As you wish, *Herr* Major."

The evenings were warm, and Father Stevan Belić experienced no trouble finding a comfortable place to sleep. He walked from Chieti, in a north-westerly direction, towards the large township of L'Aquila that lay just under one-hundred kilometres away. Flickering lights dotted the landscape as he passed small farms along the winding country road. Occasionally a dog barked, but otherwise, he encountered no one. Eventually, he found what he sought, a large detached barn not far from the road that was separated from the farmhouse. Exhausted and anxious, he crept inside and was soon in a troubled sleep.

When planning his escape, Belić knew this part of the journey was the most crucial and physically demanding. Once he stepped unobserved from the train at Chieti, the goal was to vanish into the Italian countryside. He'd left no clues to his destination or whereabouts, and anyone astute enough to pick up his trail in Sarajevo would lose it in Ragusa. If the authorities were blessed by good fortune and picked up his scent again in Pescara, they would discover he'd disappeared on a train bound for Naples and devote their resources to looking there.

The next hundred or so kilometres to L'Aquila was a considerable distance, and he would have to travel along remote country roads and rely mainly on the generosity of locals to complete his journey. Once he arrived in L'Aquila, he would catch another train to Rome and quickly vanish into its populace and labyrinth of narrow streets.

After a restless night, he woke to feel a little stiff and then spent a few minutes in solitude with a morning offering. On completion of his ritual, Father Stevan sat quietly and ate a meagre breakfast from the food he brought with him. Highlighted by morning sunlight that streamed through cracks in the barn wall, he watched dust motes contemplatively as they drifted randomly past. He sought answers and resolution to a growing unease. Uninspired by any divine guidance, his thoughts turned to the day ahead.

He took advantage of a nearby stream that meandered past the barn and cleaned himself in the cool water. Feeling a little better, he repacked his belongings, grabbed his old, battered suitcase and crept away, back onto the road to continue his solitary journey. The suitcase was proving to be awkward and heavy, and he constantly switched hands, taking frequent rests to ease aching shoulders. The sound of an approaching *carello*[3] offered some hope. Father Stevan stepped to the side of the narrow road as a mule and wagon slowly clattered around a bend. The driver delicately guided the mule past, then with a quiet word and a gentle yank on the reins, the wagon creaked to a stop. Taking advantage of the unscheduled break, the mule hung its head and immediately began foraging for grass in the centre of the road.

"Is a lovely morning to be out, Father, but why are you torturing yourself like this?" asked the driver with a wry smile. "I hope you are near your destination because if you are not, this day will be a long one for you."

Father Stevan smiled at the enigmatic farmer. "If I were

3   Carello – Cart or wagon.

anywhere near my destination, then I would not be as happy to see you," he quickly replied with a grin.

The old farmer lifted his cap and scratched his head, "Please, you are most welcome to travel with me, Father. Together we will make this day shorter."

Belić hoisted his case over the side and scrambled up to sit beside the driver. With a few gentle words and much coaxing from the old man, the mule eventually saw sense, and they rumbled off and headed up and over the hill. They talked sparingly, the farmer content to leave the priest to his own thoughts and musings. They stopped once or twice to allow the mule water and so they could tend to their own needs and then ate lunch beneath a shady tree atop a hill. Row upon row of neatly planted Olive trees thrived on the lower slopes that overlooked golden wheat fields in the flat land below. Father Stevan watched the breeze ripple through the fields while repetitiously rotating the old cross, end for end, in his hands. He sensed the farmer watching and turned to look at him.

"You are troubled. Is your worry for yourself or others?" asked the wizened old man.

Belić contemplated before replying with a rhetorical question. "When does the road end?"

"And when is a religious man not a philosopher? And you haven't disappointed me." Age lines around his eyes deepened as the old man laughed. "So, you worry for yourself." It wasn't a question.

"I think I worry too much and fear the lines between right and wrong are often very murky."

The farmer nodded in sympathy. "Does your perspective change when standing on the other side of the road, from a different viewpoint?"

Belić gave the question a moment of thought before he replied. "It does."

"And of a drunk when he stumbles home, which side of the road does he walk?" asked the farmer.

"A drunk uses the entire road and cares not for which side he is on."

"Then you should use the entire road and avoid taking a side," the farmer offered as he creaked to his feet. "That way, you will see both sides, and just like the drunk, have no problems." His smile faded. "Perhaps the answer you seek cannot be sought ..."

The priest opened his mouth to reply.

"... because the question should never be asked," the farmer quickly added with a wink.

Father Stevan watched the old man with newfound respect. He was well educated and profound, and his sense of reasoning was more than he'd ever expected from a simple Italian farmer.

"You are not just a farmer, are you?"

"And you are more than a priest, are you not?" asked the old man, his eyes twinkled in mischievous delight.

Neither answered the other's question. Deep in thought, the priest packed away his things and returned to the wagon. Soon they headed off again, and after a short time, they began climbing another hill. The road wound its way through small valleys, then up, constantly climbing higher. The mule had no difficulty pulling them up the gentle grades, and soon they crested another summit, revealing a distant cluster of buildings nestled snugly against the hillside.

"In the village is a place you can get a room. I suspect you'll want to clean up a little." offered the old man.

"Yes, I do, thank you."

"The big house on the eastern side of the village, the one with olive trees in front, ask for *Signora* Milani." The mule came to a stop. "I go this way," the old man pointed to a small track that disappeared through olive trees.

"You have been most kind," said Belić once he retrieved his case.

"Think nothing of it, it is my duty to stir the moral conscience of a man in need, especially wearing the garb of a priest."

"But I am a priest," Father Stevan defended himself.

The old man raised his eyes in question, smiled warmly and gave the reins a flick. Needing no further encouragement, the mule took the strain of the wagon and plodded off, leaving a somewhat bewildered and dishevelled man holding an old suitcase on the side of the road.

"I was thanking you for the ride!" shouted the priest after the wagon.

In response, the old man lifted his hat but didn't turn around.

The road down the hill was easy going, and Belić arrived in the village within a short time. He was greeted by a dog who was only mildly curious, and after a quick sniff, it trotted off to lay in the late afternoon shade beneath a wall. As he walked casually through the main street, he saw a man chopping wood, a woman retrieving clothes from a washing line, and he could hear the infectious laughter of children. He spoke to no one. Ahead was the house the old man described. It was hard to miss. It was a large home known traditionally as a *cascine lombarde* and similar to a Roman villa. Built of stone with a tiled roof, the house was immense. Out front, the tortured trunks of a few elderly olive trees provided shade and proudly stood sentinel. He took a few steps closer, careful to avoid deep and hardened wagon ruts carved deep into the road.

Belić stopped and looked at the house briefly, then gave himself a cursory dust off, removed his hat, and climbed the steps to knock on the door. Before he could announce himself, the solid Italian oak door swung open and revealed a striking woman.

"Good afternoon, Father," she greeted him politely, showing a perfect white smile.

Caught by surprise, Belić stumbled for words. "Uh, *Signora*, uh, *Signora* Milani?"

"Yes, how may I help you?" She inclined her head.

"Forgive me for interrupting your work; I, er, I'm Father Stevan Belić. I was told you may have a room for rent." He realised his mistake, and it was too late now to change his name to the fictitious one he had rehearsed. He felt his face redden. "It, it's just for the night, only one night," he added quickly.

Signora Milani looked him over from head to toe. She saw the dirt and his unkempt appearance and laughed. "Perhaps, Father, it would be in your interest, unless your busy schedule prevents it, that you stay for two nights. Your cassock needs some attention, as do you." She stepped back and to the side. "Please, Father, come inside." She made brief eye contact with a large man who'd been observing them from up the street and gave a subtle nod. A sign everything was well.

Sarajevo's railway station was bustling as many travellers, predominantly Serbian, were fleeing in growing numbers at an anticipated Austrian retaliation to the assassinations. The Empire looked unkindly at those who chose to murder royalty. *Oberleutenant* Koell and *Stabswachtmeister* Wolff positioned themselves at either end of the platform and began showing the photograph of Father Stevan Belić to either arriving or departing passengers. Some recognised the priest but hadn't seen him here, and most sullenly shook their heads and quickly moved on, unwilling to be seen cooperating with the Austrian authorities.

On arriving in Sarajevo, the Austrian lieutenant and his sergeant immediately reported to Leo Pfeffer, the local chief investigator and hoped for an update or news on the Black Hand members who evaded capture. Of significant interest, Major Vojislav Tankosić, while under interrogation, volunteered the name of Dragutin Dimitrijević, the person he reported to. Known by his alias, 'Apis', Dimitrijević, the suspected leader of the Black Hand movement, was arrested within hours of the major's confession. The net was closing quickly on Muhamed Mehmedbasić and the priest who were the only Black Hand terrorists still at large.

However, all was not well in Sarajevo. Anti-Serb protests broke out in response to the assassinations, and the military was employed to quell the unrest. The following day rioting continued and became increasingly violent. Pro-Austrian rioters destroyed over one-thousand Serbian houses, businesses and schools, while the police and authorities stood back and allowed the destruction and pillaging to continue unabated. For this reason, *Oberleutenant* Koell and *Stabswachtmeister* Wollf were very wary of retaliation and genuinely feared for their safety. They found the prospect of remaining at Sarajevo Railway Station unnerving, and both soldiers hoped they could quickly find a clue to the whereabouts of the elusive priest so they could be on their way.

The afternoon wore on, and after each train departed, the two Austrian's tirelessly showed Belić's photograph to all passengers with no luck. During a brief respite between trains, *Oberleutenant* Koell walked over to *Stabswachtmeister* Wollf and looked at him with a measure of hope.

"Nothing, sir, no-one even recognised him," said Wollf

despondently.

Koell grimaced and rotated slowly to look at each end of the platform, then turned back to face his subordinate. "We will stay here until the last train tonight. Keep up the good work, Dieter." Koell spun and walked back to the other end of the platform.

Dieter Wollf, unhappy with his assignment, pulled a disrespectful face at the back of the departing officer and stood from the bench where he sat to question new arrivals who walked towards him.

The remainder of the day and early evening were equally unrewarding, both Austrians suffered endlessly at the hostile glances and scowls, but no one challenged their authority or provoked them.

The last train arrived, and eager to finish their long day, the soldiers questioned the last passengers until none remained. Having completed their task, both men walked towards each other and met in the middle of the platform.

"We'll come back tomorrow," stated *Oberleutenant* Koell without enthusiasm.

Stabswachtmeister Wollf nodded.

The train's conductor appeared from a carriage to check all was clear before he signalled the driver.

"Wait!" shouted Koell." He immediately strode to the annoyed conductor. "Are you familiar with this man, have you seen him recently?" asked Koell handing him Belić's' photograph.

"I have a train to keep on schedule, I can't –"

"It won't take but a minute of your time," interrupted Koell.

The conductor was good at this job. Over the years, he had honed his skill at recognising faces. After all, someone had to remember troublemakers and ensure rabble-rousers and joyriders were kept from his train, and that responsibility fell to him. The conductor gave the photograph careful scrutiny. "Yes, I remember this face, but he was not dressed as a priest," replied Conductor Gruber confidently.

A distant yell from the engine reminded the conductor it was time to leave.

"I'll go," offered *Stabswachtmeister* Wollf. He quickly headed towards the locomotive to appease the driver. A few passengers stared curiously out carriage windows.

"Are you sure it was him?" Koell asked.

Herr Gruber nodded, "I remember him well, although something about the man didn't sit well with me. I thought at the time he was up to no good, he looked nervous. A mischief-maker."

"Do you know where he was going? His destination?"

Conductor Gruber stared at the *Oberleutenant* as if he had onions growing from his head. "This train only goes to Ragusa." The conductor scratched the stubble on his chin. "That's where he got off."

"Are you sure of this?" asked Koell excitedly as he removed a pencil and paper from his pocket.

Piqued that his judgement was being questioned, *Herr* Gruber gave the *Oberleutenant* a scathing look. "Of course."

Losing patience, the locomotive driver blew the whistle. *Oberleutenant* Koell took details from the conductor, wrote them diligently down, and waved for Wollf to return.

"You've been most helpful, *Herr* Gruber. If we need further information, we know where to find you. Thank you for your time," acknowledged Koell.

Anxious to return to the sanctity of his beloved train, Conductor Gruber couldn't board quick enough. He blew his whistle and waved to the driver, and with a cloud of steam, the locomotive lurched away.

Stabswachtmeister Wollf walked wearily towards his superior, who remained standing in the middle of the platform. "The conductor saw the priest?" he asked.

"Yes, he did and claims he was headed towards Ragusa."

Wollf rolled his eyes.

"I need to find a telephone to call Major Richter."

"Then we will go to Ragusa?"

"Unless the Major tells us not to, we will catch the first train in the morning."

CHAPTER FIVE

An endless parade of puffy white clouds drifted leisurely overhead and disappeared over the distant hills. It would be a hot day, and the priest was quietly relieved he wasn't walking. He sat on a patio in the shade of an olive tree at *Signora* Milani's villa and enjoyed the cool morning breeze that blew down from the hills. In nearby fields and olive groves, he could see the tiny figures of men at work, toiling before the heat of the day made it too uncomfortable. He took a sip of coffee and wondered if he could enjoy such a life in a peaceful place as this.

Signora Milani proved to be a wonderful hostess and insisted that she launder his clothes and tend to a rent in his cassock he hadn't noticed. As his other clothes needed washing, she thoughtfully provided him with some clean, lightweight cotton pants and a shirt, explaining that they belonged to her husband and he wouldn't object if he wore them.

When he arrived the day before, *Signora* Milani led Father Stevan to a spacious and tastefully furnished room with a large bed that surpassed his expectations. After dinner, he bathed, scrubbed, shaved and retired to his room, where he immediately fell asleep and woke just as the sun rose above the distant peaks. As he had for most of his adult life, he went through his morning liturgy, and once completed, wandered downstairs to greet *Signora* Milani, who was preparing breakfast. She showed him to a small patio and handed him a coffee.

"How do you feel today, Father?" she asked, placing a plate with some *fette biscottate* on the table along with a small pot of *marmallata*. She sat down and looked out at the panorama beyond.

"I didn't realise how tired I was."

"Please, eat," she offered.

Needing no further encouragement, he picked up the hard rusk biscuit and spread a healthy dollop of *marmallata* across it. "You've been most hospitable, *Signora*; I will leave your comfortable home tomorrow morning and be on my way."

"After breakfast, I hope."

Belić laughed. "Yes, after breakfast."

"Where is your destination?"

Belić chewed thoughtfully, giving himself time to think. "I have some church business to attend to," he took another sip of coffee. "And where is Signor Milani?" he asked, quickly changing the subject, "I have yet to meet him." Belić turned to her.

A look of sadness crossed her face. "I am a widow, my husband, Paolo is no longer with us." *Signora* Milani closed her eyes. "May he rest in peace," she said quietly, then crossed herself.

Father Stevan felt her loss. "Please excuse me, I am sorry, *Signora*. It was thoughtless of me to ask and none of my business."

"That's quite alright, you weren't to know, and I have grown accustomed to his passing."

The silence was a little awkward and uncomfortable.

"Have you a newspaper? I am curious to learn of the latest news?" he asked casually.

"Perhaps later today, a neighbour often picks one up for me on his twice weekly trip to Chieti."

The priest nodded. Again, there was an awkward silence.

"It is quite tragic, don't you think?" she suddenly asked.

"*Signora*?"

"In Bosnia, the assassination."

"Oh ... Yes, of course. But I am not up to date on the latest news, what do you know of it?"

"Only a little, other than the Prince and his wife, Sophie ... she was so beautiful ... they were murdered in cold blood. Why do people do such sinful things, Father, why is it necessary to commit acts of evil and destroy innocent lives because someone doesn't agree with their politics?"

"Uh ... Well –"

"Did you know they left behind three children aged between twelve and fourteen years old?"

Father Stevan wiped his mouth and fingers with a napkin. "I knew they had children ..."

Signora Milani was expecting an answer.

"Are you aware of how the Austrians treated the Bosnians, and they have children too?" he blurted without thinking.

She shook her head. "But that isn't what I'm asking, Father. I'm talking about killing ... It's just wrong, and there are other ways, civilised ways to right injustices without resorting to murdering innocents."

Inside, Belić was fighting with his emotions. He looked to the inquiring eyes of the beautiful woman who sat beside him. The way she held her head, the tone of her voice, and the calm way she asked questions... it was alluring and sincere, but at the same time, it was also probing, as if his answer would reveal himself to her. He felt vulnerable, and it gave him pause as he weighed his response.

"In God's eyes, murder is wrong." He returned her quizzical look. "When a policeman kills a man intent on harming others, are his actions sinful or unjust?" He was beginning to feel more composed, and just as she had done, he spoke calmly and didn't wait for her reply and continued. "God gave us the right to defend ourselves, both as individuals and as countries. The Archduke and the Duchess represented an empire that threatened the existence of a nation of innocent people." Belić looked away from her and focused on the coffee cup he held. "The Church teaches us that their deaths may have been justified under God's law, and the interpretation is not whether the deaths were wrong, but in words used to describe their deaths." He looked away from the cup and held her gaze as he waited for an answer.

Signora Milani absentmindedly twirled a small strand of hair between her fingers. "Then what you are saying, Father, is whether I believe they were either murdered or killed and that there is a difference?"

Father Stevan smiled. "In a manner of speaking, yes."

"I've not lived under oppression from the Austrians, so I cannot place myself in the home of a Bosnian woman, however, I feel taking the life of another is wrong under any circumstance."

"Then you disagree with God?"

"No, Father, for I have faith, I disagree with you."

Belić sat upright and was taken back. He fought to control his immediate response and resisted the temptation to question and have her explain herself further. He believed her answer was not to provoke or seek an argument, she answered honestly and simply stated how she felt.

He forced himself to relax. "Then you are wise beyond your years, and God is lucky to have your love and devotion."

She returned his look and remained quiet for a moment. "I have much to do today, please excuse me, Father." She slid her chair back and stood. Without another word, she picked up the dishes and left him to ponder her responses and his introspections.

For the remainder of the day, he was left alone. *Signora* Milani provided him with a fine *antipasto* lunch, and to his surprise and disappointment, she did not sit or share the meal with him. He felt an uneasy tension between them that he presumed was due to the nature of their candid talk earlier at breakfast. After lunch, he decided to walk through the village and hoped it would allow him to think and clear his head.

The village was small, perhaps ten or so homes of varying sizes. Not many people were about, and those he saw appeared busy and engaged in different aspects of farming. A few old men sat outside in the shade of an awning and chatted amiably with each other. They greeted him cordially, but as a stranger in their midst, they were understandably distant.

His thoughts returned to his last conversation with *Signora* Milani and her puzzling reaction. For some inexplicable reason, he felt compelled to defend himself to her, and it was important that she understand him. While he couldn't share with her his violent past or the role he played in the deaths of the royal couple, he did want her to understand why it was necessary, that there was a moral justification, and under Gods Law, he had not sinned. Her opinion mattered, and he sought her approval.

He passed an old woman dressed mournfully in black sitting on a bench cutting tips from green beans. He nodded respectfully and offered her a formal greeting, and continued on his way. He felt her accusing stare. *No doubt she was wondering why he wasn't out in the fields working,* he thought.

He retraced his path back through the village towards *Signora* Milani's home and was again consumed by the tension of their last conversation during breakfast. He couldn't forget the look on her face when she disagreed with him. Was she referring to him personally or to the Church's interpretation? He decided to ask her what she meant at a suitable time.

He walked around the back of the villa and onto the patio where they'd shared breakfast and entered the coolness of the house.

"I hope you will enjoy *tortellini* tonight, Father?" she yelled.

Belić turned and followed the sound of the voice to an expansive kitchen. She stood over a counter and was folding pasta shells. "I am grateful for anything you provide, *Signora*. I have simple tastes."

She smiled as she wrapped a filled tortellini pasta shell around her finger and carefully folded the ends over. She placed the finished shell on the counter and then efficiently grabbed another to repeat the process.

"Perhaps you could open the wine for us?"

"Of course, and I am grateful for anything I can do," he replied while reaching for the bottle of wine she indicated. "I am not used to such meals."

She gave him a brief look then continued humming softly as she carefully shaped another pasta shell. He found himself captivated by the repetitive process. The absence of tension was noticeable, and if the *Signora* was upset earlier, it no longer showed. He uncorked the bottle and filled two glasses before handing her one.

Her eyes sparkled. "Are you still leaving tomorrow morning?" She brushed a strand of hair away from her face and left a smudge of flour on her cheek.

"Oh... yes, *Signora*, after breakfast, I will leave."

She nodded and began humming again as she finished shaping the last of the tortellini. Then I hope you enjoy your last night here. Your cassock is clean, and I put it on the bed with your other clothes.

They talked, shared wine, laughed and ate a wonderful dinner.

Belić could feel his eyelids growing heavy and excused himself, wishing to retire early. He expected to have a long day tomorrow and wanted to be fully rested and prepared.

Everything was not well aboard the yacht *Mana* which was still berthed in Pescara. A resourceful friend, a Frenchman named Luc, who owned a local ship's Chandlery store, recommended a reliable mechanic who was called to diagnose and repair *Mana*'s engine problem. After a thorough evaluation, the mechanic explained that their marine Bolinder-Munktell diesel engine had a faulty fuel release valve, commonly called an injector. The replacement part needed to be ordered and dispatched from Sweden. The bad news, he explained, it would take three or four weeks at best before the part arrived.

While Kaha and Pam Peterson were not dependant on the engine, they needed it to keep the batteries charged which provided electricity to the yacht's lights and radios.

As requested by Kaha, the mechanic reinstalled the faulty injector, enabling them to briefly run the motor and charge the batteries until the new part arrived. They prudently decided to remain in Pescara, and as duty required, informed those who needed to be told of their change in plans.

Darkness descended over Wien's *Ringstrasse*, but evening didn't prevent everyone from working, especially at the Royal Ministry of War building. The Direktor of the *Evidenzbureau*, Oskar von Czvetassin, obsessively polished his spectacles while Major Richter sat stiffly and patiently waited for the direktor to complete his task. Pleased that his spectacles were once again clean, he placed them on his nose and leaned forward.

"Then you have some good news for me, Major?"

As always, Major Maximillian Richter sat attentively and looked impeccable. He took immense pride in his appearance, if not somewhat obsessively. He shaved twice a day, kept his hair stylish and trimmed, and used hair cream to ensure his healthy coiffure had lustre and sat precisely as it should. Any observer couldn't fail to assume that vanity played a significant part in Major Richter's visage. Little expense was spared to ensure his tailored uniforms fit his trim physique like a second skin and were free from stains, lint and other undesirable matter that could suggest the major was slovenly or uncaring of his appearance.

"We can now assume that the terrorist, Muhamed Mehmedbasić, is in Montenegro, sir. Our informants tell us he has been seen in the area, it's a simple matter of having the authorities do their job and pick him up," replied Major Richter matter-of-factly.

The direktor scratched a note on a document, closed the file and retrieved another. "Excellent, that leaves the priest, I'm surprised you haven't located him yet." Direktor von Czvetassin peered over the top of his spectacles at the major.

"The priest planned his escape thoroughly and took steps to ensure he could remain at large, sir."

"I see." The direktor drummed his fingers on the fine oak desk and thought a moment. "Where has he gone, Belgrade?"

"Apparently not. We have a sighting of him on a train bound for Ragusa. I expect an update later today," replied Richter.

"Well, that's good then. I will look forward to your report that he's been caught, and Mehmedbasić is in custody awaiting trial by the week's end," said the direktor with finality. He closed the file and smiled, an indication the meeting was over.

Major Richter didn't return the smile or move.

"Something the matter, Major?"

"Perhaps. I am concerned about why the priest fled to Ragusa.

I believe he probably made good his escape by boat. He could be anywhere by now."

The direktor's smile of satisfaction disappeared. "Could he have gone to Italy?"

"We won't know for sure until I receive more information. I have insufficient facts to know for certain, sir." The major's expression remained neutral.

Direktor von Czvetassin, pushed his chair back and stood. He walked from behind his desk to the small window that overlooked the back of the Ministry of War building and peered out. "If he's in Italy, then this could be a problem for you." He turned back to Richter.

For the first time, the major was caught out. His impenetrable façade cracked a little. "*Herr* Direktor?"

"What I'm about to now tell you is classified secret and could alter how you conduct your investigation. You need to be aware of this, and so I have total faith that what I tell you will not leave this office, understood?"

"Yes, sir." If it were even possible, Major Richter sat a little straighter.

Although designated 'Military Intelligence', The *Evidenzbureau* did not report to the Ministry of War as expected. Instead, *Herr* Direktor reported directly to the Imperial and Royal Foreign Ministry headed by Austria's Foreign Minister, Leopold von Berchtold. The advantage of such an arrangement meant that from time to time, Direktor von Czvetassin was provided with foreign policy information he would otherwise not receive. Major Richter was naturally aware of this, which was why his curiosity was piqued.

The direktor walked from the window, opened his office door, and ensured that the outer office was secure. He returned to his desk and sat.

"Prior to the assassination in Sarajevo, it was our intention to annex Serbia from the rest of the troubled Balkan region, just as we did with Bosnia and Herzegovina. Serbia has been growing extremely confident and rebellious recently, especially since they've been cosying up to the Russians."

Major Richter nodded, this information was not new to him. In fact, it was another reason the Black Hand attacked the Austrians; they hoped to prevent Austrian annexation of Serbia.

"Since the assassination, our philosophy has changed somewhat. With Germany's overt support, the Emperor believes that a military invasion of Serbia will finally put an end to the unrest in the region. Many people here believe the Serbian government knew the Black Hand's assassination plot and did nothing to stop it. Germany's Kaiser is in total agreement with that theory, by the way."

This was news to Richter. Like a chess game, his mind began moving pieces around the board, who was aligned and friendly with whom – the alliances between countries could significantly alter the dynamics of a German supported Austrian invasion. He said nothing to his superior and looked on, waiting for him to continue.

"We will send a letter to Serbia outlining a list of our demands. Failure to comply will result in punitive retaliation, more than likely an invasion," said the Direktor with finality.

"What is the likelihood Serbia will agree to all demands?" asked Richter.

"Foreign Minister Berchtold believes they won't comply, although, between you and I," Direktor von Czvetassin lowered his voice and leaned forward, "he hopes they won't."

Again, this came as no surprise to major Richter, and he understood from a political viewpoint his job was going to become much more difficult.

The direktor sensed a question on Richter's lips and held up his hand to forestall him.

"If the terrorist is captured in Montenegro, as you suggest, then an existing extradition treaty will make it straightforward to return him to Sarajevo, where he will stand trial. However, if the priest is in ..."

"Italy," suggested Major Richter, "the logical place to go."

"Yes, exactly. I'm pleased you've identified the problem. Well, that is quite a different scenario entirely. When Austria does invade Serbia, the Foreign Ministry expects Italy to remain neutral and won't interfere in our plans. If Austrian military intelligence investigators are running rampant through Italy in pursuit of a terrorist, irrespective of whether Italy approves of our reasons – or not, could provoke them into taking a side. Foreign Minister Berchtold doesn't want that to happen, and he made his feelings known to me on that." Direktor von Czvetassin eased a finger into the collar of his shirt at the memory of the Ministers rather vociferous warning and threats to cease all *Evidenzebureau* operations in Italy.

"Are you suggesting we do not pursue the priest?" asked Major Richter.

The Direktor spoke slowly and deliberately. "What I'm telling you is; the Emperor publicly wants all the terrorists to stand trial and pay for their crimes."

"But, *Herr* Direktor, we have not made any public announcement that the priest was even a conspirator, let alone evaded capture."

"And that is my point, Major. Not publicly acknowledging his existence means that we can deal with him without going through the judicial system. It's been suggested that a more effective and permanent solution would be more satisfactory – just don't do it in Italy."

Major Maximillian Richter considered his options. The room was silent. "I understand. I will do as ordered, sir," acknowledged Richter after a moment or two.

"You will do your duty, Major."

The message wasn't lost on Richter. He focused on a point on the far wall above the direktor's head as he reflected on the implied order to find and then kill the priest. If he did go to Italy, then he'd have to find a way to transport the man out of the country without drawing the attention of the Italian authorities. Richter looked down and met the direktor's gaze. He saw it then; he saw it in von Czvetassin eyes. He would be the scapegoat – he was expendable. If things didn't go to plan, the direktor would deny any involvement, and his tender bureaucratic rear-end would be protected.

Richter kept his face impassive. "How long do we have before things become sensitive with the Italians?"

"You have about a week, after that, you need to take a more circumspect and clandestine approach to bring the terrorist to justice."

"Very well, *Herr* Direktor. Is there anything else?"

"Failure is unacceptable, Major," warned Direktor von Czvetassin.

Major Richter stood, "Of course, *Herr* Direktor."

Oberleutenant Koell and *Stabswachtmeister* Wollf split up, and each walked through the township of Ragusa, covering a different area. They politely showed a photograph of the priest to as many people as possible. As before, at the railway station in Sarajevo, no one recognised or saw the man. At the ferry terminal, they questioned everyone - twice – no one identified him.

As the day wore on, the two investigators for the *Evidenzbureau* met near the docks to lament the lack of progress. *Oberleutenant* Koell looked out across the water while his subordinate, *Stabswachtmeister* Wollf sat on a bollard at the wharf and looked towards the fish market.

"Damn it! Someone must have seen him, we know he caught the train here, so, where is he?" Koell uttered in frustration.

Wollf shrugged.

"Someone here knows, they must. Let's go back to the fish market and ask again," said Koell.

"He probably dug a hole, jumped in and covered himself over," replied Wollf lacking the enthusiasm to begin traipsing around Ragusa again.

"Like on a boat," offered the lieutenant. "Speaking of which, when do the fishing boats come back?" He turned and looked at the empty moorings; only one boat was tied to the dock, and men were busy replacing a mast. He walked towards the crippled boat.

"Excuse me, when will the fishing fleet return?" he asked a man who stood against the rail of the boat smoking.

The fisherman turned and appraised the young officer before replying. "When all their barrels are full."

"When did they leave?"

"Most left about five or six days ago, won't be back in a while."

"Most? You mean they didn't all leave together?"

The fisherman shook his head, "No, sometimes a couple of boats don't leave with the others. Like us, they have a problem that needs fixing, or crewmen don't show up."

Oberleutenant Koell thought a moment. "So, the boats generally all go together, they fish in the same place?"

"This time of year, the water is warmer, and so the fish are north." He flicked the cigarette into the sea and watched as it settled onto some scum. "But all the boats go together, and each has his special place he likes to fish."

Koell nodded. "So, all the boats head in the same direction?"

The fisherman turned to the officer. "Why is this so important to you?"

Koell pulled the photo of Father Stevan Belić from his tunic and showed the fisherman.

"Have you seen this man here in the last three days?"

The fisherman looked closely at the photograph.

"I thought perhaps he was on a fishing boat," said Koell.

"A priest, on a fishing boat!" the fisherman laughed. "No, I've never seen this man before."

"He's a bad man. And perhaps a boat didn't go up north and instead took him elsewhere. Did any fishing boats not go north with the others?"

With practised ease, the fisherman retrieved his tobacco tin from his pocket and began rolling another.

The *Oberleutenant* believed the fisherman knew something. "Did a fishing boat not travel north with the others?" he repeated.

The fisherman shrugged.

Koell reached into his pocket, pulled out a small wad of *kronen,* and waved it at the seaman.

The fisherman looked at the money, it was tempting. He didn't know the man in the photo. *Perhaps there was no harm sharing what he knew about departing boats.* "Actually," said the man with a cigarette paper stuck to his lip, "one boat didn't go north, went west instead."

"West! What's west?"

The fisherman held out his hand, and Koell peeled off a fifty krone note and gave it to him.

"Dry land," laughed the fisherman. The paper bounced up and down on his lip as he pointed with his chin. "Italy. You don't travel much, do you?"

Oberleutenant Koell ignored the taunt and looked to his sergeant, who was still leaning against the bollard with his eyes closed. "Dieter!"

Stabswachtmeister Wollf pried himself from his comfortable seat and casually ambled over.

"What boat went to Italy? What was its name?" Koell asked excitedly as he pulled his notebook and pencil from his pocket.

The fisherman lowered his head, and his hand protectively cupped the cigarette as he lit it. He drew in heavily, exhaled, then spat as he expelled a piece of tobacco. He held his hand out again. Like before, the Austrian peeled off another fifty krone note and handed it over. The money disappeared into his trouser pocket as quickly as the first.

"The *Kralj Mora*, the king of the sea."

"Do you know the captain? His name?"

"You're wasting your time. Boris is a good man, he wouldn't do anything wrong; I've known him since we were boys – my entire life."

"Boris?"

"Boris Marković. Like I said, you're wasting your time."

"Why would he go over there then?" asked *Stabswachtmeister* Wollf. "What towns are over there?" He pointed with his arm.

The fisherman shrugged and dragged heavily. "Only Pescara, that's the closest." He spat another piece of tobacco from between his lips. "Perhaps he needed something from there," he suggested. "A part for repair, who knows."

"Are you sure that's where the *Kralj Mora* went?"

"Where else can he go? Only the fishing port of Pescara is west, you figure it out." He threw the butt into the water. "I have work to do."

Koell and Wollf walked away from the dock. "Do you think it's him? Did a fisherman take the priest to Italy in a fishing boat?" Wollf asked.

"Let's see what Major Richter wants us to do," replied *Oberleutenant* Koell.

A large map of Austria and neighbouring countries was pinned to the wall inside one of the rooms occupied by the *Evidenzbureau*. Major Richter cradled an arm and rubbed his chin as he stared at the map - more specifically, he focused intently on the seaport of Pescara.

He wouldn't admit it to anyone, but he had a growing and grudging respect for his adversary. The wily priest planned his escape carefully and has been successful so far. But what were the priest's intentions once he arrived in Pescara? Maximillian Richter went through the possibilities in his head. The priest could choose to stay in Pescara or leave. For the major, it was an easy choice, the priest would leave. Pescara was too close to the Balkans, and he would be in constant danger if he remained. So, then where too? The map beckoned, and Richter took a step closer. Florence, Rome, Naples, or further afield? For a priest, Rome was the logical choice, but – obvious, too obvious? No, the priest wouldn't go there. South to Naples? If discovered his options for escape were limited, no, Belić wouldn't go south. Richter made a hurried decision based purely on intuition.

When *Oberleutenant* Koell contacted him after arriving in Pescara, he would tell him to pay particular attention to all northward routes after eliminating Naples as a destination.

CHAPTER SIX

Father Stevan Belić once again stood outside the door to *Signora* Milani's home and thanked her warmly for her kindness and hospitality. He paid her the money for room and food she asked for, and he was now fully prepared and rested for the next stage of his journey.

"I wish you safe travels, Father. You've been a wonderful guest." She stood inside the doorway with her arms folded and smiled.

For some unexplained reason, he felt self-conscious, her unwavering gaze was unsettling, and he found it difficult to just walk away. He looked at her one last time; there was much he still wanted to say to her - things unsaid.

His eyes looked to her in question, and she stared back. Her head was canted at a slight angle, and her long black wavy hair cascaded freely over a shoulder. She was tall, very tall and only a few centimetres shorter than he. Her height made her elegant and emphasised her confidence. She moved slightly and leaned against the door jam, and he knew she could see into his mind - he felt a pang of smouldering guilt and looked away.

"Again, thank you very much, *Signora*. May God's angels keep you safe." He crossed himself, picked up his suitcase, turned and walked down the steps onto the road. He looked back, and she was still there, framed in the doorway and unmoving. He realised he didn't know her first name and opened his mouth to ask her when he stepped awkwardly into a deep, mud dried wagon rut. A wave of intense, debilitating pain spread upwards from his foot, and in reflex, he dropped the suitcase as he fought to control his fall. He landed awkwardly and heavily, sprawled on the hard-packed dirt and afraid to move. The blinding agony from his ankle was almost unbearable. He clamped his eyes tightly shut as the searing pain spread up his ankle, through his leg and threatened to explode outwards. His breathing came in ragged short gasps as he fought to control and manage the excruciating fire from his foot.

"Father!" cried *Signora* Milani. She ran down the steps and onto her knees beside him.

"I'll, uh, be all right, give me a mo –" He exhaled slowly. The pain was too much – intolerable, and he felt the sweat on his brow ... it began with a narrowing of his vision, the light of day fading into blackness, and then his consciousness surrendered, his mind shut down, and he passed out.

Belić blinked his eyes open and found himself staring up at the beautiful face of *Signora* Milani. He groaned and tried to sit up.

"Don't move, the doctor is coming."

"How long?" Father Stevan grimaced as another wave of pain shot up his ankle.

"You were out for a minute or two, Father." She shook her head. "That was a terrible fall." She placed a hand on his shoulder to keep him from moving. "I hope it's not broken."

Belić closed his eyes tightly. "I hope so too," he gasped through clenched teeth.

All the men in the village were out in the fields or the orchards working. A few children playing nearby heard *Signora* Milani's cry and came over to investigate, she immediately dispatched the oldest one to bring the doctor while the younger ones watched with snot noses and pained expressions.

Belić moaned again as he sought a more comfortable position.

He reached into a pocket of his cassock and pulled out the old cross, and held it firmly.

"*Signora*! *Signora*!" A man quickly approached them. "What happened?"

"Fabio, the Father fell, it's his ankle."

"This will hurt a little, Father," stated Fabio as he knelt on the ground at Belić's feet. "I'm going to remove your shoe; please try to relax as best you can, eh!"

"It can't hurt more than it does already, doctor," replied Father Stevan with a grimace.

Fabio was already carefully undoing the laces of Stevan's shoe. "I am no doctor, Father, I look after the animals when they need my attention."

"And people too," she added.

Gently, Fabio eased Belić's shoe from his foot. Stevan gasped, his knuckles white as he gripped his cassock.

"Can you move your toes, Father?"

Obediently Belić wriggled his toes.

"This is good, and can you move your foot?"

Again, with determination, Belić moved his foot as much as possible while Fabio supported his lower leg.

"Is it broken?" asked Father Stevan.

"No, I do not think so, Father, you have suffered a sprain, I think.

The two Austrian *Evidenzbureau* investigators were again on the platform of a railway station, now in the Italian town of Pescara and this time dressed in civilian clothes. Neither was happy as they spent the entire day questioning people. Typically, no one recognised the priest from the photograph they showed.

Unknown to *Stabswachtmeister* Wollf, he sat on precisely the same bench as Father Stevan sat four nights ago. "Do you think he was here 'cause someone must have seen him?"

Oberleutenant Koell didn't reply. He watched the ticket office door and saw the clerk leave for the day and go home. The replacement clerk was already inside.

"A shift change. Come, Dieter, let's talk to the new ticket seller, shall we?"

Dieter Wollf reluctantly stood and followed a step behind the lieutenant as he walked to the ticket window.

Signore Claudio Ricci was busy organising his things. He placed his lunch pail, newspaper and tobacco pouch in the corner of the tiny ticket office, just as he always did, and removed his jacket to carefully hang it on a peg on the back of the ticket office door. A speck of lint caught his eye, and with a quick swipe, he removed the offending fleck from his jacket. He reached for his visor that sat on a shelf and carefully placed it over his head. With a little adjustment, it sat comfortably, and Claudio was pleased. Not breaking from his meticulous routine, he checked the door to ensure it was locked and then lastly perched himself on the stool and cast a professional eye quickly over the items on the narrow desk in front of him. He checked each of the stamps he used and put them in order, just as he preferred. *Oberleutenant* Koell stood patiently at the window and watched Claudio complete his ritual while *Stabswachtmeister* Wollf leaned casually against the wall.

Now that everything was organised exactly as it should be, Claudio Ricci finally looked up at his first customer. "*Sì?*"

Oberleutenant Koell leaned forward and down. "Excuse me, but I'm wondering if you have seen this man recently, perhaps in the last few days or so?" He passed the photograph of Father Stevan Belić beneath the glass to the ticket clerk.

Claudio picked up the photo and looked at it quickly. Koell immediately saw a flash of recognition in his eyes.

The ticket clerk shook his head. "No, no, I haven't seen him."

"Are you sure? It's important," asked Koell.

"I told you, I haven't seen him," replied Claudio sliding the photo back. The aggressive stranger at the window spoke Italian reasonably well, but he was not a native speaker, and it was apparent he was a foreigner. Possibly German, thought Claudio as he eyed Koell with mounting suspicion. "Is there anything else you need, a ticket?"

Koell was an experienced investigator, he knew the ticket clerk was lying to him and knew the futility of trying to intimidate the man or offer him a bribe while he sat securely in his cosy office.

"No, thank you." He retrieved the photo and strode away from the ticket window down from the platform towards town.

Wollf walked up and beside him. He looked questioningly at the officer.

"He recognised the priest," said Koell.

"I can kick the door and be in that office in seconds," offered Wollf, relishing in the thought of finally doing something he was good at.

Koell walked a few paces before replying. The words of Major Richter still echoed in his head. "No, I don't think that will be best. We will not create a reason for the *Carabinieri* to come looking for us. Come, now we will eat."

Pescara was shrouded in darkness, and the town settled into its normal evening rhythm. The odd dog barked, the wail of a colicky baby broke the stillness, and a carriage or two rumbled unhurriedly past. Two *Carabiniere* ambled by and took little interest in their surroundings or, surprisingly, at the two men who loitered in the darkened doorway of a building near the railway station.

The last train from Pescara departed on time, and an elderly man began laboriously sweeping the station and emptying rubbish tins as he did every night. *Oberleutenant* Koell watched the rear of the station and saw the ticket-office lamp extinguished, he nudged Wolff. "Get ready."

Moments later, the ticket office door opened, and the clerk stepped out. He locked the door, lit a cigarette, picked up his pail, tucked his newspaper under his arm and walked away. Within seconds the two investigators caught up to the unsuspecting clerk. Immediately *Stabswachtmeister* Wollf slipped his hand through Claudio's arm as *Oberleutenant* Koell stepped in front. All three men came to a halt.

"Wha–what is the meaning of this?" Claudio looked in fright from Wollf and then in recognition to Koell. "I remember you, what do you want? Let me go!" His cigarette slipped from his mouth.

"Tell me about the priest," ordered Koell.

"What priest, I don't know who you mean?"

Oberleutenant Koell pulled the photograph from his pocket, although it was too dark to see it

clearly, and waved it at the clerk as a reminder. "This man, you saw him."

"I, I don't know wha–what you mean," stammered Claudio. "Please, leave me alone!"

Without warning, Dieter Wollf twisted his upper body and drove a fist into the solar plexus of the clerk. With his other arm, he prevented the much smaller older man from collapsing. Claudio dropped his pail and clutched his chest, panting for air. Wollf continued to hold him upright. Koell watched a moment to give the clerk time to rethink and catch his breath.

"This man, you saw him. Where was he going?"

"Who are you?" gasped Claudio before erupting into a fit of coughing.

"I will ask you one more time... politely," stated Koell, beginning to lose patience. "Where–

was–he–going!"

Claudio Ricci looked from Koell and back to Wollf in fear. "I don't know where he was going. Please believe me. Most people buy tickets to Naples, if he were getting off somewhere else, then I would have remembered. I just remember the face, that's all, please believe me."

"So, you are saying, he most likely bought a ticket to Naples?"

Claudio nodded. "*Si.*"

"How was he dressed?"

"I can't remember. I suppose just like everyone else."

"And not as a priest?"

The clerk shook his head. "I would have remembered that."

"When did you see him?" Koell asked.

"Two, no, three or four nights ago. I expect."

Koell nodded. "Was he travelling with anyone?"

"No, that's why I remember him because he made a point of keeping away from everyone else. Pietro, the janitor, he pointed him out to me – that man misses nothing. He thought he was up to no good."

Oberleutenant Koell gave Wollf a subtle nod. Obediently, Wollf released the clerk and straightened his jacket, then picked up the lunch pail and newspaper and handed them back.

"I hope my friend here doesn't have to come back to see you," Koell leaned forward to ensure the clerk understood his meaning. "We apologise for delaying your journey home. Good night, *Signore.*"

Oberleutenant Koell and *Stabswachtmeister* Wollf disappeared into the night. Still in some discomfort, Claudio Ricci clutched his chest and walked home as quickly as he could.

As requested, Koell immediately telephoned headquarters. Under terse orders from Major Richter, both Koell and Wollf were instructed to make their way to Naples and not spend any more time lingering in railway stations than was necessary. They were lucky and, so far, managed to avoid all contact with Italian authorities and were not, under any circumstances, to come under their scrutiny or to engage with them. As far as Major Richter was concerned, both Koell and Wollf were now civilians and operating outside the scope of their authority and jurisdiction. Drawing attention to themselves and the *Evidenzbureau* was forbidden.

On learning of the latest update on the priest's movements, the major made it quite clear that he believed that Naples was only a ruse, a false trail, and the priest headed northwards in the opposite direction. However, they needed first to follow the obvious and eliminate all possibilities before looking elsewhere.

As ordered, *Oberleutnant* Koell purchased two tickets to Naples on the next train south. *Stabswachtmeister* Wollf, typically unimpressed, whispered some unkind words about his superiors, the entire Austrian military, including all its officers and a handful of politicians. If anyone of importance heard his unflattering utterings, his career might have been considerably shortened.

The train journey south to Naples was uneventful. Both investigators were tired of trains and sitting for hours on uncomfortable seats staring out across the monotony of the Italian countryside.

After their arrival, they became intimately familiar with

Stazione di Napoli Centrale, Naples' main railway station, and walked backwards and forward, from one end to the other. They talked to dozens, and dozens of passengers and employees, all of whom failed to recognise Father Stevan Belić. As accurately predicted by Major Richter, the trail petered out.

If Father Stevan was aware of the frustrations currently being experienced by both Koell and Wollf, he might have smiled. His plan worked flawlessly. If given a choice and left to both investigators, they would have admitted defeat and returned home. However, returning directly home was not quite what Major Richter had in mind for his two men.

After a restful evening and indulging in a well-deserved exquisite meal, *Oberleutenant* Koell and *Stabswachtmeister* Wollf again found themselves on a train. Major Richter's orders were explicit. Both investigators were required to depart the train at each station on the route back to Pescara, find a suitable candidate and offer him a small amount of money in exchange for their help to locate the priest. If their information led to the capture of the priest, they would receive a substantial reward.

Copies of the photograph, a small amount of cash and contact information were handed out to eager informants, and after five tiring days, Koell and Wollf stepped from the train onto the platform in the small town of Chieti, it was the last stop before Pescara.

Chieti, one of Italy's most ancient towns, provided the outlying agricultural and horticultural regions with an array of support services and merchants. Like all thriving towns, the mayor's role is pivotal in developing the local economy and keeping the voting public placated. He also had jurisdiction over Chieti's municipal police department, the small but efficient *Municipal Polizia Locale*.

Through his prominence, Chieti's mayor also felt it a priority to first satisfy the needs of his large and extended family, of course, his ardent supporters and, to a lesser extent, the community.

Named after his father and his father before him, Mayor Alberto Maria Gabriele De Rosa did his best to keep the peace. He mediated with skill and negotiated policy with convincing and well-articulated eloquence. Alberto was a problem solver and a people person, and exceptionally proficient. Many would say a likeable man. However, despite his talents, few in the community rankled him more than Gianna. She had a way of needling and getting under his skin like no other. For all his exemplary accomplishments and achievements, Alberto always found himself looking over his shoulder, waiting for his younger sister Gianna to make an appearance and embarrass him. He was convinced she did so with the sole intention to harass, badger and torment.

Some years ago, Gianna decided that her only son, Gabriele, should join the *Polizia*, and she chose to tell her brother about this during a council meeting. After chairs and tables were returned upright and decorum restored, Mayor De Rosa ordered Gianna physically removed from the chambers – but it didn't end there. Fearful of physical reprisals because Gianna was not a delicate woman and carried with her, in addition to her disagreeable temperament, some considerable bulk and surprising strength. However, as always, Alberto knew deep within his heart that the only way he could prevent continued embarrassment and outright war was to do what he could to secure her son, his nephew Gabriele, a position within the *Polizia*. The mayor and most of the councilmen felt this was the only real way to appease his less than gracious and very volatile sister. Mayor Alberto Maria Gabriele De Rosa was also mindful of the election to be held later that year.

Mayor De Rosa called in a few favours, even threatened a little, and eventually, Gabriele sat and passed the police test – only just – and that is still open to debate. For the time being, harmony had once again been restored to Chieti, and Gianna was temporarily mollified.

Few, if any, would disagree that Gianna demonstrated a lack of tact and refinement, and her son Gabriele was no different. Exceedingly unpopular, Gabriele possessed few friends at school and even less as an adult.

For as long as anyone could remember, Gabriele was always known as 'Gabbi', and for his immediate family, they all incorrectly believed his name was an affectionate abbreviation for Gabriele – which it wasn't. Gabriele enjoyed nothing more than to poke around and discover things, and he was an opportunist and a forager. Not known for his kindness and generosity, a trait inherited from his mother, he would use his discoveries for personal gain and resort to underhanded strategies to solicit favours or, better still, money. A habit his job as a policeman was well suited to. It was Carlo, remarkably only five years old at the time, and Gabriele's only friend, who appropriately, first began calling him 'Gabbi', an abbreviation of 'Gabbiano' or seagull – a scavenger.

Where Gabbi's mother was generously proportioned, Gabbi was rail thin and short. It was discretely suggested that Gabbi's obnoxious personality and size was purely a result of undernourishment, a sad inexcusable condition that Gianna was directly responsible for – a sentiment neighbourhood mothers quietly propagated.

Gabbi showed little aptitude for police work and was frequently relegated to mundane foot- patrols or other tasks no one else wanted. In the interest of public safety, he was denied permission to carry a sidearm, but that didn't prevent him from owning one. He confiscated a quality pistol from a minor criminal he apprehended a year earlier and conveniently failed to turn it in. From time to time, in the privacy of his room, he waved it around with bravado, although he had never shot at anyone and certainly never fired it. Most of the time, the pistol was wrapped in a cloth and remained hidden beneath the floorboards of his room in the house he still shared with his mother.

Gabbi's police associates were just happy to be as far away from him as possible, while his superiors, burdened by the scrupulous pecuniary oversight of Mayor De Rosa, were also rewarded with fewer items crossed off their annual police budget, an arrangement that conveniently suited everyone.

Although not gifted with an outgoing, friendly disposition, neither was he a fool. Gabbi was enterprising and always on the lookout for opportunity and self-betterment. With that philosophy foremost in his mind, he observed two men harassing departing passengers on Chieti's railway station platform. Rather than go immediately to the travellers' assistance, as his training dictated and his superiors would have preferred, Gabbi watched and observed until the last passenger departed. What he saw interested him greatly. Two well-dressed men seeking something, and in Chieti, if people sought something, then he, Gabbi, nearly always knew where to look. He smelled money.

Secure with his position as a policeman, Gabbi hoisted his ill-fitting trousers and confidently sauntered towards the two men. "What are you idiots doing?" he snapped.

On hearing the voice, *Stabswachtmeister* Dieter Wollf whipped his head around and stared at the little policeman with some surprise. Few men spoke to Wollf disrespectfully, and those that did were less inclined to do so again after a little chat. His jaw tightened in preparation for delivering a vicious left-handed jab to the acne-scarred face of the diminutive policeman when *Oberleutenant* Koell stepped forward.

"Are you deaf? I asked, what are you up to!" again stated the policeman.

It wasn't by accident that Koell was an officer with the *Evidenzbureau*. He'd been thoroughly vetted and screened before he was accepted into Austria's vaunted military-intelligence establishment and was considered a bright young man with a promising future. Standing at one-hundred and eighty-five centimetres tall, the six-foot-one-inch *Oberleutenant* towered over Gabbi and quickly took the accurate measure of the man. A natural talent that Major Maximillian Richter recognised in the young officer.

Rather than appear nervous, as Gabbi expected, the tall man offered a friendly smile. "I'm so pleased to see you, officer. Perhaps our good fortune, eh Dieter?"

Dieter Wollf took a casual step or two back and to the side of the policeman. He grunted in reply.

Certainly, Gabbi lacked social graces, but his survival instincts were finely tuned. "Don't you go creeping around me, stand in front where I can see you both," he snarled, taking a step away from Wollf and pulling out his whistle.

"It's quite alright, officer, we mean you no harm," appeased Koell. "Actually, an important person such as yourself might be in a good position to help us, and perhaps even benefit in a small way."

Gabbi's eyes shifted from Koell to Wollf and back again. His curiosity was piqued. "What is it you want?"

Carefully, Koell slipped a hand into his pocket, extracted the priest's photograph, and held it out to the policeman. "We are looking for this man, have you seen him?"

"What do you want him for?" asked Gabbi, not acknowledging if he'd seen the man.

Koell shook his head and frowned. "He is a very bad criminal, and if you've seen him, and tell us where he is, then we will reward you handsomely." He looked into Gabbi's watery eyes. "Have you seen him?"

"A priest and a criminal?"

"Only a disguise, but he may not be travelling as a priest anymore," offered Koell. *It wouldn't hurt to embellish the facts a little*, he thought. "And yes, he is bad, he has committed multiple murders and is responsible for the deaths of women and children, not to forget he's injured, countless innocent people. Just Horrific," Koell tut-tutted to enhance the seriousness of the offences.

"And you believe he is here in Chieti?"

"No, we are not sure. We lost his trail between Pescara and Naples."

"What's the reward?"

"Let's say ... uh, substantial."

Never one to miss any opportunity that he could benefit from, Gabbi came to a quick decision. "I have not seen him, but if he were here, then I would know. But I will ask around for you."

"Keep the photo, and if you find him, then send a telegram to this address." Koell fished in his pocket for a pencil and wrote out the destination address on the back of the photograph, and handed it to the policeman, along with a handful of lira.

"How urgent is it you find him?" Already, Gabbi was calculating how to extort more money from these two men if he found the man they sought.

"It is important, but our generosity is proportionate to the accuracy and timeliness of the information you provide us." Koell's expression hardened. "If you know where this man can be found with certainty, then send me a telegraph, we will presume you can lead us to him immediately. Understood?"

The destination address gave no clue to who or where the telegram was destined. Gabbi was curious about the identities of these men and for whom they worked. Based on their accents, he believed they were Germans, and although he didn't show it, they frightened him, especially the thickset muscular one. Through experience, Gabbi also knew the more significant the reward, the higher the risk. These two men were serious; he'd have to be careful.

Gabbi nodded. "Did this man stay here or pass through?"

"We think he will only have passed through."

"I want to see some identification," asked Gabbi with his hand held out.

"No, you don't," replied the tall man without pause. His eyes bored into Gabbi's. "Your curiosity is better served to look for the man we seek rather than asking about us."

Gabbi swallowed. "What is his name?"

Koell knew it wouldn't cause any harm to tell the policeman the name of the priest. "Father Stevan Belić is more than likely he will use an assumed name."

"Baltic?"

"Serbian," answered Koell.

Gabbi nodded and now knew these men were Austrians. "If he came here or is still here, I will find out and let you know as you ask." He gave Koell a version of his own hardened look. "You had better not be trying to cheat me, I can make life very difficult for you and am well connected, so keep that in mind."

Koell kept from laughing, "We have no intention of cheating you, we just want this man. And your name?"

"Just ask for Gabbi, everyone here knows me."

Koel wrote his name in his notebook, although he didn't expect to hear from the scrawny little policeman again.

Having almost exhausted their cash reserves and patience, *Oberleutenant* Koell and *Stabswachtmeister* Wollf set about returning to Wien and reporting to Major Richter.

Koell began thinking of the detailed report he would need to write. The major was insistent that all the minutiae were painstakingly documented and recorded regardless of how trivial. Richter would read, analyse, dissect and then tirelessly debrief them – not at all pleasant. Koell pulled out his notebook and began briefly summarising.

Both investigators felt that the priest had successfully evaded them, and they stood little chance of ever finding him. He'd simply vanished, and as Koel predicted, even the informants in the towns between Naples and Pescara would prove to be worthless. Major Richter would have some suggestions, of that Koell was certain.

CHAPTER SEVEN

The large one-hundred and twenty-two-centimetre diameter grindstone, the shaft, bearings and its entire assembly all lay on the floor of the mill. They'd been painstakingly removed from the heavy chassis for annual repair and maintenance before the olive harvesting season in Autumn. The heavy stone used to grind the olives, before pressing, suffered a sizeable visible crack that ran through its centre. As Lorenzo told Belić, once the olives were harvested, they needed to be processed almost immediately, or the quality of the oil would deteriorate significantly – an equipment fault during the harvesting season was catastrophic.

Lorenzo was nothing short of a wizard when it came to farming and agriculture. He was also the *capo*, and under *Signora* Milani's direction, he managed her property and agricultural interests with unquestioned loyalty and dedication. Father Stevan leaned on his walking stick and watched Enzo, as he preferred to be called, inspect and oil the shaft bearings the heavy grindstone rotated on.

On the advice of Fabio, Belić began to walk as much as possible to strengthen the muscles in his ankle. Every morning he either walked around the village or visited with Lorenzo, who was always busy working here or there and would chat with him a while. In the early evening, he would walk again, often with *Signora* Milani and they would stroll through the olive groves and enjoy the cooling breezes as they swept down from the hills.

Signora Milani was insistent that Belić remain as her guest until he recovered enough to resume his journey. Over the last two weeks, they frequently talked, enjoying each other's company to the point where they'd quickly become good friends. Although discussing politics, the current state of regional affairs and her husband were delicately avoided. Belić still felt an unexplained tension at times.

Once a week, supplies were brought in, including a collection of newspapers, and Belić hungrily devoured everything he could read about the assassination of Franz Ferdinand and Sophie. He wasn't surprised but still dismayed to learn all the Black Hand members were apprehended. The papers claimed that the last remaining terrorist, Muhamed Mehmedbasić, was finally arrested in Montenegro and awaiting trial in Sarajevo. To his surprise, there was no mention or description of any other accomplices the authorities sought in connection with the assassination plot. There was no mention of him. Belić found this omission unsettling.

He couldn't accept that other Black Hand members hadn't talked about him in their coerced confessions. So why omit the details in the newspapers? This was perplexing and worrying. Over the last few days, Belić pondered over this constantly, and he came up with only one real plausible explanation. The authorities did not want to alert the public that they were actively searching for him, which would make him feel safe, and that he'd successfully avoided being caught. He knew that was pure nonsense and discarded that idea. Of course, the other perspective was also possible and more likely – if they never caught him, the authorities didn't have to admit he'd escaped in the first place. That, he surmised, meant he'd never stand trial, and if caught – he'd be executed.

Although the injury was unplanned, it wasn't devastating, he'd still managed to vanish, and the authorities would find it almost impossible to locate him. It was doubtful the Austrians would trace him to the sanctuary of *Signora* Milani's fine estate.

Although convenient, remaining here for any length of time was out of the question, and once his ankle sufficiently healed, he would quietly make his way to L'Aquila and then by train to Rome as initially intended.

As all the newspapers reported, tensions between Serbia and Austria were understandably high, and as predicted, Austria delivered its ultimatum to Serbia, listing ten non-negotiable demands. War would result if any of the stipulations weren't met, and Serbian newspapers all forecast that their country would be invaded in retaliation for the assassinations. For Belić, he was curious about other nations in the region and how they would respond to an Austrian invasion of Serbia, and most of all, how would Austria's friend and ally, Germany, react.

Enzo stood and arched his back. "I am too old for this, Father."

"There are other men here who could do this work, why must you do it?" Belić asked.

"Because I do not want a mechanical breakdown, if I do this work, then I know it has been done properly."

Belić nodded as Enzo wiped his oily hands on a rag and stepped from behind the disassembled grinding machinery. He began to walk towards the village, and Belić fell into step beside him. They remained silent for a minute or two.

"*Signora* Milani says you will leave soon as your ankle has healed," Enzo stated. He was considerate of Belić's injured foot and walked slowly.

"I am hoping that I can leave sometime within the next two or three weeks." Belić wanted to change the subject. "What of the grindstone, you can't use it like that?"

"I will order a new one. The *Signora* will be unhappy at the cost, but she can delay it no longer. It will be a good excuse for her to go into Chieti."

Ahead, *Signora* Milani, smiling broadly, walked towards them. "Have you already finished for the day, Enzo?" she asked, teasing him. She winked at Belić.

"*Signora*," Enzo shook his head at the severity of the bad news he must share with his employer, "the grindstone is no good. The crack has worsened, and we need to replace it."

"Can we buy one in Chieti?"

Enzo nodded, "Yes, but they will not have one available, so we will need to order it."

"Then next week, we will go into Chieti and purchase a new one," she said decisively.

"Very well, *Signora*," offered Enzo. "Please excuse me, I have much to do. *Signora*, Father." Enzo respectfully nodded and walked towards the barn and workshop.

"He is a good man," Belić said after Enzo was out of earshot.

"I couldn't manage this place without him. He is a wonderful dear man. Come, Father." She slipped her arm through his, and they walked towards her villa. Through the opening in the barn, Enzo watched them walk away.

It was early evening, and Father Stevan Belić sat comfortably on the sofa, with his foot elevated and reading from a book he was never without, titled *Divine Office*. It provided him with spiritual guidance and support. More recently, he turned to it in increasing frequency as he again felt the tugging of guilt seeping into his consciousness. The hymns and litanies of the *Liturgy of the Hours* weren't enough to quell the growing unease. He'd turned to the Bible and read scripture, he'd prayed, he'd asked for forgiveness and sought strength from God to overcome the oppressive feelings of shame that began to dominate his thoughts. Instead of helping, the feeling he'd betrayed his faith only worsened.

Betrayed was the word on his lips, it was a word he wrote on paper, dreamed about, and agonised over. He knew in his heart God was disappointed with him over what he'd done.

Over many years, and through a direct result of his actions, many people died. Did it matter if Franz Ferdinand and his wife, or even others, supported unjust causes? They certainly had a right to believe what they wanted, and did he, Father Stevan Belić, have a right to pass judgement on them because of their beliefs or politics?

God loved everyone, and so should he. But he had been critical, he had been caught up in the fervour of bias and prejudice and been swept away in a river of hate which led people to violent deaths. As a priest, he'd been remiss and not acted in accord with the doctrine of his church or God, and instead, sinned again and again. With bitterness, he spoke the word aloud, "Betrayed."

"Betrayed?" repeated *Signora* Milani as she entered the room. She carried a bottle of wine and two glasses and set them down on a small table before sitting beside him.

Belić felt ashamed and looked away. People expected that he, a priest in the Roman Catholic Church, conform to a spiritual standard; time had proven he was incapable of that.

"What is worse, *Signora*, failing to meet the expectations of others or your own?" He looked at a portrait painting of a distinguished elderly man on the opposite wall.

"That is easy, if you meet and satisfy your own expectations, then you can't disappoint anyone else's," she laughed. "You've had too much time to think."

He closed the open book that sat on his lap, put it aside, and reached for the glass of wine she offered. "I believe what I did was right, although others may have expected better of me, and I fear disappointed them."

Signora Milani studied him carefully and waited for him to elaborate – he didn't. She acknowledged that he was tall, dark and handsome, and in civilian clothes, it was difficult to imagine him a priest. She felt no guilt with her appraisal of a clergyman and assessed him as she would any man who interested her.

"Perhaps you allow the church to come between your heart and mind?" A small smile played across her face.

"Oh," he gave a small nervous laugh, "you are insightful."

Now it was Belić's turn to study her. He usually didn't allow himself the opportunity to analyse women, it was a pastime and temptation he could do without. But here in her home, in this setting and mood, it seemed not only appropriate, it felt right and natural. He took a healthy sip of wine to settle his disquiet.

He imagined her sitting before a painter, with her chin held high, emphasising her slender and elegant long neck. She was more than attractive; she was beautiful in the truly classic sense. He could picture her face on canvas, unblemished skin, sensual lips, long flowing hair ... and a bare shoulder. He sighed.

Her dark brown eyes frightened him. They probed and exposed his weaknesses, made him feel vulnerable and insecure. The way she looked at him with inquisitive openness and honesty, and he knew it was his guilt that made him feel unworthy. His lips were suddenly dry, and he raised the glass again to his mouth before he spoke.

"My heart and mind do not share the same space, *Signora* Milani, you are correct." He smiled to hide his unease.

"Enough of that, Stevan. Call me Natalina."

He mouthed her name slowly, "Nat–a–lin–a. Is a beautiful

name and suits you."

Signora Milani shifted her position and now sat on an angle so she could see him better; their knees touched. He felt the electricity pass between them, and he almost gasped.

"I, uh. I expect the grindstone will be expensive to replace," he finally managed to say. He needed to deflect his thoughts. He looked towards her and immediately wished he hadn't.

Her eyes twinkled in amusement. "Yes, Stevan, it will. We knew it would eventually crack all the way through, and I was prepared. Would you like to come with us when we go into Chieti?"

He wanted to say, *yes, I'd enjoy that tremendously.* "No, thank you kindly, I will take the opportunity to write some letters." He looked away and returned his gaze to the sobering face of the portrait on the wall and the dark, brooding, unblinking eyes of the figure who stared back. He felt she saw through his lie. Thankfully she moved her knee.

"He was a good man but a horrible father."

"That's your father? You look nothing like him."

"This was his farm, and he had vision and determination. He put his heart into making it work and to provide a good income, then when he died, Paolo and I returned here."

Belić risked a subtle look at her. She was focused on the painting and lost in her memories. He could see the gentle rise and fall of her chest as her slender fingers toyed sensually with the stem of the wine glass. She was captivating. He wanted to ask her about her husband Paolo but thought it best to allow her to talk of him when she was comfortable to do so.

The silence in the room was broken only by the sound of his thumping heart. "Well, please excuse me, Natalina, I, uh, I am tired and in need of sleep. It is time for bed."

Her head slowly turned from the painting, and she looked at him, her eyes sparkled and probed; again, he felt she could see through his transparency. He turned guiltily away, lifted his leg from the chair it rested on and rose unsteadily.

Belić closed the door of his room and leaned back against it, his mind was in tumult. He looked down at himself, his heart was racing, and he could feel his cheeks redden. He knew it wasn't the wine.

He clutched the book *Divine Office* protectively against his heart. It did little good and only made him question – *Who was he? What was he*? He took a steadying breath, closed his eyes and reaffirmed – "I am Father Stevan Belić, a Roman Catholic Priest. I received and accepted my Holy Orders, and I act in the power of Christ. It is no longer I who live, but Christ who lives in me. I swore obedience to my Bishop – I am Father Stevan Belić ..." He opened his eyes and remained against the door, reflecting a moment longer as his breathing settled.

He limped past the bed and placed his book on the nightstand, and continued into the small bathroom attached to his room. A large full-length mirror was affixed to the far wall, and on impulse, he stopped and looked at the reflection – at the man who stared back at him. He looked at his face, the square jaw, the deep-set eyes and the shock of black hair. He raised his hands, opening and slowly rotating them so he could assess and scrutinise – searching for visible flaws.

Carefully he removed his clothes and presented himself naked in front of the mirror. He studied himself in the minutest detail. At his injured and bruised ankle, his legs, and chest – everywhere. Time stopped. He lifted his head and courageously met his own gaze and stared objectively at his manifestation. His self-appraisal was critical and quickly turned to despondency. *What have I become?* he thought in growing despair.

From deep within, he heard a voice, a whisper of equity and yearning, and then he spoke softly, "I am a man." He didn't move and thought of Michelangelo's David and the biblical story of Goliath. "I am just a man, and I love my country and my people," he whispered. "I am David."

He paused and stared, not daring to move. He swallowed thickly as unfamiliar words formed. "I, I–am–also–a ..." He couldn't continue, he couldn't acknowledge it and knew he needed to focus on other things. The eyes in the mirror stared back knowingly – they mocked him, they judged. He closed his eyes tightly, clenched his fists and fought the overwhelming burden of shame that threatened to subjugate him.

After a heartbeat or two, he breathed out slowly and forced his eyes open. He looked into the mirror one last time as the image of *Signora* Natalina Milani began to invade his thoughts. He hobbled into the bedroom silently mouthing Nat–a–lin–a, Nat–a–lin–a. Tonight he'd succeeded in controlling his emotions; he'd won. But deep down, he knew it was a temporary victory, only a stay. She was important to him, he needed her, and he knew if he was to survive, he must be strong and overcome his weakness.

The two Austrian's disappointed Gabbi, yet he was convinced they believed the priest was here in Chieti. Sadly, he wasn't so sure. He'd wasted hours and hours talking to people and asking questions. No one even spared a second glance at the photograph when he showed it to them. When the two strange Austrians left Chieti over two weeks ago, Gabbi visited every hotel, guest–house and boarding house he knew and presented them with the photograph.

On a whim, he even visited the few brothels in the area and met with similar results. Rather than just ask people, 'Have you seen this man?' He changed tactics and inquired, 'Is this man still staying here?' It caused people to think more carefully before they replied.

Gabbi knew the two men had money, and it rankled him to no end that he wouldn't be rewarded for his efforts. But as a true scavenger, he wouldn't give up, he'd dig a little deeper, look farther afield and be more creative in his search.

Content with his narcissistic thoughts, Gabbi took a seat at his favourite café and began to read the newspaper. He ignored the idealistic chatter of locals as they squabbled endlessly about politics and the differences between socialism and nationalism. He'd heard it all before and made his point quite clear that he supported individualism, anything else was pointless and stupid.

Staring up at him in bold letters was the newspaper headline, 'ASSASSINATION MAY LEAD TO WAR.' He read the story with interest and wondered if there was any connection between the Austrians looking for the priest and what recently transpired in Sarajevo. Initially, this gave Gabbi some cause for concern. But war? He'd always been against war, not for political or religious reasons or even because he objected to war on moral grounds. In Gabbi's world, everything was simple. War restricted his freedom, war limited opportunity and war was dangerous.

Experts predicted Italy would remain neutral, as politically, there was nothing to gain by supporting Austria. If that were true, then he hoped there was nothing to worry about and could continue to go about his activities unaffected, or better still, even capitalise in some small way.

He fished the dog-eared photograph of the priest from his pocket and looked at it again. The Austrians wanted this man badly, why else send two men traipsing across Italy to find him. He would renew his efforts, and when he did find him, and the Austrians returned, he'd demand more money.

Over the coming days, Belić's foot continued to improve, and he could walk without the aid of a stick. Although a little tender at the end of each day, it always felt better after a good night's rest. The healing was taking time, more than he ever thought possible, and with it, his anxiety increased. Fabio suggested he continue to exercise and, when sitting, keep the foot elevated. Belić reassessed when he could resume his journey and now believed he could depart *Signora* Milani's home in about two weeks.

As he did every morning, he sat outside as the sun crept over the shadowed hills and revealed men already hard at work in the surrounding orchards and fields. Once the midday heat became uncomfortable, they would go home, sleep, and return later in the afternoon for another hour or two of work. It was an uncomplicated life, and part of him was envious.

"Are you ready?" asked Natalina.

Belić smiled and rose from his chair and waited for her as she slid a supportive arm through his so they could begin a morning stroll together. His ankle always felt a little tight first thing in the morning, and so they set off at a slow pace. There was no hurry, and they walked in companionable silence, taking in the mornings scents and sounds around them. He enjoyed the closeness and the feel of her tucked in at his side, occasionally he could even smell the fragrance of her hair. He was happy, content, and warming to the routine of the Italian culture and lifestyle. Of course, *Signora* Natalina Milani was a gracious and kind host, but there was more, he felt it.

"Paolo was killed just over there," said Natalina, surprising him. She pointed to a corner of the olive grove at a distant tree by a fence.

Belić said nothing, allowing her to talk. He squeezed her arm reassuringly in acknowledgement, encouraging her to continue.

"We had a neighbour, Franco, he was a good man, and he and Paolo were the best of friends. I liked both Franco and his wife, we spent many evenings together socialising."

They walked between rows of mature olive trees, the green and silver leaves beginning to sparkle as the early morning sun draped them in a golden glow. Belić said nothing and allowed her to talk at her own measure. She steered him towards the tree she pointed to.

"Paolo hired Franco to do some pruning on our trees, he had a natural ability and was quite an expert. Paolo believed he paid Franco for his work, but Franco claimed he never received any money. After a few months, the bickering became worse and affected their friendship, and they became hostile towards each other." Natalina paused a moment, and they walked on a few steps before she continued.

"One day, Franco came over to where Paolo was working. It was right here at this very place."

She looked at the ground near the tree as if searching for a lost memory.

"He was enraged and demanded Paolo pay him. They began pushing each other, and Paolo slipped and fell ... his head hit a rock, and he died instantly." Natalina stopped and released his arm, turning away to look out across the valley.

"What happened to Franco?" he asked, standing behind her.

"The police said it was an accident, and he wasn't charged with any crime."

Belić took a step towards the wooden fence that separated the olive grove from a field where sheep grazed, he leaned against the top rail and looked out, following her gaze. "And you, Natalina, how did you feel?

"I felt cheated that my husband was taken away from me, the man I loved was dead because a foolish neighbour made a simple accounting error."

"How did you respond to him afterwards?"

"I hated him for what he did. Oh, Stevan, I hated Franco and everything about him. I even hated his wife." She stepped closer to the fence beside him and looked up, her eyes moist.

He turned to face her. "Did you forgive him?"

"No, no, I did not." She shook her head.

Belić reached in his pocket and felt for the old cross. "None is righteous, no, not one." The quote from scripture, almost a reminder to himself as for her. "Have you room in your heart for forgiveness?"

"Forgiveness, for what that man did? You talk to me of forgiveness, and yet he ruined my life."

Belić nodded sympathetically and continued to look at her. She couldn't maintain eye contact and turned away. "Then there is more?" he asked after a moment of silence.

"In my anger, I had them evicted. They were tenants."

"I see... Then you felt better after turning them away?"

"No, Stevan, that's just it, I didn't, I felt worse. What I did was wrong."

"Judge not, and you will not be judged; condemn not, and you will not be condemned; forgive, and you will be forgiven."

"And that solves all – through reciting scripture?"

"You have to believe it within your heart, Natalina. Forgiveness is not a sin; it's a doorway to redemption and peace." He paused a moment. "It's the same door where you'll allow people in to touch your heart and soul."

She turned to face him and shuffled a step closer. Their eyes met, and neither turned away. She slowly raised her hand and gently touched his cheek. Belić didn't move and looked into the deep liquid pools of her eyes. He felt it then, and he knew in his heart, she did too.

He silently mouthed the words he spoke to himself in front of the mirror ... I am a man.

"A prayer?" she whispered.

He could hardly hear her over his pounding heart. "No, far from it," he smiled. "I said, I am a man."

They remained still, each looking intently at the other. He could smell her, and it was intoxicating. The unbroken silence filled with entente.

"Yes," she finally replied in a whisper, "that you are."

"I think we should go," he finally croaked.

CHAPTER EIGHT

The elderly gentleman steered the wagon slowly up Chieti's, Viale Benedetto Croce, and was oblivious to the angry shouts of other drivers who wished to share the road. He was content to navigate a safer path and one a little closer to the centre of the main thoroughfare than some may have preferred. Occasionally a motorcar spluttered noisily past and attracted curious stares from those unfamiliar with the new conveyance, but the old man ignored them too. Remarkably, he waved at those he recognised, replied to friendly greetings from those he knew and disregarded the less than savoury comments directed at him. Determined to fulfil his responsibilities and keep his passengers safe, the old man remained calm in the face of mounting hostilities.

Down some narrow streets, washing was strung between buildings to dry, and women tended to domestic tasks in the coolness of shadowed lanes. A few dogs foraged for treats and sometimes barked at perceived threats, while some children, too young to attend school, played happily.

Signora Milani sat up front beside the old man, while Enzo was reasonably comfortable in the back of the wagon and immensely grateful for the folded canvas tarpaulin that provided him with some comfort to his rear end.

She hadn't been entirely aware of the journey into Chieti; her mind had been preoccupied with other thoughts. Mostly the surprising realisation that she missed Stevan. After their talk in the olive grove the previous day, she believed he was correct, and she should forgive. Later that night, after their conversation, she pondered and analysed her out of character reactions over the death of her husband, Paolo. The evening she spent alone in the privacy of her room was emotional and accompanied only by an outpouring of grief, guilt and loneliness.

On Stevan's prompting, she reluctantly began the process of forgiving Franco, and as the anger and guilt washed away in a flood of tears and sobbing, the doorway to her heart and soul also cracked open a little. She could see Stevan in that newly vacated space standing proud and handsome, but the connection she felt was more than just a passing fancy, it was an impassioned bond that drew her in. She felt someone watching her, and in reflex, looked over her shoulder. It was just Enzo laying comfortably in the wagon. She smiled at him.

She welcomed Stevan's strength – she needed it. The long talks they'd enjoyed long into the evenings, the laughter ... she'd seen his walls come down and believed she saw him for what and who he truly is. Principled, passionate and moral, someone she respected and admired. He was an anchor and provided her with strength and courage to face her demons and resolve issues that festered malevolently inside her. She wanted to know more about this man who unexpectedly came into her life and brought so much; however, one issue remained unresolved – Father Stevan Belić was a Roman Catholic priest.

As planned, Enzo and *Signora* Milani's visit to Chieti was to purchase a new grindstone for the mill. The old man who usually made all local pick-ups and deliveries enjoyed the company, and as he always did, generously insisted they ride with him. Although today, *Signora* Milani had not been her usual talkative self and been distracted. The old man quietly believed she was thinking about love and romance, as word quickly spread among locals about how frequently she was seen in the company of her house guest. The fact he was a priest only fuelled their interest and local gossip. Personally, the old man believed nothing should stand in the way when it came to matters of the heart. If two people were genuinely in love, then any challenges they faced were not insurmountable, love does conquer all, he believed. He wished the beautiful Natalina and the priest nothing but good wishes. But Enzo was the worry. He'd seen the way Enzo looked at the *Signora* and surmised he'd been in love with her for years, but the *Signora* was blind to it. Perhaps he would offer her the benefit of his experience and wisdom with a fatherly talk when they returned to the village. After all, many would be surprised to learn he was a romantic at heart and still madly in love with his wife as he was the very first day he set eyes upon her all those years ago. *The young had so much to learn about love.*

Typically, on their trips to Chieti, and today was no exception, *Signora* Milani would spend a night or two with a dear friend, while Enzo would spend time with his sister. When ready to return home, Enzo's brother-in-law would take them both back up into the hills using his wagon and, in turn, spend the night with Enzo and his mother. While confusing to some, it was how it was always done, and no one had any reason to change what had worked well for some time.

Before Enzo could order the new grindstone, *Signora* Milani needed to go to the bank and withdraw money to pay for it. Banca Monte dei Paschi di Siena was just ahead, and without warning, the old man began to veer from the middle of the road towards the left–hand side of the street. This prompted a chorus of yelling from other wagon drivers as he aimed the mule for an open space where he could park outside the bank.

On his circuitous foot patrol around Chieti, Gabbi was on Viale Benedetto Croce when he heard yelling, and a commotion from ahead and immediately looked to the cause. He wasn't concerned for the well-being of pedestrians as they quickly leapt out of the way of the seemingly errant wagon, or for the safety of other road users who took evasive action; no, Gabbi's watery eyes were firmly fixed on the woman who sat beside the driver of the approaching wagon. He knew who she was and immediately fished in his pocket and found the tattered photo of the priest. He chastised himself for forgetting all about her, but here was an opportunity too good to miss. He knew she frequently rented a room in her villa to travellers. He hoisted his ill-fitting trousers and walked quickly to where the wagon was pulling up outside the bank.

Gabbi saw little benefit in offering anyone a greeting or a polite salutation, such courtesies he allowed others to make. He was focused purely on the money he hoped to extort from the Austrians when he found the priest. He looked at *Signora* Milani and licked his lips, he didn't see a beautiful woman, he just saw a person – a convenience to use – they were all the same to him, what he saw was money.

"Is this man still staying with you?" he barked, waving the photo for all to see. He kept his eyes on her, hoping for the slightest reaction. He couldn't have been more surprised when her eyes flashed in recognition.

Receiving no verbal reply, he asked again, "Is this man still staying with you?"

"No, who is he?" she answered, recovering quickly. Enzo leapt from the wagon and walked up to Gabbi. The old man kept his face stoic, he didn't respond and remained seated. He'd seen her reaction too.

"He's a bad one, he is. Murdered people, women and children. A cold-blooded killer!" Gabbi stated with confidence.

Enzo was tall and in superb physical condition, he towered over Gabbi and wasn't intimidated by the small annoying policeman. "What do you want, Gabbi? Leave us alone, we're busy and have things to do."

Gabbi placed the photo back in his pocket and smiled broadly – he could have jumped for joy. He now knew the priest was a guest at her home but was he still there?

Enzo reached a hand up and assisted *Signora* Milani down from the wagon.

"You've been harbouring a fugitive, this doesn't look good for you, *Signora*." Gabbi accused. He waved a bony finger at her.

"Show me the photo again?" she asked once safely on the ground. "And what's this about murdering people? I do not know this man you speak of." She shook her head.

Gabbi didn't have many details on what the priest was accused of doing, other than being a murderer, but that didn't matter, he'd lie. "He's killed important people, apparently. Women and children. I'm not allowed to disclose police business or any facts relating to the case, but trust me when I tell you, he is bad." He showed the photo to her again and decided to embellish the severity a little more. "I shouldn't tell you this," he looked over his shoulder to ensure no one was within earshot and leaned forward, "I understand he raped them before mutilating them."

Signora Milani had a hundred thoughts going through her mind

– her initial reaction was disbelief. Surely, Stevan wasn't capable of committing the horrific crimes Gabbi suggested; it wasn't possible, inconceivable. Or was it? Father Stevan, if that was really his name, could he have deceived her?

Enzo was trying to step between *Signora* Milani and Gabbi, who was becoming increasingly louder.

"Where is he? Where is he now?" Gabbi began to yell. He wanted to attract as much attention as possible.

"Leave the *Signora* alone, she has done nothing. Let her go about her business!" cried Enzo in growing frustration.

Gabbi raised his voice louder, "Where is he? Where–is–he!"

Signora Milani didn't hear the yelling, she stood transfixed outside the bank as she recalled the heart to heart conversations with Stevan. *Was he a murderer and a rapist, had he killed women and children?* She found it difficult to believe Gabbi. She turned and looked at the policeman who was trying to sidestep around Enzo.

"You are lying to me, Gabbi. It wouldn't be the first time you've lied, and it wouldn't be the last," she said.

Gabbi stopped trying to push past Enzo. "I tell the truth; why would I have his photograph if I were making this up?"

He had a valid point, she reasoned.

The old man in the wagon watched quietly. He rubbed his chin thoughtfully as he remembered the day he'd picked up the dishevelled priest alongside the road. Although, in his opinion, the priest was undoubtedly running from something, but he didn't appear to be a rapist and killer of women and children, as Gabbi claimed. He continued to observe and wondered if either Enzo or the *Signora* would tell the little policeman about the priest and give him up? Enzo would support *Signora* Milani in whatever she said. But the *Signora* was currently distressed, that was plain to see.

The more Gabbi pressed her, the more upset and flustered she became. Admirably, Enzo tried his best to get between the two of them and encouraged her to go inside the bank, but Gabbi darted around Enzo and pointed his finger accusingly at her. "He's staying at your home, isn't he? Tell me!"

Why did Gabbi have a photo of Stevan if he'd done no wrong? How could Stevan have deceived me so? Gabbi's incessant yapping dissolved into the background, and she paid no attention to him or Enzo. She still stood beside the wagon and stared vacantly. Her feelings towards Stevan were genuine, perhaps a lot more than she even cared to admit. She had allowed a stranger into her home and her heart, and now she learns that he is a wanted fugitive. And if Gabbi were to be believed, a criminal, a murderer. *Why else would the police have a photo of Stevan?* She asked herself again. What a fool she'd been. Her emotions were awash in a confusing turmoil of fluctuating sentiments that went from disbelief to anger in only a heartbeat.

She shuddered, realising she couldn't return to her home while he remained there. What options did she have? While Gabbi may embellish the truth, why would the police seek Stevan if he were innocent? She came to a decision and held her hand up. "Stop! Both of you," she commanded, "enough!"

Enzo and Gabbi stopped their jostling and shouting and stared open-mouthed at her. The old man in the wagon slowly shook his head.

"He is a guest in my home," she said quietly. Tears began to flow.

Gabbi pushed his way past Enzo. "He-he's there now? Are you sure? If you are lying to me…."

"She isn't like you, Gabbi, and if I find out you've lied to us, then you'd better watch yourself," responded Enzo as he took a threatening step towards the policeman.

Signora Milani turned from Gabbi and dabbed her eyes, ignoring the spectators who stood gawking before she walked quickly into the bank. The old man closed his eyes and lowered his head. Gabbi turned and promptly began to walk away; he had a telegram to send. Enzo turned and leaned against the wagon in frustration, he liked the priest and enjoyed his company, they'd become friends – he didn't believe Gabbi for one moment.

The *Evidenzbureau* headquartered in Wien received a telegram that contained only three words, 'Priest in Chieti'. Major Richter insisted that both Koell and Wollf return to Chieti with some urgency and depart Wien that same day.

The major was bent over a chart table and was staring over a detailed map of Italy, in particular the small town in the region of Abruzzo known as Chieti. His finger traced a line in a westerly direction from Chieti towards L'Aquila and then onwards to Rome.

"That's where he intends to go, *Oberleutenant*, Rome!" His finger stabbed the map.

Oberleutenant Hans Koell, nodded, "Yes, *Herr* Major."

'Had you done your job properly, then you wouldn't find yourself in this mess, and we'd already have him." Richter turned away from the map and gave *Oberleutenant* Koell a steely glare. "The priest may be clever and resourceful, but we are even better. Make sure you don't fail this time." The major straightened. "The emperor wants this man punished, do you understand me, *Oberleutenant*?"

"Yes, *Herr* Major."

Richter doubted Koell did understand as this situation was becoming increasingly complicated. "There are some rather sensitive developments taking place that will affect how you and

Stabswachtmeister Wollf can operate. Travelling as Swiss nationals doesn't mean people won't ask questions, I implore you to act with discretion."

"And when we find the priest?" asked Koell.

"You'll take him to the coastal town of Pescara, where I will arrange for a boat to pick you up. Once aboard, you will kill him and throw the body overboard, well away from Italian waters. Just make sure his capture and death don't lead back to Austria or Italy. Emperor Franz Joseph wants this dealt with decisively, quietly and without fuss."

"And a boat? *Herr* Major."

Richter glared at Koell. "It will be a Radio Direction Finding trawler. Fortunately, I have one in the region. You will take the priest aboard the vessel, and I repeat, once away from Italy, kill him in international waters, is this understood, *Oberleutenant*?"

Of course, *Herr*, Major," *Oberleutenant* Hans Koell acknowledged.

Richter nodded. "Have you learned anything about him, his mannerisms, habits, what do you know?"

Wollf and Koell exchanged a look. "We don't know much about him," replied Koell.

Stabswachtmeister Deiter Wollf shrugged and shook his head. Then he remembered something and opened his mouth to speak, then decided otherwise.

"You have something to add, *Stabswachtmeister*?" asked the major.

"It isn't important, *Herr* Major."

"Let me be the judge."

"Someone told me the priest fidgets constantly with an old wooden cross. But all priests have a cross, so it probably isn't important," Wollf replied.

"So now we are spies?" asked *Stabswachtmeister* Deiter Wollf with a surly frown.

Koell shrugged, "We have no choice, and it's an easy job. All we must do is find the priest, take him to Pescara, put him on a boat, kill him and then return home. How hard can that be?"

"Easy?" Wollf laughed. Both men sat in the train that was taking them towards Chieti. "Bloody trains ... uncomfortable bloody seats," muttered Wollf to himself and then turned his thoughts towards the pleasures of sleeping on a bed and not on a hard seat.

After multiple trains and endless miles, both Austrians arrived thirty-six hours later. It was late evening when the train finally rattled into Chieti, and two weary and morose investigators stepped onto the platform. It departed after the conductor blew the *all-clear*, leaving two travel-weary Austrians alone on the platform.

Gabbi accurately reasoned the Austrians would return on the late train two days later and began preparations to ensure everything went according to his plan. With the door to his room securely locked, he pried up two loose floorboards revealing a cleverly concealed compartment containing an assortment of items, including a small but growing stash of money, some pornography, and a Bayard 1908 semi-automatic pistol carefully wrapped in an oily rag. He pulled the gun from its hiding place and, with practised ease, snapped in the five-shot magazine and held the pistol out at arm's length, then with one eye shut, imagined shooting two men in quick succession.

"Bang, bang," he whispered. Imminently pleased with his exceptional shooting skills, he repositioned the floorboards and placed the loaded Bayard in the waistband of his trousers.

From his secure position in a darkened doorway across the street from the railway station, Gabbi watched the train depart and saw the Austrians alone on the platform. As he didn't want to be seen near the two men, he decided to lure them away from the station to a more secluded spot just up the street where he could conclude his business in privacy.

"Where do we find him?" Wollf asked.

"I suspect he will find us," replied Koell as he looked around the platform. "In the meantime, let's walk towards the centre of town and find a hotel." He picked up his suitcase and walked from the platform, with Wollf following a step behind.

"Did you hear that?" Wollf asked.

Both men heard it. A low whistle. "Is coming from up the street," Koell suggested. "Remember what we talked about?"

Wollf nodded and said nothing. His senses finely tuned to the surrounding area. "A signal. I think it's that policeman."

Koell and Wollf discussed the possibility of being extorted by the policeman, and Wollf's job was to ensure their safety and keep a weapon trained on him whenever possible.

Wollf switched his suitcase to his left hand, and automatically his free hand went to his hip where a *Nahkampfmesser,* the German close quarter's combat knife, sat sheathed on his belt. Both men also carried pistols, by coincidence, also Steyr, Model 1910's, the same as the Black Hand used.

Both men walked cautiously towards the sound but couldn't see into the darkness, their eyes yet to adjust to the night after the bright gas lights of the station.

Gabbi saw both men approach, and he left the concealment of the doorway. He slowly backed away from the station and occasionally whistled, luring them to a dark alley with a small gate at the far end that led to a maze of minor narrow thoroughfares used by commercial businesses. It would be his escape route.

"I don't like this," said Koell. He now nervously held his pistol inside the pocket of his trousers.

Woolf's head swivelled from side to side as he sought to locate the source of the whistling. He grunted in response.

"Here!" said Gabbi, only loud enough for the two men to hear. He repeated it again. "Here!"

"I think we are being set-up," said Wolff stopping.

"Yes, something is odd. Dieter, separate a little, keep some distance between us."

Now apart, both men continued with caution and walked closer to the source of the voice. Koell could now begin to see the outline of a figure standing against a wall. As he approached, he saw the solitary figure of a man. It was the small policeman he met almost three weeks ago. Wollf was out of sight on his right somewhere. He walked forward, reassured by the feel of the Steyr in his pocket.

"We received your telegram ... so you know where the priest is?" asked *Oberleutenant* Koell.

"Where is your friend?" said Gabbi in his high-pitched voice.

"He's coming. He's just making sure you are alone."

"Call him over."

Koell kept quiet, knowing Wollf could hear. He took a step closer to the Italian.

"Where is he?" Gabbi asked again.

Koell could hear the nervousness in his voice. "He's here, no need to worry."

"Where? Where is he?"

Their eyes adjusted to the darkness, and they could see better. Without a sound, *Stabswachtmeister* Deiter Wollf stepped up beside his superior. Koell noticed Wollf had both hands free and discarded his suitcase.

"Don't you two going playing games with me," warned Gabbi. "I expect you both, to be honest, and treat me as you promised, we have a deal remember?"

"Of course, we have a deal. So, where is the priest? Tell me, and I will make it worth your while - just as I said," Koell smoothly offered. He lowered his suitcase to the ground.

"How much?"

"I think five-hundred lire is more than fair." Koell slowly reached into his pocket and extracted a wad of folded notes.

Gabbi laughed. "I think you'll need to do better than that. I want five-thousand."

"Five-Thousand?" Koell was taken back. *That was a lot of money.*

"I don't have all day."

"Then, where is he?" pleaded Koell.

"Show me the money first." Gabbi was becoming more excited as he smelled victory and began hopping from one foot to the next in excitement.

Koell fully expected the dishonest policeman would try to rob them, and he and Wollf discussed in length how they would respond, however, their main objective was first to find out where the priest was hiding.

"Let me get the money, it's in my jacket." Koell carefully removed another thick pile of folded notes and threw the wad on the ground near Gabbi's feet. "That's it, is all we have. Now tell me, where is the priest?"

Dieter Wollf leaned casually against the wall of the alley and appeared unthreatening. With his arms folded, he cleverly concealed the pistol he held. He knew that Koell didn't want the policeman to have all their money, but they first needed to know where the priest was. He tensed, ready to make his move.

Gabbi took a step forward and carefully reached down and picked up the large wad of banknotes held in place by a metal clip. He couldn't count the money in the darkness, but he knew it was a lot, although less than the five-thousand he demanded, but certainly more than he hoped for. He could see the tall officer standing relaxed in front of him, one hand in his pocket, while the other thickset man leaned against the wall. Neither looked menacing.

"You have your money, now where is the priest?" asked Koell. He kept his voice moderated and friendly.

Gabbi began edging away from the wall, taking a step towards the gate at the end of the alley. "He has been staying at the farm of *Signora* Milani, in a village about thirty-five kilometres north of here on the road to L'Aquila. She has a large villa and often rents a room to travellers."

"And you know he is there now?" Koell asked.

Gabbi took another step. "Yes, he is still there." With deliberate slowness, he began to reach behind his back for the pistol hidden in the waistband of his trousers. He had no intention of shooting anyone, but he would level the handgun at the two men and threaten them both to remain standing until he'd escaped through the gate and into the labyrinth of alleys beyond. He hoped the darkness would hide his movement as he reached for the Bayard pistol.

While the policeman was distracted by the wad of money, Wollf slowly took a step to his right hoping to cut-off Gabbi's exit. Koell fully expected the little policeman would pull a weapon on them as he made good his escape and true to form and even in the darkness, he saw the Italian slowly reach behind his back. On seeing Gabbi reach for his weapon, he began to lower the hand that held the Steyr.

"Stop!" Koell warned Gabbi.

Gabbi reacted in fright. In a fluid motion similar to the move he practised in his room, he pulled his pistol and swung his arm forward as he began to run for the gate at the end of the alley. Held firmly in his hand was the Bayard 1908 semi-automatic pistol. It was never his intention to pull the trigger as he lacked the courage to shoot someone face–to–face. When he saw the Austrians were armed, he panicked. In abject fear and without thinking, he inadvertently squeezed the trigger.

Hans Koell saw the pistol appear in Gabbi's hand and immediately lunged to his left. The gunshot was unnaturally loud in the alley and echoed throughout the stillness of the night. While Gabbi's motions may have been heroically rehearsed in the privacy of his room, his actual shooting skills had not.

The 6.35mm bullet from Gabbi's pistol left the muzzle with about 165-foot pounds of energy and struck Hans Koell in the left bicep. The force of the impact at close range spun him around, and off-balance, he fell to the ground with a yell of pain.

Although Gabbi never intended to fire his pistol, he'd done so purely in reflex, and for only a brief instant, he felt a sensual gratification at the result and a new experience to savour.

Stabswachtmeister Deiter Wollf dropped to a knee and by using both hands, expertly lined up his pistol on Gabbi and squeezed two shots in quick succession. Even in the darkness, the double-tap was accurate, both shots entered Gabbi's chest within a handbreadth of each other, the force propelled him back into the alley wall, where he slid to the ground. With his brain unable to receive the needed blood supply from his shredded heart, Gabbi died quickly.

Already Hans Koell was regaining his feet and cursing the pain and his misfortune. In response to the sound of three gunshots that broke the peaceful silence of a warm Chieti summer evening, dogs began to bark and already questioning voices in alarm could be heard.

Wollf quickly retrieved the money clip that had slipped from Gabbi's grasp and then checked to ensure the policeman was dead.

"Down the alley," grunted Koell as he picked up his case with his good arm.

"Wait," said Wollf and ran out the alley and around the corner to retrieve his suitcase. Koell was at the open gate at the end of the alley, dusting himself off when Wollf ran up only seconds later. Both men ran through the connecting alleys and, after a few wrong turns, arrived on the main street. *Oberleutenant* Hans Koell was in some discomfort and needed his arm tended too. They decided to walk normally and not attract any unnatural attention.

They could see a small hotel a short distance ahead, it was perfect for their needs, and they checked in without fuss. Koell kept his injured arm hidden behind Wollf at the reception desk, and his lightweight jacket prevented any blood from dripping on the floor.

The 8mm bullet had not damaged bone and fortunately passed clean through the fleshy part of his bicep. Koell was lucky, and he knew it, although luck did not prevent him from feeling the intense soreness.

In the service of Austria's military, *Stabswachtmeister* Wollf had tended to more wounds on himself and others than he cared to remember, and through his experiences, knew what needed to be done. Koell remained alone in the room where he stripped his clothes and cleaned his wound the best he could while Wollf went in search of bandages and ointment and whatever else he could scrounge.

A short time later, he returned with a stolen clean sheet he found hanging from a clothesline and began to tear it into long strips before bandaging Koell's arm. Both men had hardly spoken since the shooting. Neither man spared a thought or commented on the man they killed, they felt no remorse or guilt, he was a casualty, and they were acting according to their orders. As there were no witnesses, Koell was confident the death of a local policeman would not be traced back to them.

"It will be sore and stiff in the morning," offered Wollf as he finished rinsing the blood from Koell's blazer. He hung it near an open window to dry.

"It's painful and stiff now," replied Koell with a grimace.

"Just don't move it, keep it still, and hopefully we can find a doctor to look at it," grizzled Wollf.

Koell looked thoughtful a moment. "We will need to find horses in the morning."

"Can you ride?"

"I must."

Stabswachtmeister Deiter Wollf scowled his superior officer and looked out the window.

CHAPTER NINE

The breeze offered little relief, and what wind there was blew hot air across the valley and through the small village that nestled against the hills thirty-five kilometres from Chieti. The sun blazed unforgivingly and the oppressive heat, too hot for most, drove farmers indoors where many slept, content to return to work a little later when cooler.

Not everyone was sleeping, Father Stevan Belić was writing in his journal and reviewing his plans on travelling to Rome. Having the house to himself while *Signora* Milani was in Chieti for a few days allowed him the privacy he needed to spread out his notes, maps and addresses across the kitchen table.

His ankle had healed sufficiently enough where he could walk unaided without discomfort for short periods, and he reluctantly decided to leave the following week, or perhaps even the week after. He didn't want to go, and each passing day saw his attraction towards *Signora* Milani deepen, and his emotional conflict worsen. The bond between them was consuming, and even now, he admitted to himself, he missed her and wished she was here sitting at the table with him.

Belić looked up from his journal, and his expression hardened, it was also convenient and safe here; it suited him, and if he was honest, she was useful. He chastised himself for his weakness and conflicting emotions.

The last few weeks hadn't been easy for him, and he considered his actions from every angle. He'd sinned and felt ashamed. Being here in Italy with a beautiful hostess for company made him question his values and vows. The sprained ankle was a warning from God. It had forced him to reassess his beliefs, faith and the pain he had caused others. Yet, he knew his priority was self-preservation, and despite moral conflicts, and just as he'd done in the past, he could take full advantage of those who came into his life. They were opportunities, nothing more. But the *Signora...*

He stretched, leaned back in his chair and placed his hands behind his head and looked up. "Nat–a–lin-a, Nat–a–lin-a," he repeated, "my beautiful Natalina."

A sudden urgent rap on the door disturbed his abstraction and caused him to sit up with a start. He eased his foot from the chair it rested on and limped through the kitchen and into the atrium. He swung open the heavy door and was surprised to see the enigmatic old man who'd first offered him a ride in his wagon all those weeks ago. He was fanning his face with his hat, and he looked hot and flustered.

"Is it you who seeks trouble, or does trouble find you?" asked the old man with a tired smile.

"Uh, please, come inside, it looks like you need water," offered Belić. He stepped aside to allow the old man to enter. "Are you suggesting there is trouble?"

"Young man, far be it for me to judge, for to judge only brings attention on oneself, and I have a past that will keep God busy for quite some time. However, my concerns are not for myself."

Father Stevan was filling a glass of water from a pitcher. The import of the old man's cryptic words suddenly struck home. He stopped and quickly turned, facing his guest with urgency. "What has happened?"

"*Signora* Milani has informed the local police that you are a guest here in her house."

"The police!" Belić's mouth hung open. "Why?"

"If you'd prefer, we can discuss this in great detail now, however, my belief is that you need to pack your suitcase immediately so you can leave. I expect the police will be here very soon, and they can't be far behind me."

"Why would they be interested in me? I have committed no crimes in Italy?"

"You don't have time to dwell on your misdeeds." He sipped from the glass, wiped his mouth and looked up at the priest with a grim expression. "I have an inherent mistrust for the authorities, most of all the police, and I returned home after returning from Chieti to ponder over your dilemma. My conscience wouldn't allow me to ignore you and do nothing to assist. I should have spoken and warned you two days ago. For my delay, I apologise, young man, but to amend for my lack of action, I can take you up the road, not all the way to L'Aquila but hopefully far enough so you can have a little head-start. I hope that will be enough?"

Belić's mind was spinning. *The Italian police*, he wondered? He had questions. "Why would the police be interested in me?"

"Are you free of guilt?" replied the old man. "The police are circulating a photograph of your likeness, and *Signora* Milani identified you."

Belić was crestfallen and frozen in indecision.

"I am surprised the police have not yet come, but they will, of that you can be sure, so it is best that we get a move on, eh? I will tell you what I know later, but If I am to help you, then we must go."

Belić thought quickly. "Ah, yes, of course, uh ... please wait."

He quickly returned to the kitchen and gathered his journal and hurriedly scooped up his papers, and went upstairs to his room to quickly pack his suitcase. As he didn't have much, it didn't take long. He moved as fast as possible and was downstairs in no time, standing in front of the old man. "What happened, and why would she tell the police about me?"

"I'm curious to know what you've done, but later, but please hurry."

"I wish I could talk to her before I leave."

"I don't think that will be time well spent." The old man raised a knowing eyebrow. "The last time I saw her, she was thinking less than kindly thoughts about you."

Belić shook his head in disbelief. "Why, what reason would she have? I can't believe this."

"We should hasten."

"Let me leave her the money I owe. Is the least I could do."

The old man was already heading towards the door as Belić counted a substantial amount of money and left it on the chair. "I could leave her a letter."

"No, Father, time is presently not your friend!"

Within a short time, the mule was pulling the wagon upwards and over a range of hills. When the view afforded a look down into the valley, the old man took every opportunity to glance back, fearful the police would be following close behind. Belić's mind was in confusion. *How did they find him*?

Once they crested the rise and the going was easier and faster, the old man relaxed. "I'm trying to understand why the police would be in need of a priest. If they were looking to absolve their sins or seek spiritual guidance, then a couple of excellent priests in Chieti could provide them with absolution or forgiveness. Therefore, their need to see you must be for other reasons, and from what I heard from the police, you brutally raped and murdered women and children."

Belić's head whipped around, his mouth open in disbelief.

"That would be an excellent reason to want to talk to you. Tell me, Father, why it is I have risked my life, or the very least, my freedom to come to your assistance?"

"Because I am not guilty of raping or killing women and children!" stated Belić empathically. "But I am curious why the police are involved ... you did mean Italian police?"

"What other police could there be?"

"Please, what happened in Chieti? Tell me I must know." Father Stevan pleaded.

After they woke from a restless night, Wolfe went downstairs and spoke with the hotel manager to enquire where to rent horses. After a little negotiation, Koell and Wollf rented two healthy animals, and before long, both men left the outskirts of Chieti and rode in a northwesterly direction towards an unknown village and a villa where the fugitive priest was supposed to be staying.

Stabswachtmeister Deiter Wollf hated horses. He didn't care for sitting high up on an animal on a hard leather seat. He hated having his legs chaffed, his bottom rubbed raw, and the suffering he endured from the pain in his thighs after a day spent on horseback. Admittedly horses did travel quickly, but that was the only redeeming feature that came to mind. His superior, Hans Koell, in contrast, was quite at ease on a horse, he even admitted to liking them. However, *Oberleutenant* Hans Koell was not doing well today as the constant movement and jostling were causing him considerable distress and the wound on his arm began to bleed again. For two hours, they'd been riding and made good time, but now Koell needed to stop and rest.

Some distance ahead of the two Austrians, *Signora* Milani, Enzo, and Enzo's brother–in–law Carlo were cautiously approaching her villa. Upset and unsure what to do about the priest, *Signora* Milani delayed her return home by a day. It was decided that Carlo would take her directly to Enzo's small house, which was set back from the road, near her stables, where she would wait with Enzo's mother, while Enzo went to her home to find Father Stevan and explain to him that he needed to leave immediately. Something Enzo wasn't happy about doing.

She hadn't spoken much during their journey. Her despondency was heightened by sadness, an emptiness, and a feeling of heartache and loss. It made her feel lonely, but not too lonely that she still didn't feel anger. It simmered rancorously beneath her composed façade. If Belić was at her home and encountered the beautiful *Signora* at this moment, he would have witnessed the full extent of an infuriated and betrayed Italian woman.

Fortunately for Father Stevan, he was some miles away when *Signora* Milani, with the help of Enzo, stepped down from the wagon and made her way to Enzo's home.

"The house is empty, *Signora*. All I found was this," He held the money Belić left for her. "I went upstairs to his room, and it was empty, all his things have gone."

She took the money he held out and looked at the notes. Stevan paid for accommodation for every night he'd stayed and then a little extra. "Was there a note?" she asked.

Enzo shook his head. "Perhaps you should look, *Signora*, I did not see one, but it is safe to go home as he has gone. I will keep watch over you."

She turned and smiled at him. "Thank you, Enzo."

She was busy cleaning the room Father Stevan slept in and scolded herself for allowing her feelings to surface ... and then to be taken in by the stranger? He was a deceiver, and he claimed to be a catholic priest? She laughed at the irony. If she could lay her hands on him now, he would know how she felt, of that he would be certain. She released the pillow she was strangling and instead vented her anger on the clean sheets as she woefully made his bed. His bed ... overcome by a flood of emotions, she sat down on the bed and buried her head in her hands.

The sound of her sobbing was disturbed by a loud knock on the door. "Enzo," she said. *Coming to check on her.* With her anger and heartbreak temporarily forgotten, she wiped her tears with her apron and headed downstairs to answer the door.

Signora Milani opened the door expecting to see Enzo, instead, she was greeted by a large man and a grimace, which may have been his attempt at a smile. She looked past the man and saw another, a companion on the road holding two horses.

"*Signora* Milani?" asked the big man.

Immediately she noticed his accent and guessed he was German.

"Yes, how can I help?"

"We were told you frequently rent rooms to travellers, perhaps you have a room for *Ober*– uh, I mean my friend and I?"

Signora Milani looked again at the man on the street, he was standing behind one of the horses and couldn't see him well. She noticed Enzo standing up the road watching from a distance.

"Uh, just the one night," he added. His small eyes constantly flicked here and there.

She didn't like the look of the man or his friend, something about them didn't seem right, and she had a sense of foreboding.

"Please, *Signora*. We are weary and for one night only. We will pay you well," said the man.

"Forgive me, I have no rooms available at the moment, however, you are welcome to attend to your horses with some feed and water," she replied, feeling somewhat reassured with Enzo's presence. "The stables are around the back."

The man looked around and said nothing for a heartbeat or two. "Please, we have money and can pay you."

Signora Milani shook her head, "I'm sorry." For comfort, she gave a quick glance towards Enzo again. "You can bring your horses around the rear of the house, is all I can offer you."

The man's face hardened. "Thank you, *Signora*."

Stabswachtmeister Wollf awkwardly walked from the step. The effects of hours in the saddle resulted in chaffed thighs, a bruised rump, and a more dour disposition than normal. He shook his head subtly to *Oberleutenant* Koell as he approached. He also gave the man standing a little way up the street close scrutiny.

As *Signora* Milani watched the two strangers lead their horses around the side of the villa.

Enzo quickly approached. "*Signora*, who are those men? The tall one, he has blood on his arm, did you see?"

"He did?" she gave him a look of surprise. "I don't' know who they are. The man said they are travellers and just wanted a room for the night."

Enzo looked at her in question.

"Don't worry, I said no. They're just watering their horses, but please, Enzo, stay close. I do not like these men."

They walked through the house and through a rear door and observed both men as they tended to their horses at her stable. She could see the tall man was indeed injured and favoured his bloodied arm. He looked up and saw her watching, he began to walk over.

"*Signora*?" he yelled, then turned and spoke over his shoulder to the other man who had been at her door, he followed the taller man.

She felt Enzo tense beside her.

"I can handle this Enzo, please let me deal with him."

Enzo nodded and took a step backwards.

"I am sorry to trouble you, *Signora*. My friend tells me you have no rooms available for tonight. Can I change your mind? We have money if that is what worries you." He gave Enzo a long hard look, then turned to look inside the villa, not meeting her eyes. The heavy-set man slowly approached and stood near Enzo.

"No, as I told your friend, I can't accommodate you both. I'm sure you understand." Natalina's expression hardened. She could see a vein pulsing on the side of the tall man's neck. The look on his face and the blood on his arm unsettled her. "You may tend to your horses and water them," she added, "but then you must go."

Before she could say more, the taller injured man stepped forward, surprising her. "Where is the priest?" he snapped. All semblance of civility was gone. "I know he is here, fetch him."

Immediately, Enzo stepped forward. "What is the meaning of this?" he asked. He stood with his hands on his hips, his anger evident at the disrespect shown to his patroness.

Wollf took a step closer to Enzo and, without warning, and just as he'd done to the ticket seller at the railway station, drove a fist squarely into his solar plexus. Enzo collapsed to the decking gasping for air.

"Stop this!" she cried as she crouched to attend to him.

"Check the house," ordered Koell to his sergeant. He now held a pistol threateningly in his good hand. "I want to know where the priest is."

Signora Milani gasped when she saw the gun. "He isn't here. He's gone. And I want you to leave too," she cried, helping Enzo to his feet and eyeing the weapon nervously.

"When did he go?"

"I don't know; he was gone when we arrived back from Chieti a short time ago."

"Where? Tell me where?" Koell demanded.

She shook her head.

"You," said Koell to Enzo, "what do you know of the priest?"

"He doesn't know anything about him, leave him be," the *Signora* pleaded.

"Let him talk." Koell had the pistol aimed at Enzo.

Enzo was breathing hard and gasped, "I do not know - anything – except – we expected him here - when we came back - from Chieti - and he was gone – that is all I know."

Stabswachtmeister Wollf returned and shook his head, "The house is empty, no sign of him."

"Inside." Koell pointed with the gun. Once they'd all entered the villa, *Oberleutenant* walked to a chair and sank gratefully into it and scratched his head. "If he left here today and headed towards Chieti, then we would have seen him on the road. If we didn't see him, he could only have gone in the other direction towards L'Aquila unless he turned off somewhere. Did he take a horse or wagon?"

Signora Milani looked at Enzo for confirmation, he shook his head. "No, nothing was taken, he must be on foot," she said.

Wollf knew what the lieutenant was thinking, "You can't travel anymore today. I will go. You remain here and have your arm looked after by the beautiful lady. He turned and gave the *Signora* a salacious all–over look.

Koell knew the sergeant was right. He couldn't travel anymore today, and he needed to have his arm taken care of. "Go, find the priest and bring him back – and hurry, Dieter."

Wollf walked outside to the horses, tightened the saddle girth, mounted awkwardly, and headed towards L'Aquila.

Signora Milani was frightened. She'd seen men like this before and knew they were capable of doing anything. The two strangers were brutal and cold, unfeeling men. The tall one with the injured arm sat at the table and kept his pistol within easy reach. He was obviously the leader, the other heavier man was the enforcer, familiar with violence, and she knew, without doubt, would kill without a second thought.

"Is there a doctor here?" Koell asked.

"There is no doctor," she replied.

"Who is the person in the village who tends to your medical needs?"

Signora Milani's eyes involuntarily flicked to Enzo. "Tell me!" insisted Koell.

She knew the futility in lying to the stranger. *Perhaps if he was looked at, he would leave quicker.* "We have a man who looks after the animals when they need care," she offered.

Koell looked up at the *Signora*, his eyes blazed and bored into hers. He said nothing and continued to stare for a few heartbeats. Finally, he turned to Enzo. "Fetch this animal doctor, bring him. I will have the *Signora*, so I know you will not want to see her come to harm. If someone rides away to get help, I will see."

Enzo was a big man, and a lifetime working on farms made him strong and tough. His mind was working furiously as he weighed up his options. He knew if he leapt at the man, he could easily overpower him. It was the gun that frightened him.

"*Signora*, sit!" Koell kicked a chair out from the table with his foot and shifted the pistol to aim directly at her.

Any thoughts of jumping the stranger were shattered. Enzo

nodded. "I will be back with Fabio. Please do not harm the *Signora*."

"Go!" Koell waved an arm.

The old man encouraged the mule with soothing words and goaded him up the last incline before reaching the summit. The mule responded willingly and picked up the pace.

"The function of a citizen and a soldier are inseparable," said the old man to Father Stevan, again satisfied with their speed.

Belić looked at the old man.

"Benito said that. Wise words and very appropriate in your case, don't you think?"

"Benito?" questioned Belić.

"An up–and–coming young politician – Benito Mussolini. Although he's a fascist, he has some interesting views."

Belić hadn't heard of him. "You were very kind to assist me today, why is it you chose to do so and risk life and limb?" Belić smiled at the old man.

"When I picked you up, and after spending a few hours with you a few weeks ago, I knew you weren't the type of killer Gabbi suggested. Of course, the villagers gossip and talk and told me you were a good man, whereas I have little faith in whatever that nasty little policeman says. His involvement alone was cause for me to question his accusations against you. But innocent you are not, eh?' He looked to Belić and grinned. "I know you are from the Balkan's, your accent. The only reason you'd flee is over what recently happened in Sarajevo. Am I right?" He didn't wait for a reply and continued. "And you choose nationalism over faith?"

The mule pulled the wagon closer to the upcoming summit.

Belić thought a moment before responding. "I support the right of the people, my people, to be free from exploitation and social injustice." Belić maintained eye contact before continuing with pent up frustration. "Emperor Franz Joseph appointed Prince Ferdinand as head of the military, it was he who intended to invade Serbia and deny my people the right to enjoy their own culture and freedoms, and this isn't just my opinion. Even Pope Leo sent a letter to his Bishops on political issues known as *Rerum Novarum*, he outlined all this in detail. And yes, I support this belief."

The old man pulled on the reins, and the mule obediently came to a stop and immediately lowered its head and began foraging for grass on the roadside. "And this led to your decision to involve yourself with that organisation, the – ?"

"Black Hand."

The old man remained quiet and waited for an answer.

"I stand by my decision, yes, but I deeply regret the loss of his wife, and I grieve over her death. It is, uh ... unfortunate that people must die, but it was necessary, and I pray God will forgive me for my sins, for I have to live with them."

The old man reached behind him and dug around in a canvas sack, eventually finding the newspaper he sought. He carefully unfolded it and handed it to Belić.

Belić stared at the headline – he didn't move or speak. The words, in bold ink, glared up at him. Belić closed his eyes and mouthed a silent prayer. When he was finished, he crossed himself, opened his eyes and looked again at the bold type that disturbed him. WAR DECLARED BY AUSTRIA, Hostilities Commence.

The old man watched the priest carefully, and in a voice no louder than a whisper, he said, "The death of Prince Ferdinand and his wife really didn't accomplish anything, did it? Now, look what has happened, in retaliation, they invaded Serbia anyway."

Belić nodded, his expression solemn.

"But you couldn't have known the Austrians would react as they did, you aren't gifted with such powers, for you are just a man.

You did what you thought was right – you had the conviction of your beliefs and an admirable quality, although I do not agree with your methods." The old man scratched at the stubble on his chin. "What will you do now?"

"I, I really don't know, I must think." Belić turned away.

"You'll have plenty of time to do that because this is where I will leave you. I must get back, or it will be dark and travelling on this road at night isn't wise. If you continue and make your way down the hill, you can't see from here, but a few farms are around the corner. Sleep up here amongst the olives tonight, then in the morning, make your way down, and I believe a farmer will rent you a mule or a horse so you can be on your way."

Belić looked visibly upset, the news of war in his homeland struck him hard. "Yes, thank you very much for your help and wisdom."

"You are welcome young man, I wish you well," said the old man.

Father Stevan carefully alighted the wagon and stepped gingerly onto the uneven track. He looked up at the old man. "I apologise; I don't know your name."

"Andrea, Andrea Mussolini."

Belić smiled. "Is Benito your son, the one you quoted?"

"No, my nephew." Andrea raised a finger. "And remember, don't go down to the farm below till morning, stay here the night where it is safe. Good luck, Father." The old man snapped the reins, and the mule turned around at the crest and began the easy descent down. Father Stevan Belić stood motionless on the summit, his mind in a state of flux and confusion. Finally coming to a decision, he looked around.

The view was spectacular. Back in the direction from where he came from, he could see dotted farms, the blur of olive trees and even some grapevines in conspicuous straight rows. There were fields dominated by yellowed grass and even the speck of the odd goat and flock of sheep that grazed far below. On the other side of the summit, he saw more olive trees, but here the hills were steeper and rockier with no shelter at the crest. The nearest trees were twenty metres back down the hill. Resigned to spending the night outdoors beneath the branches of an olive tree. The comfortable bed at Signora Milani's home was nothing more than a distant memory. He picked up his suitcase and walked towards the olive trees.

The wide twisted trunk of a mature olive tree, about ten metres back from the road, was where he decided to rest. Remembering the days of his youth in Serbia, Belić began pulling long grass and twisted them together and placed them on the ground to create a mattress. He'd almost finished when the sound of a human voice drifted up to him.

With some urgency, he immediately lay flat on the grass behind the tree and waited. A short time later, he heard a horse snort as it plodded up towards the summit. Again, he heard the voice – it was a curse. Belić froze in fear; the profanities he heard were in German, and if he could have pressed himself into the earth and disappeared, he would have. Careful not to draw attention to his movements, he began to place the pulled grass over him.

The rider and horse slowly walked up the road, and then they were directly opposite him; Belić didn't move. The rider's head vigilantly swivelled from side to side taking in his surroundings. Belić closed his eyes and kept his face pressed to the ground. He could feel the gaze of the man sweep over him, and he waited for the yell of discovery that was sure to follow. Then the horse and rider moved on, it walked steadily up the road and then once near the summit, it stopped. Belić risked opening his eyes. The rider, a thick, muscular looking man, twisted in the saddle and began to look around. With deliberation and from the elevated position on the horse, he began to survey the area.

Belić feared the man could hear his pounding heart. The rider cursed again and then stiffly dismounted. Father Stevan watched as the man, safely on the ground, stretched his back. It was plainly obvious he was no equestrian.

He looked around and led the horse a few steps back down the hill to the remnants of an old tree and lashed the reins to a dead branch. He was only ten metres away – so close, and yet the man had still not detected him. Thinking ahead, Belić realised that when the man came back and mounted the horse, he would be staring right at him, he'd be completely exposed. He had to do something.

The big man fumbled with his trousers, and accompanied by a groan of pleasure, the sound of urine splashing on the ground reached Belić's ears. He dared not move. Once relieved and buttoned, the man lit a cigarette and began to walk stiffly up towards the summit. Belić finally breathed out, he hadn't been aware of it, but he had been holding his breath.

A stone was digging into his ribs, and he risked easing into a more comfortable position. He rolled on his side and onto a fallen twig – it snapped. Not loudly, but enough to attract the attention of the man – he stopped and turned. Luckily the trunk of the tree hid him. Had the man walked another few steps, he would easily have seen him. Deciding it was unimportant, the man continued to the crest.

Stabswachtmeister Deiter Wollf stood with his hands on his hips and looked down into the valley on the other side of the summit. He could see the empty road winding down the hill and then disappear around a corner into the distance. The olive groves were well-tended, and he determined there must be a farm nearby that he couldn't see. The grumpy old man in the wagon he'd questioned not long ago hadn't seen anyone, although he did say there were farmhouses nearby.

It was late afternoon, and searching further was out of the question. Not only was he sore, but it would also be getting dark within the next hour or so, and he should return to the villa. He rubbed his tender buttocks and welcomed the few minutes of respite of not being astride the horse.

"*Wo bist du?*" he said to no one. Where are you?

He took a few steps over the crest of the hill, hoping to glimpse a little of what was around the corner and into the valley further down. He knew the priest was nearby; he could feel it. He took another step, then another. He threw the cigarette to the dirt and ground it with his foot.

His horse snickered, and Wollf whipped his head around. He couldn't see the animal as he was over the crest, and it was out of sight. He began to run back towards the summit and saw a man astride his horse, cantering away and clinging to a suitcase. While he couldn't see his face, Wollf knew he'd found him.

"*Oaschloch!*" he yelled.

He cursed again and reached for his pistol. In a single practiced motion, he dropped to a knee and simultaneously cocked and, using both hands, raised the weapon. With his eyes expertly tracking the fleeing horse and rider, he sighted carefully and gently squeezed the trigger.

CHAPTER TEN

The Steyr Model 1910 pistol still pointed unwaveringly at *Signora* Milani as Enzo sat on the floor as ordered. His eyes never left the Austrian military intelligence officer, and with knees drawn to his chin, he glowered at him with resentment.

Hans Koell removed his shirt and sat at the table in the kitchen of *Signora* Milani's home while Fabio cleaned the gunshot wound to the best of his ability. He wiped the blood away with water and soap and carefully inspected the entrance and exit wounds for foreign matter. Once satisfied, he applied a solution of carbolic acid to the affected areas to reduce any chance of infection and lastly, before applying the bandage, he liberally smeared a Thuja salve over both wounds.

"You've done a good job," commended Koell to Fabio once he had finished bandaging the arm.

Fabio wiped his hands on a cloth and looked at his patient. "I had little choice, did I not?"

Koell shrugged.

"Anyway, if it works on the horses, then it must work on you."

"Now your arm has been bandaged, you can go and leave us in peace," suggested *Signora* Milani angrily.

"I am hungry, and my companion will return soon so you could make some food, *ja*?"

Koell was exhausted and hungry and needed sleep. He felt the effects of a long day and was waiting on Wollf, who had yet to return. He turned to the *Signora*. "Do you have a clean shirt that will fit me?"

She didn't want to help this man but hoped if she could give him the things he needed, it would only encourage him to leave. "Yes, perhaps, but if you want me to look, then please put the gun away."

Koell fixed her with a steely look, then moved the gun and pointed it at Enzo.

As Fabio put away his potions, ointments and salves, the *Signora* quickly went upstairs and found a simple cotton shirt to fit the tall Austrian. She returned downstairs and flung the shirt on the table, and stood with arms folded glaring at him.

"Some food? Cook!" Koell rose slowly from his chair and moved his bandaged arm. It felt much better. "Doctor, help me with the shirt."

She walked into the kitchen, threw some wood into the stove and began rummaging for food as Fabio picked the shirt from the table and held it open for the Austrian. Unseen by Koell, Fabio made eye contact with Enzo.

Slowly Koell eased his wounded left arm into the sleeve and held the gun on Enzo with his good arm. Once his arm was through, he transferred the gun to his other hand and then began to slide his dominant right arm into the remaining sleeve. For a brief instant, the gun wavered and pointed away from Enzo, and Fabio reacted. With Koell's good arm halfway into the sleeve, he jerked the shirt down, trapping his arms and nimbly stepped behind him.

He did two things very quickly. With his right arm, he encircled Koell's throat and squeezed tightly, and with his left hand, he struck Koell's injured arm. If he hoped Koell would drop the weapon, then Fabio was disappointed.

In reflex, Koell's training took over. He drove his right elbow hard and backwards into Fabio's side, which caused him to release the pressure on his neck. Fabio doubled over in pain. Without pausing, he pivoted, slipped out of Fabio's grasp, and swung the

Steyr pistol around, which was now pointed directly at the top of Fabio's head, who was bending over in pain from the blow to his kidney.

Enzo was in the process of standing and couldn't move or react fast enough to help his friend. On hearing the commotion, *Signora* Milani looked up at the same time as Koell pulled the trigger. Enzo froze as he watched bits of flesh, bone and brain matter fragment outwards. The gunshot seemed unnaturally loud in the confines of the villa.

Signora Milani screamed and sank to the floor, burying her head in her hands and began sobbing. Enzo slid back down to the floor, his mouth open in horror. Fabio's body crumpled over, twitching. He was dead.

Mayor Alberto Maria Gabriele De Rosa had one of the worst days of his life. Not only was his nephew Gabbi dead – murdered – slain in cold blood in a darkened alley, but he also had the unenviable task of informing his sister of the death. An undertaking he could only accomplish with the fortification of alcohol. After two hours and two and a half bottles of wine later, he could no longer avoid the unpleasant task and arrived at Giana's door to share with her the unfortunate news.

Just as he predicted, Giana began to wail and howl as a grieving mother would and rained upon him a series of painful blows that would leave a few marks and bruises for days to come. She cursed him and the police department for failing to protect her darling son from criminals and murderers, and just for good measure, she blamed the entire township of Chieti and central Italy for her sorrow; Pope Pius X was fortunately spared. Thankfully, her tirade ended when she threw herself on the floor and surrendered to exhaustion after a tearful episode of hysterical vehemence. Had Giana been dainty and slender in form, Mayor De Rosa may have been more compassionate and assisted her to her bed. Already somewhat battered and still in lingering pain from her assault, he left her in the tender care of a neighbour and returned to the police station to receive a status update and finish the third bottle of wine.

The police conducted a comprehensive investigation throughout the following day, and by late afternoon, Mayor De Rosa was again briefed on the outcome. The police determined that two strangers arrived by train the previous evening and checked into a hotel about twenty minutes later. Considering the hotel was only a five-minute walk from the station, that left fifteen minutes unaccounted. In the morning, the same two men rented two horses and were last seen heading towards L'Aquila.

As head of Chieti's metropolitan police, *Capitano* Luigi Gallo patiently explained to Mayor De Rosa that those facts didn't prove the strangers were guilty of murdering dear little Gabbi. Yet, as he went on to explain, the unusual incident a day or so earlier also had significance.

The police spoke to eyewitnesses who recounted in extraordinary detail how Gabbi had been in an altercation with *Signora* Milani and her *capo*, Enzo, outside the bank. On his own volition, Gabbi took it upon himself to locate a man, apparently a Catholic priest, and believed *Signora* Milani knew of him. He accosted her outside the bank and accused her of knowing the priest's whereabouts. With unrelenting pressure, she finally admitted the priest was, in fact, a guest in her home. Chief Gallo believed this incident and Gabbi's murder were related, and the two strangers most likely went to see *Signora* Milani about the mystery priest. He didn't think either Enzo or *Signora* Milani were guilty of murdering Gabbi. The two strangers were the link, and as *Capitano* Gallo advised, they should send an armed contingent to *Signora* Milani's home first thing in the morning to apprehend the suspects. Mayor De Rosa enthusiastically agreed.

However, further ailing Chieti's Mayor was another very sobering issue. Gabbi's employment wasn't strictly by the books, and the unusual circumstances around his death could bring him some unwanted attention from the federal authorities, namely the *Carabinieri*.

The Polizia Locale in Chieti have limited authority and are under the mayor's jurisdiction, while *Carabinieri* are under federal command. If the *Carabinieri* became interested in Gabbi's murder and wrested control of the investigation from him, then the mayor knew any chance of re-election would be slim, especially if they misinterpreted his familial loyalties and some of his other questionable practices as being corrupt. Mayor De Rosa didn't see himself as a malefactor; his position as mayor offered him some advantages that were convenient and, he believed, necessary.

Mayor De Rosa explained all this to his old friend *Capitano* Gallo, and he unequivocally agreed that he would also be implicated and urged the mayor to keep the entire affair under wraps as best they could. This was why *Capitano* Gallo would accompany and lead the contingent of men heading to *Signora* Milani's farm very early the next morning. The editor of the local newspaper was Luigi Gallo's brother-in-law, and a quiet word in his ear would ensure the media would never publish the story and the whole sordid affair would never come to the attention of the *Carabinieri* or the general public. The current state of unrest in the Balkans saw the *Carabinieri* a little jumpy, and thus extra care would be needed to ensure they remained uninformed. Perhaps there were other more important things they could concern themselves with, hoped Mayor De Rosa.

It was still dark when one by one, six armed men on horseback rode quietly from Chieti. Three men represented about half of Chieti's entire police force, and the other three were Luigi's deputised relatives. They regrouped just out of town and headed quickly in a north-westerly direction on the road to L'Aquila.

Even though *Capitano* Luigi Gallo headed a tiny police department in a small town, he was no fool. He was naturally curious, nimble of mind and intelligent. If employed by the police in a larger municipality, he would easily have risen in rank and been promoted to either Police Chief or become a decorated detective – Mayor De Rosa was eternally grateful for Luigi's assiduity.

In some detail, Luigi outlined his plan to his men the previous evening. Even the mayor was in attendance and listened attentively with the aid of another bottle of locally produced wine.

It was elementary, Luigi explained. Firstly they must ride out of town unobserved – Chieti's residents must not know of their departure. Once they arrived at *Signora* Milani's farm, hopefully just before daybreak, they would secure the perimeter by surrounding the house and prevent anyone from leaving. He told his men to be observant and be on the lookout for two rented horses, an indication the strangers were at her home, and to be extremely cautious as the men they sought were likely to be armed. Luigi would then approach the house and ask the *Signora* about the strangers. If the men were guests, then surrender was their only option, and both would be arrested and brought back to Chieti for questioning. Everyone understood the potential danger they were exposed to and their assigned roles. In addition to the assortment of weapons they carried, each was given a set of handcuffs, as the Chieti police department only owned five sets, *Capitano* Gallo went selflessly without.

Something pressed uncomfortably onto his nose, and with a start, Father Stevan Belić blinked open his eyes. The grey of dawn provided enough light to see the outline of a man looming over him.

"Don't move or make a sound," whispered the man. The shotgun pressing onto Belić's nose emphasised his point. "Do you have a weapon?"

Belić wanted to shake his head but dared not. "No, none," he said. It sounded nasal.

"I'm going to move this gun, and you're going to roll over and lay on your stomach. Do you understand?"

"Yes," he replied. Belić was puzzled, the man with the shotgun wasn't Austrian or anyone local he recognised. *Then who was he*, he wondered?

The barrel pressed onto his nose was withdrawn, and Belić, careful not to make any sudden moves, rolled onto his front as ordered.

"Put your hands behind you," commanded the voice.

Again, Belić complied and immediately felt what he assumed was a pair of handcuffs locked onto his wrists. He felt the man pat him down and search his pockets for weapons. Finding none, the man reached down and hauled him painfully to his feet.

"Please, my suitcase," Belić appealed.

The man grunted, picked up the case, and led him from the barn and towards the road near *Signora* Milani's home.

The previous evening was a blur for Belić. He'd watched in absolute terror as the lone Austrian rode up the road and then dismounted, leaving the horse tied to a dead branch of a tree near where he lay. Then to his surprise, the man had left the horse unattended and walked away just over the crest of the hill and was momentarily lost from sight.

Belić knew when the man returned and mounted the horse, he would be discovered. He felt he had no other option, and although somewhat reckless, he dragged his suitcase with him and crawled from beneath his meagre grass concealment towards the horse. It took mere moments, and then realising he couldn't be seen, he rose and ran the last few metres. He quickly untied the reins from the tree when to his horror, the horse snorted. With one hand gripping his case, he mounted the horse and spurred it into action, heading back down the hill towards *Signora* Milani's farm, some kilometres away. There was no plan, he'd not thought it through and acted purely on impulse and a need to survive.

The accuracy of the gunshot truly surprised him; he didn't expect the man with a pistol to almost hit him while he fled. The bullet struck his suitcase, the impact almost flinging him from the quickly moving horse. Belić felt blessed.

It became too dark to ride quickly on the narrow road, so he allowed the horse to find its way, which was back the way he had come with the old man only an hour or two earlier. He'd been riding for about two hours when the familiar outline of *Signora* Milani's villa came in sight. Unusually, lights were still on in the house, which added to his sense of unease.

He was tired and hungry and resisted the temptation to knock on the door. Firstly, he was unsure of the welcome he would receive from Natalina, and then he didn't know how many other Austrians were looking for him.

He cautiously made his way silently past her villa and down

behind Enzo's home and towards the barn and stables. There he saw another horse, and one he knew didn't belong to the *Signora*. There were at least two men, certainly one very unhappy gunman high up on the hills without his horse, and another here, presumably in her home.

This left Belić in a dilemma. He unsaddled his horse in the darkness, gave it water and knew there was little he could do until daylight. Then, in the morning, sneak into the olive grove, and from concealment, watch the house until he could decide what to do. A soft bed of straw was inviting, and overcome by exhaustion, he was soon fast asleep. The man with the shotgun rudely interfered with his plans.

The rising sun in the east dissolved shadows into recognisable gloomy shapes of men, horses and activity. Horses were all tied against a fence a little way up the road, and from what he could determine, a group of armed men stealthily surrounded *Signora* Milani's home. The man with the shotgun ordered him to sit against a fence about thirty metres from her villa.

He could see a man ushering a woman away, he couldn't see clearly, but from the direction he was taking her, it must be Enzo's mother. He was sure he could hear her sobbing.

Belić focused on the sound of approaching footsteps.

"And who might you be?" asked the voice.

He looked up to find a large middle-aged man in the uniform of the Polizia Locale standing before him. Resigned to his capture and fate, Belić thought there was little need to hide his identity anymore. "I am Father Stevan Belić, sir," he answered respectfully.

The policeman nodded. "Ah, the elusive priest."

"Yes, sir." Belić wasn't wearing his cassock, so he was surprised the police knew who he was. He had questions of his own – so many things he wanted to ask. Before hé could open his mouth to begin asking, the policeman spoke again, this time to the man with the shotgun.

"Watch him carefully." He turned and walked away, back towards *Signora* Milani's house.

"Who is he?" Belić asked. He heard the policeman pound heavily on her door.

"Luigi, uh, *Capitano* Gallo," replied the man with the shotgun.

"What is happening? Why are you here? Is it because of me?"

He didn't reply. Both men watched the *Capitano* at the door.

Again, the *Capitano* banged on the door, this time louder. "*Signora* Milani!" he shouted.

It wasn't completely light, and Belić still found it difficult to see clearly.

"*Signora!*" repeated the policeman more urgently. The *Capitano* must have heard a noise that alarmed him because he fumbled awkwardly to lift the flap on his holster to reach his pistol. Once free and cocked, he held the weapon steady and aimed at the door. The man with the shotgun nervously shifted his feet beside Belić.

Suddenly *Capitano* Gallo took a step backwards and leapt from the step onto the road.

"*Fuoco!*" he yelled. Fire! He took another step back and looked up and down the length of the house. "It's a diversion, look sharp everyone, he's coming out!"

"She's in there, you've got to help her out," pleaded Belić to the man with the shotgun.

Alerted by the warning yells of fire, residents began leaving their homes and were surprised to see police and men with guns in their quiet village. The police shouted warnings for residents to keep away, and it did little good.

Belić could already see a flickering light coming from inside the villa. The policemen all stood ready, but yet no one made any attempt to enter. "Please, *Signora* Milani is in there ... do something!"

Two deputised relatives of *Capitano* Luigi Gallo came running from behind the house in a panic. "Luigi, it's on fire, the house is burning," one yelled.

"We know that, now get back!" cried the *capitano*, "It's a diversion, go back to your posts."

Belić was becoming increasingly agitated. While the man with the shotgun focused on the house, he awkwardly rose to his feet. "Please, let me go into the house and get her. Take the handcuffs off, and let me get her."

The man with the shotgun looked uneasily at Belić, and he didn't know what to do.

"Take me to the *Capitano*. Ask him if you can take the handcuffs off, and I will go in and get her. I won't escape, you have my word, please."

Just then, Enzo's mother reappeared from behind her house and began screaming, "Enzo, Enzo, my boy Lorenzo, he's in there! Please, someone help!"

"Please," Belić appealed again in a quieter voice.

Another female voice began yelling for Fabio. Belić was more puzzled. *What were Enzo and Fabio doing in the house at this time of the morning? Had they been there all night?*

The man with the shotgun made up his mind and nodded. "Come." He quickly pushed Belić forward, and they jogged to the *Capitano,* who still covered the door. "Luigi, there are people in there we must rescue them, we can't let them burn," implored the man with the shotgun to his cousin. Already thick smoke began billowing out.

"What's he doing here? Take him back," ordered the *Capitano* with a wave of his arm.

"He wants to go into the house and rescue whoever is in there. We can't leave them, Luigi!"

Capitano Gallo was hesitant. "I can't send anyone in there until I know it is safe. Go back to your position, now!"

Villagers were yelling, and some brought buckets of water while Enzo's hysterical mother was being restrained by a neighbour, her wails and pleas to save her son becoming more and more frantic. Gallo was losing control of the situation, and he knew it. More people began yelling, and fearful children started crying. Things were fast becoming unmanageable.

Capitano Gallo was conflicted, he knew he had a duty to save those in the house, he also knew there were at least two armed and dangerous men inside. He couldn't risk sending anyone into the house until he knew it was safe to do so.

Two quick gunshots silenced the yelling. Where only seconds ago confusion and pandemonium prevailed, everything became eerily quiet.

Nearly one–and–a–half kilometres away, high on the hill overlooking the valley and the small village, *Stabswachtmeister* Deiter Wollf watched anxiously. He could see flames from a house that he knew was the farm of *Signora* Milani. Too far away and too dark to discern details, he knew with certainty what was happening below. When he heard the unmistakable sound of gunfire, he winced and shook his head.

Wollf knew the fire was deliberately lit to create a distraction, and therefore, presumably, the *Oberleutenant* was outnumbered by an unknown force and trapped inside the house. Once the fire took hold, he knew Koell would use the distraction to escape, however, the two quick shots he heard were distinctive and not the sound from a Steyr handgun, they were shotgun blasts. Someone just fired both barrels, and the only reason to do that is to shoot at a fleeing target. As there were no answering shots, he wondered if Koell was hit and was still alive? Wollf sat down and leaned against the trunk of an olive tree and gave his precarious situation serious thought. His orders were clear, and the only course of action he had was to contact Major Richter in Wien as quickly as possible for instructions on how to proceed.

The nearest telegraph office was in Chieti, and perhaps the fire was the distraction he needed to circle unseen around the village and head back towards town. Other than the *Signora* and her big friend, no one knew what he looked like, so he had an advantage. If Koell was dead, then that was unfortunate. He never really liked the man anyway – actually, truth be known, he didn't like any officers.

If Koell was alive and taken prisoner, he couldn't singlehandedly rescue him, so that didn't affect his plan. Clear to his objectives, Wollf stood and began to walk down the track to find a way around the village to reach Chieti as quickly as possible.

"No one move, hold your positions, wait for the other one!" yelled *Capitano* Gallo. He looked nervously around him. At the sound of the gunshots, the villagers moved back and quietened down. Enzo's mother was still sobbing and yelling for her son. Thankfully, someone considerately led Fabio's wife away.

"He's dead, he's dead!" cried Enrico, another of Luigi's cousins. He came running from behind the house. "Vito killed him!"

"Go in the house, save them!" yelled Belić. "You can't leave them to burn!"

Capitano Gallo raced after Enrico to the back of the house to investigate, leaving the man with the shotgun and a policeman out front. Flames were licking up the far side of the house, and a window exploded from the heat, sending flames and a cloud of sparks upwards.

"Do you have a key to the handcuffs?" Belić asked.

"Yes, but I will get into trouble if I release you," replied the man. "There is another man still inside, it is dangerous."

"I will not run away, I want to rescue those in the house, please." Another window blew out, and flames shot hungrily from the open space. Everyone watching knew the entire building would be engulfed in minutes. The man placed the shotgun on the ground and dug in his pocket for a key. Within seconds, Belić was free and, with urgency, ran for the front door facing the street. His tender ankle forgotten.

He bounded up the steps, quickly removed his jacket and wrapped it protectively around his hand and tried the door. Even with his hands covered, he could feel the heat – as expected, the door was locked. He kicked the door as hard as he could – it didn't budge. Two other men, locals emboldened by the priest's actions and carrying buckets of water, ran up to help. They put the buckets down, and on the count of three, kicked together and the door splintered near the lock. Another kick saw the door fly open. Immediately the incoming draft fanned the flames. The roar of the blaze was almost deafening.

Belić paused and peered inside and suddenly felt the shock as a bucket of water was thoughtfully thrown over him. He took another step towards the inferno. "Natalina! Natalina!"

He could see the far wall, and the ceiling was well alight, which he feared could collapse at any moment. Once inside, he quickly looked around and didn't see anyone. He took a few more tentative steps using his arms to shield his face. It was so hot. He felt a presence behind him, and a glance saw both locals with grim, determined expressions follow him in.

He saw a movement in the far corner near the stairs, a pair of legs. "Over there!" he pointed and then ducked as a sheet of fire flared out, threatening to envelop him. It was Enzo, and he was tied securely to the stair bannister. Then he saw Natalina and his heart skipped a beat. One of the men who was closest ran over to untie her, she wasn't moving. Both had rags in their mouths. The other man was searching for Fabio.

Other villagers began a bucket brigade and were tossing bucket after bucket of water through the open doorway. It did little to stop the blaze but may have slowed it somewhat. It helped and gave Belić time to untie Enzo.

With the gag removed, Enzo began coughing. "Where is Fabio?" shouted Belić. Enzo couldn't speak. He shook his head, and soon as his arms were free, he pointed towards the kitchen, which was engulfed in flames. Belić risked a quick look at Natalina as she was being carried out to safety. She, too, was coughing.

"Is Fabio in the kitchen?" queried Belić as he finally untied the last knot.

Enzo tried to speak and couldn't. Belić leaned down as Enzo tried again.

"*Morto*," he croaked and began coughing.

"I don't like what is happening," stated Kaha as he looked up from the newspaper he read, "his death will lead to all sorts of problems."

"And it all makes sense to me too, and now I understand the urgency to why London wants us in northern Italy," Pam said.

Kaha nodded, threw the newspaper aside, and stared out across the marina. "And to me too. I just wish that diesel injector would arrive so we can be on our way. Sitting here in Pescara with nothing to do is maddening."

Kaha and Pam had spent the last two days cleaning the bottom of their boat to remove marine fouling, the unwanted growth that accumulated on the hull beneath the waterline. Usually, he'd pay someone to do the unpleasant task, but as they had nothing else to do but wait, they decided to do the job together. It was challenging and arduous work, but feeling good over their efforts, they now relaxed in the early morning sun on the deck of the *Mana*.

"Do you think the rest of Europe will enter into war," she asked.

Kaha turned away from the marina to look at his wife; he nodded. "Before, I wasn't so sure, but now... I think war is inevitable, and our role is crucial."

They sat silently, each lost in thoughts over a quickly developing European conflict.

"Come below, Kaha, it's too hot to be outside," she stated. "You can help me with lunch."

The interior was almost totally ablaze, everything that could burn was engulfed in flames. The heat was unbearable, and Belic knew that if he and Enzo didn't leave, they would succumb to smoke and heat. Locals continued to pour endless bucketsful of water through the destroyed doorway, which slowed the fire's progress and provided a small corridor to safety. The heat became intolerable, and everyone finally retreated, leaving only Belić and Enzo. With strength he didn't know he possessed, Belić hoisted Enzo over his shoulder and stumbled through the heat and flames and finally through the door and outside to eager hands willing to take him.

He collapsed to his knees. His scorched jacket was smoking, his hair was singed, and his hands were red and slightly burned – his eyes streamed tears. Never had fresh air felt so good as he breathed in lungsful. His chest hurt, his ankle was sore, and all he could think of was Natalina, and was she unharmed and safe?

Capitano Luigi Gallo stood over the ailing priest. "Fabio, where is he?"

Belić looked up at the policeman and shook his head. "Dead – in – the – kitchen," he wheezed, then he began a fit of coughing. "Nat–a–l–," he coughed again.

"Is there anyone else in the house?" asked the *capitano* with concern creeping into his voice.

Still on his knees, Belić was bent over hacking. During a brief moment of respite, he sat up and shrugged his shoulders. Someone brought a cup of water for him, and he drank greedily to ease his seared throat. The *capitano* stood with his hands on his hips and studied the surrounding area, he knew another Austrian was still around.

"Come, you need to be taken care of." The *capitano* helped the priest to his feet.

"*Signora* – Milani?" croaked Belić.

"She's being taken care of, and she is lucky. Overcome by smoke, I think. I will talk to her and Enzo soon. I will give them a few minutes to recover." The *capitano* gently grabbed Belić by the elbow to lead him away from the house, which was about to collapse. "Are you sure it was only Fabio left in the house, no one else?" he asked again.

Belić nodded and wheezed, "Why?"

"We believe there is another man, and we can't locate him."

Immediately Belić stopped walking and turned to the policeman. He pointed up the hill.

"He – he, is there." He coughed again. "I took – his – horse."

"When?"

"Last – night." Belić rubbed his eyes which were stinging and watering profusely.

Capitano Gallo cursed, then realised what he had said. "Sorry, Father. How far away was he from here? Can you describe his appearance, and was he armed?"

Belić cleared his throat. "About seven kilometres, and – yes, a pistol. A big – man."

"And you took his horse? Then he must still be on foot?"

Stevan nodded.

"Vito! Get that dead Austrian onto the horse and bring the men to me now!" The *capitano* turned back to the priest. "One of my men killed the stranger in the house when he tried to escape, those were the gunshots you heard. He set fire to the house to create a distraction, then tried to run into the olive grove."

He turned from the priest as his men approached. "Listen, the other man is in the hills." *Capitano* Gallo pointed in the direction. "He is armed and probably on foot and less than seven kilometres away. Just be careful, the man is dangerous, but please try not to kill him, and if you do manage to find him, bring him to Chieti." He indicated to his regular policemen. "You three go and find the other man, and Enrico, Vito and I will take the priest to town. Father, can you ride?"

"I'd like to – to see *Signora* Milani," Belić asked, his voice slowly coming back to him.

The *capitano* watched his three policemen as they made their way to their horses. Vito and Enrico went back towards the stables to saddle the horse Belić rode. Chieti's police chief would return the rented animals to their owner once they were safely back in town.

"No, not possible," replied *Capitano* Gallo sternly. "She's in no condition to talk, and when she can talk, it will be to me. I want you to sit at the fence, drink water and rest. Soon as I am finished talking to her and Enzo, we will leave, and you are coming with us."

Capitano Gallo looked towards the stables and shouted to Vito,

"Put the handcuffs on the priest, with his hands in front, *pronto*!"

Belić said nothing and looked despondent.

It was just becoming light when Dieter Wollf crept through the olive grove bordering the village. As he correctly guessed, all attention was focused in the opposite direction, towards the fire. He could hear yelling, a woman crying hysterically and even individual voices of men. He could see a tall plume of black smoke rising at an obscure angle from what was once a fine villa, and curiously he saw a few men in uniform. They looked like police which explained Koell's actions. But what were the police doing at the villa? How did they know to go there? Again, he shook his head and doubted Koell was alive.

Wollf skirted from tree to tree and kept low. Within a few minutes, the village was behind him, but he wasn't safe yet. He needed to climb the hill, and the only way to do that was to remain amongst the olives where he was afforded shelter. He kept the road in sight and slowly climbed the steep incline using the trees to stay hidden.

He was breathing hard and stopped for a rest when he saw three policemen on horseback leave the village to head along the road from where he had so recently come. No doubt in search of him, he thought. Despite his fatigue and feeling hatred towards the priest for stealing his horse and making him walk most of the night, he smiled. When he caught the priest, he'd give him a beating he wouldn't forget.

The Italians didn't know where he was, but there was something else – he'd seen his horse, and then the priest being handcuffed. There was only one place they would take him, he guessed, and that was to Chieti. Perhaps the situation wasn't that bad after all. Richter would be most pleased.

CHAPTER ELEVEN

Father Stevan Belić stared up at the spider web of cracks in the ceiling and thought of the recent events that dominated his life. He compulsively rotated the ancient wooden cross in his hands and took solace and comfort from it. He used it as a reminder; it was a link to his faith, conscience and God. He thought of the deaths of Prince Ferdinand, his wife and those injured when the bomb exploded beneath the automobile in the motorcade. Even Fabio, the caring Italian animal doctor who tended to his sprained ankle and became a friend – sadly another innocent victim.

His past was finally catching up with him, and now he was confined to a small room in a police station in Chieti awaiting his fate. He'd never been locked up before, and now his life was in the hands of his gaolers, or was his life in God's hands? He wasn't sure.

They'd treated him kindly, even courteously. They allowed him to bathe and wash the soot that caked him from head to toe, and to his surprise, they even brought a doctor to tend to his burns and look at his reinjured ankle. Someone took his soiled clothes to have them laundered, and they had brought him food and drink and asked if he needed anything special. He politely asked for a national newspaper and thanked them for their thoughtfulness. It could be worse, he thought with a wry smile, it could be an Austrian gaol.

But one thing they hadn't done was talk to him. Every question he asked, they remained silent and unresponsive. He wanted to know how Natalina was. When he saw her last, she didn't look well and was suffering from the effects of smoke. She'd lost her home, she lost everything but the clothes she wore, and he felt responsible. She may have been useful to him, but it wasn't fair that she lost everything because of him.

He expected to be interrogated and harshly queried, especially since they seemed to know a lot about him. Perhaps they would do so tomorrow, he thought. He took a long deep breath and resigned himself to an uncertain future. He slowly eased from the bed and lowered himself onto his knees, bowed his head and prayed for forgiveness.

Enjoying the privacy his position afforded, *Capitano* Luigi Gallo reclined back in his chair and nursed a glass of Port. The bottle, perfectly positioned in the centre of his desk, rose like a cenotaph, a monument to a great thinker. *If Plato were here now, what would he have to say?* questioned Luigi as he took another sip of the ruby-red beverage. But as Plato himself said, 'wise men talk because they have something to say; fools, because they have to say something'.

The priest was locked in a secure room in another part of the building and was being held unjustly, or more specifically, to satisfy the needs of Mayor De Rosa. Truth be told, thought Luigi, he didn't have anything to say to the priest that didn't make him feel like a fool. Luigi raised his glass and toasted Plato for the irony.

The paradox as he saw it was quite simple, the priest had not committed any crime or broken any laws, certainly not in Chieti anyway. As far as he was aware, the priest was not under any suspicion of having violated any of Italy's laws. He hadn't even been in Chieti when that fool Gabbi was killed. Although technically, he may have stolen a horse, and even that was debatable. He wasn't even in *Signora* Milani's home when Fabio was shot, neither, as far as he was aware, was the Serbian aiding and abetting any criminal activity, the man was a priest for heaven's sake, and now, against his will, he was arguably being illegally detained in a locked store-room at a small-town, central Italian police station.

However, two men, Austrians and probably military men, sought the priest. Whatever he'd done to earn their displeasure must have been quite serious. The papers they'd found on the dead man indicated he was a Swiss national, pure rubbish, thought Gallo as he upended his glass.

And now the priest was bait. He would try to keep him in custody for as long as possible because the longer he was here, the more likely the remaining Austrian, or perhaps more of them, would eventually come.

Luigi would question the priest, and if willing, he may answer honestly. Perhaps he could offer some insights as to the identity of the violent Austrians. To fully discharge his duties as head of Chieti's small but effective police force, Luigi knew he needed to investigate both Gabbi and Fabio's murder and bring those responsible to justice, and he would do so to the best of his abilities.

Capitano Luigi Gallo reached for the bottle and refilled his glass, and stared at the photo of the priest he took from the dead Austrian.

The glass arced through the air and shattered against the wall into countless shards. Liquid splashed against photographs, including the venerable Emperor, over files, books and documents. The usually intransigent Major Richter was incensed, he was livid, and his ice-cold facade disintegrated, just like the glass into sharp cutting slivers.

He stormed through his office door, leaving it ajar, "Clean up that mess!" he barked to his cowering secretary and then proceeded into the operations centre.

A hapless *leutnant*, an analyst, was in the wrong place at the wrong time. "What are you standing around for, you fool? I want a detailed relief map of central Italy placed on that wall in two minutes!"

The *leutnant* made the simple mistake of standing when Major Richter entered the room and immediately became the target for his rage. Richter spun and left the room as quickly as he entered and headed towards the bathroom.

He splashed water over his face, and as he habitually did, thoroughly washed his hands and then meticulously dried them. He placed both hands on the sink, leaned forward and stared into the mirror. He noticed his eyes were a little bloodshot and his skin more pallid than normal.

Two experienced investigators bungled a simple task! Richter shook his head in disgust. And now, one of them was dead. How did they let that happen? What on earth had they been doing?

The face in the mirror stared coldly back at him. Which reminded him; he'd have his secretary write a condolence letter of sympathy to the *Oberleutenant*'s grieving widow.

But what had just transpired was unheard of, seethed Richter, his anger still palpable. That sycophant, the *Direktor* of the *Evidenzbureau*, Oskar von Czvetassin, had the gall to dress him down, berate and humiliate him and then order him into the field like a lowly, still wet–behind–the–ears junior officer. It was outrageous.

Richter recounted the conversation.

"The Emperor demands retribution," insisted the *direktor*.

"We are at war, *Herr Direktor*, my department is understaffed, and my people have been busy working on the Russian codes as you ordered," he reminded his superior. "I have no time for this, use other men more suited to this task."

It did little good, the *direktor* was totally inflexible.

"I care not for excuses, or your shortcomings, and inability to complete this assignment, major. The Emperor is unimpressed with your performance and lack of results, he's holding you accountable and wants you to complete this mission personally, and I wholeheartedly agree!"

He could have leaned forward and throttled the *direktor*. He'd been tempted. Never in his exalted military career had he been spoken to in such a demeaning way.

Even as a junior officer, those more senior had tactfully avoided upsetting him. Perhaps he may yet allow himself the pleasure of dealing to the *direktor* and inflict some pain on him after he caught the assassin priest.

But now he needed to prepare, the *direktor* ordered him to Italy and required him, no, ordered him to leave today. Richter stared at his reflection; he saw the pulsing vein on his neck and grimaced, his lips compressed into a bloodless gash. *That damned priest*. His right fist shot out and collided with the mirror – it shattered.

Major Richter rewashed his hands and licked the blood from his knuckles as he returned to the operations centre. On the wall, just as he demanded, a map of central Italy was affixed. He kicked a chair out from behind a desk and sat down to study Chieti and familiarise himself with the surrounding area down to the minutest detail.

"You! Clean up the mess in the toilet!" he snarled at the *leutnant* who sat diligently working away at his desk. Everyone else wisely left the room to avoid the wrath of their volatile superior.

Richter found comfort in the pain from bloodied knuckles.

Thirty minutes later, Major Richter was back at his desk and re-read the first report *Oberleutenant* Koell wrote after he and Wollf first returned from Italy. He'd already read it countless times, but this time he looked for particulars. He slowly turned the pages, one by one, until he'd reviewed everything again. He leaned back in his chair and considered the facts. As an investigator, he wanted information from the priest, specifically, who were the subversives, the planners, the support people and sympathisers of the Black hand organisation, and ultimately where did they obtain their funds – was the church involved? However, he didn't expect the priest to divulge anything without some coercion, he needed leverage. But something about Father Stevan Belić stirred some memories – past events.

He opened the detailed report again and casually flicked back through the numerous pages. Two words leapt out at him, *Kralj Mora*, the fishing boat in Ragusa. The fisherman had a son. Richter smiled, this was precisely what he sought. Although the fisherman didn't know it, he and his boy would help him catch the priest. Richter smiled, the word 'bait' seemed very appropriate.

Father Stevan Belić was more than just a priest, he wasn't about hymn books and rosary beads, he was sure of it, he just couldn't prove it – not yet. He looked at his bloodied knuckles and thought of how he would torment and torture the man when he was captured. One of life's pleasures. As in a game of chess, he planned his moves with meticulous precision. He had a plan.

He put the report aside and composed a series of coded messages that outlined his detailed orders and then handed them to his secretary, insisting they be telegraphed immediately by the signals office. She was to wait until the messages were transmitted, then retrieve all copies and destroy them. Reassured everything was in order, Major Richter locked Koell's report in his case along with all the other files pertaining to the Black Hand and was about to leave the building to pack, change his clothes and make his way to the railway station when the thought came to him. It was a fleeting recollection of something he'd read some time ago.

He returned to his office, searched through a series of documents, then removed half a dozen files from a filing cabinet and placed them with the others in his briefcase. He had no time to read them now and would review them during his journey.

In addition to the newspapers Belić asked for, they brought him a small table and a chair so he could read in a civilised way. What he learned horrified him. Defending its borders, Serbia fired shots at Austrian troops at the Danube. England proposed peace talks that France and Italy supported. The *tsar* had yet to make Russia's intentions clear, but if the Russians rallied against the Austrians in defence of Serbia, then Germany undoubtedly would enter the fray. And according to the pundits, if the *Kaiser* mobilised his army, it was predicted England could also enter the war. It all hinged on alliances, treaties, and promises.

What shocked him the most was the news from Sarajevo, all the members of the Black Hand were tried and found guilty and were to be executed, except the three young Bosnians who were deemed too young. It didn't matter, he knew death awaited them anyway, the three young radicals were afflicted by tuberculosis.

Belić folded the papers carefully and lay back down on the bed as he considered all the news. He believed that Russia's *tsar* would come to the aid of Serbia. Would Germany come to the assistance of Austria? He thought it was the most likely outcome. On the other hand, if England went on a war alert to halt a German advance through Europe, the German *Kaiser* may hold his military back.

A knock on the door preceded the lock being turned, and the youthful face of a policeman stood awkwardly in the open doorway.

"Father, this way, please," politely requested the young man.

Belić thought a moment and prepared himself for what was to come. This was the defining point in time when he'd learn of his fate.

"Father?"

Belić nodded and slowly eased from the bed and followed the young man to a non-descript door. The policeman knocked once, opened the door, stepped back and allowed Belić to enter.

It wasn't an interrogation room as he'd expected, it was the *capitano*'s office.

Capitano Luigi Gallo quickly stood and smiled warmly. "Father, please, have a seat. Are you comfortable? Are you in need of anything?"

"Under the circumstances, I'm being treated very well thank you, and your staff have been most helpful and considerate," replied Belić cordially.

Gallo returned to his chair once the priest was seated. He nodded and studied the priest carefully.

"You have a great deal of money in your suitcase ... I wouldn't expect a priest to have that kind of cash," commented Chieti's police chief.

Belić raised an eyebrow, "Have I done something wrong?"

"Look–"

"I wasn't always a priest, and that money represents my entire life savings," Belić interrupted. He kept his face impassive and returned the quizzical stare. Neither man looked away.

"I can do this all day if you'd like," offered Belić, unimpressed with the games the *capitano* was playing.

Gallo's eyes hardened, then creased into a smile. He fished in a drawer of his desk and extracted two small glasses and his favourite bottle of Port. "Your money is safe, but I must question such large amounts. I'm sure you understand."

Belić watched the chief open the bottle.

"Perhaps you'd care to join me in a drink, Father?"

Belić inclined his head as the *capitano* passed him a glass. "To the unfortunate casualties of war," toasted Gallo.

Belić raised his glass in acknowledgement and remained silent.

"Chieti is a quiet town, Father. Normally we have a few problems with drunks, a minor theft here or there. Some local boys getting into trouble, but nothing bad." He took a sip from his glass and licked his lips, savouring the sweetness of the drink. "Suddenly, one of my policemen is shot and killed, and two strange men are seen in the vicinity. A villa is torched, burned to the ground, and a local is found dead, shot inside while a stranger is killed while trying to escape. What do you make of that?" The question was rhetorical.

Father Stevan was surprised, he didn't know about the death of a policeman.

"When we investigated the murder of our policeman, it led us to the home of *Signora* Milani," continued the *capitano*. He kept his gaze firmly on the priest, ignoring his look of surprise. "There we find you comfortably asleep in her barn, and you'd ridden there on a horse you stole from a man we are quite keen to question regarding the death of our police officer. A man we have yet to locate." Gallo raised his eyebrows and expressively turned his palms up. "Now, what are we supposed to think, eh?" *Capitano* Gallo paused a moment. "If I were a gambling man, Father, which I am not, I would wager that you could assist us with our inquiries and help us bring the remaining man to justice."

"*Capitano*, I have never met those two men you speak of. Actually, I'm as curious as you are to discover who they are. The closest I came to those men was when one of them followed me and probably would have … uh, killed me if I had not taken his horse."

Belić paused and looked at the *capitano*. "Am I being charged for theft? Could I make amends, pay for the rent of the horse? I'm willing to do what is right, but my actions were motivated purely for the need to survive and not for self-gain."

Capitano Luigi Gallo nodded, "I see." He breathed in through his nose, then exhaled noisily, and raised both hands again. "No, you are not being charged for stealing the horse, Father, you are a central figure in an ongoing murder investigation, and I just want to know who they are and what it was you did to have two men come after you, why would that man have wanted to kill you?" Gallo cocked his head and picked up his drink.

"The man whose horse I took ... do you have any idea where he is?" Belić asked, evading the question.

Gallo shook his head and then drained his glass.

"And *Signora* Milani, is she well, and how is she doing?"

"Like you, she suffered mostly minor burns, nothing serious, but she is distraught and emotionally ... Father, you know how women get ..."

"Fabio's mother?"

"Ah, yes, she isn't doing well." Again, the *capitano* shook his head in sadness. "But Father, why don't you tell me something." He topped up Belić's glass and looked expectantly at the priest.

Belić was thinking furiously, he still wasn't sure how much he should share with the likeable *capitano*. "May I go to the funeral?"

"You what?" sputtered Gallo, almost spraying a mouthful of Port over his desk and the Belić.

"Fabio's funeral, I want to attend."

Somewhat composed, the *capitano* looked again at the priest taking measure of the man. At first, he thought it an absurd request ... then again, it may not be a bad idea. It may draw out the Austrian. "Let me think about it. But, Father, you were about to tell me about your involvement..."

Father Stevan nodded and repositioned himself on the chair. "What I was involved with appears to have far-reaching political implications beyond what you or this town can cope with. It is best for you and Chieti that you do not know what I have done and allow me my liberty so I can leave and spare this town from continued violence. They will come for me, and I do not want to see any more people suffer. If I am not to be charged with any crime, then is it not my right to be allowed my freedom?"

Capitano Luigi Gallo was waiting for the priest to make that request. "You are a link to an ongoing murder investigation," he repeated. "For your safety, and until we can determine the true nature of your involvement, we will keep you secure." He waited for the priest to argue. He didn't. "You said, 'they' will come for you.' Who are they? What can you tell me? Give me something, Father?" pleaded the *capitano*.

Belić was toying with the old wooden cross. He looked down at it, seeking strength. Finally, he looked up and cleared his throat. "I believe those two men are Austrian, probably military intelligence. They will stop at nothing to find and kill me." Father Stevan paused a moment, then continued. "When I say they will stop at nothing, I mean, and concerning the fine policemen here in your small police force, they will probably kill anyone, without thought or remorse who stand in their way. The recent death of your associate supports my belief, *capitano*."

Capitano Luigi Gallo remained quiet as he digested the priest's words.

"I only saw the one Austrian whose horse I borrowed, then only from a distance. He is a big man, muscular, looked like a brawler. Blonde hair clean-shaven and wore a brown jacket and black trousers. I can't tell you more, other than he is armed and shot a hole

179

in my suitcase. I think it was a remarkable shot considering I was on a moving target and already some distance from him."

"Military Intelligence, eh? And as you say, probably quite dangerous."

"Absolutely." Belić emptied the glass of Port as the *capitano* leaned back in his chair and rubbed his chin.

"A large muscular, blonde brawler, eh?" echoed *Capitano* Gallo. "And will you share with me what you did to anger Austrian military intelligence?"

"No, not yet." He raised the glass to his lips.

Less than twenty-five metres from where *Capitano* Luigi Gallo and Father Stevan Belić chatted in Gallo's office, sat another man, comfortable in the shade of an awning at a café. He was cleverly positioned to see the entrance to the police station while he sipped an espresso coffee and read a newspaper. For all outward appearances, he seemed to be in no hurry and was savouring the solitude, as any man would who'd decided to read the newspaper and prefer to remain undisturbed while doing so.

A closer inspection of the man would reveal he had not the appearance of a salesman, nor of a man on holiday enjoying leisure time, his physical presence and constant dour expression did not advertise a friendly outgoing disposition – fair warning to those wishing to intrude on his solitude.

Without moving his head, Dieter Wollf lifted his eyes and scanned the road near Chieti's police station again. His back was protectively against a wall, and he felt secure, knowing no one could approach him without being seen. He'd previously scouted the maze of alleys and streets in the neighbourhood, and if the need arose, he could disappear instantly. He'd explored all his escape options and planned his route to the step.

A waiter at the café innocently inquired about the gentleman's prolonged stay in Chieti. In reply, Wollf grumbled he was waiting for a relative coming from Venice and experienced an unexpected delay. The explanation seemed to satisfy the waiter, who no doubt immediately reported the information to the café's proprietor. He didn't.

For the last two days, Wollf had not been in an agreeable mood, not since the priest stole his horse and he'd been forced to spend an entire day and night walking back to Chieti. He returned to his hotel without encountering the front desk clerk or manager and hurriedly packed Koell's belongings and then his own. Carrying two suitcases, he left the building through a rear exit and found another hotel not far from the railway station that suited him perfectly. At the appropriate time, he would destroy the dead officer's possessions.

Once checked in to his new room, Wollf left the hotel and sent a coded telegram to the *Evidenzbureau* in Wien and returned a few hours later for a reply. The news that Major Richter was coming here to Chieti was astonishing, not only did Wollf dislike the man, he was frightened of him. The thought of spending time in the major's company did not sit well. He hated officers, most of all Major Maximillian Richter.

Wollf felt the presence of someone at his side. He'd been daydreaming, a mistake, and hadn't detected the person approaching. Automatically his right hand dropped to the pocket of his jacket and grasped his pistol. He slowly looked up from the newspaper and saw a young girl, her clothes were soiled, and she held out a dirty, grimy hand begging for money. He shook his head, then gave her his best smile. Frightened, she ran away. He shrugged and then noticed a *Carabiniere* on a bicycle coming towards him. He kept his hand in his pocket and tensed, ready to make a move. At the last moment, the Federal Policeman veered away and stopped outside the Polizia Locale station. Leaving the bicycle outside, the policeman straightened his uniform, removed the bicycle clip from his leg, repositioned his hat and strode confidently into the building. That was unusual, thought Wollf, wondering why a *Carabiniere* was visiting the local police. He threw some money on the table and left the café, and found another position to observe that offered him better concealment from down the street.

Father Stevan was listening politely to the *capitano*'s dissertation on the changing face of Italy's political landscape and a European war when a knock on the door interrupted his vociferous discourse, both men turned to look as the young policeman entered.

"Excuse me, sir, and sorry to disturb you, but I have a *Carabiniere* here who insists on personally delivering a message to you."

Gallo's expression changed from annoyance to puzzlement. "Show him in."

The junior *carabiniere* entered *Capitano*'s office and, without preamble, began his rehearsed communique. "Are you *Capitano* Gallo, sir?" His eyes flicked down at the priest, then back at the *capitano*.

Luigi nodded and winked at Belić. "See, not everyone in Chieti knows me."

Assured he was addressing the right person, the young *Carabiniere* continued. "*Maggiore* Da Camino sends his regards and requests the pleasure of your company at your earliest convenience. I, uh, I am to escort you, sir."

"Earliest convenience?" Luigi laughed. "And you will escort me!" he bellowed, then turned to Father Steven. "Oh my, the *carabinieri* are asserting themselves, aren't they?"

The young man was unfazed and entirely at ease with the importance of the responsibilities he'd been tasked. "Yes, sir."

"Wait outside," snarled *Capitano* Gallo.

"And shut the door behind you!" the *carabiniere* about-faced and strode from the office.

Belić watched him leave.

"Six months ago, he would have been a snot-nosed, pimply-faced youth hanging from his nanny's skirts, now look at him ... his family buys him a commission, he spends an afternoon training, and now he's ordering me around." Gallo shook his head. "Give me back the good old days, Father. That's when officers were trained properly and earned respect to lead men."

Father Stevan had an uneasy feeling in the pit of his stomach. He said nothing.

"I suppose I had better go and see what the fuss is about. Anyway, I don't want that boy snooping around here for the high and mighty Da Camino." He rose from his chair and walked from behind his desk, only to hear another knock at the door.

The door opened, and the young policeman, one of Gallo's men, entered. "I was told to give you this, *capitano*."

Gallo unfolded the note and scanned it. "How did you get his?"

"I went to get food from the café over the road. The waiter told me to see you received it urgently, sir."

"Very well, thank you."

Capitano Gallo read the note again and then stared blankly at the far wall. After a few heartbeats, his eyes refocused, and he turned to the priest. "Remain here." Gallo walked from the office and closed the door. Belić was left wondering.

A few minutes later, the door opened, and the same young policeman entered. "This way, Father."

"Where is *Capitano* Gallo?" Belić asked as he was led back to his small room.

"He'll be back later."

The young constable locked the door, and Belić was alone in his small room again. He heard a noise outside and pressed his ear to the door, and thought it sounded like a chair scraping on the floor. *Is there a guard outside his room?*

Capitano Luigi Gallo slowly exited through the door of Polizia Locale and onto the street. Outside, impatiently waited the arrogant young *carabiniere* with his bicycle. Gallo stopped, patted his pockets and then turned around and re-entered the building. He returned a minute later, all smiles. "My tobacco," he volunteered to the puzzled young man.

Under the pretext of having forgotten his tobacco, Gallo had, in fact, looked towards the café and scanned the surrounding area. He didn't see the Austrian but suspected he was still nearby.

Ten minutes later, they entered the spacious old building which housed the *Carabinieri*, Italy's military police and civilian police authority. Every time the *capitano* came here, he felt envious of them, for this building was everything his Polizia Locale building was not. Carved into stone over the entranceway, a sign boldly stated, *Arma Benemerita*, The Meritorious Corps. Unconsciously, Luigi adjusted his uniform, and with a wet finger, stroked his moustache. "Lead the way, boy."

"Ah *Capitano* Gallo, how good of you to come and see me," smoothly welcomed *Maggiore* Da Camino. He rose from behind his oversized desk and walked around to shake Gallo's hand.

"*Maggiore*," Gallo nodded once. "Wasn't like I had a choice, was it? You sent the boy to see me and insisted I come." He shook the limp hand of the major.

Maggiore Da Camino ignored the comment and gestured theatrically to an ornate armchair. "Please, take a seat."

Luigi accepted the offer, eased into the lightly cushioned chair, and studied the *Carabinieri* commander carefully as the major sat in a matching chair directly facing him. He didn't like the little commander, and he always had a sour taste in his mouth after meeting with him. The man was no more a soldier or policeman than Gabbi was. Another incongruous man whose noble family bought him a commission and status without having to earn it, he thought.

"How can I help you, *Maggiore*?"

"It seems we have a common problem."

Gallo's eyebrows lifted in question. "We do?"

"Word has come from the Reggio Calabria that Giuseppe Canolo has come this way to establish a foothold for the Ndrangheta[4]."

"These types of criminals fall mostly under your jurisdiction –"

"Giuseppe Canolo is being sought by the *Carabinieri* in the region of Calabria for murder, extortion, blackmail, need I go on?" interrupted Da Camino waving his arm in the air.

Capitano Gallo remained silent.

"My superiors have notified me that Canolo is a fugitive and involved in organised criminal activities, part of an extensive lawless crime family, and we would be quite pleased to see his capture."

This wasn't news to Capitano Gallo. "*Maggiore* Da Camino, of course, my small, understaffed, underfunded police department is

4   Ndrangheta is a noted Mafia-type criminal organisation based in the Calabria region of Italy.

more than willing to assist, you know this. Send the paperwork to the office as you normally do, but why did you really bring me here? I have much to do," appealed *Capitano* Gallo.

Maggiore Da Camino studied his manicured fingernails for a moment, then looked towards the Chieti's police chief. "We find ourselves in difficult times, do we not?"

"Ah yes, very difficult?" repeated Gallo innocently.

"Why yes, certainly the outbreak of fighting in the Balkans and the effect it has on the rest of Europe will prove challenging for us all, will it not?" asked *Maggiore* Da Camino.

"I believe Italy's neutral position should preclude us from antagonising our neighbours and entering into war," offered Gallo.

"Oh? I beg to differ, *Capitano*. We've been instructed to upgrade our state of readiness. More training, recruiting and added responsibilities. In fact, our entire military is on a similar alert, but the Polizia Locale don't have to worry about those things, do they?" smiled the major.

"I think being prepared is reasonable considering what is happening on our borders," offered Gallo.

The major laughed. "You don't think our new alert status is in preparation for defending those borders, do you? You're a little, uh, *jejune*[5], to assume that."

Gallo ignored the jibe. "Yes, I do. What other reason could there be?"

Maggiore Da Camino inclined his head. "I have it on good authority that Italy will not remain neutral as you naively suggest *Capitano* Gallo."

This time Luigi laughed. "Then for what other reason?"

Maggiore Da Camino crossed his legs and brushed some imaginary debris from his finely tailored breeches. He didn't

5   Naïve, simplistic

answer. "I understand you've been quite busy the last few days."

"We are always busy, *Maggiore*, what are you referring to exactly?" Gallo felt tense and did his best to hide it from Da Camino.

"A shooting, was it?"

"And what of it? We are handling everything nicely." *What interest does the Carabinieri have in this, and how did they find out about Gabbi*, he thought?

"That's what we are trying to ascertain. I heard the man who was shot was, er, an Austrian?"

Gallo silently breathed out a sigh of relief. "We are still investigating the matter, and why is this of concern to you?" Luigi was instantly suspicious.

"Therein lies the problem, *Capitano*." *Maggiore* Da Camino uncrossed his leg, scooted forward on his chair and leaned in. "We, and by that, I mean Italy, has a vested interest in ensuring we keep our neighbours, ah. our allies happy. It isn't in Italy's interest to go upsetting them, now would it?"

"When you say *them*, you really mean Austria, Hungary, Germany?"

Da Camino smiled.

Capitano Luigi Gallo looked past the major and focused at a point on the far wall. He didn't see the beautiful works of art that hung with prominence and festooned the major's office, his mind was working furiously as he digested what the major implied.

"Are you telling me that Italy's war preparations are to ultimately support the Austro–Hungarian Empire and Germany in this tragic crisis?" Gallo asked.

The major smiled and said nothing. He didn't need to; Gallo knew exactly what Da Camino was alluding to.

"I believe you are currently questioning a man, a Serbian, I believe, in connection with the shooting, is this right?"

Now it was the *capitano*'s turn not to reply. He was trying to think how the major discovered all this. He was confounded and becoming angrier by the second.

"It would be in the best interests of Italy if we kept the Austrians appeased, wouldn't you say? Keep them happy and give them what they want, after all, as you just said, they might become our allies," Da Camino slickly offered.

"What is the official position of the *Carabinieri*?" asked *Capitano* Luigi Gallo, doing his utmost to reign in his temper.

Maggiore Da Camino leaned back in his chair and crossed his legs again. "I don't know yet, my lead investigator will be returning to Chieti tonight, and I will speak with him tomorrow and consider his recommendations. I, uh, hope we see eye-to-eye on this *Capitano*?"

"Oh yes, *Maggiore* Da Camino," offered Gallo, almost choking on his words, "and have you spoken to the Austrian authorities about this?"

"I speak to a lot of people, *Capitano*," said the major evasively.

"I see, then I don't believe there is any need for *Carabinieri* involvement, is there?"

"That depends on what my investigator suggests." *Maggiore* Da Camino gave Luigi a smile that contained no warmth.

"I'm sure an important man such as yourself has more pressing matters to attend to. But if you wish to investigate further, I'll be more than happy to send over any documents you require along with paperwork on Giuseppe Canolo."

"Wonderful." for the space of a few heartbeats, both men stared at each other, "Would you care for a beverage before you go?" asked the *Maggiore* breaking the silence.

"No, thank you, I should leave, I have a meeting scheduled with the Mayor. Budget issues, you know how that goes," replied

Gallo, unable to resist the temptation, "I've asked for two more sets of handcuffs, and the Council refuses to allocate money." Gallo feigned a look of displeasure.

The major tut-tutted. Not realising the *Capitano* was playing him.

"It was a pleasure to see you again, *Capitano* Gallo, we should have these talks more frequently."

"I think so too, *Maggiore*."

Luigi retraced his route back towards the station with both hands buried deep in his pockets as he contemplated the implications behind the slimy Da Camino's unspoken words and suggestions. *He wants me to drop my pants, bend over, and accommodate the wishes of Austria,* he thought. Of no doubt to Gallo was Da Camino's desire to align himself with Austria–Hungarian Empire, believing Italy would become allies. But Italy openly declared their neutrality. Da Camino was dangerous and putting his aspirations of career and political advancement before his sworn duty.

He was suddenly struck by the realisation of what would happen – he stopped. The Austrians would come with the *Carabinieri,* and they would demand he hand over the priest, they would take him and disappear, and he'd never bring the man to justice who killed Gabbi. The priest would never see his day in court, and the Austrians will probably just disappear after killing him. Anyway, he kind of liked the priest and wanted to help him if he could.

He had no justifiable legal reason to detain Belić and probably should've already released him, but he let his ego get in the way, and now the man's life was perhaps in danger. At least one Austrian was watching the police station, were there more? He wondered if there was a way to release the priest so he didn't fall into Austrian hands, and at the same time, lure in the big Austrian who had escaped capture. He laughed. Da Camino would be incensed if he arrested the Austrian who was suspected of killing Gabbi.

As he approached the Polizia Locale, he closely watched his surroundings and hoped he would stumble on the man his nephew at the café identified. The shrill sound of a distant whistle reminded him the late afternoon train had arrived.

CHAPTER TWELVE

Pescara, Italy, 1914

The early morning sun glistened on the calm waters that gently lapped along the golden beaches of Pescara. Enjoying the morning coolness before they began their day, a handful of people, mostly tourists, casually strolled along the water's edge. One or two dedicated fishermen were positioned strategically on the beach and along the break–wall. They'd been there since before dawn but unlikely to stay much longer when the heat of the day made it uncomfortable. With patience and to the vocal protest of screeching gulls, they'd reel-in their lines, pack their tackle and depart, only to return the following morning and try again. The cloudless sky hinted that today would again be another scorcher.

A few small fishing boats found what little breeze there was and zigzagged here and there, while in the distance, the bow wave of the approaching ferry from Ragusa interrupted the antics of the smaller craft who were obliged to steer clear of the larger ship. The bow wave decreased in size as the ferry slowly neared the inner harbour. Passengers lined the rails in anticipation of reaching dry land after a fourteen-hour voyage.

At an oceanfront *ristorante* and beneath the expanse of large colourful umbrellas lining a sizeable patio, people, mostly couples, sat and enjoyed their breakfast, sipped espresso or nursed hangovers as they stared bleary-eyed at newspapers that headlined the latest current events and detailed the horrors of a developing European war.

At first glance, one couple seemed no different than others and sat at a table that afforded them an unobstructed view of the harbour, approaching ships, and even disembarking ferry passengers. The man and his wife each read a newspaper and looked relaxed and comfortable. Occasionally they would talk to each other, casually look around, share a laugh and continue reading. What separated them from others was their attentiveness to their surroundings.

The ferry docked with precision, and within minutes, passengers were checking through immigration and then beyond to waiting friends or family. The blonde-haired woman casually lowered her newspaper to the table and raised the small espresso cup to her lips, and sipped unhurriedly as she studied debarking passengers as they passed by her. She could tell most were local, a few tourists, but no one worthy of a second glance. Many seemed relieved to be here in Pescara and escape the volatile Balkans region that threatened to erupt in violence any day. More people passed, just ordinary folk, and then one person caught her attention.

What drew her interest to him was his rigidity and the way he held his head. With his chin slightly raised, he had an imperiousness about him. Even though he wore civilian clothes, she knew he was undoubtedly a military man and, through his bearing, certainly an officer. She leaned over to her husband and smiled, then whispered into his ear. To an observer, they shared an intimate moment.

"I know that face, the man with the light hat and beige jacket," she said quietly.

Kaha kissed her cheek, sat up and unobtrusively looked towards the man she identified. From his vantage point, the man's hat obscured his face in shadow, but then he casually turned towards them before looking away.

"That's, uh, uh, the Austrian major, Maximillian, for the life of me, I can't recall his last name. What the dickens is he doing here?"

"Maximillian Richter?" she clarified. They'd both studied endless photographs of ranking intelligence and military officers as part of their induction into the British Secret Service.

"Yes, that's the chap, Austrian military intelligence," replied her husband. "Is odd that the Austrians are here in Pescara. Very strange." Kaha scratched his chin. "Why would a senior *Evidenzebureau* officer be here? I suppose we should notify London immediately; they'll want to know."

"I'll go to the yacht," she said, standing and placing her napkin on the table, "Will you watch him?"

Kaha nodded as he placed some *lire* on the table, "I'll meet you there later. And please check the boat thoroughly before you go below," he cautioned her. This was a security task he typically performed himself. "Oh yes, and lock the hatch from inside." He leaned forward and embraced Pam as he kept an eye on the disappearing back of Major Maximillian Richter.

Pam quickly made her way back to their seventy-three-foot yawl moored in Pescara's inner harbour. Aboard the yacht, cleverly hidden behind a wood panel at the navigation station, sat a powerful and small wireless transmitter-receiver. There she would code and transmit her message to the Secret Service Bureau in London and sign off with their designated code names Anchor and Chain. Usually, communiqués were sent at night when the effective broadcast range increased dramatically due to atmospherics, however, today, the message would be relayed. As protocol demanded, she would wait for a reply.

Surveillance was typically performed by teams. One person would follow the target for a short distance and then switch over to another, this minimised the risk of a double-sighting, where the target saw the person following him more than once and aroused suspicion.

Kaha didn't have the luxury of having a large team, he was alone in a foreign country without support, and he was about to follow a person believed to be a high-ranking intelligence officer from the Austrian military. This was a perilous situation, and he knew it. Some would argue, even foolish.

Rather than immediately follow the target, Kaha loitered some distance behind and, with an experienced eye, scanned the surrounding area to see if he had associates following. The major was still visible ahead of him, and thankfully he paused at a store to look at the merchandise before moving on.

Determining it was safe, Kaha followed discreetly and never looked directly towards the Austrian, as people had a way of sensing if someone was watching them – Kaha took no chances. There were plenty of pedestrians about, and he always kept himself partly obscured and never put himself in full view of the Austrian major.

The target stopped again, this time, he browsed for hats and tried a couple on.

He already wore a hat and certainly didn't appear to Kaha that he needed another. With realisation, his heart began pounding, and he could have kicked himself; he'd been careless. Seeing a store selling fruit, Kaha decided to employ his own surveillance countermeasures and began selecting a few apples from the street–side stand and forced himself to relax.

The major employed counter surveillance measures and stopped twice to look at hats, and to anyone watching and paying attention, he appeared to be innocently shopping – this was a ruse. Called a theme, and under the pretext of browsing, he could easily confirm if he was being tailed and not let the followers know they'd been identified. Kaha suspected the major knew he was being followed as he was being particularly cautious, which meant there could be others following him at a discrete distance.

Nonchalantly, Kaha glanced behind, back down the street as he paid for his apples. He extracted one from the bag and rubbed it on his arm, polishing it to a sheen as he casually observed pedestrians and shoppers. He saw no one that looked out of place, unexpectedly looked away, or paused suddenly without warning. From his peripheral vision, he saw the Austrian finally move away from the hat vendor and quickly cross the street.

Kaha sauntered along the footpath munching on his apple and didn't follow the Austrian across the road. He maintained a respectful distance and continued to avoid looking directly at him.

He saw another vendor selling fruit and stopped to inspect pears. The distance between them was widening, but Kaha was still worried about being detected – it was better to be cautious. He knew the chance of successfully following this man without being seen was tenuous, especially with one only person performing the surveillance.

From the Austrian's direction, Kaha surmised he was heading for the railway station, which was only a five-minute walk. Leaving the pears, Kaha walked back onto the footpath, quickly confirmed where the major was, then ducked down a side street, and once out of sight, he began to jog. He tossed his apples away and picked up the pace, turning left and running down a parallel street, hoping to find a vantage spot where he could watch the station and the approaching target.

Something didn't feel right, his sixth sense alerting him to danger. Kaha had been around long enough to know not to ignore the sensation. Responding to his gut feeling, he suddenly veered away from the footpath and turned left into a narrow lane dissecting two tenement buildings and surprised a woman hanging out her laundry. Without thinking, he quickly removed his blue coloured shirt, threw it out of sight, stepped closer towards her and leaned against a wall. Wearing a singlet, light-coloured trousers, and with his olive complexion and black hair, he appeared to be Italian and having a pleasant conversation with his woman. She opened her mouth to speak, but thankfully, she was too astonished by the sudden appearance of a handsome man to say anything. Kaha forced his most charming smile as his heart began thumping when he heard someone briefly slow behind him and momentarily pause before running on. Now he knew there were others with Major Richter or at least one other person. He had been seen, and fortunately, not identified because he had successfully kept his face hidden. It now required a risky change of plan.

The sighting of the Austrian intelligence officer in Italy was of some concern, and he knew his superiors at the Secret Service Bureau would be more than curious as to the reason. The dilemma remained, how to observe the major without being seen and identified. He'd been fortunate so far, but would his luck hold? He leaned with his back against the wall and rested his hands on his thighs as he considered his next move. The perplexed woman hanging her washing took a step back and looked at him with suspicion and unease.

This time, and with a genuinely warm smile, he returned her look, and in barely passable Italian, he said, "A woman ... her husband..." and shrugged.

She wasn't impressed.

Determined to find out where the Austrian was headed, Kaha left his shirt in the alley and briskly walked towards the railway station. On impulse, he stopped at a clothing store and quickly bought a new shirt and hat. Not his preference in style, but certainly, it changed his appearance. Feeling more confident that he could remain undetected, he arrived at the station and was rewarded with the sight of the major purchasing a ticket.

Kaha never saw the man who was with the Austrian, his back had been turned when he ran past the alley and could not identify him. But he was here somewhere. Rather than risk compromising himself by searching for the man, he decided to end the surveillance.

Supported by his newly purchased gaudy shirt, he assumed the role of a confused holidaymaker. He waited as the Austrian officer walked back across the street to a café where he sat down, presumably to wait for his scheduled departure time.

Forcing himself to relax, Kaha went to the ticket window and slid some lire under the glass. "*Mi scusi, signore*, that man who just bought a ticket, where is his destination?" Kaha's Italian wasn't perfect, but then it didn't need to be; he was a tourist after all.

The ticketing clerk looked at the money, then up at the traveller.

"Yes, the money is for you. Is important, please *Signore*." Kaha smiled, showing a mouthful of even bright teeth.

The clerk looked to either side, but no one was near the window to see the offered bribe, he smoothly pocketed the money. "Chieti, the train departs mid-afternoon."

"*Grazie, Signore.*"

Now he knew the destination. Kaha decided to return to the yacht, and hopefully, London would have responded to Pam's message by the time he arrived back.

It was a typical mid-summer afternoon in Chieti, the sun shone brilliantly, and along with it came the oppressive heat. A stifling thirty-three degrees, he'd overheard a traveller say to another. The train had just departed Chieti's railway station, and Major Maximillian Richter stood in the shade on the platform, although it wasn't any cooler, but at least the sun wasn't sucking the life from him.

He felt self-conscious and unimportant. Out of uniform and dressed in civilians wasn't something he enjoyed. Civilian clothes made him look like a bookkeeper, and it's difficult to instil fear and command respect when not wearing a crisp uniform that displayed rank. Although dressing like a bookkeeper had its advantages, no one spared him a second look – he was anonymous – almost. But someone had recognised him and followed him in Pescara and managed to slip away. This wasn't good. He removed his spectacles and gave them a thorough polishing before replacing them carefully back on his nose.

To add to his humiliation and against all his protestations, *Direktor* Czvetassin had insisted he travel to Italy alone. Although, and through a contact in the Italian underworld, he'd hired a local thug to meet him in Pescara to keep watch and ensure he wasn't followed. Again, his hunch had proven to be correct. Unfortunately, the thug was less than capable, lost the man who he was tracking and neither could he be enticed to journey with him to Chieti, claiming he was sought by the local police. So be it, thought Richter, I'll manage without him.

Richter continued to survey his surroundings from the shade provided by the railway station roof. Chieti was much like any other small Italian town and situated on a low hill alongside the Pescara River. The city was dominated by a Gothic cathedral, although nothing like the grand architecture in Wien, and hilly rugged terrain rose either side of the township … but the people here were nothing more than just simple peasants, and he had no time for them. Richter's nose twitched, and he found the unfamiliar smells bothersome and vulgar and hoped to be away from here within a day or so.

He saw some movement in his peripheral vision, turned slightly, and recognised *Stabswachtmeister* Wollf as he stepped from concealment. Richter lifted his hand and looked at his watch; Wollf was precisely on time. He was pleased, he liked his men to be punctual. Richter picked up his case, stepped into the hot sun and walked towards him.

"She's not doing well, Father," said Enzo.

Belić stared at the wall and thought of how Natalina must be feeling. The guilt and the inability to do anything was frustrating.

"She doesn't hold you responsible –"

Belić quickly focused on Enzo. "Why not? I came here to this peaceful place and brought with me nothing but pain and suffering to innocent people–"

"Listen," Enzo leaned forward, interrupting, "you didn't shoot Fabio, and you didn't set fire to her house. Those men, they did it, and they chose to do it." He sat back in the chair. "I believe you when you tell me you didn't murder women and children, and I don't' know what you did to have those men come after you, that is your business."

Belić nodded. "Thank you, Enzo. And otherwise, how is she?"

"She feels you lied to her." Enzo was uncomfortable and wanted to change the subject.

Belić looked down at the cross he rotated in his hand.

With a heavy sigh, Enzo looked around the small room. "What are they going to do with you?"

Suddenly the door opened, and *Capitano* Luigi Gallo stepped in. "Enzo, how are you feeling, better, I hope? And the lovely *Signora* Milani, she is recovering?" Luigi shook his head sadly. "I am sorry for the loss of your friend Fabio. Such a waste," offered the *Capitano* with a sorrowful shake of his head.

Enzo offered a smile. "Thank you."

"I, uh, need to speak with the Father, Enzo."

"Yes, I apologise for intruding, *Capitano*," said Enzo as he rose from the chair. Luigi pressed against the wall to allow him to pass in the cramped room. "And thank you for allowing me to visit."

"Think nothing of it, come and see us anytime." Gallo patted him on the shoulder and smiled in a fatherly way.

"Thank you for your visit, and please tell *Signora* Milani I asked after her," said Belić.

"I will."

Capitano Gallo watched Enzo leave and then closed the door and sat on the recently vacated chair. He removed his hat and threw it on the bed, and patted his head with a handkerchief. "It is hot today, Father."

Belić shrugged.

"I need to talk with you."

He got no response from the priest.

"Father, we need to talk, both of us have a problem. Are you listening?"

Belić turned to the police chief. "I'm sorry, *Capitano*, please continue."

"It is not wise to attend Fabio's funeral – I am sorry."

Belić opened his mouth to speak, but *Capitano* Gallo raised a hand to forestall him. "The *Carabinieri* have taken an interest in you, and if that isn't bad enough, I expect they will demand I hand you over to them, and if I do, they will turn you over to the Austrians."

Belić looked shocked. "The *Carabinieri*, why?"

"That doesn't matter, what is important is one of the Austrians, the man whose horse you took has been watching this building. He's not made any attempt to enter here yet, and that leads me to the conclusion he's waiting, others may come. If the Austrians come here with the *Carabinieri*, then I am legally bound to hand you over, and they *will* release you to the Austrians. Do you know what that means?"

Belić nodded. "Yes, I do."

"Good, it also means I will not be able to arrest Gabbi's murderer, and I made a promise to the mayor I would." Gallo neatly folded his handkerchief and returned it to his pocket. "Now, I've given this a great deal of thought, and I think there might be a way to make this work for both of us."

An old rattling fan swivelled backwards and forwards on its pedestal and succeeded only in circulating hot air, it failed to offer relief from the heat of any kind, most of all to *Stabswachtmeister* Wollf. Two of the three men in Major Richter's hotel room were uncomfortable and were sweating profusely because of the heat. The only coolness in the room came from the major whose intense, unblinking gaze bored into the skull of Wollf as he looked downwards at the floor. Deiter Wollf just received a tongue lashing from Major Richter about not capturing the priest and allowing him to fall into the hands of the local police. As the major reminded him, he had bungled the only real opportunity to catch the fugitive.

The other silent occupant, Johan Bekker, sat on a chair near the open window, and like Wollf, had discarded his jacket and shirt and sat only wearing his trousers and an undershirt. He'd listened dispassionately to the tirade as the major unloaded on Wollf and concluded that Maximillian Richter was indeed a strange and unconventional man.

Herr Bekker had a diverse career. To the *Evidenzbureau,* he was an informer, a fixer, a contractor to do whatever task required of him. He lived a quiet life in Naples and supplemented his income with petty crime, extortion and anything else he could do. For a man of his extraordinary talents, Naples provided him with everything he needed. The telegram he'd received a few days ago insisted that he make his way to Chieti with expediency and would be briefed on arrival, however the last person he expected to see was Major Richter himself.

Wollf shifted uncomfortably in his chair, and other than the vibrating fan, the room was quiet. Major Richter turned his attention from Wollf to Bekker. "Anything you wish to say, Bekker?"

Without moving his head, he flicked his eyes towards the major. "No, nothing."

Soon as the major looked away, Johan Bekker pulled a tortoiseshell comb from his pocket and began pulling it through his jet-black shiny mane with practised ease. Once finished, he licked his palms and patted each side of his head.

"Now tell me, has the police station been under constant surveillance?" asked Richter, giving Bekker a sideways glance and a scowl.

"Yes, *Herr* Major, we have been constantly watching in four-hour shifts," replied Wollf.

Richter blinked a couple of times. "When will Gunter be

replaced?"

"In an hour, then Johan will take over," Wollf added quickly.

Gunter Meyer was another useful petty criminal that Major Richter hired from time to time. Like Johan Bekker, Meyer was an Austrian patriot who lived in Italy and most frequently involved himself in any criminal activity that generated an income. Gunter also responded quickly to Richter's telegram and arrived in Chieti shortly before the major.

"It is too late to do anything today, but tomorrow morning, you," Richter nodded at Bekker, "will accompany me, and we will pay a visit to *Maggiore* Da Camino, who commands the local *Carabinieri*. It is imperative that he cooperates with us and pressures the local police to hand the priest over." Richter turned his head to look at Wollf, "I'm expecting another person to help us, and all going well, he's bringing a ... er, a package and will arrive from Pescara on the early evening train tomorrow. You'll recognise him, so make sure he gets a room and keeps the package safe, then come and find me." Richter paused a moment and gave *Stabswachtmeister* Wollf a long cold look. "Can you do that simple task, or will you fail in that too?"

Wollf sullenly met the major's stare. "Of course, *Herr* Major."

"Meanwhile, I suggest you both rest and continue to keep the police station under observation. Now off you go."

The sound of the lock being turned disturbed Father Stevan Belić's sleep, he looked at his wristwatch and could see it was only 5:00 a.m. One of *Capitano* Gallo's policemen entered the small room and looked apologetic.

"Is something wrong?" Belić asked, rubbing sleep from his eyes.

"Good morning, Father. I don't know what is going on, but *Capitano* Gallo gave me precise instructions, and so I must do as he asks."

Belić stretched and noticed for the first time the bundle of clothes the young policeman carried.

"The *Capitano* fears for your safety and asks that you put on these clothes. He gave me a note for you to read and asked me to ensure you do exactly as he requests." The young man handed over a sealed envelope.

The grey of dawn brought much relief to Gunter Meyer. It was that time of morning that was neither night nor day, and he knew his four-hour shift watching the police station would end soon. Already there was a little activity in the streets as people began their morning routines. The position from where he observed the entrance to the Polizia Locale was cleverly situated, he could see the faces of everyone coming or going from the building, even during darkness, the exterior lamp attached beside the police station doorway briefly illuminated the face of each person who passed by or entered the building.

It had been an uneventful shift; no one left or entered the Polizia Locale during the four- hours he'd been watching. It took all his willpower to not sit back against the wall and take a nap, but he'd resisted and continued to remain vigilant.

He'd been given a few photographs that made it possible to identify the fugitive they called the 'Priest', and if the priest left the building, he was to follow. In addition, he was to report any abnormal activity and odd comings and goings. Although, according to Gunter, that was difficult because other than the shift changes, he wasn't aware of the everyday routine. But with the mind of a criminal, Gunter's senses were finely tuned to distinguish abnormal behaviour from ordinary. He'd been told by the big oaf, Wollf, that during the morning shift change, he could expect to see at least two policemen enter the Polizia Locale just before 6:00 a.m. and shortly after, another two policemen, just finishing their work shift would leave.

Already Gunter could make out the form of two policemen walking up the street. With his head only centimetres above the wall, he observed as the two men approached the building and walked inside. As they passed beneath the light attached above the doorway, he briefly saw their faces. Gunter fished in his pocket, pulled a photo of the priest, and to refresh his memory, studied it as best he could in the early morning gloom.

A few minutes later, laughter drew his attention to the entranceway again, and he saw the form of two policemen exiting the building. The first man walked by the light, and Gunter observed the man was too young to be the person in the photograph. Just as the second man was about to step into the light, a voice from inside the station called out, and he turned his face away to look back inside the building. In response, the policeman yelled back, and as he stepped through the circle of yellow light, he raised his hand to and adjusted the position of his peaked cap. Gunter never saw his face clearly. Both off-duty police officers walked down the road towards home and bed, their night shift had ended, and Gunter was envious.

An hour later, Gunter was relieved by Johan Bekker and reported no unusual activity, and as expected, two policemen entered the building at 6:00 a.m., and shortly afterwards, two men left.

Capitano Gallo's cousin Vito and Father Stevan walked away from the Polizia Locale and headed towards the railway station. To

Vito, the priest appeared to be relatively calm and unaffected by their subterfuge.

"You did well, Father," laughed Vito.

"I almost forgot to adjust my hat if it hadn't been for your reminder," said Belić with a laugh

"You'd make a fine policeman; you wear the uniform like a natural."

"I'd prefer to remain a priest," offered Belić sourly.

Directly in front of the railway station was a small fountain. On the other side, facing the station, was a collection of small stores that included a café, a bakery, a cobbler, and a Doctor's office. Vito led Belić past the bakery and rapped loudly on the door of the cobbler. As they waited for someone to open the door, Father Stevan read the painted sign on the window, *'Fissiamo Suole'*, and grinned.

"Ah, yes, you like, Father? That was my idea," offered Vito. "We Fix Soles."

"And he repairs shoes too?" Belić smiled.

"It's my cousin, Gino, you know him from *Signora* Milani's villa."

Just then, the door opened, and Belić recoiled, it was the big hulking man who held him at gunpoint at *Signora* Milani's Villa. This time he didn't have a shotgun and opened the door with a big welcoming smile and urged them quickly inside. He stuck his head out through the open doorway, looked both ways down the street, then closed and locked the door after him.

Belić could smell leather and the musty odour of feet. Rack upon rack of shoes lined the walls of the cramped shop, some new, others used. A work area along the rear wall was lined with tools, leather and a host of items used to make and repair footwear. A doorway led to adjoining living quarters at the rear, and Belić guessed Gino lived here with his family.

"We meet again, Father. Although this time under different circumstances," he held out his hand in greeting.

"It's a pleasure to meet you again, Gino, and under friendlier circumstances. I am grateful for your help." They shook hands, and Belić unconsciously rubbed his nose where Gino had poked it with the shotgun.

"You can thank Luigi, uh, *Capitano* Gallo, he is the one who has arranged all this. Come, please, I think we should begin our day with a zabaglione[5], something special for you, no?"

Gino led Belić and Vito through the rear door and into a private living area.

"Father, you must not leave this shop at all, do you understand?" insisted Vito.

Belić nodded.

"Luigi will come here in a short while and explain to you what he has in mind. Remain out of sight and do as he asks, he's a clever man is our Luigi." Vito beamed with pride. "You can relax now, no one knows you are here."

"My clothes and suitcase?"

"They will come, do not worry," offered Vito.

The smell of coffee reminded Belić of his time at Natalina's. He couldn't stop thinking about her. Most of all, the guilt he felt at being responsible for all that had happened, and of course, the deception. And these people, these kind and generous Italians, held no hard feelings towards him. It only compounded how he felt.

"Can you repair shoes? I could put you to work," grinned Gino,

6   Zabaglione – A special Italian beverage made from coffee, egg yolks, sugar and marsala.

bringing two cups of zabaglione.

"I have a hole in my suitcase, do you think you could repair it when it arrives?"

CHAPTER THIRTEEN

Michael Sykes stuck his head through the open doorway. "Excuse me, sir, do you have a moment?"

"Yes, hang on, let me finish this first ... uh, take a seat," came the reply, followed by an arm that waved him to a chair.

Carrying a thick file, Sykes walked into the office, sat as requested, and patiently watched Mansfield Smith–Cumming, the Director of the Secret Service Bureau, finish the letter he was writing. Pleased with his work, the director screwed the cap on his fountain pen and reached for another. He tested the pen on a blotter and quickly scrawled the letter 'C' in green ink at the bottom of the page. He replaced the fountain pen in an open desk drawer, picked up the completed letter, and waved it in the air a few times to help dry the ink.

"Marge!" he shouted.

Within seconds his attractive young secretary entered the office and looked in question at her boss.

"See, this gets sent off, will you!"

He handed the letter to her, sat back in his chair with a squeak and reached for the gold-framed monocle that hung around his neck and affixed it to his right eye. He looked up at his guest. "Now, what's up, Michael?"

"We've got something interesting here and not really sure what to make of it." Sykes scooted his chair closer to the director's desk and extracted a document from the file he carried, and looked at it briefly. "Those boffins over at MI8 have received *sigint*[7] from the

7   Sigint. Signal intelligence.

French, sir. Seems they intercepted a flurry of radioactivity from the town of, uh ... I have it here somewhere ... ah yes, Chieti, in Italy. That in itself isn't cause for any real concern, but we just received a message from 'Anchor and Chain' who are presently in the Italian seaside town of Pescara, which coincidental is only ten miles from Chieti."

"Pescara? What on earth are they doing there?" asked the director.

"If you recall, sir, Anchor and Chain were tasked to go to Venice, they stopped in Pescara to effect repairs ... something about their motor."

"They're still there?" Sykes raised his eyebrows in response. "Oh, yes, I recall now, carry on," requested Mansfield Smith–Cumming.

"It appears that Anchor and Chain ran across our dear old friend Maximillian Richter, who stepped off a ferry that came from Ragusa."

"That scoundrel. What's Max doing away from the comforts of Wien?"

"Yes, well, that's what we've been wondering too. But there is more."

The director looked intently at his resourceful intelligence analyst.

"We received a subsequent message, and apparently, Anchor followed Richter to the Pescara Railway station where he purchased a ticket to Chieti," informed Sykes.

"And what of the intercepts from the French, have we been able to decode them?" asked the director as he leaned back in his chair.

"No, not yet, sir. We feel the intercepts and Richter's visit to Chieti are related."

"I suggest you take those intercepts to the Admiral Ripley

building in Whitehall, Naval intelligence is setting up some cryptographers there, room 40, I believe."

"Oh, Room 40 is operational?"

"We can thank the bloody Hun for that, our entry into this fracas has sped things up a tad."

"And about Anchor and Chain, sir?"

Mansfield Smith–Cumming, repositioned his monocle and scratched his chin. After a few moments, his chair creaked again as he leaned forward and placed his elbows on the desk with his hands clasped. "Are Anchor and Chain still at their yacht?"

"Yes, sir, they are standing by for orders," replied Sykes.

Director Smith-Cumming looked thoughtful. "Do you have any recommendations?"

"I believe something is going on in Chieti, and we need to know what is so important it would cause Maximillian Richter to leave the comfort of his lair."

"And I concur, Michael," offered the director, "Do we have anyone in the area other than Anchor and Chain?"

"No, sir, we do not."

"Very well. As they are more or less stuck there ... send a message to them and request they proceed immediately to Chieti and find out what the devil is going on. Caution them, Michael, make sure they know Richter is a psychopath. Stress to them, they must not engage with him and are only to observe and report. Understood?"

"Yes, sir," replied Sykes.

"Anything else?" asked Mansfield Smith–Cumming.

Sykes stood from his chair and gathered his file. "No, sir."

"*Capitano, Maggiore* Da Camino is here to see you, along with another man."

Capitano Gallo quickly brushed biscottate crumbs from his

shirt and desk and grabbed a file from a small stack so he could appear busy reading when they entered. "Send them in, Enrico, and remain outside the door."

This was the meeting he'd been expecting. He knew the *Carabinieri* would come for the priest, and the man with him, he hoped, was the big Austrian.

Capitano Gallo rose from his chair, dislodging a few more crumbs he'd missed. He smiled and held out his hand in greeting to the *Maggiore* as he walked into the office, followed by another man, but not the big muscular man he expected.

"Good morning *Capitano*," offered Da Camino, shaking Gallo's hand. "I am sorry to disturb you so early, but we have some important matters to attend to."

The stranger did not accept the offer of a handshake, and Gallo took a moment to look at him closely as he waited for *Maggiore* Da Camino to introduce him – he didn't. Realising no introduction was coming, he waved them both to chairs. *Definitely an Austrian* thought Gallo, *but not Gabbi's killer.*

The unidentified stranger had yet to speak and stared malevolently at Gallo with cold, unfeeling eyes.

"I'm here to serve the needs of Chieti, how can I help you?" asked Chieti's chief of the local police once he was seated.

"I need the Serbian priest you currently have in custody, the man we discussed a day or so ago. Some rather distressing information has come my way that affects our national interests, and it is necessary to have him under our authorisation for questioning."

Capitano Gallo nodded in agreement and smiled warmly. He glanced at the Austrian, who in turn stared mutely back. "I understand, *Maggiore*," Gallo turned his attention back to Da Camino, "Absolutely, I'm only too happy for us to work together

212

in mutual cooperation. What else can I do to assist the *Carabinieri* with their needs today?"

"That is all, just the priest," stated *Maggiore* Da Camino.

"Good, you make it easy for me," *Capitano* Gallo smiled and stood from behind his desk.

"Thank you for coming to visit personally, *Maggiore*, but ah, who is your friend?" he asked.

"National security, *Capitano*, you know how it is." Da Camino inclined his head, then he and the Austrian rose from their chairs and paused.

"Please forgive me, is there something else?" asked Gallo, trying to appear concerned.

"The priest, Gallo, get the damn priest." All sense of civility was gone from the *Carabiniere* officer as he lost patience.

"*Maggiore*, please, there is no need for rudeness, I told you I would hand him over."

"Now, if you please, we are waiting, and I have men outside ready to escort the prisoner."

Capitano Gallo shook his head slowly, "I am sorry, *Maggiore*, forgive me if I was unclear, I am a little confused, it is early and, it will be another hot day today, you know how it is." Gallo offered a conciliatory smile that offered all the warmth he could muster. "You can take the priest on, uh ..." He turned to study a grubby calendar on the wall. "Thursday next week, how is that?"

The Austrian shifted his position, and his eyes narrowed.

"Hand him over, Gallo. We're not here to play games, I have the authority to –"

"Of course you have the authority," interrupted the *capitano*, his voice contained an edge that was most unfamiliar to the *Maggiore*, "however, the priest is an integral witness in an ongoing investigation. Handing him over to you now would be a dereliction of my duties. When this case has been resolved, then you may have him, as is the right of the *Carabinieri*. Now, since there is nothing else, then I hope you have a pleasant day." Gallo stood, his face hardened and his eyes bored into Da Camino and held his gaze.

The Austrian stirred.

Ignoring him, Gallo called out to Enrico, who he knew was standing just on the other side of the door as planned.

Almost instantly, Enrico replied. "Yes, *Capitano*?"

"Please see *Maggiore* Da Camino and his associate out?"

In anger, the Austrian spun and strode quickly from the office, the *Maggiore* gave Gallo a cold look. "You'll be hearing more from me about this," he spat, then left *Capitano* Gallo's office.

Luigi remained standing long after they departed, finally he sunk into his chair and mopped his brow with a handkerchief. He thought long and hard and came to a sensible conclusion. He must, for all outward appearances, keep things normal and not deviate from his routine. They were watching him, and any unusual activity would draw attention to his deception.

Following a knock on the door, Enrico entered. "Are you unwell, *Capitano*?"

"No, no, I am fine." Gallo looked up at his cousin. "The man with Da Camino, he is a strange one, eh?"

Enrico raised an eyebrow, "I thought he would punch a hole in the wall when he left here, he was furious. Are you worried about *Maggiore* Da Camino and what he will do when he finds out the priest isn't here?"

"No, Enrico. The *Maggiore* is playing a game, he has no reason to hold or question the priest, and he knows it. The priest has broken no law, committed no crime, and isn't a threat to anyone. The *Maggiore* is trying to receive favour from the Austrians, and he will abuse his authority and deny the priest legal process if he holds him and hands him over to the Austrians. That is why he is angry because he can't do anything but voice his displeasure and yell at me." Gallo laughed. "Enrico, you should have seen his face when I told him he could have the priest on Thursday – next week." Gallo began to laugh.

Enrico joined in for a short time, both men were just cousins again, laughing as they did when they were teenagers.

"At midday, I will go as normal to have my lunch, but I will detour to Gino's afterwards and talk to the priest. I hope he can get away safely without the Austrians finding him. I would hate to think what that man would do to him if he got his hands on him."

Vito went home to sleep, and Gino explained to Father Belić how he made the best women's shoes, and they came from many kilometres away to buy them.

"One day, Father, I will sell my shoes to all the women in Italy." Gino looked down at Belić's feet and turned his nose up. "Perhaps you could do with some new shoes, Father?"

A bell on the shop door rung as it swung open and interrupted Gino's sales pitch. Cautiously, Gino left his private rooms and walked out front. Belić could hear loud voices and then some laughter. Within moments he returned with *Capitano* Gallo carrying a bag.

"Unless you wish to remain a policeman, I suggest you change your clothes, Father," smiled Gallo as he tossed him the bag.

"My suitcase?"

"Do not worry, someone will bring it here later this afternoon. Sit, Father, we need to talk a little, yes?"

Belić sat as ordered, and Gino returned to the store.

"Now listen to me carefully, you must do everything I say, do you understand?"

Belić nodded. "Of course, *Capitano*."

"Just as I predicted, the *Carabinieri* came to see me this morning, perhaps only two hours after you left with Vito. *Maggiore* Da Camino brought with him a tall and rather severe looking man, I think an Austrian. But I do not know who he is, do you?"

Belić shook his head, but he had a suspicion where he was from.

"Yes, a strange man ..." Gallo looked across the room at a small ornamental statue of the Virgin Mary that sat on a shelf, one of many that sat strategically throughout the house. "The man frightened me ... his eyes ..." He swallowed and then turned back to the priest. "Anyway, they demanded I release you into the care of the *Carabinieri*, of course, I refused. They think you are still locked up in my storeroom."

"Thank you, *Capitano*, I appreciate what you are doing, I – "

"Don't thank me, you're not safe yet." Gallo reached into his trouser pocket and handed Belić a train ticket to Naples. "At seven this evening, a southbound train will come from Pescara and stop here. You will wait for Gino's signal that everything is clear, at the very last second, you will leave Gino's store, walk across the road and board the very last carriage, that's the carriage closest to where this shop is. It should take you about one minute. Do not loiter or look at anyone, keep your head down and do not run and draw attention to yourself. The conductor will wait for you to board before he gives the all-clear to the driver. But you must be on that train tonight because I cannot protect you any longer."

"Why are you doing this ... helping me and putting yourself in danger?" Belić asked. The old cross slowly rotated in his hand.

"Because I put you in this situation and should never have had you detained, you did nothing wrong while here in Chieti. I allowed the mayor to pressure me into holding you. It was wrong, and I apologise."

"You did nothing wrong, and there is nothing to apologise for. I am grateful for your kindness, thank you, *Capitano*." Father Stevan reached out, and they shook hands. Moments later, Gallo was gone.

The rest of the day was spent in quiet reflection while Gino attended to his duties in the store. As the afternoon wore on, Father Stevan considered his options and decided to continue with his original plan and head to Rome, where he felt he could effortlessly disappear.

As he waited, Belić read through Gino's newspapers with growing unease. Europe was volatile and ready to erupt. As predicted, Russia made its intentions very clear and came to the aid of its ally, Serbia, and subsequently declared war on Austria. This came as no surprise to Belić. However, the twist came from the aggressive Germans.

France was bound by a treaty to assist Russia, which posed a challenge for the Austro–Hungarians and German military. They didn't want to fight a war on two fronts, with France in the south and Russia in the north. The Germans believed they could quickly defeat France and decided to attack them by mobilising its army through Belgium. Belgium already declared its neutrality and quickly denied permission for German armed forces to pass through their country. In response, the Kaiser thumbed his nose at the Belgian's decision and sovereignty and invaded them anyway.

Indeed, the crisis was escalating beyond what anyone had thought possible. Further complicating the situation and called upon to honour a hundred-year-old treaty, England entered the fray and came to the support of the Belgians and, like France and Russia, it was now at war with Germany and the Austro–Hungarian empire.

To make matters even worse, the Ottoman Empire joined its

forces with Austria and Germany, which created a powerful and disturbing alliance.

Thankfully, for the present, Italy remained neutral, thought Belić, with some relief. He placed the newspaper on the table and leaned back on the chair. *What a mess.*

Dressed in nondescript civilian clothes, Father Stevan Belić stood safely inside the door to Gino's shoe shop with his newly repaired suitcase and waited for the train that was expected to arrive at any minute. As promised, *Capitano* Gallo delivered Belić's suitcase in a box earlier that afternoon, although a few items of clothing now showed clear evidence that a bullet had passed through them, noticeably Belić's only pair of spare socks. Much to his relief, his money had not been taken. Gino offered the priest his suitcase, but Belić politely declined. Instead, Gino spent half an hour repairing the case for the priest as Belić watched over his shoulder.

Gino stood casually in the street, kept a wary eye for any suspicious strangers, and would signal Belić when he could safely cross the road and board the train. Precisely on time, the shriek of a whistle warned Gino the southbound train was quickly approaching from Pescara.

Around the corner and hidden in the early evening shadows, *Stabswachtmeister* Dieter Wollf also waited for the train to arrive, he'd carefully positioned himself so he could see the platform and any passengers who disembarked while remaining inconspicuous. He knew the police were searching for him, but they couldn't identify him, so for the time being, he felt reasonably safe.

On orders from Major Richter, he was to meet a man with a

package. He knew the man and had worked with him many times in the past, he was a Turk and called himself Mr Yavuz. Wollf heard the whistle as the train drew near and again looked around to ensure he wasn't being observed.

The train slowed and chugged along the tracks and eventually ground to a halt. The conductor nimbly stepped off the train and assisted an elderly couple from a carriage, a dozen other people disembarked, and a few others waited to board. It was a routine stop, and as expected, the train would be stationary for no longer than five minutes.

Kaha and Pam Peterson, or Anchor and Chain, as known by their British Secret Service designated code names, stepped onto the Chieti Railway Station and looked around with curiosity.

Kaha could see a few people leaving the station, one or two were walking along the street, deep in conversation, and they observed a very large bearded man standing in front of a cobbler's shop. Trained to look for suspicious or odd behaviour, Kaha's glance returned to the man outside the cobbler's when the door opened, and another man carrying an old suitcase began walking quickly across the road to the train. He kept his head down, and Kaha couldn't see his face. A slight movement in the shadows around the corner drew his attention to another large man, but he was too far away to see clearly.

Pam had her arm hooked through her husband's and looked up at him. "Do you see him?"

"Yes." "He's trying to remain hidden," she suggested.

"Let's walk towards him and get a closer look." Kaha swivelled his head back to the cobbler's, but the bearded man who'd been standing outside was nowhere to be seen. There was something very familiar with the man and the suitcase, Kaha couldn't put his finger on it. Then it dawned on him.

"The fishing boat," Kaha whispered.

Pam looked up at her husband's face, but he'd turned to look at the man with the suitcase as he walked along the platform.

"It's the same man we saw step ashore from the fishing boat," he added.

Pam turned back to look and saw the man board the last carriage just as the conductor blew his whistle and gave the all-clear."

Belić took a seat and leaned against the window, keeping his face hidden best he could. He saw the tourist couple standing on the platform looking around, but now they began walking away, Belić breathed out and began to relax.

Just as the train lurched forward and began to pull away, his vision was momentarily obscured by two departing passengers. A man and a boy passed the window directly to the side of him. The man was unnecessarily rough as he tugged on the boy's arm and then saw the man clip the back of the boy's head with his hand. It was apparent, the boy had no desire to be going to Chieti. Belić felt pity for the young lad. The boy, expecting another smack for his reluctance to comply, flinched and turned away as the man again yanked aggressively on his arm. The priest and the boy locked eyes through the window, tears streaked down his face, and Belić recognised him immediately. He leapt from his seat, it was Zoran, Boris's son. What was he doing in Chieti, and with that stranger? Belić ran for the door, but already the train was gathering speed, and it was too late to leap off. He reached for the emergency stop button, but his hand paused mid-way. Why was Zoran here, and who was the man with him?

The setting sun cast an orange glow across the distant hills in the west, and the temperature dropped significantly, it was pleasant to be outside at this time of the day, and Kaha and Pam were in no hurry. They strolled, taking in the sights of Chieti and pointed out various buildings and landmarks of interest, and to anyone watching them, they appeared to be nothing more than affluent tourists enjoying a holiday.

A short distance ahead stood the man who had tried to remain hidden in the shadows. Kaha could see he was a large man with a big muscular chest and thick arms, he stepped from the doorway and raised an arm, signalling to someone behind them. Ignoring him, Kaha stopped and pointed to the cathedral's spire that rose majestically over the town. With his arm, he continued to point at other landmarks and slowly turned so he could look behind. A man pulling the arm of a boy approached. The boy resisted and tried to break free, yelling at the man who held him firmly.

Pam leaned against Kaha and raised her chin, her mouth only centimetres from his ear. "He's rather aggressive with the boy," she whispered.

Pretending to be amused at something his wife said, Kaha laughed and kissed her on the forehead. The man and boy were almost beside them, while the big man waited a couple of metres away. The boy continued to struggle and again yelled at the man in a language that he and Pam were unfamiliar with. In response, the man spoke.

"Thank God you are here, take this whelp from me, but hold him tight," said Mr Yavuz to Dieter Wollf, ignoring the boy's pleas and relieved to be free of him. The boy began to cry.

Although the man spoke quietly, Pam was close enough to have heard most of what he said and immediately turned away from the two men so they couldn't see her face. "I think our hotel is this way, dear."

"How much of that did you overhear," asked Kaha when they were safely out of earshot.

"A little, I think the boy was speaking a Balkan language."

Kaha looked ahead and could see the big man leading the uncooperative boy away with the other man walking beside them.

"Were the other two speaking German?"

Pam looked thoughtful. "Sort of. Yes, an Austrian dialect. Do you think they could be Austrians and involved with Richter? But the boy, what does he have to do with them?"

"Let's keep them in sight and see where they go."

Along with other passengers from the train and all walking in the same direction, they followed at a discrete distance. The sun was slowly disappearing beyond distant hills when both men and the boy disappeared into a hotel.

Capitano Gallo had only just arrived at work and sat behind his desk when Enrico knocked and entered. "The *Carabinieri*, *Capitano*, they are back and demand we immediately release the priest to their custody."

Gallo gave the matter only a moment's thought, "Is *Maggiore* Da Camino, or the other man with them?"

"No, there is only the *tenente* and three *Carabiniere*, but they do not look happy, *Capitano*. What should I do?" Enrico looked worried.

"Send the *tenente* in and then unlock the storeroom door and then keep close until they have gone."

Enrico left the office only to return a minute later with a very stern-faced young officer.

Capitano Gallo made no effort to greet the *tenente* formally and remained seated. "How may I assist you today, lieutenant?" Gallo noticed the man was armed.

"I am here to take custody of your prisoner, sir."

"I'm afraid that isn't possible."

"*Maggiore* Da Camino instructed me not to leave here until you have released the priest into my custody." The *tenente* looked defiantly down at *Capitano* Gallo.

Gallo nodded. "Yes, I expect he would say that." He sighed heavily. "You may find our headquarters a little uncomfortable for an extended stay, your own building has more room and better amenities. Even our modest gaol is nothing more than a simple storage room containing toilet paper and old Christmas decorations. We have no facilities to billet you or your men, however, you could take turns sleeping in the storeroom, it is empty at the moment."

The *tenente* was unaware that the *capitano* was just playing with him and failed to comprehend the context of what he'd just said. "Sir?"

"Our storeroom is empty, lieutenant, the prisoner is no longer here. Go look for yourself." Gallo waved at the door.

The *tenente* looked unsure, puzzled.

"Go on, have a look, search the entire building if you must."

With realisation dawning on him, the *tenente* quickly turned and barked out orders for his men to follow. Just as he feared, the storeroom door was open and the room empty. He commanded his men to search the entire building while he went back to the *capitano*'s office. Without knocking, he thrust open the door and entered.

"Where are your manners?" *Capitano* Gallo stood quickly and glared at the *Carabiniere*. "When you are satisfied that the man you seek is not here, then leave. Do I make myself clear, lieutenant?"

"Where is the prisoner, what have you done with him?" Not

easily intimidated, the *tenente* stood aggressively in front of the *capitano* with a hand on his holstered side-arm.

"On conclusion of our inquiry, we found that we had no reason to hold the priest, he committed no crime and had done nothing wrong to warrant being held against his will and denied his freedom. Just as the *Carabinieri* have no legal right to detain him. We released him, and he did not inform us of his destination." Gallo's eyes bored into those of the *tenente*, challenging him.

The Polizia Locale headquarters in Chieti was not housed in a large building, and it didn't take the *Carabinieri* long to discover the priest wasn't there. The *tenente*'s anger was palpable, and his face red as he glared at the *capitano*. Unable to maintain eye contact, he turned away.

"You know where the door is, see you close it on your way out. That will be all." *Capitano* Gallo sat.

Undecided what to do, the *tenente* remained standing.

"Enrico, show this man to the door!"

Enrico, just like his other cousins, was a big powerful man, he stood in the doorway, paused a second and grabbed the *tenente*'s elbow to lead him away. The lieutenant shook himself free and finally stomped from the office and outside to the street, three frustrated *Carabiniere* followed.

"I'm sure we'll hear more about this," said Enrico once the *Carabinieri* had all left.

"I don't think so, Enrico. The *Carabinieri* had no legal rights to hold the priest, and it is just Da Camino's pride that's been offended. He's only indulging for Austrian favour, that's all," said Gallo. "However, I do think this would be a good time to keep a close lookout for that big Austrian."

CHAPTER FOURTEEN

The Hotel Teate in Chieti wasn't particularly grand or remarkable in any way, its address on Via Colonnetta offered more convenience through its location rather than the sparse amenities it provided. At one time, the hotel may have been generously considered luxurious, but it is doubtful anyone alive or of sound mind would describe the hotel as anything more than just barely adequate.

Only a five-minute walk from the railway station, Hotel Teate was, if nothing more, accessible and convenient for the travel weary. The rooms were neither large nor small, however, they were clean. An important detail the hotel proprietor, Signore Angelo Romano, was quite fastidious about.

Typically the twenty or so rooms had a minimal occupancy, and most guests were budget-conscious people from outlying areas who had business in Chieti, and of course, travelling salesman also appreciated the hotel's thrifty tariffs. If two rooms were booked mid-week, Signore Romano considered the hotel busy.

He frequently reminded new guests that a few very important dignitaries once stayed at the hotel, including a distinguished gentleman who was once a neighbour of Giuseppa Verdi, the sister of the famous composer Giuseppe Verdi. He had stayed for three nights in 1870 when one of the horses pulling their carriage became lame. A horseshoe haphazardly nailed above the front desk was unquestioned evidence supporting Angelo's outrageous claim.

Presently Signore Angelo Romano was beside himself with worry and frantically attempting to find housekeeping staff. His only housekeeper, who was also his mother-in-law, refused to clean more than two rooms a day. This dilemma posed a significant problem for the hotel's proprietor. Presently, he had guests in six rooms, and it was only mid-week. This upturn in business was unheard of.

He placed the newly arrived tourist couple on the 2nd floor, where the rooms featured a larger bed. The stern Swiss gentleman, who arrived the previous day on the afternoon train, demanded a room on the ground floor near his associates. Per instructions, Proprietor Romano assigned the Turk and his son, who had also just checked in, a room beside a visiting manure salesman on the ground floor.

Major Richter pulled the watcher from the Polizia Locale and called everyone together for a briefing in his hotel room. While he waited for them all to arrive, he'd briefly interrogated the uncooperative young boy who now lay tied, gagged and blindfolded on the bed, and at long last, finally appeared to be sleeping. He'd been curious as to the relationship the boy had with the priest. Unwilling to be cooperative, the boy immediately began screaming for help. A quick belt to the side of the boy's head quietened him down.

Beside the major, on a small table, lay a handful of files he brought from Austria. He'd read them and studied them repeatedly, seeking all the information he could about the mysterious priest. He wasn't thrilled about losing him again and would let his men know of his present mood in a colourful rant once all were assembled.

"The priest was on the train that just departed," continued Major Richter in a more moderate tone. "How do I know this?" He waited for a response, but none was forthcoming. "Because the boy told me – he claims he saw him. He wouldn't answer my questions but was quite willing to tell me he would be rescued. He claims he saw the priest through the window on the train, and then with childish naivety, the boy had the guile to threaten me."

The Turk sitting near the window smirked.

"Apparently, the priest and the boy's father will come and kill me," added Richter.

No one laughed.

"Sir?" responded Johan Bekker.

Major Richter turned to the questioner, his lifeless eyes bored into the man.

"Do we know if the priest saw the boy? Or is he making good his escape while we sit here?"

Richter chewed his bottom lip thoughtfully as he decided how to answer. "From what the boy said, the priest saw him alright. I'm convinced the boy's father and the priest are acquainted, and if so, then I expect the priest to return." Richter was pleased with himself, the expense of kidnapping the boy was worth it.

Hotel Teate was old, but high ceilings and conduits in each room allowed air to circulate freely and kept the temperature comfortable and cool. It was to one of these conduits that Kaha now had his ear pressed against. He'd heard the screaming of a youngster, the sound carried up through the vents, and he now waved for Pam to kneel on the floor beside him to listen. For a while, all was quiet, then they began hearing voices wafting up from the room below.

"You listen, I can't understand them," he whispered as his wife joined him after throwing a pillow on the floor for her to kneel on.

They remained quiet as snippets of conversation drifted up. After a few minutes, Kaha stood and allowed his wife to continue to eavesdrop.

"My notebook," she asked during a brief lull in the conversation.

Kaha sat on the bed and waited patiently as she scribbled notes. Occasionally she'd wince or react to something being said. After what seemed an age, she stood to ease her aching knees and rubbed them.

"Did they stop?" asked Kaha.

"Not sure, for the last few minutes, they quietened down, and I can't hear them anymore."

"Were they German?" asked Kaha as he placed the discarded pillow against the vent and slid a chair against it, holding it in place.

"They spoke a Bavarian dialect which is the type of German that Austrians speak. But whatever
was going on, the person doing the talking was irate and upset."

"Could it be Maximillian Richter?"

Pam shrugged, "No way of knowing."

"What was he talking about?"

"Well, that's what was peculiar, he kept referring to a priest, and that the others who were in the room had lost him. He instructed someone in the room to look for the priest." Pam flipped a few pages in her notebook. "Oh yes, he mentioned the boy, said he'd already proven to be useful as bait."

"Bait?" Kaha's eyebrow knitted together in puzzlement as he tried to determine what Major Richter was doing. 'And that's it? Nothing more?"

She looked at her husband. "I think he beat the boy, Kaha."

Kaha's mouth tightened. He shook his head and remained silent for a moment or two. "Do we know for sure it's the same boy as we saw?"

"No, I'd be speculating. I didn't hear full sentences, only snippets here and there. Oh, and there was mention of a farm, an olive orchard, I think he said." Pam closed her notebook and placed it on the bed. "Kaha, I'm worried about the boy, I think he may be kidnapped."

Kaha stared at the far wall. He remembered the big man waiting for the smaller man and the boy to arrive on the street a little while earlier, he knew a killer by his eyes, and the big man was definitely a killer and probably military. "I agree with you, but this whole situation is odd, Pam."

She returned to the bed and reviewed her notes. "Olive groves, a priest and a boy, what do they all have in common, and does this have anything to do with Richter?"

"I think we need to find out who is in the room beneath us," Kaha said as he rubbed his wife's knees. "Perhaps I will have a little chat with the man at the front desk."

Belić stared vacantly out the window as the train rattled through the countryside. The sight of young Zoran in the hands of the small man shook him to the core, and the image of the boy being tugged by the stranger left a painful mark on his conscience. It could only mean one thing; the boy had been kidnapped, and the Austrians were using him as leverage. He chastised himself for underestimating the Austrian resolve and for involving Boris with his escape plans. Now Zoran was in peril, and Boris, who would undoubtedly search for his son, would also be in imminent danger. He shook his head at the thought of how furious Boris would be. The Austrians were military men, and any others who were aiding them were likely to be nothing more than street thugs and criminals. Boris, nothing more than a simple fisherman, wouldn't stand a chance against them. On the other hand, the safety of Rome's streets beckoned, he stared out the window at the passing countryside.

In the province of Perugia, Popoli was approximately 40

kilometres southwest of Chieti and where the train was scheduled to make its next stop. Belić pondered his dilemma. He was already well on his way to freedom and could easily turn his back on Zoran and Boris and disappear.

The conductor entered the carriage and walked down the aisle, informing passengers of the next stop. "Popoli, Popoli," he repeated, "next stop Popoli."

Belić watched the back of the conductor as he entered the next carriage. He shifted in his seat, made himself more comfortable and closed his eyes.

"The one place the priest is familiar with is the Olive farm, and that's where we will take the boy. You and you," Major Richter pointed to Dieter Wollf and Gunter Meyer, "will leave Chieti, unseen, later this evening," he shot a scathing look at Wollf, "as I said earlier, you will go with Gunter and wait on the road that leads to the widow's farm on the outskirts of Chieti. The rest of us will make a spectacle leaving town in the morning, and we will pick you up once we are clear. We will make sure people see us leave, the boy will be the bait, and eventually, the priest will follow. He will know where we are headed.

"But the local police will also know where we are going," added Wollf.

"As long as they haven't identified you, then there is no reason for the police to be interested in us. Are you concerned about a few local village policemen?" snapped Richter.

"Of course not, sir, but –"

"Then I urge you worry about getting out of town without being recognised," interrupted the Major coldly.

Dieter looked away, "Yes, *Herr* Major."

"I suggest the rest of you get some sleep as we have a busy day tomorrow."

Britain's Secret Service Bureau was busy recruiting staff and employing more resources to meet the growing demand for intelligence in a new and dangerous European war. Of significant concern to the British Admiralty was the maritime strength of the Imperial German Navy. Sir Mansfield Smith-Cumming had little success in establishing a network of agents in Germany and instead relied heavily on the intelligence provided by agents who were either stationed in neutral countries or occupied territories.

The bureau was divided into two divisions – navy and army, and each section was respectively engaged in foreign espionage and domestic counter-espionage. For the director, Sir Mansfield Smith-Cumming, this was a headache. Especially for his two agents, Anchor and Chain, who were tasked with obtaining maritime intelligence and were now engaged in central Italy with matters more relevant to the army, the other division of their intelligence-gathering operation.

Laying on the desk in front of the Director was an extensive file on Major Maximillian Richter, and he arrived at the conclusion that Richter's visit to Italy was significant – and he wanted to know why. For what reason was the Austrian investigator traipsing around neutral Italy? The director's reverie was interrupted by a single knock, and his secretary stuck her head around the door.

"Sir?"

"Yes, Marge."

"Allan wishes to see you; he says it's urgent."

"Of course, it's bloody urgent, I was the one that requested he come." Smith-Cumming shook his head at his peculiar but brilliant analyst, Allan Reed. "Very well, show him in," sighed the director taking the opportunity to stretch his back. He hoped the analyst could provide some answers.

"I did the best I could with the short notice you gave me," said Senior Analyst Allan Reed as he entered the office.

The director noted his rumpled jacket and dishevelled appearance. "Have you been here all night?"

"Have I? Oh yes, I expect I have, sir, but please read this." He handed a file across the desk to his superior.

Smith-Cumming knew the eccentric analyst might have had his oddities, but he was superb at his job. "When we are finished here, see you go home, Allan. I don't want you here any longer than is absolutely necessary, you need rest, eh. Now, what have you got for me?" He reached for the file and began to read as Allan slumped into a seat and waited.

After a few minutes, the director closed the file and looked at Reed. "How dangerous is this priest?"

"Very... which is why Maximillian Richter has been sent to kill him. But Richter isn't alone, he's with several contractors that the *Evidenzbureau* hires from time to time. Mostly petty crooks and hoodlums."

Smith-Cumming leaned back in his squeaky chair to give the matter some thought. The noise the chair made caused Reed to giggle. He took immense delight in childish sounds.

"Why is it that the Austrians kept the involvement of, uh Stefan Bellick–"

"Stevan, Stevan Belić, sir."

"Oh, yes, thank you, but why keep his involvement a secret?" asked Smith–Cumming."

"Good question, sir. Well, you see, it appears the Austrian's made it quite public they caught *all* the Black Hand group members immediately after the assassination of Prince Ferdinand and his wife. By publicly admitting they never caught the priest and allowed him to escape, simply shows they erred. I expect the Emperor's pride has something to do with it. It also allows for them to quietly eliminate the priest and not have to put him through the courts."

"Is he just a simple priest loyal to his country, or is he truly dangerous?"

"According to our asset inside the Austrian Foreign Ministry, they say he is extremely dangerous and ultimately responsible for the deaths of many prominent people. Apparently, those are Major Richter's very words, sir."

Mansfield raised his eyebrows and leaned forward, placing his hands on his desk. "Do we have a file on Belić?"

Allan giggled again at the sound of the chair. "Only what I've just created, but nothing on him previously. Up until a month or so ago, he didn't exist."

Ignoring the childish giggles, the director smiled, "So we don't haven't any useable background on this Belić chap, is that right?"

"Correct, sir, he is previously unknown to us."

Mansfield Smith-Cumming drummed his fingers on the Admiral Nelson's old desk and reflected on this new intelligence. "Good work, Allan, now go home and sleep."

"Yes, thank you, sir," said Reed as he stood and picked up his file.

"Oh Allan, one more question." The analyst turned and looked to the director. "Why is it that the Austrian's are devoting such resources to finding and killing this priest? Surely, a simple priest would require a low-level response."

Reed stood awkwardly, his head twisted from side to side as he formulated his reply. "Two reasons, sir. Firstly, he has information they want. Secondly, he poses a threat to Austria. I can conclude that he may not be just an ordinary priest."

"Because he is responsible for the deaths of many people? An assassin?"

Reed shrugged. "That is what Major Richter believes."

"Whose deaths, and then who the hell is he?"

Reed shook his head. "I really don't know." He waited as the director browsed over the file. "Is that all, sir?"

"Ah, yes, thank you. Now go home." Mansfield Smith-Cumming watched him leave his office.

"Marge!" Moments later, his secretary appeared in the doorway as the analyst departed. "Be a good girl and get Michael Sykes in here, will you?"

"Of course, sir."

"You wanted to see me, sir? asked Michael Sykes.

Mansfield Smith-Cumming was standing near the window and looking out towards the Thames. Rain splattered the window making visibility almost impossible. He turned slowly and walked back to his desk.

"Have a seat, Michael," he said as he eased himself into his chair. It squeaked. "Marge! Get this bloody chair fixed!

"Yes, sir," came the muted reply from her desk in the anteroom.

Sykes was suppressing a smile. Marge had quietly informed him that the analyst had just left, and he knew the oddities of Allan Reed all too well.

"And you can wipe that grin off your face," instructed the director curtly.

Michael Sykes's expression returned to something more acceptable.

"Now tell me, have we heard from Anchor and Chain within the last twenty-four hours?" asked the director.

Sykes shook his head and was instantly curious as to where this was leading.

"I was afraid of that. Then we have no way of contacting them until they return to their boat?"

"I believe so, sir." Sykes leaned forward in his chair. "Is there a problem?"

"Damn," said Smith-Cumming under his breath and then scratched his chin. "I'm afraid we may have dropped Anchor and Chain in the shit."

CHAPTER FIFTEEN

Kaha and Pam rose early that morning and took turns listening by the air vent opening, hoping to hear any fragments of conversation that would help them understand why Maximillian Richter was in Italy. The boy was a piece of the puzzle they had to yet understand.

"I think they are preparing to leave," said Pam.

"Checking out?" he clarified.

She shrugged her shoulders. "Should we go to the police and tell them about the boy?"

Kaha nodded. "I think it may be a good idea, however, if we determine that Richter is involved with this boy, then that changes everything."

"So, what you're saying is we shouldn't help the boy by going to the police because of Richter, and that our work is more important than that of a kidnapped boy?" Pam was becoming upset.

Kaha looked into his wife's eyes and spoke slowly and clearly. "There is nothing more important than the welfare of the lad. If Richter is mixed up in this somehow, we might be able to free the boy ourselves and still find out what Richter is up to."

"And we can do this better than the police?"

"I wouldn't place much faith in the ability of a small-town police force. You saw those men, they're killers, the police wouldn't stand a chance against them."

Pam considered the options and looked up at Kaha, "If you think we can, I agree."

"Good, I'm going to go downstairs and have a look. Maybe I can see what they're up to."

Kaha and Pam were in the hotel lobby and asking the hotel proprietor for a recommendation on where they could obtain breakfast when the small man Kaha previously saw with the boy came through the hotel entrance and disappeared down the corridor. Kaha ensured he kept his back turned to the man and watched him as best he could from a courtesy mirror. The proprietor, *Signore* Romano, was busy explaining where a ristorante that served a European type breakfast was located when the man reappeared, again pulling on the young boy's arm. A few steps behind them, Maximillian Richter, followed carrying only a small bag. Again, Kaha made sure his face wasn't seen and continued to ask questions about the location of the ristorante as Major Richter passed him and exited the hotel.

"Looks like you have vacant rooms again," Kaha offered to *Signore* Romano and then turned to see Richter climbing onto a wagon that waited outside.

"No, no, they will be travelling for a couple of days and returning," replied Angelo Romano.

"Are they sightseeing?"

The proprietor frowned, "Perhaps, I do not know. They told me they would return in a day or so and not to bother cleaning rooms." Signore Romano was relieved he didn't have to find another housekeeper.

Kaha nodded. "My wife and I will do some sightseeing while here, that's why I ask." This time the Signore Romano nodded as if he understood. "Where could I rent a wagon?"

The proprietor reached under the counter and handed Kaha a brochure. "This business has everything you need."

"Thank you, *Signore*." Kaha smiled in appreciation as he quickly glanced at the advertisement for horse and wagon rentals.

Angelo Romano was anxious to return to his breakfast and was only too pleased to say goodbye to the talkative Englishman and his wife. Due to a recent upturn in business, he was having some interior painting done, and workers would be arriving soon, which would demand his full attention. "You are very welcome, *Signore* Peterson, anytime."

Kaha pocketed the brochure and casually strolled onto the street, in the distance, he saw the wagon disappearing. He returned quickly to the lobby and told Pam what he saw.

"I'm going to search their room."

Pam raised her eyebrows. "They may come back, Kaha."

"You keep watch from our room, if you see them return, then tap on the air vent a few times, I should be able to hear it. But I won't be long; we can't miss this opportunity."

Kaha leaned forward and kissed his wife on the forehead.

It took Kaha only moments to unlock the door with a special lock-pick. It was a hardened piece of wire with a ninety-degree bend at one end, much like the letter 'L'. In his haste, he failed to see the tiny thread of cotton that fell from the door when he entered the room. It was a tell-tale, a simple warning placed by Richter. Kaha used a similar technique on the *Mana*.

The room was immaculate; nothing was out of place, and it appeared that no one had slept in it the previous night. Kaha didn't touch anything and stood in the centre of the floor and studied the room layout carefully. A suitcase sat on a low table against the wall. Both single beds were neatly made, and the same brochure given to him by the proprietor about horse and wagon rentals lay on a chest of drawers near the door. A coffee table with two worn chairs sat at the other end of the room.

He continued to study the furniture and chairs' position; he was looking at details and memorising everything. When he left the room, it would appear just as it did now – untouched.

The room was neat, too neat. Something wasn't right. Someone went to extraordinary lengths to make the room look this way, even the ashtrays were clean. Why, he wondered?

He walked to the suitcase and bent down to study it. He looked behind it, to each side, and he lifted it gently to peer beneath, just in case Richter had left markers that would tell him it had been tampered with. Satisfied that all was well, he attempted to open the case, only to discover it was locked. Kaha rummaged in his pocket and took out a smaller version of the pick he used to gain entry to the room. In seconds, both locks were opened, and the contents of the case were visible. Carefully he pressed down on the clothes and felt nothing odd and then lifted them to look underneath. Socks, underwear, a clean shirt, trousers and tie, all ordinary items you would expect. He checked for a false bottom but found nothing.

The bathroom was the same, and it was as if the maid had just given the room a thorough once over. Kaha walked back into the bedroom and surveyed it one more time. He looked under the beds, behind the chest of drawers and even pulled the empty drawers out and looked underneath them, he looked everywhere, even behind the picture frames. He pulled the pillows from the chairs and investigated them thoroughly, then replaced them precisely as they had been – there was nothing to be found.

Kaha scratched his head. He'd been here too long and should leave, and he knew Pam would be anxious too. But he felt he missed something and would have one last look around. He was puzzled and again looked at the beds one last time – then made a decision.

Like everywhere else he'd searched, there was nothing to

find in or under the first bed. However, when he completely lifted the mattress on the second bed, he found more than he bargained for. Spread out beneath the mattress were a handful of files. They were written in German, and even though Kaha couldn't read the language, he could see they were official files from Austria's Military Intelligence organisation, the *Evidenzbureau*.

Pam would have to look through them and determine what they were and if they were important. Kaha saw no point in making the bed until he returned to replace them. He scooped up the files and placed them under his shirt, tucking them awkwardly into the waistband of his trousers. The hallway was empty. He quickly exited the room, locked the door, and walked away feeling reassured he wasn't seen.

Kaha leaned against the window and peered out onto the street below as he smoked another cigarette. Every now and then, he turned to watch Pam, who was studiously going through each file in succession. When focused on her task, Pam would silently mouth the words she read. he could see her lips moving as she skimmed through the documents. He found it delightful, just another in a long list of reasons why he loved her so.

"Kaha, I think these documents are quite important."

Kaha extinguished his cigarette in an ashtray and walked over to her.

"These files are all about murders, recent killings in Europe. Look, see this one." Pam held up a document from the file she was reading. "You remember this, it was only last year ... Franz Schuhmeier, he was a socialist member of the Austrian parliament and was murdered, gunned down. This file is the complete report. It's so detailed. But the margin notes are what's interesting."

"Does it say who did it?" asked Kaha.

"Yes, it says a man called Paul Kunschak was found guilty. Apparently, he was the brother of another politician. But here ..." Pam pointed to handwritten notes that covered the document. "It questions the final analysis and findings. He even put a question mark after the killer's name."

"Are these Richter's notes?"

"I don't know, probably. All the files contain margin notes, and they're all written by the same hand. Look at this one." Pam replaced the document into the file folder and picked up another. "Dimitar Nikolov Petkov, he was Bulgaria's Prime Minister, murdered by anarchists in Sofia seven years ago."

"Yes, I recall when it happened. Are all the files about people who've been killed?"

"Yes, all of them. There's a couple of people I have never heard of. The information in each file is incredibly detailed and talks about informers and intelligence gathering sources."

"Assassinations?" asked Kaha.

"I don't know, I would have to read each document carefully. We need to get these files to London. The information is too important, it's a gold mine."

"That's what I was thinking. Means we need to go to the boat and radio London immediately."

"Richter will be beside himself when he finds these files missing. Will he know we stole them, and will he come after us?"

"It wouldn't take a genius to deduce the English couple took them." Kaha returned to the window as he considered the problem. "We can't even leave Pescara until *Mana* has been repaired, and that won't be for another two weeks or so at best."

Pam rose from the chair and stepped up to Kaha.

He wrapped his arms around her. "So, the big question is, Pam, what do these files have to do with why Maximillian Richter is here in Chieti with a boy?"

"Is he a hostage and being used as leverage, somehow?" she asked.

"That's what I'm beginning to think."

Mayor Alberto Maria Gabriele De Rosa inspected the shallow bowl of spaghetti placed before him with more than casual interest. He carefully rotated the dish and found a loose spaghetti noodle, and with his fork, carefully cut through it. He leaned forward and scrutinised the severed end and, with an appreciative nod, let the relieved waiter know all was well. The noodle end had a tiny spot in the centre that indicated to the discerning mayor that the spaghetti was not overcooked and was indeed safe for human consumption. Heaven forbid that Chieti's distinguished mayor be presented with a sub-standard pasta dish – it didn't bear thinking about.

Opposite him sat Chieti's Chief of Police, *Capitano* Luigi Gallo, who watched the mayor's inspection ritual with amusement. Gallo knew the kitchen would serve the dish exactly as the mayor preferred, and he felt no need to dissect the pasta and offer comment and risk upsetting the *capocuoco*[8]. At the end of the meal, he would offer praise to the chef as he always did.

Mayor De Rosa spun his fork, winding a precise amount of spaghetti around the tines and then enjoyed his first mouthful, Chief Gallo followed suit, and both men ate in silence for a minute or two.

"You know that *Maggiore* Da Camino came to see me this morning." The mayor looked up at Gallo for his reaction. "He wasn't pleased and had some unkind things to say about you."

Gallo continued to spin his fork, and once he had the required amount of pasta secured, he placed it carefully in his mouth. He chewed thoughtfully. The dish was superb, but then it always was.

8   Head chef.

"Did he lodge an official complaint?"

Mayor De Rosa shook his head. His mouth was full.

Chief Gallo laughed. "I didn't think he would, he couldn't."

The mayor wiped his mouth with a napkin. "He claimed the *Carabinieri* have been given instructions to be on the lookout for the priest."

Luigi shrugged. "He could send an army; they won't find him."

Both men sat in companionable silence as they ate. "Were you aware that a wagon was seen leaving Chieti this morning? I believe that man who you suspect of being an Austrian was in it along with another man and a boy?" offered the mayor.

"I'd heard something, but no details," replied Gallo. "All I know is that the big man, the one who killed Gabbi, wasn't on it."

The mayor's fork froze halfway to his mouth as he thought of his sister. "Do you know where they were going?" he finally managed to ask with a shaky voice. Four pasta threads became unbound and now hung suspended beneath the fork. A potential catastrophe was unfolding.

This time Gallo shook his head.

Mayor De Rosa stared at the dangling pasta. "I think they were headed towards Natalina Milani's villa."

This news caught the normally unflappable chief of police completely by surprise. "Are you sure?" He rested his fork in the bowl.

"Yes, absolutely. But I can't think why they would want to go all the way out there, can you?"

Truth be told, Chief Gallo couldn't think of a valid reason either. If he'd learned anything, it was the Austrians who were here in Chieti for one reason, to find the priest. And he'd departed Chieti on a southbound train. So why were they heading back out to

Signora Milani's farm? Obviously, they believed the priest might be hiding there. "A boy? You said there was a boy on the wagon?"

"There were two men, one was tall; I think he was the one that visited you with the *Maggiore*, the other was a smaller man with a boy." A casual twist of the wrist saw the noodles return to their correct place, and a calamity averted.

Chief Gallo's *pranzo*[9] lost its appeal. He dabbed at his mouth with a napkin. "How did you come by this information?"

"They drove past me, I saw them with my own two eyes," replied Mayor De Rosa, having fully regained his composure and control of his pasta noodles.

Chieti's chief of police wasn't listening; he was staring out the *ristorante* onto the street beyond.

"Luigi, your *pranzo*," reminded the mayor with a look of concern.

"Could the big Austrian man have been hiding in the wagon?" finally asked the chief.

"No, no, not possible, I could see inside the wagon as it went by."

Capitano Luigi Gallo leaned back in his chair and clasped both hands together over his belly.

The Austrians were up to no good – he knew it. And what irked him more than anything was the fact they had not attempted to hide their intentions. Riding out of town in full view was deliberate.

Mayor De Rosa tore a piece of bread and began enthusiastically scraping at the small lake of sauce that remained in the bottom of his bowl. He looked across the table at his friend, "Are you going to finish your spaghetti?"

Pangs of hunger rumbled through Stevan Belić's stomach,

9   Lunch

reminding him he hadn't eaten in a while. As the uncomfortable twinge of hunger receded, it was immediately replaced with a knot of worry over the welfare of Zoran and the need to continue with as much speed as possible. He sat astride a horse he'd rented from Popoli and stared out at the hilly terrain that lay before him. He squeezed his heels into its flanks, and it responded willingly to his expert touch and began to canter towards the road that snaked upwards into the Abruzzo Appennines, a range of mountains dissecting Italy's east and west coasts. The route he had chosen would safely bypass Chieti, which lay to the east. On Belić's right, he could see the towering peak of Monte Amaro, but he wasn't going anywhere near there, he was headed towards the small village he knew so well, nestled in the hills where he would find Enzo, and he hoped, *Signora* Natalina Milani.

As tempting as it was, he knew returning immediately to Chieti was out of the question. The *Carabinieri* wanted him, and so did the Austrians. Returning to the police station would be foolish. Enzo was the only person he trusted who could wander through Chieti and not arouse suspicion. He could be his eyes and ears until he could determine where Zoran was kept and then inform *Capitano* Gallo of the kidnapping. Enzo was his only friend and the only one he could trust.

He'd been travelling since daybreak and had already put many kilometres behind him, and he figured there were still two or three more hours of riding ahead before he reached the small community with its olive groves and cluster of homes that were so familiar to him. While the road he travelled on was not considered major, it was heavily used, and he encountered many people, mostly locals, who offered a friendly wave and a kind word as he passed them by.

Directly ahead lay the quaint hilltop village of Brittoli. Again, Belić's stomach complained. He slowed his horse to a walk as the first homes came into view and began searching for a place where he could purchase food, rest and water his horse.

Houses were clustered protectively around what was originally a medieval castle and had since been modified and built into a palace. An old stone retaining wall lined one side of the narrow road, and small homes, typical of the region, were perched above and below him. Each with an expansive view of the surrounding countryside.

Up this high, the village was exposed to the elements, noticeably the wind. It swirled up the hills and over the houses and brought with it the sound of raised voices. Belić paused to listen but couldn't make out what was being said. Whatever was causing the commotion was around the next corner and out of sight. With a heavy sigh, he placed the old wooden cross back in his pocket and urged the horse on, cautiously he rounded the bend and immediately wished he hadn't.

An ageing priest stood in the middle of the road, with his black cassock flapping against his thin legs as he held the wide-brimmed cappello romano firmly to his head. He waved his other hand expressively as he conveyed his displeasure at two mounted *Carabiniere* who prevented him from going about his business. Belić immediately felt apprehension and pushed aside his thoughts of food. He couldn't turn around and leave without drawing suspicion to himself, and there were no places for him to detour – he must pass by the priest and the *Carabinieri* who blocked the road. He quickly looked for other options – there were none.

The gist of the argument was obvious; the police were insisting the priest prove who he was. It was too late for Belić to turn back, he could only continue and pray they let him pass.

Belić suppressed his anger at not being more careful, he'd impatiently blundered into a village without first ensuring it was safe to do so, and now he could only hope the *Carabinieri* were sufficiently distracted by the angered priest and not pay him attention.

Both policemen glanced at him briefly, nodded in greeting, then turned their attention back to the priest who was explaining, as if talking to children, that he was the local parish priest of San Carlo, one of two churches in Brittoli, and any local would confirm it if the lazy *Carabinieri* only made an effort to ask someone.

His heart was pounding and he felt the hair on his neck rise. It was him the *Carabinieri* were searching for. He kept his head down and hoped his peaked cap would keep his face in shade. His horse became skittish, it sensed his anxiety and began lowering and twisting its head wanting to turn. Belić patted its shoulder and spoke soothingly, encouraging the animal forwards as one policeman considerately moved aside and thankfully allowed him to pass.

Finally permitted to go about his business, the indignant priest threw a hand up in the air in obvious disgust and turned and walked away muttering under his breath about fascism, the two admonished *Carabiniere* now focused their attentions towards the stranger on horse–back as he drew level with them.

"*Signore*?" a *Carabiniere* questioned.

Belić felt the first beads of sweat trickle down his back. He wasn't sure they were talking to him and he didn't want to find out, he kept going.

"*Signore!*" yelled the policeman, louder and more insistent.

Belić let the horse take another step or two then twisted in his saddle to look back. The sun was behind him and his face still in shade. Both *Carabiniere* remained astride their horses, from their expressions they didn't look happy and were very suspicious. He knew he'd been caught and there was no escape.

His horse was already tired after the morning's journey, and the horses the *Carabinieri* rode looked fresh, it would be futile to attempt to flee, and if he did, they would certainly catch him without effort. He reigned in his horse and waited.

One policemen extended an arm and curled his finger, rudely indicating Belić should turn back and come to him. He realised then, both were very young, inexperienced, and arrogant. No wonder they'd upset the local priest. He felt a measure of sympathy for the man.

As ordered, Belić turned his horse and took a few steps towards the waiting *Carabiniere*. He kept his head low. "How can I help you?"

"Come closer," yelled one, hoping for a better look. Belić complied, and moved a little closer, the policemen were now about five metres away. "What is your name, and where are you going?"

"Forgive me, I am in a hurry, my mother is sick and I am going to be with her during her last moments." Belić, knew it was a weak excuse, but he needed the policemen to relax and not feel threatened by him.

"Your name?" repeated the policeman.

"Christiano Costa, perhaps you know me, I make the finest shoes in Italy," Belić grinned. He Remembered the conversation he'd had with Gino. "Perhaps you need shoes, eh. For your woman? I make the best shoes in all Italy."

The *Carabinieri* turned to talk to each other, and Belić heard them laugh. Obviously they had little interest in women's shoes.

Finally, they looked back to him. "Climb down from your horse, *Signore* Costa."

Belić knew this wasn't going at all well. For the time being they hadn't identified him. There was still a slim measure of hope.

Slowly, he eased himself down from the horse, threw the reins over the branch of a low hanging tree, and tied a loose knot. He rubbed his tender buttocks with one hand as both *Carabiniere* also dismounted. Out of habit he pulled the old cross from his pocket. Belić couldn't help but notice both policemen were each armed with a sidearm. In addition, a rifle in a scabbard hung from each saddle. One held the reins of both horses while the more senior of the pair unbuttoned the flap of his holster and walked over. In his hand, he held a photograph.

Belić didn't need to see the photograph to know it was of him. There was no way he could talk his way out of this situation. His mind worked furiously as he thought of a plan. Casually he slid over half a step, keeping the approaching policeman between himself and his partner holding the horses. He knew he needed to get just a little closer.

"What's that in your hand?"

Puzzled, Belić looked down, he'd forgotten he held the old wooden cross. "Is nothing, just a memento, a talisman."

Belić took another step closer, the *Carabiniere* was now only a metre away. He raised his hand to show them the old cross, and as expected the policeman's eyes followed. The inexperience of the young man showed, he allowed the stranger to come too close.

Without warning Belić lunged forward and grabbed the young *Carabiniere* by the shoulders, spun him around, then quickly pulled the pistol from his open holster and jabbed it into his back. The photo fluttered from his hand onto the road. Shocked into immobility, the other policeman holding the horses wasn't sure how to respond.

"Throw your pistol to me," Belić ordered. He kept his voice low. "I will shoot."

The *Carabiniere* slowly unbuttoned the flap of his holster and carefully slid the pistol up and out with his fingers and tossed it to the ground near Belić's feet.

"Now lay down on the ground. Both of you."

The *Carabinieri* were understandably unwilling to comply. And if they knew who Belić was they showed no puzzlement at the unusual behaviour of a Catholic priest.

"I won't ask again."

"Don't hurt us, we both have family," one pleaded as he lowered himself to the ground. The other quickly followed.

Keeping a safe distance, Belić carefully picked up the pistol and snatched the photo the *Carabiniere* dropped and stuffed it into his pocket. He sidestepped around both prone policemen, retrieved the reins of their horses, and led them towards his own. He quickly untied the reins and mounted. He didn't bother to warn them not to follow, he knew they wouldn't listen to anything he said.

Without another word and his hunger pangs forgotten, Belić rode off leading the two horses, he looked back one last time before he lost sight of them and saw they were already on their feet.

Now he was in a predicament, but he also knew the *Carabinieri* did not immediately know his destination, so he had some time.

Once the village of Brittoli was safely behind him, Belić switched horses, and rode for another half-hour as quickly as he dared. The road wound higher into the hills and the few people he encountered stared at him curiously.

A fork in the road proved to be an ideal spot to release the *Carabinieri* horses. He unsaddled both animals, then with his knife he severed the thick bulky girth–strap on each saddle, then removed their bridles and threw them away. He wasn't going to make life easier for them. Both rifles had the bolts removed, rendering them useless, and were tossed into the trees, along with both pistols. The two horses, now free from constraint were only too happy to playfully gallop away and then begin foraging for food. When the *Carabinieri* found their horses, as they were sure to do, they wouldn't be effective without saddles, bridles or weapons. He smiled for the first time that day.

CHAPTER SIXTEEN

Two approaching people disturbed the foraging seagulls squabbling over food scraps littering the dock. In vocal protest, the gulls launched themselves safely skyward to avoid the unwelcome intrusion as the couple walked towards them. Self-preservation was far more important than nourishing empty bellies. Not daunted, they circled noisily overhead and waited impatiently for the danger to pass so they could return to the dock and devour the tasty morsels that still lay in wait for them.

With a grimace, Kaha kicked at the fish entrails, scattering them haphazardly into the sea. This caused a fresh bout of excitement as the gulls dove down to retrieve the delicacies that now bobbed in the calm waters of the Pescara Marina. Pam wrinkled her nose and nimbly stepped around the stain where the offensive offal had lain.

They each carried a suitcase and walked single file down the gangway towards their yacht, *Mana*, which was berthed at the end of the dock in a space generally allocated for larger boats. When they arrived, Pam stopped near the stern and placed her suitcase on the dock beside Kaha's. She waited for him while he walked forward and began to inspect the yacht carefully. He checked the bow, both spring and lastly, the stern lines, ensuring the Flemish flake coils were still neatly wound beside dock cleats. His eyes moved over the deck, checking for signs of disturbance during their absence. Slowly he walked back towards the stern and automatically looked aloft to each of the two masts before using a dock-step to climb onto the teak deck.

He stood motionless and listened, his eyes constantly moving, looking for evidence that someone may have come aboard. After a few heartbeats, Kaha stepped to the small deckhouse or 'doghouse' as he referred to it and looked behind the companionway hatch. Hidden from view, he'd previously attached a small thin piece of cord with a small clip to the hatch. If the hatch was moved, the string would detach from the clip and provide a simple and effective indicator to show someone had been aboard and gone below. After a quick look, he was relieved to see the twine was still fastened at both ends. He released the clip, then unlocked the companionway hatch before sliding it open. Confident that everything was secure, he walked back to the gunwale to receive each suitcase from Pam and helped her climb aboard.

The inspection wasn't complete. He entered the doghouse, then descended the companionway ladder and immediately turned to his right towards the navigation chart table. The chart table had a lift–up, hinged lid where navigation charts and other sundry items were stored. On the rear right corner of the desk was an inkwell where a bottle of Indian ink sat. Kaha leaned forward and checked the position of the bottle. The letter 'K' of the word 'ink' was perfectly aligned to an almost invisible scratch on the desk. It hadn't been moved.

At the Secret Service Bureau, the technical experts, or 'Boffins' installed a powerful experimental and highly advanced vacuum tube 'De Forest Radiophone', a wireless radio transmitter-receiver, behind the wall panelling on the starboard side of the navigation station. Powered independently by batteries, the De Forest Radiophone conveniently did not integrate into *Mana*'s electrical system. To access the hidden radio, the ink bottle needed to be removed, which released a small spring-loaded pin, and then the chart–table desktop raised. A concealed steel rod was easily extracted from inside the desk, allowing the wall panel to slide open and expose the radio. The entire procedure took only seconds and was cleverly designed and hidden. Another less powerful but functioning, limited range, 'Spark-Gap' radio, generally found on luxury cruising yachts, was in full view, exactly where it should be and situated directly in front of the navigation desk. Its bulky size and complex array of knobs and dials dominated the confined space. Both radios shared the same antennae, which extended up the rear mizzen mast, then spanned across to the top of the mainmast.

It was evident that no one had been aboard their yacht, and Kaha thought it safe for Pam to go below.

Again outside, he moved the suitcases from the dock and into the cockpit rather than take them below as they hoped they would immediately return to Chieti a little later. Immediately Pam began the tedious task of coding an urgent, priority message she would send directly to London. The message would contain only highlights of Richter's files and provide an update on their observations of the major, his associates and the unusual appearance of a boy. Kaha and Pam both believed the boy was abducted and in imminent danger. They would also request permission to return to Chieti and continue their surveillance of the Austrians and free the boy.

It was almost dark when Pam finally completed coding the lengthy message. Kaha went on deck to keep a lookout while she began to transmit the extended communique on the De Forest Radiophone. As protocol demanded, they had to wait for a receipt of their message, which would include information about when they could expect a response that detailed their orders.

Kaha lit a cigarette and walked forward towards the mainmast, and gazed outward. As far as he could tell, everything was quiet inside the Pescara marina. Beyond the sea wall, a trawler with a single tall funnel that sprouted amidships plied her way northwards. There was a minimal wake, and the small ship travelled slowly, barely making steerageway. *Obviously, in no hurry*, he thought. He finished the cigarette and flipped it over the side and hoped Pam had finished transmitting, they'd been warned against transmitting for long periods as the Austrian navy had Radio Detection Finding, or RDF boats patrolling these waters. It would be easy for them to triangulate the location of a radio signal, transmitting from a stationary position in a marina. After what seemed an age, he went below and, to his relief, saw Pam had completed broadcasting and was now reviewing the files they liberated from Major Richter.

As expected, they received a reply a few minutes later. It was succinct; they were to standby to receive instructions at 22:00 hours local time. It would be a two-and-a-half-hour wait. They were both hungry and decided to visit a nearby *ristorante* and eat.

"While we have Richter's files, we should carry weapons so we can defend ourselves, Pam. And I want you to carry one too." Kaha knew Pam disliked carrying a pistol. "Someone may have followed us back to the boat, and it is probably best to be over cautious and be prepared. Just in case," said Kaha smiling.

Pam looked concerned as if she was about to protest. Then her look softened. "Yes, you're probably right," she replied.

Kaha opened another hidden compartment, one of many throughout the boat that hid their pistols and ammunition. Wrapped in cloth, he took two almost brand-new Remington Rand Model 1911A1 semi-automatic pistols and ammunition and handed one to Pam, who expertly checked the mechanism, quickly loaded the weapon and flicked the safety to on before placing the bulky gun in her carry bag. Kaha positioned his weapon in a special holster in his back, under his shirt.

As protocol demanded, the *Mana* was to be secured anytime they were not aboard. The De Forest radio was again concealed, the hatch locked, and the twine re-attached. Kaha quickly looked around and again noticed the trawler beyond the sea wall, this time, she was much closer to the marina but changed direction and was now headed south. He made a mental note to keep a watchful eye on it and hoped daylight would give him a better opportunity to study her if she was still loitering in the area. Their suitcases remained in the cockpit and couldn't be seen from the dock, they were safe for an hour or two. Determining everything was as it should be, the happy couple strode arm in arm down the dock to enjoy a meal.

By the time Kaha and Pam were seated at their favourite table, an unobtrusive rowboat with three men slowly entered the marina. Two men rowed, and another sat at the tiller. Forward, three fishing poles jutted over the bow, and three bulky satchels and a knapsack lay at their feet. A bucket with half a dozen dead fish was the only other item in the boat.

The men didn't speak; the only sound was the rhythmic cadence of the oars as they dipped repetitively into the water. The man at the tiller was attentive to his surroundings, and while his head didn't move much, his eyes roamed everywhere. He consulted a handheld compass and checked its reading. He hadn't lost his way; he was interested in a particular boat that they had yet to identify and had previously been given a compass bearing to help find it.

The rowboat angled towards two larger boats moored to the end of a small pier, then went past and headed towards the adjacent dock, about a hundred feet, from where *Mana* lay. They passed the big yawl, gave it a careful look, briefly chatted and agreed that the sizeable two-masted yacht was the boat that interested them. They made a slight course correction and entered a vacant slip about three spaces from the end of the dock. The two rowers clambered out once they tied the boat to a cleat; one man began to walk along the gangway towards the shore to ensure they could go about their duties unseen, while the other headed in the opposite direction towards the *Mana*. Both men walked casually and drew no unwanted attention, but then again, they appeared to be recreational fishermen, and there weren't many people about to question their activities, even if they did seem to be unusually quiet.

After two or three minutes, both men returned to the rowboat, where a quick discussion ensued, and it was decided it was safe to proceed with their objective. Time was of the essence, and their orders explicit. This time they retrieved the satchels and one fishing pole, and all three men climbed onto the dock. Two men walked to the *Mana*, and the youngest, with the pole, walked some distance down the gangway and began to fish. He was the lookout.

It took Hans a bit longer than usual to pick the lock on *Mana*'s companionway hatch, but to his relief, he eventually felt the latch click. He slid the hatch open, and both men descended below.

They began a quick systemic interior search and found nothing of interest and were about to lock up and leave when Otto, sitting at the navigation station, lifted the desk lid to look a second time. With the light from his lamp, he flicked through a few charts and found a notebook. It contained nothing more than notes about tides, water depth, diesel fuel usage figures and, at the end, was a doodle. The word 'Richter' was written, then circled and circled again and again.

"Psst," Hans looked up. "Here, see this," offered Otto holding up the notebook, he pointed to the word 'Richter'.

Hans nodded. Now they were positive this was the boat that had transmitted the message. It was the confirmation they needed. "But where is the damn radio?"

Otto shrugged. Both men knew the Spark Gap radio was not the radio used to transmit the signal they'd detected. There must be another.

"Perhaps they took it with them?"

"Come, we have to hurry," ordered Hans, ignoring the question. With a minimum of fuss, the two *Feuerwerkers*, or ordinance technicians, began placing each satchel that contained three sticks of dynamite in three separate places. One satchel near the diesel fuel tank near the stern, another by the mainmast amidships, and the last satchel forward. Hans was concerned that it wasn't enough dynamite, but they hadn't expected to destroy such a large yacht. Primer charges were wired to each satchel, and then the wires were combined. A length of detonator cord was fed through an outboard facing port which they would retrieve soon.

After hiding signs of their incursion, Hans locked *Mana*, and both men headed to the rowboat. A low whistle signalled the lookout to return, and just as quietly as they arrived, the three men rowed out of the slip. The detonator cord hanging out of the port was attached to a reel and then slowly spooled out as they rowed towards the adjacent dock. They found the space between the bow and stern of both larger boats they had passed earlier – a perfect place to hide and wait.

The detonator cord was attached to the plunger, and the connections were double-checked to ensure they were tight. When the plunger handle is depressed, an electrical charge builds up through a magneto inside the box. At the end of its downward travel, the handle triggers a switch, and the stored current sends an electrical charge down the wire to the blasting caps used to detonate the dynamite, but the *Feuerwerkers* wouldn't depress the plunger yet, they had to wait.

The youngest, with his fishing pole, climbed onto the dock, again he was charged with the responsibility of being a lookout and would warn of anyone approaching the *Mana*. Their orders were clear, they must detonate the charge when the owners were aboard. It had taken them approximately an hour to search and wire the yacht, and now they needed to be patient.

Father Stevan Belić was exhausted, he'd spent a long day on horseback and added many kilometres to his journey after leaving false trails for the *Carabinieri* to follow. It was dark as he finally approached the burnt shell of what was once *Signora* Milani's fine villa. The acrid smell of burnt wood assaulted his nostrils, and even under the light of the moon, he could see exposed blackened timbers and immediately felt guilt; he was responsible for the destruction, and he felt sad for her. Adding to his dour mood, he knew his unexpected appearance was likely to cause her some anguish.

He reined in close to where he'd previously twisted his ankle, dismounted gingerly from the horse, and looked around as he stretched his back. The street was unusually quiet, lights burned brightly through open windows of nearby homes, and he could hear snippets of muted conversations. With his sensed heightened, he cautiously led his horse towards the house where Enzo lived.

Something didn't feel right, the horse snickered, and Belić paused. He stepped back towards the horse and stroked its neck. He could see the mare's ears twitch; she'd heard something.

Belić waited but saw nothing, he had no reason to feel unease, but a sixth sense warned him something wasn't as it should be. Perhaps returning during daylight might be better, he thought. The sight of seeing Zoran with tears streaming from his eyes and being dragged from the train unsettled him, and the frightened expression on the young boy's face as the small swarthy man pulled his arm reminded him of Boris and their special life–long bond. He knew he needed to speak with Enzo urgently, and throwing caution to the wind, decided to proceed. Ahead, was a crude rail fence where he could tie the horse while he reconnoitred.

An explosion of light and intense pain was the last thing he felt before everything went black and he passed out.

With a curse, *Stabswachtmeister* Dieter Wolff launched a savage blow into the midriff of the fallen priest, then for good measure, he delivered a few more. Unable to protect himself, the unconscious priest's body absorbed a series of vicious kicks and brutal punches. At one point, Wolff sadistically smashed his pistol into the priest's mouth.

Breathing hard and having temporarily expended his rage, Wolff straightened, holstered his weapon and while he took a quick rest to catch his breath, remembered the long walk in the dark after Belić stole his horse. He cursed the priest and spat, then bent down to pick up his arms and began to drag him slowly toward the house where Major Richter and the others waited. The major would be pleased, his plan to entice the priest back to the village had worked flawlessly.

Kaha leaned back in his chair and patted his belly. "I think I'm growing accustomed to this lifestyle."

"And you're growing fat, look at you," teased Pam, reaching over to affectionately rub his stomach, she pecked him on the cheek.

He returned the kiss and raised his hand, looking at his wristwatch, "I think we should leave now; I don't want to miss that message." With a groan, he sat upright, reached for his wine and drained its contents in a single swallow.

It was only a five–minute stroll back to their boat, and Pam's arms were linked through his, she was pressed snuggly against him as they walked unhurriedly, enjoying the peacefulness of a serene Italian summers evening.

Yachts of all shapes and sizes creaked at their moorings. Occasionally, a halyard would clatter against a mast, its predictable cadence measured by the flow of the incoming tide rocking against wooden hulls. In step, the couple walked parallel to the marina towards the gangway where *Mana* was berthed. The rhythmic and familiar sound of moored boats broken only by their footfall. They entered through a narrow gate onto the gangway and paused only so that Pam could untangle herself from her husband as they entered the marina. An unexpected disruption caused nearby yachts to tug at their lines, their fenders bumping into unyielding docks. A few halyards rattled in protest, the broken rhythm caused Kaha to stop.

"What is it?' whispered Pam.

Kaha held up his hand, his head swivelled from side to side, his eyes trying to see through the darkness. "I don't know ... was odd. Something disturbed the boats when we walked on to the dock." He shrugged. "Seems normal now." He reached for her hand, and they both continued warily to their yacht twenty metres away. Kaha saw the glowing tip of a cigarette on the other dock, it was difficult to tell, but the person appeared to be night fishing.

On reaching the stern of *Mana*, Kaha released her hand, and obediently Pam waited while he completed his security routine. He took his time. Using available light from the moon and a nearby light, he walked slowly and silently, his eyes flicked over the deck of *Mana*, aloft to the masts, then down to each of the four snaked Flemish Coils that lay at measured intervals along the dock. Nothing was amiss, and all was well. He checked the tightness of the bowline, then turned and repeated the process in reverse as he headed towards Pam, who still waited patiently near *Mana*'s stern. He froze, then took a step backwards and glanced again. He'd missed it the first time. To see better, Kaha crouched and looked at the coil from the stern spring line.

He was a man of habit, ingrained into him from an early age, Kaha was always taught to coil the lines that tethered the boat to a dock cleat by creating a tight spiral of the excess line or tailings. This was called a Flemish Coil. By force of habit, he began the spiral from the inside out in a clockwise rotation, and it was natural for a right-handed person to twist the line in this direction. The coil wound beside the dock cleat at his feet was rotated in an anti-clockwise direction. In the hours since he'd last checked the boat, someone had disturbed the coil, probably inadvertently kicking it, and then rewound it backwards. Probably a left-hander and could be nothing more than a kind gesture from a well-meaning sailor who had disturbed the coil – purely innocent? He straightened, and to appear normal, walked casually, the last few steps towards Pam.

"Someone has been here," he whispered, "Might be nothing, but take a few steps back down the gangway and have your pistol ready."

"Kaha, what is it, what's wrong?" she whispered in growing alarm.

"Just do it, I'll explain later."

As told, Pam eased slowly away, and Kaha reached for his gun beneath his shirt. He took a deep breath and slowly exhaled before he nimbly climbed the dock-step onto *Mana*'s deck. Their two suitcases were still sitting in the cockpit where they'd left them and appeared undisturbed. He walked to the companionway hatch and leaned over to inspect the tell-tale. In the darkness, he had to look closely to find the twine thread he'd fastened to the clip. It wasn't attached, but the companionway hatch was still locked. The twine couldn't separate from the hatch unless the hatch was opened. In this case, somebody must have picked the lock, and slid the hatch forward. Kaha's heart began to thump in his chest. Something was horribly wrong. Twisting to check on Pam, he could see her dim outline. It gave him comfort to see she was crouched on one knee, with both arms outstretched in a defensive firing position and held her pistol at the ready.

Feigning tiredness, he pushed himself away from the hatch, stood straight and stretched. Alert to his surroundings, Kaha looked outwards, turned his head slowly from left to right and looked out across the water. What he saw made his blood run cold. A thin, straight line, almost invisible, and caught in the reflection of moonlight, trailed from *Mana*'s bow along the surface of the water and disappeared in the direction of the adjacent dock near where he'd seen the man fishing. He knew exactly what it was.

Resisting the temptation to immediately flee and fighting to remain calm and not draw attention from anyone watching, he carefully made his way across the deck towards the dock. When he was a step away, he used his thick, powerful legs to leap on to the dock towards Pam.

"Run, Pam!" he yelled.

He was almost at her side when an enormous explosion drove the air from his lungs, and he slammed into her, the concussive shockwave from the immense blast lifted them from the dock and flung them both away. Debris and flames shot out and skywards. Had Kaha been able, in the brief flash as the *Mana* exploded, he would have seen the singled funnelled trawler, beyond the marina, loitering close to the harbour entrance. He didn't see a rowboat containing three men skulking away in the darkness.

Mana's remains were unrecognisable. The mahogany hull planks were designed to prevent water from entering the boat and were not constructed to withstand internal forces pushing outwards. The seventy-three foot yawl mostly disintegrated. With large sections of her hull missing, she sank immediately and lay with a broken, twisted keel on the silty bottom of the Pescara Marina. Her two masts that once towered regally from a great height above the deck were now mutated stumps that peaked at unnatural oblique angles from the water. Bits of decking, canvas, frayed lines, and planks floated in the soupy water. Flames still flickered from floating debris in a few places, but most of the fire quickly burned itself out. A few nearby boats in the marina were severely damaged, and others now contained souvenirs that littered their pristine decks, mementoes from what was once a beautiful and elegant yacht.

The dozen or so people who sat expectantly in the smoky conference room of the Secret Service Bureau in London were waiting for their director, Mansfield Smith–Cumming, to appear before the meeting could begin. There was some speculation and certainly rumours, as one would expect from a dedicated and small staff occupied with the sole task of obtaining information. Those who knew the purpose of the meeting remained tight-lipped, while others propagating unsupported theories did so with an enthusiasm that highlighted fertile and active minds.

The door opened, and the director finally entered; his face belied his dark mood, and Marge, his personal secretary, followed in his wake, clutching a pad and pencil to her ample bosom. A few people made to stand, but Smith–Cummings waved them back to their seats as he took his customary position at the head of the table. All conversation ceased, ending the speculation and rumours. Everyone sat a little straighter.

"Michael?" Smith-Cumming nodded.

Michael Sykes removed the pipe from his mouth, placed it on an ashtray, and reached for a cardboard file. He opened it, flicked through a few pages before closing and putting it reverently back on the table. Out of habit, he cleared his throat, a call for silence, but the room was already deathly quiet.

"At 21:00 hours last evening, Anchor and Chain failed to acknowledge a scheduled radio transmission. We have reason to believe there is a legitimate cause for concern."

"Likely to be a faulty radio, those vacuum tubes are finicky little sods, not to mention the salty air causes all sorts of corrosion," interjected Peter Bething, one of the bureau's technical experts.

A few heads nodded in agreement. "That's what we'd first considered, too," replied Sykes.

"How do we know they received the initial transmission? Could they not have known the time of our broadcast?" asked a voice. "They may have been mistaken."

"Atmospherics?" someone asked.

Smith-Cumming turned to Marge and inclined his head. She immediately rose and walked to the front of the room and rolled down a political map of Europe.

"Anchor and Chain are currently in the seaside town of Pescara, Italy," offered Sykes.

Marge pointed with her pencil to central Italy and placed the pencil tip on the coastal town of Pescara.

Sykes continued. "On time difference, they are one hour ahead of us, and we received previous acknowledgements to our transmissions from them earlier yesterday afternoon. This tells us there wasn't an issue with the time difference, and ..." Sykes turned to look at Peter Bething, "at the time, their radio was operating as it should. Could the radio have malfunctioned in-between transmissions?"

"Possibly," replied Bething, "but highly unlikely. Perhaps an atmospheric anomaly may have restricted their broadcast range ..." Peter Bething scratched his thinning scalp, "but I would have heard if that were the case by now."

"We agree with you, Peter," continued Michael Sykes. "They have spare vacuum tubes with them and a back–up, Spark Gap radio, even if it does have limitations. So, we can discount technical difficulties with their radio."

Peter Bething nodded in agreement. The director listened intently, comfortable to let his people share their knowledge openly without undue influence or pressure from him.

"However, more troubling is a radio intercept that came to us this morning. It's been reported there was a significant explosion near Pescara..."

Understanding the relevance, a couple of people gasped.

"It could be anything," someone suggested.

"...although unconfirmed, it states the time of the explosion at 21:45 hours, Pescara local time."

"Have we been able to contact anyone in Pescara to confirm this?" Bething asked.

"No, not yet, we're still trying," Michael replied.

Mansfield Smith-Cumming adjusted his monocle and leaned

forward, contributing for the first time. "Allan, do you have any thoughts on this?"

All heads turned to Allan Reed. He fidgeted nervously with a lock of hair at his temple. He giggled. "Logic would preclude us from discounting that the *Mana* was, in fact, a target. We know RDF ships are operating in the area, and we know the Austrian Navy have been rather aggressive as of late." He removed his finger, that his hair spiralled around and raised it. The room was deathly quiet. "When was their last recorded transmission?" he asked after a heartbeat or two.

Peter Sykes reached for his folder and searched for a copy of the radio traffic log. "Here, I have it. Um, it looks like 19:30 hours for an acknowledgement, and before that, they sent a transmission at ... "His finger moved up the page. "Yes, 18:50 hours, forty minutes earlier."

"So, Chain sent a message, and it took almost forty minutes before an acknowledgement was sent to them indicating we'd received their message. Then, in turn, they acknowledged that message, and that was sent at 19:30 hours?" asked Reed, seeking clarification.

"Yes, it was an unusually long transmission time," answered the Director. "It needed de-coding, hence the delay."

Reed lowered his finger and placed his hand out of sight beneath the table. "Yes, yes," he said, "It's entirely probable that the long transmission was detected by an RDF vehicle of some type. Since it's unlikely the Italians were responsible, that leaves the Austrians and the Germans. But again, it would be redundant to believe they'd have a land-based RDF vehicle patrolling the streets of a seaside town in neutral Italy." He giggled, finding his statement amusing. No others shared his mirth. "Then that leaves a marine vessel, a radio finding detection ship. As the Austro–Hungarians control most of the northern Adriatic, that eliminates the Germans. There can be no other possible explanation, it was Austria."

"Then you're suggesting somebody detected their transmission?" confirmed Sykes.

"Of course, and the Austrians took deliberate offensive action," Reed added with confidence.

Mansfield Smith-Cumming nodded and looked to another face. "Fuse, what would it take to destroy the *Mana* with explosives?"

Quentin Markham, or 'Fuse' as he was affectionately known, was the resident expert in explosives and demolition. "For a wooden-hulled yacht, it'd be easy like. Ya gotta get inside the guts of the boat. But that ain't hard; I could do it before ya could knock back a pint. But the trick is to make sure you break the old girls back, snap the keel." Fuse clapped his hands together; the resounding smack caused a couple of people to jump. "I'd lay me charges in three places like, near the engine, then another amidships, in the bilge, and the other f'ward."

"What would you use and how much?" asked Michael Sykes.

Fuse looked at Sykes like he was an imbecile, "Four sticks for each charge, five sticks if ya wanna make a show of it."

"And you could do this by yourself?

"Yep, but two or three people would make it easy like, don't forget ya gotta layout the detonator cord, then put the boat back the way it was so the explosives weren't discovered, so yeah, with three people, wouldn't take bloody long at all."

"Would the radio be completely destroyed?" asked the Director.

"Well, sir, that depends on how well the radio is protected and how close the nearest explosive charge was. But if you're concerned about the radio not working, then you'd be worry'n for nothing, trust me, sir, the radio won't go." Fuse laughed.

"No, no, that isn't what concerns me ..."

"What the Director means," interjected Allan Reed, "could the Austrians salvage the remains of the radio?"

Fuse momentarily lost his bravado and scratched the stubble on his chin, "Well now, that I couldn't say."

"I have to agree with the logic, sir. The explosion can only be the *Mana*," said Michael Sykes. "Anchor and Chain have been compromised and, uh, may have perished with their boat."

All the room's occupants stared at their superior.

Mansfield Smith Cumming heard all he needed. Only a few here at this meeting knew the full details of what Anchor and Chain were doing in Pescara, and he wanted to keep it that way. It was the nature of this business that death was sometimes a consequence, and he accepted that with some reluctance. However, privately he had faith and would not succumb easily to the notion that Kaha and Pamela were deceased.

A knock from outside in the hallway disturbed his introspection. Marge rose and opened the door to find an attractive young woman with a message. As required, she signed the receipt and was presented with a nondescript sealed envelope which she handed to the outstretched hand of the director. "From Room 40, sir."

The creative minds of the speculators were again quietly advancing their theories as Mansfield tore open the envelope and read the transcript. His face betrayed no emotion as he handed the missive to Peter Sykes to read. All chatter ceased.

It took all but a moment to reach a decision, he accounted for all contingencies, and this meeting only supported what he already concluded. Mansfield Smith-Cumming rose from his chair and reached behind, placing each hand on the small of his lower back and then arched back to stretch. "Captain Leech, what is the status of the naval blockade in the Otranto Straits?"

Happy to be called upon for his naval expertise, Captain Leech, stood unnecessarily. "Uh, the Austrians are basically confined to the northern areas of the Adriatic Sea, sir. However –"

"You can sit, captain, you're not at the admiralty now."

"Yes, sir, thank you, sir," replied the Royal Navy liaison to the British Secret Service as he returned to his seat.

"Then tell me, how far north can we safely travel into the Adriatic?" asked the director.

"Sir, the Austrian navy is largely limited to their ports. Smaller vessels, not so much. With their battleships – "

"What about submarine activity?" interrupted Smith-Cumming again.

"The Austrians have considerable U–Boats of their own, and numerous German U–Boats. They've become a bit of a pest, sir."

"Thank you, captain. Then I presume Royal Navy ships are venturing north into the Adriatic, beyond the blockade?"

"Yes, sir. In so far as much – "

"Captain Leech find out where the Mediterranean fleet is, then get me someone at the admiralty. I want to know if the Royal Navy has a small ship close to Pescara we can use. Under the guise of a breakdown, I want them to enter the harbour and pull that bloody radio from the *Mana* before the Italians, or the Austrians do."

"Yes, sir," Leech replied. He stood and quickly exited the room.

"You have more information, sir?" asked Peter Bething.

Smith-Cumming leaned forward with both arms on the table, his expression was grim. "We have a confirmed report that the *Mana* was destroyed by an explosion at 21:45 local time while tied to a dock in Pescara."

"Aw Christ!" someone said. A few others sat shaking their heads.

Ignoring the outburst, the director continued. "Mrs Marsden, who is our Military Liaison Officer at our Rome embassy? Isn't it, ah, what's his name, Levin, John Levin?"

"No, sir, Captain Levin broke his leg playing polo, he's on medical leave. Its Commander Bruno Bottini," informed Lilly Marsden, the only remaining woman in the room.

"Even better. Get hold of Bruno, I want to fully update and brief him as soon as possible. I'm going to have Bruno make a little trip to –"

"Pescara," interrupted Lilly, who was writing furiously on her notepad.

The Director turned to look at her, "No, I want him to go to Chieti."

CHAPTER SEVENTEEN

Belić tentatively blinked open his swollen eyes as he felt a cool, wet cloth applied to his face. The throbbing at the back of his head pounded incessantly and, combined with the pain from his mouth, made him feel nauseous. It took a few moments for his senses to focus, and he tried unsuccessfully to push aside the agony that consumed his entire body. He ran his tongue over his teeth – one was surely broken, others were loose and he tasted blood.

Even concentrating on breathing didn't help, and he immediately felt a sharp stabbing pang shooting from his ribs when he tried to inhale deeply. One, possibly two, were broken. He tensed involuntarily, which caused him more discomfort, and he gasped. He knew he was hurt badly and needed medical attention. He closed his eyes again and tried to remember what had happened. He could only recall walking to the fence to tether the horse, then nothing.

"Father?"

Belić instantly recognised the familiar voice of *Signora* Milani – *Natalina*. He swallowed away the blood and willed the pain to leave. Again, he tried to open his eyes and saw nothing but the cloth covering his face. He knew that he sat propped-up on a chair, the hardness of the back and seat only adding to his discomfort. The wet cloth was still gently dabbed over his eyes, preventing him from seeing. With care, he slowly raised his hand, relieved to find his arm was still functioning, but even that movement hurt his ribs and chest. He tried to move the cloth so he could see and felt a wrist, a slender familiar wrist – It was Natalina who was administering to him.

An involuntary groan escaped his torn lips, and he felt the coolness of the wet cloth slide away. With caution, he risked opening his eyes and saw the room for the first time. Standing before him was the beautiful *Signora*. She looked at him coolly, assessing his injuries, as his eyes slowly focused on her. In return, her mouth did not expand into a welcoming smile of warmth or pity. He didn't blame her, what could he expect?

His body hurt. How it ached, and as each of his faculties began to respond, he became acutely aware of other people in the room and where he was. He was in Enzo's home.

Natalina moved to the side and revealed a man, a stranger sitting on a chair. He watched impassively and stared with cold, unblinking eyes, unconcerned and unfazed with the sight of a severely beaten and bloodied man. Belić tried to ease himself into a more comfortable position, the foolishness of his decision apparent when the movement caused sharp, searing pain to shoot up his back and explode in a consuming flash of brilliant white light in his head.

Before the priest could fall from the chair, Natalina rushed forward and held him in place. Unperturbed, the stranger didn't react.

"Damn you," she yelled, "he's a priest, for God's sake! You can see he is injured, he should be in bed having his injuries attended to, not sitting in a chair for your cruel amusement!" She turned to look over her shoulder and shook her head in disgust at the lack of feeling the man demonstrated.

Major Maximillian Richter finally offered her the courtesy of a smile, but it conveyed no compassion or warmth. He turned his attention to a fleck of lint that lay on his trousers and casually brushed it away.

Belić regained consciousness, groaned and coughed up blood.

With agonising slowness, he lifted his head and grimaced through the pain. Blood and saliva dribbled over his chin, and he managed to speak a single word. "Zoran?"

Ignoring the question, Major Richter looked at the priest. "*Signora* Milani, perhaps a cup of tea would be welcome unless Mr Belić prefers a coffee?"

She gently dabbed his chin with a bloodied cloth.

"Water," breathed the priest.

"Yes, a good choice ... considering." Richter nodded at *Signora* Milani. The major scooted his chair a little closer to the stricken priest and finally appeared to take an interest in the wounds he'd received – although not from concern. Congealed blood caked the priest's matted hair. Both eyes showed signs of bruising and were almost swollen shut. Although some blood ran from his nostrils, his nose didn't look like it was broken. His lips, however, were a different story. They were almost shredded, especially in the centre. A lower front tooth was broken, its sharp edges contributing to the carnage of his mouth. Holding a cup to his lips would be a problem for the priest, thought the major.

"I apologise for the beating you received, *Herr* Belić," said Major Richter, "I'd hoped we could chat politely without the need for such violent behaviour."

Belić blinked in response.

"But you managed to upset the wrong person when you took his horse, and I can't be entirely responsible for his actions. My advice to you is, cooperate and don't anger him again."

Belić remained silent, trying to regain his strength. He felt another person in the room, behind him, but he couldn't see. "Zoran?" he managed to squeak."

Richter nodded, acknowledging Belić. "For now, the boy is being looked after and is safe from harm, however –"

Belić closed his eyes tightly as another wave of intense pain shot up his body. This time he managed to remain upright and not slip into the inviting blackness. Again, he sensed movement behind him but couldn't turn his head to look.

"– If you cooperate, then the boy's safety is assured. His ... uh, welfare lays in your hands and becomes your responsibility. You answer my questions truthfully, and I will ensure the boy remains unharmed."

The priest forced his eyes open and looked directly into the face of the man before him, and met his unblinking gaze. The man was cold, lifeless, like a soulless corpse. Belić closed his eyes and quietly began to pray when Natalina reappeared.

"Drink this," she offered and held the glass to pour warm water into his parched throat.

"I think I shall give you some time to rest," suggested the man. "It is late; sleep will help you regain your strength, and we will continue with our pleasant chat in the morning."

Belić remained quiet and thoughtful as Natalina lightly dabbed at the water that spilt over his mouth and chin.

"*Stabswachtmeister* Wollf, please assist *Herr* Belić to a bed."

Behind the priest, Wollf moved.

Maggiore Da Camino sat behind the grand expanse of his desk and studied the portrait on the wall of his father astride a valiant courser. The portrait inspired and motivated him to fulfil his dreams of becoming a national hero, a leader of men, someone who children looked up to and men both respected and feared. Chieti had not been the posting he'd hoped for, and opportunities for advancement within the *Carabinieri* and even in national politics slipped away into the abyss of futility. Or had it?

The appearance of the influential Major Maximillian

Richter reignited his passion and dreams and then just as quickly extinguished them. He held *Capitano* Gallo responsible for the embarrassment he suffered over the failure to apprehend the man Major Richter desperately sought. Gallo was a righteous interfering fool, he was nothing more than a bumbling small-town policeman with no ambition or initiative.

Da Camino saw unabashed potential in the European conflict. Currying favour with the powerful Austro–Hungarian Empire certainly had benefits. Friends openly suggested Italy would be forced to honour the Triple Alliance treaty they were a signatory of, and remaining neutral was out of the question. When Italy joined with Germany and Austria, he, *Maggiore* Lukas Da Camino, would be recognised as a true patriot, a fine son of Italy, but… if only he could redeem himself to Major Richter.

An open bottle of a delightful Portuguese Madeira beckoned, and *Maggiore* Da Camino poured a liberal amount into a small glass and considered the information he was given earlier. He raised the glass and took a small sip, savouring the dryness.

A source had come forward and informed him that Chieti's mayor, Alberto De Rosa, applied pressure on *Capitano* Gallo to apprehend the Austrian suspected of murdering his nephew and insisted he send a small contingent to the village where Major Richter and his men were presumed to be and apprehend the man.

Da Camino licked his lips. A slight window of opportunity presented itself. He could warn the Austrian Major before Gallo sent his men. He replaced the cork in the bottle, drained the glass and called for his adjutant.

Lights blazed over the marina where the beautiful yawl, *Mana*, once proudly floated. Admittedly, what remained of her was still partly visible and distinguished by a grotesquely misshapen and shortened main–mast. Most of the mizzen–mast floated nearby and was still attached to what was left of the hull by a lifeless cluster of halyards and shrouds. Her bow pointed unnaturally skywards to the heavens and her bowsprit, largely untouched, gestured to the Gods like a solitary protesting finger, an exclamation of pain during her last throes of life. *Mana*'s stern feared no better and lay twisted and jammed into the jetty, surrounded by an oily sheen that blanketed the water, and the pungent, sickly smell of diesel fuel filled the air. Still attached to a pole that jutted rudely from the stern and over the dock hung what was left of Italy's national flag. A closer inspection revealed the flag was singed, perforated, and the bottom third was missing – severed like an unwanted limb.

Water now lapped where the teak deck should have been, and on the dock, the Flemish flaked coils were still neatly wound uselessly to their cleats. It wasn't a pretty sight, and the spectators who stood nearby were solemn, they whispered to each other in respectful tones and shook their heads at the destruction and sadness at what now remained of a living and breathing entity. Those who knew the ocean and boats could feel it – it was part of the bond between man, the sea and the ships they sailed on. The death of a ship was not a pretty sight, no matter how small or large the vessel.

At the extreme edge of the lights arc, a cork boom was stretched across the marina to constrain the debris and flotsam that bobbed forlornly. Books, photographs, bits of wood, large planks, canvas, cushions, rope, clothes and even a few bottles littered the immediate area.

Earlier in the morning, many hours after the violent blast, men in small boats plied backwards and forwards, beyond the boom, picking up larger pieces of wood and wreckage that were blown outward during the explosion. They also had the gruesome responsibility of searching for bodies.

The *Capitaneria di Porto* responded quickly to the reports that a tourist yacht had exploded inside the marina. He initiated an immediate search for the likeable couple who owned the yacht, but so far, no one had found a body, let alone any human remains. The search continued throughout the night and all day without success. He'd received orders from the *Carabinieri* to keep people away from the wreckage and ensure lights illuminated the area during evenings until the completion of a thorough investigation. The dutiful Harbour Master wasn't of a mind to over analyse these unfortunate accidents, pleasure boats did not erupt in a violent explosion on their own accord, and as he knew, such misfortunes were frequently the result of carelessness and inexperience.

The Harbour Master stood on elevated ground near the jetty and surveyed the marina with a practised eye. An unlit cigarette hung miraculously from his bottom lip, and both hands were buried deep in the pockets of his trousers. His peaked cap was tilted upwards and sat at a rakish angle, and nestled in an unruly nest of curly black hair. To a bystander, he looked untroubled, but today *Capitaneria di Porto*, Antonio Conti was far from relaxed. Not only did he have to contend with the destruction of a beautiful yacht and the mess that needed cleaning, but a small English warship in need of emergency repairs was due to arrive sometime late this afternoon, and he needed to find a suitable berth to accommodate its thirty-eight-metre length and allow for sufficient manoeuvring room. He looked outwards beyond the marina and watched a trawler slowly making its way south. He'd seen the boat before and recently. Why was it loitering in the area, he wondered?

Antonio jostled the coins in his pocket and made a logical decision. After the explosion, and for safety reasons, a few boats moored nearest the *Mana* that were damaged were moved elsewhere, this opened a sizeable space at the end of the dock adjacent to where *Mana* lay. It was perhaps a little too close to the wreck, but he had no other option. The *Carabinieri* investigating the accident would be unhappy to have an English warship moored in the immediate vicinity, even if it were only an auxiliary trawler. Antonio shrugged – what will be will be.

He pulled a hand from his pocket, holding a well-used brass cigarette lighter. He flicked open the cap with his thumb and depressed the little hammer igniting the wick. He tilted his head to the side, closed an eye and lit the cigarette, puffing a time or two before he was happy. He closed the cap with a snap, put the lighter back in his pocket, and began jangling his loose change again. He turned around and walked away in a cloud of smoke.

Not far away, in the salon of a motor–launch, two pairs of eyes watched Antonio depart the jetty.

Kaha had been on the dock and about four metres from their yacht when the detonation occurred. Propelled by the concussion wave, the violent blast drove him forcefully into Pam, essentially shielding her from flying debris and thrust them outwards. They narrowly missed hitting the hull of a boat as they flew through the air and splashed in a tangle of arms and legs into the marina between two moored yachts. A spinning plank hit him squarely on his back and head, rendering him unconscious before he hit the water.

Although dazed and with her ears ringing, Pam was unhurt. In reflex, she had tightened the grip on her purse and, to her amazement, noticed she still firmly held it. Its hefty sodden weight reminded her that she still carried the pistol. With concern for her injured husband, she fought to keep his head above water and had the presence of mind to drag him away from the wreckage and swim into the dark recesses of the marina. Once she had judged they were far enough away, she looked for a boat where they could hide.

A large motor launch was the obvious choice; its square transom and ladder made access easier. However, dragging the inert body of her husband up the ladder built onto the transom was another matter. Undaunted, she wrapped her arms around his chest and attempted to haul him up and succeeded only in raising his chest above the water. At one point, he slipped from her grasp and slid back down, briefly submerging. A desperate hand on his collar saved him from disappearing.

Focused entirely on the task, she failed to hear the soft footfall as a man stepped aboard the launch and was still oblivious to his presence as he purposely walked aft in her direction. She nearly leapt overboard in fright as two muscled arms appeared from the darkness, gently pushed her aside, grabbed Kaha and, with relative ease, lifted him from the water and over the transom and onto the deck of the launch.

Pam was shocked, and her heart pounded, not just from the effects of the explosion and being blown from the dock into the marina or even from the physical exertion of trying to lift Kaha, but from the surprise appearance of a burly man. The stranger laid Kaha gently face-down on the deck, and then for the first time, Pam saw a glimpse of his bearded face as he sat back and whispered a few unintelligible words into the darkness. She heard a muted reply and then saw two more men quickly walk along the dock and step quietly aboard.

The stranger began probing Kaha for injuries. After a minute or two, he spoke quietly in Italian, his voice deep, resonant and calming. He patiently explained and showed her the large knot on the back of Kaha's head, the splinters embedded in his back and other minor contusions. He made no comment on the empty holster in Kaha's waistband, and she noticed his two associates kept themselves hidden from view from anyone on the dock.

More and more people began arriving and stared in wonder at the destruction and after-effects of the dramatic and thunderous explosion. For the time being, Pam's hiding place was secure, and no one came close to discovering them other than the surprise appearance of the stranger and his two friends.

When Pam tried to thank the man, he shrugged and said it was nothing, telling her it was his duty to come to aid anyone in need of help. His unusual accent distinguished him as being Balkan and not Italian.

A movement in the water caught her eye, she turned to study the object and saw it was one of their suitcases floating past. Seeing her look, the stranger reached for a boat–hook that lay clipped beneath the gunwale, leaned outwards and expertly snagged the suitcase and hoisted it on deck. At least they had a change of clothes – they were very fortunate.

Kaha's shirt was shredded, and his back, bruised and tender. Using the available light and on closer inspection, she realised the stranger was correct, she could feel that he had many bumps and wooden splinters embedded in the skin, but no deep wounds. She began removing the wooden slivers, one–by–one, but with her mind still dazed and reeling ... it was all too much, and with a lightness of head, she finally succumbed and collapsed into the arms of fisherman, Boris Marković.

When Pam regained consciousness, only a minute or two later, Kaha was sitting up and feeling the back of his head, he was still a little dizzy and feeling nauseous. She tried to stand and go to him, but the stranger told her to move slowly and carefully lest she lose her balance and also suffer an injury. He assisted her to Kaha's side.

The sizeable and dramatic explosion drew a growing crowd, and Pam knew they must hide or risk discovery. People were running onto the docks and yelling frantically. Thankfully, their attention was focused on where the explosion occurred. While temporarily hidden from casual view, a thorough search would quickly reveal them. As if reading her thoughts, the stranger indicated to the main salon, and one of his men promptly went to the door and found it secured. He delved into his pocket for a tool, and as everyone watched, the door was opened in seconds. With a minimum of fuss, Kaha and Pam were both helped inside, and the door quickly closed.

"We were lucky you happened to be here to help us," said Pam.

The man shrugged. "Such is the way of life."

Kaha looked at the man in the darkened cabin. "Yet you haven't asked about the explosion," he said weakly.

Surprising them, he spoke in heavily accented English. "I think it time we go."

"Can we at least know your name? I am Pamela Peterson, and this is my husband, Kaha."

The man remained quiet for a few seconds. "Is pleasure to meet you both, I am sorry for loss of fine boat, and you lucky not seriously hurt, eh. I Boris Marković." In the darkness, he reached out and shook both their hands. "But, er, we haves business to attend to, and so now we go."

He spoke to his two friends, and they moved to the door. Boris stopped and turned around. "I unsure why you remain hiding ... you have reasons, and I will er, I will not asks. I tell no ones you are here."

"Again, thank you very much," replied Pam.

The three men departed as quietly as they had come.

"He's finally leaving," said Kaha as he watched the Harbour Master walk away. Pam peered between the curtains and watched. "Something has been bothering me that I can't put my finger on," Kaha said. "When I saw the face of that man last night –"

"Boris, he said his name was Boris Marković, but he offered nothing else," interrupted Pam. "I'm finding it hard to remember all the details ... I'm still a little dazed." Pam closed the curtain and raised a hand, and gently stroked the side of his face. "I'm worried about you, Kaha."

He reached up and took her hand. "I'm feeling better all the time. I, I, just wish I knew what happened last night. I've been wracking my brain, trying to understand –"

"You saved our lives... and if you hadn't seen that detonator cord ..." Pam shuddered.

"Bastards! It could only have been that trawler beyond the marina, it must be a marine RDF boat." Kaha moved into a more comfortable position. "I've been trying to figure it out. The only time they, whoever *they* are, had the opportunity was when we went to dinner. That's when they must have sent men ashore to wire the *Mana* with explosives." Kaha looked into the face of his wife. "They were waiting for us to return and climb aboard... That's when they were going to detonate the charge. "Kaha shook his head. "We were lucky, Pam, very lucky, they were going to kill us."

"And lucky Boris and his men showed up when they did."

"Yes, he was hiding something as well, they didn't want to be seen either. What was it? Did he say anything to you? Did he give a reason?" Kaha asked.

"He only gave me his name as Boris Marković, and he's certainly a Balkan, that's all I know."

"Let's hope he doesn't talk to the *Carabinieri*, the last thing we need is to have them interrogate us as to why our boat was targeted and blown up. It won't take a fool to realise we're hiding something." Kaha's eyes opened wide. "That's it! Now I remember, he had that fishing boat. Do you recall the night we watched the man sneak off the boat carrying a suitcase? We walked over to them and asked about the weather, and they weren't interested in talking to us. That man, Boris, is a fisherman, and he was sneaking back into the marina last night when the *Mana* exploded, that's why he didn't want to be seen, he's a smuggler, or ..." Kaha paused, leaving the sentence unfinished.

"Or what? Do you think he could have blown–up *Mana*?"

"No, I don't think so, it was just a coincidence he was there. Why come to our aid and offer help when whoever blew the boat up tried to kill us? If it was Boris, then we'd already be dead, no it wasn't him."

Pam pulled her hand away from his and swept a strand of hair away from her eyes. "I was all prepared and was going to tell him you had an unpaid gambling debt and bad men were looking for you, that it was them who blew–up the *Mana*."

Kaha began to laugh.

Pam didn't. "C'mon, lay down on the settee, I'm going to dress your back again." She reached for the first aid kit she had found in the launch as Kaha eased himself face down on the settee.

"Gambling debt," he repeated and began laughing again.

"Keep still," she scolded him and then added, "You know we have to find a way to radio London."

"Yes, I'd thought of that, a telegram is all I can think of unless we contact the British Embassy somehow."

"And the boy and Major Richter, what will we do about them?" she asked.

"I think there is little we can do at this time; our main priority is to notify London. Then wait for instructions."

"Then we will just ignore the boy?"

Kaha twisted his head to look at his wife. "What do you suggest? We have to obey protocol, and I cannot see London ordering us to continue to keep tabs on Richter, can you?"

Pam looked crestfallen. "We can't stay here either."

"I suggest we remain here for the day, then tonight when it is dark, we quietly leave and then find a way to notify London and check into a local hotel.

Clothes were hung out to dry and filled all the available space in the salon. Even the contents of Pam's purse, and Kaha's wallet, which thankfully he still had, were drying in the sun.

She nodded and began to weep. "What's wrong, sweetheart?" asked Kaha as he pushed himself into a sitting position. "Our home ... the *Mana*, it's gone. We nearly died ..."

"But we didn't, and we are still alive, and, mostly unharmed. It could have been worse, a lot worse. But we will buy another boat, and it will be better and a little bigger." Kaha wiped away her tears with his thumb. "We still have each other, and that is the main thing, eh?"

Pam smiled, wiped her eyes with the back of her hand and then leaned forward to kiss him. "Now, lay back down and let me finish."

CHAPTER EIGHTEEN

The plumb bow of an English warship, the HMT *Bangor Castle*, nosed into the Pescara Marina amidst clouds of thick black diesel smoke that spewed from its single, tall and slightly raked funnel. The thirty–eight-metre auxiliary trawler barely made steerageway as she slowly past moored yachts and launches of varying sizes and designs. On deck, sailors were lowering fenders and readying mooring lines as the trawler's captain ordered a one–hundred and eighty-degree turn to port, which would lay the *Bangor Castle* alongside the dock, and much closer than he expected, to the wreck of the *Mana*.

Lieutenant Burton Sanders, RNR, Captain of Her Majesty's Trawler, *Bangor Castle,* saw the cork boom spread across the marina and smiled inwardly. This was better than he had dared hope when given the unusual orders to make best speed for the Italian coastal port of Pescara and simulate an engine malfunction. His smile disappeared as they crept closer and saw the detail and carnage of what must have once been an impressive yacht. He deftly removed the pipe clamped between his teeth.

"Watch your helm, Jack," he warned the quartermaster, who'd also been looking at the wreck and begun to deviate from his course.

"Aye, cap'n."

"Take her in, nice and slow ... that's right ... nice and easy," coached the captain. "Nothing flashy, remember we have a defective motor."

"Very, well, sir," replied the helmsman.

The clatter of feet climbing the ladder to the bridge warned the captain of a visitor. "How we doin, captain?" asked the newly arrived guest.

"I don't think the Italians have seen this much smoke in the air since Mount Vesuvius erupted." The captain clapped the ship's chief engineer on the back. "Nice job, Glen."

"I'll be happier when we can burn the diesel cleanly. This mission is a little nerve-wracking."

"Yes, and for me too, I can't say I feel good about being this far north in the Adriatic, the Austrian naval presence here worrys me a tad."

"Is that what's left of the yacht we're supposed to do a minor salvage job on?" asked Sub–Lieutenant Glen Hornby, pointing to the wreck with an oil-stained finger.

"Yes, that's the *Mana*, or what's left of her." Hornby, as many others did when they saw the wreck, shook his head in dismay. "We'll shut the motor down soon as we're secured to the dock."

"Right'o, cap'n, I'll go back down then," replied the subaltern as he made his way towards the ladder.

Lieutenant Sanders returned the pipe to his mouth and continued to scan the surrounding area and immediately saw the distinctive uniform of a *Carabiniere* walking along the dock to where they would berth. *I hope he's here to welcome us and not here as a guard*, he thought.

"There's a *Carabiniere* walking on the dock."

Kaha turned around, "Are they searching boats?" He made to stand.

"No, they don't appear to be doing anything except … oh dear, wait a moment, there's a warship about to moor to the dock."

"A what?"

"Kaha? You should come and look at this, it's a warship, and it's mooring to the dock."

"My God, it's English!" exclaimed Kaha with surprise as he saw a brief glimpse of the naval ensign as he kneeled on the settee and peered between the curtains. "What the dickens is the Royal Navy doing here? Looks like they've got some problems though, look at the smoke she's pumping out."

Kaha and Pam continued to watch in silence as the warship slowly edged up to the dock and stopped; a cloud of thick black smoke followed. Immediately sailors leapt down and began securing lines and making her fast.

"That's why the *Carabiniere* is there, to ensure that they do not break neutral country protocols." Kaha closed the curtain and turned to Pam. "That's a spot of good fortune, isn't it?"

"You mean cause they have a radio?" she asked hopefully.

"Yes, and we need to get aboard that ship and have them send a message to London."

"Will the *Carabiniere* let us past so we can go aboard?" Pam asked.

"Normally, it wouldn't be a problem, but because the *Carabinieri* are also searching for both Mr and Mrs Peterson, they may object to us going aboard an English warship and instead prefer to hold us for questioning."

"What should we do then, we can't stay here?"

"No, we can't," replied Kaha, "but others can."

"Pam looked away from the British trawler and turned to her husband. "What do you mean others can?"

"Luc."

"Luc Lemaire?" questioned Pam. "He's a rascal, would you trust him?"

"Ordinarily, I'd be circumspect, but in this case, I think we can.

After all, he is a friend. He's as patriotic as anyone could possibly be, and as France and England are allies, then we know where his loyalties lie. But because he's a ship's Chandler, gives him a legitimate excuse to go to the warship."

"So, then we should go to see Luc?"

"I think it's our best option. We can wait until it's dark and go and see him. The only thing we don't know is how long that trawler will be in Pescara for, so we do need to hurry."

Signora Milani wiped away the blood, bound his chest in bandages, and applied salve to his tattered lips and other contusions. She nursed him throughout the night, the pain that consumed him kept him from sleeping for anything longer than short stretches at a time. Each time Father Stevan drifted off, he'd wake to the torment of nightmares. At one time, he woke and asked her for the wooden cross he kept in his jacket pocket, the agony of reaching for it himself too much to bear. Once he held it, inevitably rotating it end–for–end, he relaxed.

Not trusting the elusive priest, Major Richter kept a constant guard rotation in the room on four–hour watches. Frequently the man fell asleep, and during those times, Natalina talked, she whispered to Belić of their past conversations, reminded him of the things he said and asked him why he lied and misled her. She scolded him, her anger patent. He could only lay quietly on the bed and look up at her with swollen, puffy eyes. Because of the injuries to his mouth and face, he couldn't tell her of his feelings, he couldn't share with her the anguish and guilt he felt, and as much as he wanted, he couldn't tell her what and who he was. He could only listen and endure. She wasn't a happy woman.

As the hours passed, he felt her warmth, her hand holding his, her breath on his sore bruised face – like the soothing breath of an angel. Sometimes he kept his eyes closed and took in her smell, her natural fragrance and the feel of her skin on his as she idly toyed with his fingers, it kept him alive, and it gave him hope.

He prayed for forgiveness and sought solace from his faith, most of all, he wanted spiritual guidance. It was then that God spoke to him. He knew it with absoluteness, he felt and accepted it. It came with a blessing of unclouded calm and peace that descended over him like pure radiant light. The pain of his body had not diminished, it was still significant but now manageable, and he could acknowledge that his feelings and affections for her were real – they were unfeigned, and he accepted them with joy, it was God's gift, and he knew it to be love.

During the long evening, something passed between them. It was to Belić, an unusual sensation, unfamiliar to a priest but not to a man. It was tangible, powerful and prevailed over him like a benediction. She felt it too, he could see it in her face, the way she gripped his hand, the heat from her body, and she didn't hide her tears, nor could she run away from her emotions as she previously did when he was a guest in her home. Unspoken, she held his gaze and saw beyond a broken, flawed priest and recognised the frailty of love from an injured man.

With her hand tightly clasping his, she eventually drifted off into a fitful sleep, and he lay on the bed and stared at the darkened ceiling of Enzo's home. She did not know about him and the man he'd become. His acknowledged feelings for her were real, but so was his objective and need to survive. Because of him, she was also in danger, and he didn't want to see her hurt anymore. He knew what he must do, and it made him sad – yet another wound, another mortal blow to his tormented and fragile soul.

Sensing his guilt and unease, she stirred and woke. To her protest, he carefully shifted his position slightly and leaned his head towards her, and despite the pain, kissed her cheek. He knew it would be the only kiss she would ever receive from him. She did not recoil in horror, instead, she returned his kiss with a lingering caress of her own. The heat of her lips pressed onto his skin – it seared him and left an indelible imprint of her sentience. What passed between them at that moment was veritable, he saw through her eyes and into her heart. A tear fell from her eye and splashed on his cheek like an explosion of consciousness, an awakening.

How would she react when she learned about him? he wondered. He shouldered aside the weak sentiments and prepared himself for what was to follow.

Now, he feared nothing, not the man who'd beaten him senseless and almost killed him, not the cold, unfeeling Austrian who stared malevolently with a dark vacant hole where his soul should have been, or the Church who were so eager and quick to judge and condemn. More importantly, and with resolve, he cast his feelings of guilt aside and, with unspoken words, decided to accept his predicament. He would face his accusers and spare Natalina.

When the first signs of dawn broke, Belić felt remarkably better, although exhausted, he had regained some strength but was not free of pain. He looked over at Natalina, she was asleep and still clasped his hand.

The door opened, and Major Richter, trailed by Dieter Wollf, strode in. Immediately Mr Yavuz, who was currently on guard duty, rose sleepily and somewhat guiltily from his chair and onto his feet.

Richter looked over at Belić and saw the stirring form of

Signora Milani. "Take her into the other room and bring the boy," he ordered as he walked to the window and parted the curtains to peer outside. Natalina struggled as the Turk, Mr Yavuz, held her wrist and pulled her from the bed. "Please, don't hurt her!" gasped the priest. His voice barely rose above a whisper.

"I can see you are a little better," said Major Richter drawing the curtains closed, "I think it's time we continued our discussion." He pulled the chair Mr Yavuz recently vacated, dragged it closer to the priest, and sat down.

Belić managed to pull himself into a more upright position. "Water," he croaked.

Richter nodded, "Have the *Signora* bring water and tea for us."

Wollf acknowledged the order and walked out of the room, leaving the two men alone.

"We're going to begin by recounting your involvement with the assassination of Prince Ferdinand and his wife."

"You already know everything," Belić offered. His swollen eyes stared into the unblinking face of the major.

The Turk brought Zoran into the room. When he saw the battered body of Father Stevan, he began to cry and covered his face with his hands.

"Have they hurt you, Zoran?" hissed Belić, barely able to constrain his anger.

"Where is papa, I want papa?" appealed Zoran between sobs.

Major Richter inclined his head, and the Turk led Zoran from the room, leaving them alone again.

"Let him go, there's no need to involve the boy, I will tell you what you want to know. Just, return him to his father." Talking was difficult for Belić, and he struggled to form words with his lips and mouth in such bad condition.

"As I explained, the boy's well–being depends on you.

Cooperate and tell what I want to know, and the boy can go home."

Belić continued to glare at his captor. "What of Enzo and his mother, have you harmed them also?"

"They are quite comfortable, Father. I am not a monster as you would believe, but I must follow orders and do what is necessary to make my superiors happy." Major Richter reached into his jacket pocket and extracted a notebook and pencil. He glanced down at it and flipped a few pages looking for a space to write.

"Who are you?" croaked Belić.

The major looked up from his notes and stared at the priest for a heartbeat or two before replying, "I am Major Maximillian Richter of the *Evidenzbureau.*"

Belić swallowed, he knew of the *Evidenzbureau* and heard of the reputation of Major Richter.

Richter tapped the pencil on his notebook as if trying to decide which question to ask first, he frowned and looked troubled. As if coming to a decision, he asked his first question calmly, almost in a friendly manner. "You are an ordained Roman Catholic Priest?"

Belić nodded in agreement. He wasn't fooled, he knew what Richter was doing. The questions were designed in such a way as to appear unthreatening and to encourage him to talk. Richter knew the answers to the questions he asked.

"Your age, ah, thirty-four?"

Again, the priest nodded.

The major raised his eyebrows in question. The corners of his mouth tightened imperceptibly.

Got him, thought Belić.

"You lie! Thirty–six!" Richter knew exactly how old he was.

Belić took satisfaction in seeing the arrogant major become upset. By He'd make him work hard for every question he answered.

The major closed his notebook with a sigh and placed it and the pencil on the dresser beside the chair. He slowly stood and took a step closer to the bed, leaned forward and stared at Belić.

Even though he knew it was coming, the blow came with lightning speed, it wasn't a closed fist, it was an open palm that hit squarely on the centre of his chest and caught him totally by surprise. Belić screamed, his eyes filled with tears as he gasped for air. Each tortured breath sent sharp shooting pains through his entire body.

"Don't play games with me," warned the major, he spoke through clenched teeth.

Belić closed his eyes and willed away the pain as Richter returned to his seat and retrieved his notebook. In the background, he heard Natalina crying. He thought he could hear Enzo's voice, but then it abruptly stopped.

"We'll try again. How old are you?"

It took a moment before he could answer, when he did, he replied, "Thirty–six."

The major didn't smile. The questions went on for an hour. Natalina brought tea and water for them both and gave Belić a worried look. Richter asked simple questions about the Bishop of his church, about the Black Hand organisation, who were its leaders, how did they recruit members, where did they train, how did they obtain their weapons and where did the money that funded them come from? Belić answered honestly, he suspected the major knew the answers.

Belić was beginning to tire when the small Turk, Mr Yavuz, charged into the room. Major! Major Richter, a policeman approaches!"

The major stood, clearly annoyed at the intrusion. "Stay here with the priest, *Herr* Yavuz, and gag him. *Stabswachtmeister* Wolff, bring the *Signora* in here. Gag her as well," the major decisively ordered. He left the room and walked calmly to the door. "*Herr* Meyer, bring me the farmer."

Richter cracked the door open and peered cautiously outside. As the Turk accurately informed him, a lone *Carabiniere* approached the village. He appeared uncertain and pulled his horse to a stop and stared at the destruction of *Signora* Milani's villa.

Gunter Meyer pushed Enzo towards the major.

Richter gently closed the door and turned towards Enzo. "You will go to the *Carabiniere* and ask him what he wants." He leaned threateningly towards him. "I have the woman and boy, if you alert the policeman, then I will kill either one of them." His unblinking eyes stared malevolently. "Understood?"

"*Si*, I will do as you ask."

Major Richter stood behind the door and slowly opened it. Enzo stepped outside and began to walk to the *Carabiniere*.

"Is the boy secure?" asked Richter.

"Johan is with him and the old lady, Major," replied Gunter as he peeked through the curtains. He watched as Enzo and the *Carabiniere* spoke. "The farmer comes back."

In moments Enzo was standing in the doorway. "The *Carabiniere* is here for you. He has a message from Major Da Camino."

"Ah, the *Carabinieri* commander." Richter pushed past Enzo and strode out onto the road.

"Major Richter?" the *Carabiniere* asked.

Richter held out his hand. "You have a message?" he asked, ignoring the question.

The young policeman looked nervous, intimidated by the presence of the Austrian officer he'd heard so much about. "Ah, are you Major Richter, sir?"

"Give me the message," the major quietly insisted. "I am Richter."

The *Carabiniere* reached into his tunic and extracted an envelope. He nervously handed it to the major.

"Does Major Da Camino require a reply?"

"N, no, sir."

"Wait here." Richter turned and walked back to Enzo's home. The young policeman waited as ordered. Once inside, he tore open the envelope and read the message as Gunter watched. Once read, he folded the letter, his face remained impassive. "*Stabswachtmeister* Wollf, *Herr* Yavuz?"

"*Herr* Major?" Both men were quickly at his side.

"Seems we have a change of plans," he looked at Wollf, "We must leave here immediately, and I want you to ride back to Chieti with the *Carabiniere*, then go immediately to Pescara. No one will bother you if you ride with him."

"What has happened?"

The major was staring at the wall.

"Major Richter, why must we leave?"

The major turned to Wollf. "The local police are sending a small detachment of men here to arrest you for the murder of the policeman. They were to arrive today, but now they will come tomorrow."

Stabswachtmeister Wollf looked confused.

Richter ran his fingers through his hair. "Seems there was an explosion in the Pescara Marina, a boat blew up. Pescara's Chief of Police is the brother-in-law of Chieti's police chief, and he sought his advice, hence his delay in coming here."

Detection Finding ships fell under Richter's area of responsibility, and it was only natural he would use all available resources to assist with the completion of the mission. The major was also puzzled; explosions were unusual in a peaceful marina. The only logical reason that made sense to him was if the RDF boat he dispatched to Pescara to pick them up and take them back to Austria was involved. It made logical sense, he reasoned. If he was being followed, then it is likely that they, whomever is broadcasting and sending messages, would be in contact with their intelligence agency. Richter afforded himself the luxury of a smile, he was pleased, this was the reason he had the *Trabant* monitoring Pescara's radio broadcasts while he was here.

The trawler had standing operational orders to patrol the area around Pescara and monitor any unusual marine broadcasts. If the trawler accurately determined that any coded transmissions were associated with the Triple Entente, they were to isolate the signal source and take any necessary steps to destroy the radio and sink the boat, including its radio operators, to prevent any further transmission.

Mr Yavuz wasn't a stupid man, he'd remained alive through cunning and by being observant. When he kidnapped the boy from Ragusa, he fully expected his father to come searching. His mouth opened in realisation. "Could it be the fishing boat? The boy's father's boat."

"What do you mean? You told me there was no possibility they could trace the boy's whereabouts."

"I told you, sir, that it was unlikely– "

"Then you have been lucky, *Herr* Yavuz," snapped Richter. Although he doubted the Turk's assertion and believed it was his RDF trawler, *Trabant*.

Wisely Mr Yavuz kept his mouth shut.

"And when I arrive in Pescara, *Herr* Major?" Wollf asked.

Richter focused his attention on *Stabswachtmeister* Wollf. "You will signal the trawler, *Trabant*, and have them prepare to take us aboard as soon as we arrive. I do not wish to linger in Pescara with all those village policemen sniffing around. Leave now."

"Yes, *Herr* Major." Wollf hid his smile, he was pleased to finally return home.

Richter gave Wollf a stern look. "I do not wish for you to encounter the local authorities; it won't do either of us any good if you are arrested. Therefore, you will do your best to remain out of sight. We will meet you near the marina when we arrive."

Major Richter gave Wollf all the details on signalling the trawler.

"And our prisoners, Major Richter?" The Turk asked.

"We will take the boy, the woman and the priest with us. The boy offers us leverage. The woman can see to the wellbeing of the priest until I do not need them both anymore." Richter looked around the confines of the small house they were in. "Prepare to leave as soon as possible, I want to be well away from here when Chieti's police arrive.

"And what of the farmer and his mother?"

"Leave them, they can do us no harm," instructed Richter.

CHAPTER NINETEEN

As darkness descended on Pescara, so did an approaching weather front. Boats tugged restlessly at their mooring lines as a developing storm edged closer. The sound of halyards slapping against masts broke the stillness and quiet of the marina. Not far away, on dry land, and less than a hundred yards or so, the sound of protesting boats was replaced by the swishing of leaves as the wind rippled through a few gently swaying trees. Propelled by increasing gusts, litter tumbled up the street, and forgotten laundry flapped horizontally like colourful pennants from clotheslines stretched between balconies.

From somewhere, a dog barked, and a harsh voice quickly subdued the excited animal but couldn't silence the sound of laughter that drifted from a myriad of seedy bars that populated the waterfront area of Pescara. A Few people were out this evening, but no one paid any attention to the couple who slowly walked from the marina.

Instead of turning left on Viale Primo Vere, towards the distant drunkenness and revelry, Kaha and Pam walked straight ahead onto Lungaterno Cristoforo Colombo, which ran parallel to the Fiume Pescara where many commercial vessels were moored. Directly facing the river, a line of buildings that housed businesses supporting Pescara's maritime industry disappeared up the street. Even in the darkness, one structure stood out from the others, evident by a large white sign boldly and simply stating, 'Chandlery'. It was to this building that Kaha and Pam were headed.

Lights burned from the upper storey as Kaha and Pam passed the darkened front entrance, then turned left into a narrow lane and quickly walked around to the rear of the building and climbed a rickety staircase. On reaching the small landing at the top, Kaha rapped loudly on the heavy wooden door.

"What do you want?" eventually yelled a heavily accented voice from inside.

"It's us Luc, Kaha and Pam!"

"Who?"

"Open the door, damn it, it's Kaha and Pam!"

A heavy wooden bar was removed, a complex series of latches and locks were rotated, pulled and slid into place before the door finally creaked open. "*Sacré bleu!*" cried the voice. "You are dead!" the man stared, open-mouthed in surprise.

"Will you let us in or spend all evening gaping with your mouth open?"

His mouth closed, and the small, portly man rushed out and warmly embraced Pam, held her by the shoulders and gave her a thorough once over. His one good eye looked up at her, then down, and double-checked with a final look upwards. Then he leaned forward and kissed her on both cheeks before turning to Kaha. Ever expressive and emotional, Luc then delivered a welcoming kiss to his right cheek, then the left before declaring they were both alive.

All the locks were repositioned and the wooden bar replaced in its cradle across the door. "But you are supposed to be dead!" Luc shook his head in astonishment and led Pam inside his residence, with Kaha following.

"Sylvia, Sylvia!" yelled Luc as they walked into his spacious apartment. "You won't believe who is here."

Kaha met Luc Lemaire and his lovely Portuguese wife, Sylvia, years earlier when sailing in the Mediterranean. They began a lasting friendship and have remained in contact since. As part of their duties to the Secret Service Bureau, Kaha and Pam needed to cultivate connections that could provide them with valuable maritime intelligence, and Luc had been quite helpful in that regard. Although, he was completely unaware that the couple were operatives for the SSB and thought of them as nothing more than harmless tourists with more money than they needed. Because of this relationship, Kaha and Pam decided to come to Pescara to provision their boat and where they can have the *Mana*'s engine repaired.

During an unfortunate childhood accident, Luc lost his left eye when poked with a stick and wore an eye patch with the same jaunty demeanour as you'd expect from a pirate. Adding to the mystique, he claimed to have lost his eye in a dramatic barroom brawl. Few doubted that assertion as Luc was a belligerent drunk, and for a small man, quite adept with his fists. Indeed, anyone who talked despairingly about Napoléon Bonaparte or his beloved France found this out. Only those closest to him knew the real reason he wore the patch.

Despite his social shortcomings, Luc was a loyal and more–or–less trusted friend and a true French patriot. When temperate, and with Sylvia's help, he ran his ship's Chandlery business efficiently and profitably. Luc knew almost everyone when it came to the seafaring community, and other than the local bars, his warehouse was the focal centre for maritime gossip and rumours that provided a great source of intelligence.

"*Revenons a nos moutons,*" said Luc with a grin. He looked down at the glass he held, then emptied it with a single swallow and fixed his one good eye on Kaha.

Kaha turned to Pam in question.

"He said, let's return to the matter at hand."

"*Mon amie*, you've told me this unbelievable story, but you left out the part where you tell me why someone would want to blow up your boat?"

"I'm sorry, Luc. I'm unable to tell you that because I don't know."

"Leave him, Luc," said Sylvia. "If Kaha finds out, then he'll tell you."

Luc nodded despondently. "*Ces't la vie*, why is it all the best parts of a good tale can't be told?"

Everyone laughed, and Luc topped up their glasses.

"But the police can help, non?"

"Can I tell you a little secret," Kaha said.

Luc's eye opened wider. "If you must." He edged closer to Kaha.

"We do not want the police to know, I, uh, had a problem, a gambling debt, and uh, well, I paid back the money, and then they wanted more and told me it was interest, and I refused." Kaha shrugged.

"*Oui, oui*, do not inform the police, it is best to keep quiet about this," offered Luc with understanding. "But I have another question." Luc turned to Pam. "How was it you were able to drag that big *lourdaud* out of the water?

This time Pam turned to Kaha.

"Go ahead, you can tell him."

"I couldn't lift him from the water, he was too heavy, and at one point, he slipped from my hands and almost disappeared," said Pam. "I struggled, and then a saviour, a pair of arms, reached down and plucked him right out of the water and laid him on the deck."

"Just like that?" said Luc disbelievingly. "Who was this angel from God?"

"He was a big strong chap, we think he's a fisherman," volunteered Kaha.

"A Balkan, and he told us his name is Boris," added Pam.

"Boris Marković?" questioned Luc.

"Yes, that's him," Pam said.

Kaha looked towards Luc.

"He was here last night, he came to see me, and it was shortly after the explosion."

"Why would he come to see you?" Kaha asked curiously.

"I know Boris well. He always buys from me when he can't get bits and pieces he needs in Ragusa. But he never mentioned that he helped you, even when we talked about the explosion. He's a good man."

"I think so too, and he probably saved your life," said Pam giving Kaha a gentle poke in the ribs.

"He must have needed some items for his boat, is that why he came to see you?" Kaha asked, pumping for more information.

"*Non, non*, he came to ask me about his son, he said he's gone missing and even believes the boy's been kidnapped. He asked me to ask around and. er, to keep an eye open." Luc laughed at his joke.

Pam and Kaha didn't respond, they turned to each other, then back to Luc, who looked puzzled.

"What did I say?" Luc raised his hands, palms up.

"A boy, how old?" asked Pam raising her voice.

"Uh, twelve years old, I know the boy, he's been here many times. His name is Zoran. Why the interest, have you seen him?" Luc scooted to the edge of his chair and leaned forward.

"If it's the same lad, yes, we have seen him, and we even know where to look for him."

"Then we must tell Boris right away," Luc stood.

"Do you know where he is?" Kaha asked.

"*Oui*, but of course, in a bar not far from here."

"Listen, Luc, the men who have the boy are dangerous. They aremilitary men, Austrian's –"

"*Salauds*!" exclaimed Luc.

"Luc! That's enough," admonished Sylvia.

"We think they are dangerous men, but tell me why Austrians would kidnap the son of a Dalmation[10] fisherman?" Kaha asked.

Luc sat back down again. He shook his head, "This I do not know."

"I don't think it's a good idea if I go with you, and someone may recognise me and report that to the police. Could you bring him back here, where I can talk with him privately?"

Luc's one good eye moved alternately between Pam and Kaha. "*Oui,* I can do this," he replied slowly. But … there is more?"

"Luc, we need you to do something for us, and it is important." Kaha scooted closer to Luc.

With his curiosity piqued, Luc raised both eyebrows.

"We will give you a message and ask if you can deliver it to the English captain of the trawler that arrived this afternoon. Can you do this for us?"

"Tonight?"

"Business hours would be more believable to the *Carabiniere* who is at the dock."

"Does this have anything to do with the war?"

Kaha shrugged.

"I see." Luc looked thoughtful for a moment. "Then I will do this for you, for England, for France, eh." He raised his glass to toast. "*Vive La France!*"

10   Dalmatian – A person from Dalmatia. Ragusa was a part of the Kingdom of Dalmatia and ruled by the Austro-Hungarians until 1918 when it became known as Kingdom of Serbs, Croats and Slovenes.

"*Vive La France!*" they all repeated and drained their glasses.

"Now, I will find Boris and bring him here, please wait, *s'il vous plaît.*"

Pam and Sylvia talked quietly together, and Kaha stood at the open window watching the street below. The curtains tugged and flittered on its hanger as the wind continued to build in strength. The more he thought about it, the more convinced he was that the fisherman's missing son was somehow tied to the priest. He hoped Boris could provide some answers.

Luc had been gone for about thirty minutes when he heard footsteps climbing the outside stairs.

The surprise on Boris's face was unmistakable when he saw Kaha and Pam. "Our course cross again, do they not?" stated Boris.

Kaha could see Boris's look of worry. "They do," Kaha replied with a warm smile.

"Luc tells us your son is missing. Tell us about him, what does he look like?" asked Pam with some urgency and forgoing a greeting.

"You have seen him?" immediately, his expression brightened.

Stabswachtmeister Dieter Wollf rode back to Chieti in the company of the *Carabiniere* messenger without experiencing any difficulties. He entered the Teate hotel unseen by climbing over a wall and left his horse tethered to a rail outside. He knew the animal would be returned to its owner. It was easy to enter his room and retrieve his case as few people were about in the mid-afternoon heat. The tricky part was getting to the railway station, however, with patience, he took a circuitous route and eventually purchased a ticket without anyone recognising him.

He was tired, grumpy and sore when he stepped from the train in Pescara and immediately sought a ristorante where he could enjoy the first decent meal in days and rest for a while. At 8:00 p.m., an hour before the scheduled time to signal the RDF boat, Wollf paid his bill and walked in the darkness towards the breakwater wall at the entrance to the Pescara River as Major Richter ordered. He was in no hurry, and because he had time to spare, he couldn't resist the temptation and visited a waterfront bar to down a couple of beers before continuing.

Boris held his head in his hands.

"Why is Major Richter interested in Zoran?" asked Kaha.

Kaha was speaking privately with Boris, Luc and Sylvia were in the kitchen talking with Pam.

After a brief pause, Boris looked up. "I know not this major, but I think is because of Stevan," he finally said.

"Is he the priest?"

He nodded. "Father Stevan Belić."

"What would a priest have done to the Austrians that would have them send many men to Italy to look for him?"

Again, Boris remained silent as he wondered how much he should tell the Englishman. "I not sure, but, er, I have idea. I think he involved with Black Hand peoples who kill the prince and wife. The Austrians never catch him, and Stevan go to Italy as he plan. I take Stevan from Ragusa to Pescara in *Kralj Mora*."

"Is that your fishing boat?"

Boris nodded.

"I remember that night, we were moored not far from you, and I saw the priest leave your boat after *Capitaneria* di Porto Conti visited."

Boris nodded. "Yes, I remember this."

"Please, give me a minute to talk with my wife, Boris," Kaha asked. He called for Pam, and they stepped to the windows on the other side of the room.

"It all makes sense now," whispered Kaha. He looked over his shoulder and saw Luc and Boris talking.

"And we need to notify London of this too. Will they allow us to help him?" asked Pam.

Kaha shook his head, "No, I doubt it."

"What can we do, anything?"

"Nothing really, we can't do a thing, Pam," Kaha stated. He walked back to Boris and Luc.

"There is little that Pam and I can do to help you, Boris. We suggest that you go to the police in Chieti, explain what happened, and tell them the Austrians have your boy. They were staying at the Hotel Teate. Have the police speak to the proprietor, Angelo Romano, he knows where they went, it was somewhere in the country to the north."

Boris stood. "This is good news, now I know where to begin to look. I will do as you suggest. But now I must go to my men and arrange to go to Chieti. Thank you very much." Boris held out his hand to Kaha.

They shook hands. "Let me walk out with you." Kaha had a couple more questions he wanted to ask in private.

Boris thanked Luc and Sylvia, and then Kaha and Pam followed him outside and down the stairs. They stopped and talked on Lungaterno Cristoforo Colombo, the street that ran parallel to the Pescara River outside the main entrance to the Chandlery.

Boris looked up at the clouds that raced overhead. "I am pleased not to fish tonight, it will be day or two before the weather better."

Pam walked across the street to look at the boats noisily banging into their fenders and kept a lookout while Boris and Kaha spoke.

Kaha nodded. "Boris, this is important. Do you know the exact role the priest played in the assassination?"

"He not tell me, he said, er, better for me not to know these things."

"What about the trawler that's been loitering around here for the last few days or so, what do you know of it?"

"I know this boat is called *Trabant*, it is Austrian radio boat, not good." Boris gave Kaha a long hard look, understanding dawning on his face. "They blow boat up, they do this to you, yes?"

Pam spotted a solitary man carrying a case walking slowly along Lungaterno Cristoforo Colombo towards her, he would pass them by within half a minute. Even in the dark, the hulking form of the man looked familiar.

Kaha wasn't sure how to reply and was deciding how much to tell Boris when Pam quickly walked over.

"Kaha, it's him," she said urgently.

"Who?"

Boris looked puzzled.

"The big Austrian we saw near the Hotel Teate, the one who took Zoran from the smaller man."

Kaha and Boris turned to look towards the man about ten metres away. As he came closer, Kaha recognised the big shoulders, hair, and gait. Pam was right. He looked further up the street and didn't see Major Richter, his friends or the boy, the man was alone.

Kaha turned to Boris, but it was too late.

"*Wo ist* Zoran!" Boris screamed and began to run at the Austrian.

"Boris, noooo!" yelled Kaha.

Alerted, the Austrian stopped immediately, dropped his suitcase, reached into his pocket and smoothly pulled a pistol. The charging Croatian was almost upon him as he raised the gun.

Kaha saw the weapon and reacted instinctively. Time slowed, and training took over. He spun and pushed Pam to the ground and reached behind his back for his pistol.

Boris was almost upon the Austrian when the big man hurriedly pulled the trigger

For a large man, the Croatian fisherman was fast. Seeing the pistol being levelled at him, he dove for the ground a split second before the sound of a gunshot filled the night.

Flame spat from the barrel of the Austrian's handgun, and Boris grunted. He'd been hit but still managed to keep his momentum going and scrambled along the ground, trying to avoid being shot a second time. The Austrian stepped backwards and swung his arm round to take another sighting on the rapidly moving target trying to evade him.

Kaha yelled again, "No!"

A dog began barking nearby as the Austrian turned to Kaha, who was raising his weapon. Seeing the threat, he dropped to a knee and, with both hands, began to swing his pistol away from the fisherman and target the new danger.

Kaha stood side-on, with his arm horizontal and fully extended, aiming at the Austrian. He waited for a heartbeat, hoping he didn't have to shoot.

Again, the sound of a gunshot filled the night and drifted away in the wind. More dogs began barking, and people yelled in question from nearby homes. Both men still stood. Boris stopped scrambling on the ground, and Pam watched in wide-eyed, open-mouthed fear. Above the Chandlery, the curtains opened, and Luc and Sylvia stood in the window looking down. The boats tied to the dock in the Pescara River still banged tirelessly against their fenders.

It seemed like an eternity for the Austrian to slowly topple backwards.

Kaha turned to Pam, she was rising from the ground where he'd pushed her. Seeing she was unhurt, he turned his attention to the

Austrian and jogged over. He was unmoving, the bullet had entered his chest, and his brain, unable to receive blood from his shredded heart, ceased to function. Even as Kaha bent down, he saw the lifeless eyes staring up at nothing. He was dead. Kaha quickly went through his pockets, searching for papers or documents.

Boris slowly rose to his feet.

"How badly are you hurt?" asked Kaha as he pocketed the Austrian's pistol and wallet.

"My shoulder, not bad, but painful," grimaced Boris.

"Pam, get Luc, quickly."

She didn't need to, Luc was still at the window staring down at them, then rushed away to come down to the street.

Pam tended to Boris and led him away as Kaha retrieved the Austrian's suitcase when Luc appeared.

"*Mon Dieu*, what has happened here?"

"He pulled a gun and was going to kill Boris," stated Kaha as he bent down to retrieve all the shell casings.

"And you have a gun?" Luc looked at Kaha for a heartbeat or two. "We need to get rid of the body before *Carabinieri* arrive." He looked around. "Quick, let's throw him in the river."

"The river?" questioned Kaha.

"Where else?" shrugged the Frenchman.

Kaha picked up one of the Austrian's arms, and Luc grabbed the other. Too heavy to carry, they dragged him to the dock only a few metres away and unceremoniously threw him into the Fiume Pescara.

"Quickly, we must go, hurry," Luc urged.

Already they could hear voices as people approached.

Kaha and Luc peered anxiously from above and watched as a *Carabiniere* walked past the Chandlery, searching for the source and cause of the two gunshots. In the dark and without any physical evidence, it was difficult to ascertain where the shooting took place.

Pam and Silvia were tending to Boris. He'd been lucky, the bullet had only grazed his shoulder but left a painful reminder of his rash and impetuous decision to charge the Austrian.

"Perhaps tonight wouldn't be a good time to deliver your note," stated Luc wryly as he watched the policeman search the area.

CHAPTER TWENTY

Less than three–hundred metres from where Kaha and Luc peered out the window, Lieutenant Burton Sanders, RNR, Captain of HMT, *Bangor Castle,* stood on the bridge of his thirty-eight-metre auxiliary trawler and watched two of his men climb down a rope ladder secured to the outboard side of his ship and slide into the choppy water inside the marina.

Everyone heard the earlier unexplained gunfire, and since then, the *Carabinieri* tasked to maintain a close watch on the small British warship became uneasy and attentive, this didn't bode well for Captain Sanders and the successful completion of his unusual mission. In response, he instructed Able Seaman Derek Taylor, the only crewman who spoke passable Italian, to engage the young *Carabiniere* in idle chatter and keep him distracted.

Earlier, Captain Sanders received a coded message that detailed where to find the experimental radio and how to access and remove it from its secure compartment inside the *Mana*. Of importance were any codebooks that hadn't been destroyed, and all the small, fragile glass tubes called valves, that survived the blast.

The full extent of the damage was unknown, and there had been no way to determine if the radio existed in one piece or if it had been totally destroyed. The message had been succinct – in no way was the experimental De Forrest radio or any of its components to fall into the hands of the Italians.

Soon after they arrived in Pescara, Captain Sanders observed men in boats investigating the cause of the explosion. But as yet, no attempt had been made to begin salvage, although he expected that would change very soon. According to the *Carabiniere* on the dock, the bodies of the yacht's owners had not been recovered, and various marine experts believed they had perished inside. Sanders spared a thought for his men and what they would encounter when they submersed into what was left of the yacht.

As luck would have it, the changing weather worked in their favour and masked any sounds his men made while they attempted to remove the radio from the partially submerged yacht. Usually, the water inside the protected marina was glassy and smooth, but tonight the wind had whipped the tranquil water into a small chop favouring the two Royal Navy seamen as they cautiously swam the short twenty metres to the wreck towing a small inflatable raft they would put the radio in.

Captain Sanders raised his arm and looked at his wristwatch, the luminous hands indicated his men had already been gone for thirty minutes.

Sanders sighed, then stepped to the starboard side of the bridge and risked a quick look down at Able Seaman Taylor. Judging from the laughter, the seaman shared some off-colour banter with the Italian. He moved away and out of sight from the dock and glanced briefly up at the evening sky. Clouds still obscured the moon, and when he looked towards the wreck, there was nothing to see. So far, so good. With apprehension, he looked at his watch again.

Rather than go below to his small cabin and wait, Captain Sanders remained on the bridge and paced backwards and forwards, anxiously waiting for his men to return. Occasionally he heard a splash and wondered if the noise was generated by his men or just the natural disturbance on the water caused by the wind.

"Any word?"

The voice startled Sanders. He'd been so focused on his men he failed to hear the quiet approach of Sub–Lieutenant, RNR, Glen Hornby as he climbed the ladder to the bridge.

"A bit jumpy are we?" added Hornby, patting his commanding officer on the back.

"I hate this, we're not trained or equipped for these types of missions, Glen."

Sub–Lieutenant Hornby bent down and lit a cigarette in the shelter of the coaming. Once lit, he straightened and turned outwards towards the ocean. Captain Sanders joined him; neither man spoke.

Gusts of wind rattled around the trawler's superstructure and funnel, and from somewhere unseen, an intermittent banging could be heard. On hearing the sound, Captain Sanders looked to the source, but all he saw was blackness and a sprinkling of lights.

"How long have they been gone?" asked Hornby, breaking the silence.

Sanders raised his wrist. "Almost an hour. They should have returned by now."

"I wouldn't worry yet, Bull's a good man, they'll be fine."

Both officers looked towards the *Mana,* willing their men to appear. Then unexpectedly, from the darkness, brief glimpses of white appeared. Hornby nudged his captain. "Do you see?"

Both officers began to see the detail of two men swimming sidestroke returning to the trawler.

"I'm going below, Glen, have them report to me in my cabin soon as they're dry and warm."

"Aye, aye, cap'n," replied Hornby flicking his cigarette overboard and following Sanders down the ladder.

"Come!" yelled Captain Sanders.

The door opened, and two men entered his sparse quarters.

Each man was wrapped in a blanket and grasped a steaming mug of Her Majesty's Royal Navy issued coffee, spiced with rum – their teeth chattered.

Sanders stood from the berth he sat on and indicated both men sit.

"Is bloody cold, sir, we wanted to stay longer, like, but bugger me, after an hour in the water, me gonads have shrunk," offered Chief Petty Officer Gerald 'Bull' Buller.

"At least you're both back safely," smiled Sanders. "What did you find?"

Able Seaman Kitchen held onto his mug with both hands and listened.

"We found the bloody thing, cap'n. Is still there, or most of it is. But one of the ribs of the yacht was torn away and now lays across the front of the radio. Can't see a bloody thing, is all by feel. We moved a bunch of planks out of the way, but we can't move the bloody rib. We'll need a saw to cut through the damn thing before we can pull the radio out."

Sanders scratched his chin. "How difficult will that be?"

"The bloody ribs are white oak, sir, hard as nails."

Sanders nodded. "Did you find any remains, uh, body parts?"

"Nope." Bull turned to his shipmate. "Pete, did you see anything?"

AB. Kitchen looked up from his mug. "No, nuffin."

"How long will it take to cut through the wood and remove the radio?"

"Well, cap'n, I figure about … oh, another hour or so. But the water's cold, when we warm-up, we'll go back, give it another go," replied Bull dutifully.

"No, not tonight, you won't, look at the both of you. We'll have to wait until tomorrow night. Get some kip, and hopefully, this wind will keep up until then. Good Job, Bull, Pete." Sanders nodded in gratitude.

Petty Office Buller and Able Seaman Kitchen stood to leave.

"Oh, one more thing, did you find those valves or codebooks?"

"Aye, think so, we found those valves but couldn't get to them all until the radio has been removed. Couldn't see anything that looked like a codebook cap'n."

"Very well. Good night gentlemen."

Captain Sanders stepped to the porthole and looked out into the darkness as the two sailors left the cabin.

With the utmost care, Enzo and *Signora* Milani assisted Father Stevan into the canvas-covered wagon and placed him on blankets and pillows. Zoran accompanied them along with the Turk, Mr Yavuz, who sat sullenly and kept a watchful eye on them all.

Pleased to be released, Enzo was worried about what the major would do with the *Signora* when he no longer had use for her. His protests to release her fell on deaf ears. As he watched the Austrian's depart, he considered what to do.

Major Richter sat up front, beside Johan Bekker, who was given the duty to drive the wagon. A curious small group of villagers watched dispassionately as the wagon slowly creaked away. They had no idea what took place in Enzo's home during the last twenty-four hours, and suspecting something amiss and not wishing to become involved, prudently kept away. Gunter Meyer took the horse and scouted ahead of the group once they departed the small village.

Major Maximillian Richter timed his departure from Enzo's home perfectly, and they arrived in the outskirts of Chieti just after nightfall. As hoped, no one paid them any attention.

The wagon rumbled to a stop outside the Hotel Teate, and Major Richter gave strict orders no one must leave the wagon until he returned. After brushing the dust from his clothes, he entered the hotel and informed Signore Romano he wished to checkout and pay the bill.

Angelo Romano was disappointed to see his guests check-out but nonetheless was happy to receive payment. After exchanging money and pleasantries, he watched his guest walk towards his room to collect his things. He was surprised to see the guest come striding down the hallway carrying his suitcase and looking very unhappy.

"Who was in my room?" snarled Major Richter. "Someone entered the room while I was absent, who was it?"

Signore Romano looked on in puzzlement. He knew it wasn't his mother–in–law, it couldn't be her, he thought as the unhappy guest glared at him. "*Signore*, I am not aware that anyone entered your room. Could you be mistaken, was there theft?"

Richter held the proprietor's gaze. He couldn't tell the proprietor that *Evidenzebureau* files were stolen. "Nothing was taken. Did you see anyone acting suspicious, other guests perhaps? Someone came into the room, I want to know who?"

Relieved nothing had been stolen, Angelo Romano shrugged. "As I told you *Signore*, this is a good hotel, with the finest reputation … I can't think of any reason –"

"Enough!" Richter snapped, losing patience. There was nothing he could do, although throttling the little toad was an option he considered. In frustration, he shook his head and strode outside to the waiting wagon and allowed the others to retrieve their belongings while he stewed. The loss of the files was serious and would require some explanation.

Chaperoned by the Turk and with instructions to hurry, *Signora* Milani was allowed to go inside and freshen up.

The plan was to leave Chieti once they retrieved their belongings from the hotel and begin the road journey to Pescara. However, Major Richter knew they wouldn't make it there that night. Instead, he had Gunter search on the road ahead for somewhere they could eat and sleep, even the horses needed a rest. He was only too pleased to be gone from this backwater of civilisation and return to the culture and sophistication of Wien. His mood worsened.

While he waited for his men and the *Signora* to return, Richter recalled the sighting of a single man following him in Pescara a few days ago. Unfortunately, they hadn't been able to identify who it was, and the man cleverly slipped away. Richter had a fleeting thought and wondered if the explosion in Pescara that the *Carabiniere* told him about was related to the man who followed him and his missing files. He removed his spectacles and cleaned the lenses carefully on his handkerchief. *No, the theft was not a coincidence,* he thought.

He wasn't overly concerned and knew it wouldn't affect his departure from Italy, he'd planned meticulously to ensure that every contingency was covered. The woman and the priest would be tossed overboard once he had extracted the information he sought, and the boy would also conveniently disappear once he'd served his usefulness. For now, the boy offered them protection.

The *Signora* and the Turk returned carrying his travelling valise, and after Bekker and Meyer retrieved their belongings, the small group departed Chieti.

For Father Steven, the journey to Chieti was painful. Luckily, he had slept for most of it. At one time, he needed to relieve himself, and after much pleading, the major eventually conceded, only after the Turk said he needed to go as well. It took careful handling to help him down from the wagon, and eventually, in some privacy, felt relief. He considered escaping but realised it was pointless. Resigned to his fate and barely able to walk, he gingerly hobbled back where he was assisted back into the wagon, and their trek continued. He knew with certainty that death awaited him, and the fact that Natalina was with them meant her future looked bleak as well. He hoped Boris would find them soon.

Capitano Luigi Gallo leaned back in his chair, placed his hands together in a steeple beneath his nose, and contemplated what he learned. The two visitors in his office, Enzo and the old wagon driver, Andrea Mussolini, looked at him with some distress. After a moment's thought, he removed his hands and placed them on top of a pile of paperwork on his cluttered desk and leaned forward. "The big man, Enzo, do you have a name for him?"

Enzo looked uncertain and shook his head. "I don't speak the language, and they spoke German the entire time unless they talked directly to us. But at one time, I thought I heard the big man referred to as Lupo."

"Lupo, as in Wolf?"

Enzo nodded.

Luigi stroked his full moustache.

"What will you do about those horrible men who have the boy, *Signora* Milani and the Father?" asked the old man.

"Andrea, this is a problem for me. The *Carabinieri* will protect the Austrians and undoubtedly turn a blind eye to anything they've done –"

"But you are the Chief of Police, you have a duty," appealed Enzo.

Capitano Gallo scratched the nape of his neck. "I wish it were that easy, if I knew the *Carabinieri* would not involve themselves in this matter, then that would change everything. But..." He sighed loudly, "They will interfere, of that, you can be assured."

The three men sat in silence. Police Chief Gallo was silently fuming the *carabinieri* had double-crossed him, the slimy toad Da Camino had sent someone to warn the Austrians of his plans, and now the Austrians had fled Chieti and taken *Signora* Milani. The explosion in Pescara was a distraction he didn't need.

"Then I will go. If you can't do anything, then I will find a way to rescue the *Signora* myself," said Enzo rising from the chair.

"No, Enzo, this is not wise," cautioned Andrea looking up at the younger man. He reached up and grasped his wrist.

"Enzo, Enzo, sit down. I'm trying to think of a solution to this," insisted Gallo.

Enzo ignored the request and remained standing as he waited.

"Luigi, I have known you for many years, you are a clever man," began Andrea, "I am sure there is a way for you to convince the *Carabinieri* there are more important things they should be doing while you use your talents to bring back *Signora* Milani, and perhaps even the priest and boy."

Gallo frowned and looked down at the stack of paperwork on his desk. The top corner of a document bearing the seal of the *Carabinieri* was visible. He slid the paper from the pile and glowered at it. He remembered now, this was a document written by *Maggiore* Da Camino outlining the details of the fugitive and criminal Giuseppe Canolo from Calabria. The man was involved in murder, extortion, blackmail, theft, and more. Gallo scanned the remainder of the document and saw the entire list of crimes he was accused of. It stated Canolo collaborated with a gang they called

Ndrangheta, and they wanted to expand their area of criminal activity northwards. Gallo slowly shook his head. Signore Canolo was indeed an evil man and one the *Carabinieri,* specifically, *Maggiore* Da Camino wanted badly – very badly. Gallo didn't move and stared blankly at the document as an idea began to form.

Enzo saw the change in expression on the chief's face and slowly sat.

"Enrico!" bellowed *Capitano* Luigi Gallo.

CHAPTER TWENTY-ONE

The line between ocean and sky was almost indistinguishable. Wind-blown wave–tops broke free from the ocean's grey and for a fleeting second reached upwards, vainly hoping to touch the bleakness of the sky above before being blown horizontal and dissolving into spray and then nothing. Of the same dull hue, neither the sky nor ocean revealed a beginning or end, it was a drab fresco – an unfinished painting waiting for only detail. Created by a cycle of atmospherics and driven by a waning weather front, the wind still blew with undeterred ferocity, but each passing hour saw its energy slowly dissipate.

Closer to shore, at the entrance to the Pescara River, where fresh water and waste drained endlessly into the welcoming embrace of the sea, flotsam and effluent met at its confluence. Repelled by the tide and encouraged by the outfall, items of past use bobbled resiliently, they tumbled and turned and collected in common ground, banging and scraping like restless companions ensnared, neither entirely in sea or river – in no–man's land.

Undaunted by the weather, an early morning pedestrian saw the object as he walked along the seawall that divided the river from the marina. Caught in accumulated debris, he almost passed it by until it rolled over, and for a fleeting moment, they made eye contact. In horror, the man stared unbelievingly at it. Because it moved, he assumed it was still alive and unable to climb down to help, he ran off with some urgency to find help. The authorities, namely Pescara's Polizia Locale and the *Carabinieri,* arrived soon after. With little enthusiasm and some distaste, they stood on the seawall and looked at the bobbing and bloated corpse of *Stabswachtmeister* Dieter Wollf.

A short distance up the street, above the warehouse with the bold sign that said, 'Chandlery', Luc Lemaire stared curiously out the window and watched the proceedings.

"They found the body of that Austrian pig," he said.

Kaha walked towards the window, paused and watched as someone with a long boat hook snared the twisting corpse and pulled it towards dry land. A small group of men gathered and stood ready to assist the police in carrying the body onto a waiting dray. With nothing better to do, a few spectators gathered and watched dispassionately, sharing fanciful theories and hypotheses on the cause of death.

In addition to Pam and Kaha, Sylvia insisted that Boris spend the night with them. His crewmen, who'd been scattered about various bars, took care of themselves, while at least one probably spent a restless night aboard the boat.

The resilient Croatian fisherman joined the others at the window with his dressing changed and seemingly no worse for wear from his wound. "Are we in danger?"

"*Non, non*, without a witness, the *Carabinieri* have nothing," Luc assured him confidently.

"Perhaps now might be a good time to pass my message on to the English ship," advised Kaha.

"After breakfast!" shouted Sylvia from the kitchen. "Come and sit down!"

"*Ma chérie,* she has spoken," shrugged Luc with a grin.

Luc left the Chandlery and ambled down Lungaterno Cristoforo

Colombo to the mouth of the Fiume Pescara, where the body was discovered. There wasn't much to see, the authorities removed the corpse and transported it away, only a lone policeman remained behind interviewing locals. Luc nodded in greeting and walked past, then turned right, which would take him to the docks towards the small Royal Navy warship.

As expected, Luc wasn't challenged by the *Carabiniere* and gave him a friendly wave as he walked up to the HMT *Bangor Castle* and approached the English sailor on watch duty. As only a Frenchman can, and with heartfelt emotion, he sympathised with the crew for the unfortunate mechanical breakdown that brought their fine vessel into Pescara. The *Carabiniere* lost interest and turned away. With a wink and without attracting attention, Luc dropped the sealed envelope into the sailor's hand, quietly informing him that the message was for the captain. He offered to wait for a response. As requested, the sailor promptly disappeared into the ship and handed the message to the captain.

Written by Pam, the sealed written message was simple.

> *To the Master of the Bangor Castle,*
>
> *My wife and I were the owners of the yacht, Mana, which was destroyed a few nights ago in the Pescara Marina and we were most fortunate not to sustain any serious injuries.*
>
> *We have some matters of utmost importance we wish to discuss with you, however, in the interests of our ongoing wellbeing and safety, we remain in the trusted care of the gentleman who delivered this letter, Monsieur Luc Lemaire.*
>
> *As the proprietor of the local Chandlery, it would be appropriate for you to visit Monsieur Lemaire and his fine establishment, and we anticipate, make your acquaintance at your soonest.*

Yours, sincerely,
Master and Mistress, Kaha and Pamela Peterson.

Luc was astounded when only moments later, Captain Sanders emerged. He politely introduced himself and asked to visit the Chandlery immediately. As protocol demanded, Sanders informed the *Carabiniere* of his destination, and the two men walked up the gangway.

Boris was in search of his crewmen. Against all the advice, he insisted on going to Chieti on the mid-afternoon train to locate and retrieve his son. Once preparations were made, he promised to return to the Chandlery before they departed.

Luc allowed Kaha and Pam the courtesy of speaking with Captain Sanders in the privacy of their upstairs apartment while he and Sylvia went downstairs to begin their day.

Kaha appraised the naval reserve officer as he entered Luc's home. Not a young man, he estimated he was in his early fifties. The captain had a bookish quality with an intelligent, open face. Kaha liked the man immediately and extended his hand.

"Captain, I'm Kaha Peterson, and this is my wife, Pamela."

Lieutenant Burton Sanders removed his cover, slipped it under his left arm and took a step forward and clasped Kaha's outstretched hand and smiled warmly, then turned and politely shook Pam's hand, nodding his head in greeting. "Mr Peterson, Mrs Peterson, is a pleasure to make your acquaintance. I'm Lieutenant Burton Sanders, commanding officer of Her Majesty's Auxiliary Trawler, *Bangor Castle.* Uh, how may I assist you?"

They each took a seat in the living room. Once comfortable,

Captain Sanders looked at his hosts with open curiosity and some trepidation. *Reports stated the owners of the luxury yacht had perished, if so, who were these people – imposters, or were the bulletins unsubstantiated?*

Kaha leaned forward with his elbows on his thighs. "Please, forgive the unusual request to meet with you, Captain, I understand a mechanical breakdown forced you to enter Pescara."

The lieutenant didn't answer immediately and chewed his bottom lip as he considered his response. "Yes, my engineer tells me it's a minor repair that requires a part to be machined. I expect we'll be on our way again soon."

Kaha looked thoughtful. "You are presently moored only twenty yards or so from what was once our beautiful boat."

"Yes, your letter stated that. If I may ask, what er, happened?"

After a moment's pause, Kaha turned and gave Pam a look. She nodded imperceptibly.

"Are you aware of who we are, who we work for, Captain?"

Captain Sanders inclined his head, then looked up and made eye contact with Kaha. "Perhaps you should identify yourselves." He held Kaha's gaze.

"We are Anchor and Chain," answered Kaha quietly.

Sanders immediately exhaled, it was a long, drawn-out breath. He shook his head. "You've no idea the pressure we've been under. Apparently, you're both supposed to be dead. This is why we're here. We were given orders to make best speed for Pescara."

"What?" exclaimed Kaha.

"Yes, we uh, feigned a breakdown. Our mission is to remove *Mana*'s radio and report on your status. London apparently believes you were both killed in the explosion and feared your hidden radio would be discovered and fall into Italian hands. But what in dear, God, happened?" Sanders leaned forward.

Pam stepped over and stood behind Kaha, she placed a hand on his shoulder.

"There's an Austrian RDF trawler, she's – "

"I've seen the blasted boat, she came sniffing around us when we first approached Pescara," interrupted Sanders. "They couldn't do anything, of course, because this is a neutral country, and we were both in Italian waters. But yes, I know the boat all too well."

"Good, she's been loitering around here for the last week or so. We think they detected a transmission from us and sent a crew ashore to wire the *Mana* with explosives while we were having dinner ashore. We'd found signs someone had been aboard the boat... and when I saw the detonator cord... we just ran for it."

"Bloody lucky, I'd say," responded Captain Sanders with a sympathetic shake of his head. He reached into his pocket for his pipe and tobacco pouch and began the therapeutic task of filling the bowl.

"We were hoping you could radio London for us, give them a status update and wait for an answer," Pam added.

Sanders tamped the tobacco with his thumb, placed the pipe in his mouth, and returned the pouch to his pocket. "Well, it seems I can be of some assistance to you. My orders are quite clear..." He fumbled for a box of matches, extracted a match and lit it. He began sucking on the pipe, drawing the flame down into the packed bowl. After a few puffs, he threw the match into an ashtray and looked to Pam and Kaha. "In the unlikely event you'd survived, we were to immediately extract you – er, once we'd recovered the radio."

"You came here to rescue us?" asked Pam.

Sanders smiled.

"If you haven't located the radio yet? I can help."

Sanders laughed, sat back in the chair and crossed his legs. "We found the darn thing. But during the explosion, one of the ribs dislodged and now lays across the front of the radio, making it impossible to remove until we can cut through it."

"Those ribs are white oak, bloody hard wood."

Sanders grimaced. "So I'm told."

"How did you manage to get over to her without being seen?" asked Kaha.

"Last night, sent two chaps who swam across, poor fellows, froze their bollocks off."

Pam raised her eyebrows.

"Oh, I, er, apologise, Mrs Peterson."

Kaha smiled. "She's heard worse from me, Captain."

Sanders face was obscured in a cloud of smoke. "We intend to go back tonight, cut through the rib with a saw, take the radio –"

"You may want to take those valve thingys and our cypher book," Pam suggested.

"Yes, we've located the valves, but again, we can't get to them until the radio is out of its hidey-hole."

"And then you'll leave?"

"I think we'll shove off an hour or so before the sun comes up. We'd rather not make it obvious we're leaving. And we'll need to find a way to get you both aboard without the policemen on the dock seeing you."

"Why don't we grab a dinghy and row out towards the marina entrance just before you leave. You can pick us up on your way out, it will be dark, and no one will see." Kaha looked back and up at Pam. "Are you comfortable with that, honey?"

"Yes, but I still need to compose a message for London, and I don't have a cypher book." Pam turned to Captain Sanders for help.

Another cloud of smoke enveloped the captain. "We are using complex Trench cyphers, Mrs Peterson," replied the captain in a voice barely above a whisper.

"That's what we use too."

"Very well, when I return, I will have a message relayed to London and inform them we have located Anchor and Chain. I suggest you send your message once you are secure aboard the *Bangor Castle*."

"How will we know you were successful in retrieving the radio and are ready to depart?" asked Kaha.

"Yes, good point." Captain Sanders quickly gave the matter some thought. "We'll turn our navigation lights on, and I think that should work nicely."

"I guess we'll be going back to England, Pam," said Kaha as he reached up and placed a hand on hers.

"And I should be getting back to my boat," said Captain Sanders rising to his feet.

"Please, take these with you," offered Pam, handing him a large bag of freshly baked pastries. "I'm sure your crew will enjoy them."

Gunter Meyer watched the back of a British naval officer as he entered the marina towards the small warship tied to the end of the dock. He didn't know much about warships, but he knew enough to know Major Richter would be interested in the untimely appearance of an English naval vessel.

He reigned his horse to a stop, swung a leg over the saddle and dismounted awkwardly. It had been many years since he'd ridden a horse for any length of time, and his body hadn't responded well. With his feet firmly on the ground, he took a deep breath, ran his fingers through his tousled hair and looked outwards, past the sea wall and beyond to the bleakness of the ocean. Major Richter sent him ahead to meet *Stabswachtmeister* Wollf to reconnoitre and hopefully catch sight of the RDF trawler *Trabant*. The visibility was poor, and he couldn't see much, although the ship was scheduled to swing by closer to the Pescara coast around midday, so he wasn't overly concerned.

There was plenty of activity along Lungaterno Cristoforo Colombo. Fishing Boats that foolishly braved the weather and ventured out in the early morning had already returned with empty holds. Men stood in small groups complaining, some gesticulated wildly, pointing to things unseen, others laughed or nodded in agreement. Gunter heard snippets of conversations here and there and learned a body was discovered earlier this morning, murdered, if he heard correctly. In irony, he shook his head solemnly – people weren't even safe in a small town such as this. What's the world coming to, he mused?

He imagined his report to *Herr* Richter, – *Major, other than the weather, a small warship and a murder, everything is normal in Pescara.*

Gunter attracted no unwanted attention other than two dogs who trotted over to inspect him briefly. Finding nothing of interest and wary of the four powerful horse's legs, they wisely moved on.

Major Richter wasn't far behind, perhaps fifteen minutes or so. While the major required him to wait for his arrival, Gunter decided he should ride back and warn the major of the English warship. Better to be safe than sorry.

With no sign of the *Stabswachtmeister*, Gunter placed a foot in the stirrup, grabbed the mane with his left hand, and bounced three times, hoisting himself onto the saddle and winced as his chaffed calves rubbed against the stirrup leathers. He dug his heels into the horse ribs, squeezed, and looked one last time over his shoulder and out to sea, again he saw nothing. He faced forward and rode up Lungaterno Cristoforo Colombo towards Major Richter and the wagon.

When Johan Bekker signalled that he saw Gunter approaching on horseback, Major Richter, fearing the worst, ordered the wagon to a stop. He glanced rearward and saw the *Signora*, she looked attentive and equally curious while her charge, Father Stevan, slept. Zoran sat quietly, and even though *Signora* Milani did her best to communicate to the boy, he'd been unresponsive and surly.

The Turk, Mr Yavuz hardly spoke, and looked at the *Signora* frequently from beneath hooded eyes, he made her feel nervous and self-conscious.

Major Richter looked in question as Gunter Meyer approached and stopped beside the wagon.

"There's a small English warship in the Pescara marina, *Herr* Major! It is moored to a dock."

Richter wasn't in the best of moods, he held back a snide remark and gave himself time to think. He removed his spectacles and again obsessively cleaned them with his handkerchief. "Have you seen the *Trabant,* and where is *Stabswachtmeister* Wollf?" he finally asked, unable to conceal the edge to his voice.

Gunter shook his head, "I have not seen him, *Herr* Major, or the ship, the weather makes it difficult to see far."

Richter stared into the distance as he considered the information.

Johann Bekker began combing his hair.

"What type of ship is this English warship you speak of?" Richter snapped, turning to face Gunter.

"Is a ship," Gunter shrugged, "not a large one."

Richter fixed Gunter with an icy glare. "I want details!" he barked.

At the sound of the Major's raised voice, Belić stirred and groaned.

"Go back and wait for me at the dock, signal the *Trabant* at midday when you see her and brief me on this English ship when we arrive, and find Wollf; this is what I pay you for!"

Gunter swallowed. "Yes, *Herr* Major." He yanked the reins savagely and kicked hard into the horse's ribs. With its eyes wide in fright, the horse leapt forwards and galloped dangerously down the road back towards the Pescara marina.

Major Richter removed his hat and wiped his brow with his handkerchief He was becoming increasingly alarmed and concerned. This mission should have been straightforward, and again when he'd placed his trust and faith in others to do their job, they failed. And where was *Stabswachtmeister* Wollf and the *Carabinieri*? That fool of a major promised a *Carabinieri* escort through Pescara, and now as they approached the small coastal town, they were nowhere to be seen.

He gave orders to continue towards Pescara.

What Richter didn't know was that Major Da Camino had far more important things to do and was currently sitting in his office awaiting news of the capture of Giuseppe Canolo, the fugitive criminal from Calabria.

An informant unexpectedly came forward and reported seeing Canolo, along with other iniquitous associates in the village of Sulmona. Apprehending Canolo would certainly advance Da Camino's career – this was an opportunity too good to miss. He dispatched all available men to head south and seize the villain with some urgency.

The thought of aiding the Austrians completely slipped his mind.

Increasingly, Major Richter was convinced other forces were

involved – but who? His sixth sense warned him that he'd missed something and more would go wrong. As the wagon continued its painfully slow journey through the outskirts of Pescara, Richter began to systematically analyse his movements in Italy from the day he first stepped aboard the overnight ferry from Ragusa – step by step.

He recalled the lone man that overtly stared at him aboard the ship. Was it more than a just physical attraction? As quickly as the thought entered his mind, he discarded the idea. The man had no finesse and was too overt. *Obviously, a homosexual.*

The Evidenzbureau trained him thoroughly in the art of tradecraft, and one prime component was observation. He learned to pay attention to his surroundings and discern innocent behaviour from clandestine or covert actions. Again, his mind went over each miniscule detail the morning after the ship docked. He remembered the couple at the *ristorante*. He saw the woman look at him with more than insouciant interest. When he casually turned to look back at her, she diverted her eyes and faced her husband. To some women he was a handsome man, so in itself, largely a relatively harmless gesture.

Then when he walked to the railway station, that idiot thug he'd hired, who'd been trailing from a discrete distance, identified someone following him. Whomever it was, cleverly managed to evade him. Why was he under surveillance, and by whom? French, Russian, even the English? The thought preyed on his mind since, but he had no answers.

The train journey was uneventful, and then once in that horrible town, Chieti, there was nothing suspicious or alarming until the discovery of his missing files – *or was there*? He'd been taught not to ignore coincidences. If he saw a face in a crowd, then later saw the same face again, he must assume the worst and perceive that person as a credible threat. Lives depended on keen observation and being attentive to the surroundings. Major Richter nodded, *of course, the woman*, he realised.

She'd been in the hotel lobby when they departed the hotel. It was the same woman who looked at him in Pescara when he first arrived, and he could picture her face with ease. The Major shifted in his seat as he contemplated this new realisation. He could only assume that if the woman was an agent, then the man she was with was also an agent. It was them, they had stayed the same hotel, and with ample opportunity, he knew with certainty – stolen his files. Richter closed his hand into a fist and hammered down on the wooden seat beside him. *I've been so foolish*, he chided himself.

Johan Bekker reacted to the unexpected anger and turned to his superior. Richter ignored him, and so he shrugged and continued to drive the wagon as they wound through the streets of Pescara. A few automobiles were about, children played, and people were going about their business, no one spared the covered wagon a second glance.

The train departing Pescara was scheduled to leave mid-afternoon, and rather than allow his men to remain idle, Boris organised them to perform routine maintenance on the boat. There were nets to repair, the tiller had excessive play and needed disassembling to fix it properly, and everyone was busy and distracted, which Boris wanted. With everyone gainfully occupied, he headed back to the Chandlery to speak with the Englishman and his wife to learn more about what they knew about the people who had Zoran.

Once again on Lungaterno Cristoforo Colombo, Boris paused and instinctively looked up at the sky to gauge the weather. It was unusual, although not unheard of, to have the bora winds blow across the Adriatic at this time of year. The weather front finally passed, and even though the wind was still potent, he knew that things would begin to return to normal within the next twenty–four hours.

He noticed a man standing beside a horse near the seawall looking keenly out to sea. Purely in reflex, Boris followed the man's gaze. Like a ghost from the greyness, the Austrian RDF trawler appeared.

Standing about ten metres behind the man and his horse, Boris was puzzled when the man began to walk closer to the seawall, and then to his consternation, waved at the ship. More surprising was the response of the trawler when it flashed a signal lamp - twice.

Boris began to walk away from the man and turned to look back every now and then. The trawler appeared to have altered course and was now heading parallel to the beach and towards the marina entrance. He found the behaviour of the trawler odd and unexplained, and *why was the man signalling the Austrian ship*, he wondered as he scratched his chin through his thick beard?

Feeling the presence of someone watching him, Boris looked upwards at the Chandlery and saw the Englishwoman at the window, she gave a small smile and waved. Despite his worry and anxiousness, he smiled back, they were good people.

Kaha met Boris at the door and welcomed him inside Luc's home. Pam greeted him warmly and returned to the window as the two men sat on a settee facing each other.

"You look worried, Boris. Out on the street before, I felt your sadness," said Pam from across the room.

"I will be much happy to have Zoran back. Yes, I am worry for him, he is but a boy, what does he know of bad men. He is too young to worry about these things."

"We'll do what we can, Boris," added Kaha.

Boris's lips compressed, and he looked down.

Kaha knew it must be difficult for him and could see he struggled to control his emotions.

"That Austrian radio ship is back," Boris stated, wisely changing the subject.

Kaha's eyes opened wide in surprise. "Really, what the dickens are they still doing hanging around?"

Boris turned towards Pam. "Is man with horse still there?"

"There's a man with a horse walking towards the marina, is that the man you mean?"

Boris nodded. "He signal trawler, and they reply with light."

"He did what " Kaha shot to his feet and strode to the window. "When did this happen?"

"Just as I walk here, two minute ago."

Kaha looked out the window towards the ocean. From his elevated position, he could easily see the trawler through the haze as it motored along the coastline, and the man and horse were too far away to discern details.

"Will they enter the marina?" asked Pam.

"What do you think, Boris?" said Kaha.

Boris shook his head. "No, he not come in marina."

Sylvia appeared from the rear of the apartment. "Are you coming, Pam?"

"Yes." Pam walked to Kaha and kissed him on the cheek. "I won't be long, we're just going to the market to buy food for all the hungry mouths that need feeding. And don't worry, no one will recognise me under this hat."

Kaha returned the kiss and spoke quietly to his wife. "Be careful, and pay attention, and please don't be long." He squeezed her hand.

Pam smiled, and Kaha watched her walk to the door where Sylvia waited. He was unsure of the wisdom of having her venture out.

Capitano Luigi Gallo was agitated and a little frustrated. He'd hoped to depart Chieti with his small force earlier in the morning, however, Major Da Camino did not respond quickly to the news that the fugitive Giuseppe Canolo was seen in the village of Sulmona. If the major hadn't taken the offered bait, this would have affected his plan considerably. Luckily, Da Camino finally sent a contingent from Chieti, but because of the delay, Gallo was now fearful that the Austrians would escape Italy before he arrived in Pescara.

It took all his persuasive skills to prevent Enzo from recklessly riding alone and attempting a foolhardy rescue of the *Signora* and the boy. Such an ill-advised response would have put himself and everyone else in imminent danger. The Austrians were not to be trifled with and were dangerous men. However, he eventually conceded and allowed Enzo to travel with them, and as Gallo thought, it wasn't a bad thing, he needed all the help he could get. Once they arrived in Pescara, he would immediately call on his brother–in–law, Mario Bonano, who also happened to be Pescara's chief of the Polizia Locale and solicit his help.

Not far ahead were the food markets and just a little farther, the waterfront region. Major Richter looked for threats or anything unusual as the wagon slowly rumbled down Pescara's narrow streets. So far, the journey was without incident, the priest remained quiet, and the *Signora* dutifully ensured he was comfortable. The boy typically remained sullen and uncommunicative, which suited him just fine. Through necessity, they stopped a couple of times, each without incident and made good travelling time.

Alert to danger, the major was taking nothing for granted. He anticipated complications and would be pleased to finally meet up with *Stabswachtmeister* Wollf and *Herr* Meyer, who he fully expected to be waiting for them near the marina.

Richter scanned the faces of everyone they passed, he assumed nothing and was taking no chances. His pistol was concealed, and within easy reach, he'd told his men to expect trouble and gave permission to use their weapons if the need arose. He looked over at Johan Bekker, he too had his pistol tucked away and within easy reach. He knew the Turk, *Herr* Yavuz, in the wagon's rear would also be alert and his weapon at the ready.

Major Richter decided to take a less direct route through Pescara and travel away from the main thoroughfares, it meant he'd encounter more local pedestrians but less likelihood of being seen by anyone watching or waiting for them on the main roads.

As they approached the market, the streets became busier, a few automobiles arrogantly honked and demanded people move out the way, children played in small groups as their parents either shopped or sold wares, and thankfully, they were ignored.

A little further ahead was the turn that would take them to the waterfront and marina, they were close. Two women stepped onto the road and would safely cross in front of them. As he'd done countless times that morning, Major Richter looked at each of their faces. In reflex, the first woman looked up as the wagon approached, purely an instinctive reaction, and he quickly surmised she posed no threat. Dismissing her, Richter's gaze immediately shifted to the second woman. Her face was obscured, and in shade from a large hat she wore, he couldn't see details and was about to look elsewhere when, like her friend, she turned and raised her face towards the oncoming wagon. He instantly recognised her. This was the third time he'd seen the woman – and this was no coincidence.

Just as quickly as she looked up, she turned away without reacting. *Where was the man he'd previously seen her with?* Immediately Richter's heart rate increased. The anger at losing his intelligence files resurfaced, and only discipline prevented him from immediately leaping from the wagon to challenge the mysterious woman. He wanted his documents returned. In the space of a few heartbeats, he scanned the area around him and saw no one resembling the man he previously saw her with. He wouldn't let her get away – not this time.

"*Herr* Bekker, the woman in the over-sized hat, you see her?" Richter whispered, twisting away to hide his face from the woman in case she looked at him again.

Bekker nodded. "*Ja*, I see her."

"Quickly, stop here, this is a problem for us."

Pam immediately recognised the Austrian major and did her best to hide her response. She stepped after Sylvia and grabbed her elbow as she heard the wagon grind to a halt behind them. "Run, Sylvia, quickly!"

When he saw the *Trabant* acknowledge his wave, Gunter Meyer walked towards the marina to wait for the boat that would come. He kept an eye open for Wolff but couldn't see him anywhere. He assumed the man was in a bar or, better still, had spent the night with a woman. He grinned at the thought of the major screaming at the wayward sergeant when he returned.

He tried to look casual, like a tourist admiring all the beautiful boats, but deep down, he was nervous, something didn't feel right, and it took all his willpower to keep from leaping astride his horse to ride away and return to Florence and the big city life he loved so much.

He thought again of Wollf, where was he? he wondered. Cautiously, he cast a furtive glance around and still saw no sign of the big sergeant or the major and the wagon, although he knew they were close. Again, he turned and looked out to sea and saw the trawler cruising near the marina entrance.

A fisherman leaned his fishing rod against a handrail and rolled a cigarette. Gunter sauntered towards the man.

"*Buongiorno*," greeted Gunter.

The fisherman grunted and nodded as he unsuccessfully tried to light his cigarette. The wind proved to be too strong. Gunter cupped his hands around a match, and the fisherman sucked, eventually, a puff of smoke signalled the cigarette was finally alight.

"Weather's still rough," replied the fisherman, unenthusiastically.

Gunter turned and leaned on the rail beside the fisherman and looked out to sea. "Any luck?"

"Huh?" replied the fisherman.

"Catch anything?"

"Oh," he replied, "no, too much silt in the water only thing anyone has caught around here was the body they found at the mouth of the river."

"Oh yes, I'd heard something earlier. What happened?" Gunter casually asked.

The fisherman dragged on his cigarette. "Someone found a body early this morning, right over there." He pointed with a yellow nicotine-stained finger towards the river.

"You knew him?" inquired Gunter. He recalled the overheard conversation with the locals earlier.

The fisherman shook his head, "No, they don't know who it is. He was shot, though. Was a big man, probably a foreigner."

"Shot." exclaimed Gutner, "How do you know?"

"The *Carabinieri* told us. They asked if anyone had heard a gunshot or seen anything."

Gunter was finding it difficult to remain calm. He paused to give himself time to think. "Uh, where did they take the body?"

The fisherman shrugged and dragged heavily on his cigarette, looked at it once, then flicked it to the ground and scraped his foot across it. "*Addio.*"

"Yes, goodbye," answered Gunter. He watched the fisherman pick up his rod and bucket and walk away. He was lost, deep in thought and never heard the wagon approach.

"Where is *Stabswachtmeister* Wollf?"

Gunter looked up in surprise and saw Major Richter looking at him questioningly.

CHAPTER TWENTY-TWO

They lost everything when the *Mana* exploded. Clothes, papers, a few memento's, but other than photographs, what hurt the most was losing the boat itself. Kaha loved the *Mana* and felt a special bond with her. He'd devoted countless hours restoring and bringing her back to the splendour and grandeur she deserved. She was rigged so two people could sail comfortably in all sorts of weather, and below deck, she was hospitable and warm – *Mana* was their home. He delighted in the way she looked, with her long, swept bow and elegant stern, and although heavy, she handled well in rough weather and could still sail fast – and now she was gone – destroyed. He felt grief and heartbreak, much like the passing of a dear friend.

There was little he could do other than remember the good times, the journeys and adventures they'd shared. At least he had the memories. Kaha shuddered and allowed his thoughts to return to the present and the uncomfortable feeling of anxiousness that gnawed at him while he waited for Pam and Sylvia to return. He stood at the big window, leaning against the frame with his arms folded and stared down at the street below. "They should have been back by now."

Luc stepped up to stand beside him. "They are doing what women always do, they talk, and they buy things, then talk more, *non*?"

Kaha wasn't sure about that. "Which market did they go to, Luc?"

Luc waved an arm and pointed. "Is not far, beyond those

buildings and up the street. Why do you want to know this? You wish to go there?"

"Perhaps."

"I go with you," Boris stated from the settee where he sat.

Kaha continued to look outside. He scanned the street in both directions and still didn't see them and wondered why they had not returned. Something was wrong, he felt it, and he couldn't stand idly by and just wait; he felt the pressing need to do something. He tapped his fingers nervously on the window. "Let's go for a walk Boris."

Earlier, Pam and Sylvia gave Boris firm instructions not to aggravate his wound. With hands on their hips, they teamed up and firmly insisted he wasn't allowed to help his men about his boat, he was to rest. Boris didn't have much else to do until the train departed. He nodded, rose from his seat and walked towards his two friends.

"You worry for nothing," added Luc, shaking his head. Wait a little longer, eh?"

"They should have been back by now, Luc. I'm concerned."

"What happens if you are seen? Then you have some questions to answer. *Non, non, mon ami*, I think they will be back soon.

Kaha looked at Boris, who shrugged. "No one will take any notice of two men walking, and we won't be gone long."

Luc gave Kaha a long hard look. After a heartbeat or two, his expression softened. "Very well, go, but be careful, eh." He turned and walked towards the door. "I must go below to see if my lazy employees are doing their work."

Boris handed Kaha his knit cap. "Wear this, now you look like fisherman." He grinned as Kaha placed it on his head. "And you like smell of fish."

The two men followed Luc, who disappeared into the Chandlery, then walked onto Lungaterno Cristoforo Colombo, which paralleled the river, then turned to the right and ran alongside the marina.

"Come, this way," suggested Boris turning towards the marina.

Kaha kept the hat pulled low, and he felt comfortable that he could escape casual scrutiny.

As both men rounded the corner of the Chandlery and headed along the marina, Kaha spotted a covered wagon ahead. It was parked near a gangway that led down to the docks, and he could make out the form of a few people near it. A man and a woman climbed down from the rear and assisted another person, yet unseen.

"Papa!" cried a distant voice.

Boris stopped immediately.

"Papa!"

Ignoring the outstretched arms of the woman trying to help him climb down from the wagon, Zoran appeared from the shadows of the wagon interior. He leapt down, avoided the Turk and began to sprint towards his dumbfounded father. Caught unawares, Mr Yavuz lithely twisted to reach for the fleeing boy and missed – he grabbed nothing but air. He cursed.

"Zoran!" Boris yelled and began running towards his son.

Caught in indecision, *Signora* Milani hesitated a moment, then seizing the opportunity, she ran towards the man Zoran had called out to – his father. "Help us, please!" she yelled.

Kaha paused as he assessed the situation. He recognised the wagon and the man's face trying to stop Zoran. But not the woman who just yelled. Sensing there were more Austrian's nearby, he reached behind for the pistol in his trouser waistband.

Mr Yavuz, angry that he allowed the boy to escape, cursed again, only to see *Signora* Milani lunge past. He leapt for the woman and tackled her to the ground just as the boy flew into Boris's arms.

From the front of the wagon Major Richter appeared holding a pistol at his side, he watched dispassionately as the boy reached his father. But what caught his attention was the other man. Even wearing the hat, Richter knew who he was. He was the man at the hotel, the same man he'd seen with that woman. He smiled and spoke quickly to Johan Bekker, who still remained out of sight.

The Turk grabbed a handful of *Signora* Milani's hair and began hauling her roughly to her feet. She fought him bravely, her hands reaching for his face, but she was no match for him, and he easily avoided her wild attempts to scratch. He pushed her towards the priest, "Help him," he snarled.

Beside the major, Bekker stepped into the open.

"I want the files!" yelled Major Richter in clear, precise English.

Kaha's mouth opened in horror when he saw the other man appear with his arm around the throat of Pam and began to pull her down the gangway. As she turned, Kaha saw the glint of a knife pressed into her back.

"Pam!" yelled Kaha.

"The files!" Richter shouted.

Ignoring the major's demand, Kaha took a step forward and raised his pistol, hoping for a clean shot at the man holding her. He knew he could probably hit him, but cast aside the notion as being too risky. If he took a shot and missed, he could hit her instead. It was then he saw the gun in the hand of the smaller man who had wrestled the woman to the ground, and then another Austrian appeared from behind the wagon, he too, carried a weapon and extended his arm with a handgun.

"Boris, get behind that building!" he yelled and began running for shelter. His mind was working furiously as he considered all his options. Sadly, the realisation hit him there was little he could do to rescue Pam. He counted four armed men, a woman and another man who appeared injured. He was outmanned and outgunned.

How did Pam get caught by Richter, and how did he identify her? *It must have had something to do with those files,* he thought.

He chanced another look and saw Pam being taken down the gangway, soon he wouldn't be able to see her unless he moved.

Someone fired at him, and a chip of wood flew from the side of the building where he crouched. Boris was at his side with his arm protectively over Zoran's shoulder, and they moved further back for protection.

"Who is the injured man, is that the priest?" Kaha asked as he ducked back out of sight.

"Is Stevan," replied Boris, "Father Steven Belic. I did not think to see my friend again," he added dismally. "And now, man also has your wife. You know him, the one who yells about files?"

Kaha looked down at the boy and shook his head in response to Boris's question. "Does he know where they are going? Did he overhear anything that can help me?"

Boris turned to his son and spoke to him in his native language.

The sound of fast-approaching horses ended the conversation as seven mounted and armed policemen arrived. Kaha quickly hid his pistol.

Additional shouting from the adjacent dock alerted Kaha that the lone *Carabiniere* stationed at the *Bangor Castle* had reacted to the gunfire. He responded with two quick shots of his own, the sound of shooting echoed around them as the Austrians continued to return fire and target anyone visible.

From horseback, *Capitano* Luigi Gallo could see armed men quickly retreating down into the marina docks. He reigned in his horse and yelled to his men to back away to a safe distance until he could assess the situation. Dismounting quickly, he shouted instructions. "Enrico, ride to *Capitano* Bonano, have him bring men and weapons, hurry!"

Gallo saw two men and a boy sheltering behind a wall and ran over to them.

Kaha scooted over, making room for the Italian policeman.

"What is going on here?"

"That man has my wife."

Gallo stood and risked a quick look towards the gangway, he glimpsed the priest and the *Signora,* who was assisting him but not much else, they were the last people to walk down the dock. Earlier, Enzo had explained everything that had happened while the Austrians were at his home. Then the unmistakable form of the Austrian Major appeared, along with another woman, a stranger, and apparently the wife of the man beside him. He cursed. This was a mess.

"Do you know where they are going? asked Gallo.

Kaha couldn't answer as Luc came running from the side of the building.

"Get back!" Kaha shouted.

Seeing Kaha, Boris, the boy and the policeman, he ignored the warning and stubbornly joined them.

"They took Pam. Sylvia managed to run and hide, but they have Pam," Luc said, gasping for breath. He wasn't used to moving his body quickly.

"Yes, I saw her," replied Kaha. "Where is Sylvia?"

"Sylvia is here and safe now, but why did they take Pam? What do they want from her?"

Both Luc and *Capitano* Gallo waited for an answer.

Ignoring the question, Kaha took charge and spoke decisively.

"We need men to flank them by taking positions on the dock, either side of the one they are on, they are trapped, unless ..." Kaha stood and risked taking a step into the open, he was looking out beyond the seawall. He saw the Austrian RDF boat near the marina entrance, but it wasn't entering.

"Unless what?" questioned Gallo, also standing.

"That's it, they're meeting a boat, the bastards are escaping, that is why they're heading down there!" Kaha left the safety of the wall and began to run in a zig-zag pattern. In puzzlement, the others watched as he kept his body stooped. Another wild shot rang out, but it came nowhere near hitting him. Kaha reached a place that allowed him a protected view of the marina entrance and remain out of sight from the Austrians. There it was, he could see it. A small motorised launch entered the marina and made its way at speed towards the dock where the Austrians now waited.

Copying Kaha, *Capitano* Gallo ran up and stood at his side.

"There, see it?"

Gallo looked where the Englishman indicated. He saw it too; a launch was quickly making its way into the marina.

Someone took another shot at the two men; they ducked as the bullet ricocheted away.

Kaha pointed, "And over there, do you see? Two men are protecting the rear." *How could he get Pam back?*

Gallo risked another hurried look and saw two men on either side of the dock crouching behind a sizeable boat for protection.

Another shot caused Kaha and the *capitano* to duck, but it wasn't aimed at them. He risked another look. One of the Austrian rear-guard lay slumped over the hull of the boat. Even from a distance, Kaha could already see the red spreading stain seeping out from beneath the body.

"The *Carabiniere*!" exclaimed Gallo.

He raised a meaty arm and pointed. Kaha could see the *Carabiniere* had climbed onto the cabin of a moored boat. The elevated position gave him a temporary advantage. Even as they looked, the lone Austrian returned fire, forcing the *Carabiniere* to slide back out of sight. On his left, he could make out figures running for safety on the deck of the English trawler. For the time being, they weren't doing anything. Nor did they understand what was happening.

Kaha's mind raced as he considered all his options. He knew he needed to act fast, as already Richter and his men forced Pam aboard the launch. Even as he watched, and with a burst of speed, the launch surged away from the dock and was heading out of the marina where the Austrian RDF trawler waited.

"What will you do? In a few minutes, they will be gone," questioned *Capitano* Gallo.

Kaha could see Pam and another woman aboard the launch, they were being used as shields. He hammered his fist on the wooden handrail and stared out to sea.

"Vito!" yelled Gallo and waved his arm.

Cradling his rifle and keeping low, Vito began running towards Gallo.

"Luigi, what is happening?" asked Vito when he arrived.

Gallo quickly explained how they were pinned down by a single Austrian gunman. "You have a shot from here."

The last surviving gunman began to move further down the dock and was yelling at the departing Austrians, he wasn't happy about being abandoned.

"Throw down your weapon!" *Capitano* Gallo yelled.

In response, the Austrian took another poorly aimed shot.

There were no options available to Kaha. In minutes Pam would be aboard the Austrian trawler, and any hope he had of releasing her was over. Even if he wanted to exchange Pam for the files, he couldn't, they'd been destroyed in the explosion aboard *Mana*.

Vito unslung his Vetterli-Vitali, model 1870/87 rifle and positioned it across the handrail and sighted carefully along the length of its eighty–six-centimetre barrel. Kaha wasn't paying attention to the policeman, he was staring across the marina at the departing launch and Pam. His jaw was clenched tightly, and his eyes narrowed.

"Now Vito," coached Gallo, "quickly."

Gunter Meyer was incensed – enraged. Major Richter deserted him. After all he'd done for the *Evidenzbureau,* and now they just left him to die. He'd shown loyalty, risked his life, and time and time again, he'd done all that was asked of him. He'd done Richter's dirty work, and this is how they thanked him. He was furious.

He kept his body low as he stumbled farther down the dock. There was nowhere to run, there was nowhere to hide, he was alone and would die. The acceptance and realisation brought him clarity and focus. He raised his pistol, and for stability, laid his arm across the bow of a moored boat and took aim at the departing launch. Richter strategically hid behind the two hysterical women. If he could shoot one of the women, he may get a shot at the major. With one eye closed, he stared down the short muzzle of his pistol and aimed at the blonde-haired woman. The distance was rapidly increasing.

He waited for the boat he leaned on to stop pitching. The wake from the departing launch caused all the nearby boats to rock. Fuelled by hate, he had all the patience he needed.

The sound of two simultaneous gun-shots almost melded together as one. Kaha watched in terror as Pam slumped to the side and fell out of sight. "No," he yelled, "Pam!" He began running down towards the dock.

Below them, Gunter Meyer was dead and lay sprawled on the dock with the back of his head missing.

"Well done Vito," complimented *Capitano* Gallo. He hadn't seen Pam fall.

The launch began randomly zig-zagging. As it turned, Kaha could see Pam laying in a crumpled heap at the feet of Major Richter, who was now fully exposed. The other woman in the boat must have spoken harshly to the major because Kaha watched as the Austrian slapped her face. She fell against Pam. Kaha raised his hands to his face and sunk to his knees in despair.

"*Oddio!*" exclaimed Gallo as he turned to look at the departing launch.

Leaving Zoran in the care of Luc, Boris ran up to investigate. His sharp eyes took in the scene in a heartbeat.

"She lives, I see this – she moves," exclaimed Boris.

Kaha looked helplessly at the departing launch, its erratic course allowed him to see the distant form of Pam, but he couldn't tell if she lived.

CHAPTER TWENTY-THREE

Capitano Luigi Gallo was arguing with his brother–in–law, Chief of Pescara's Polizia Locale, Mario Bonano. They stood some distance away, and as witnessed by a waving of arms and some shouting, their quiet chat took a turn for the worse and became less agreeable. Kaha watched anxiously, hoping for some news or a sign of action – anything to help him get Pam back. From what he could discern, the argument between both police chiefs seemed to be centred around the reluctance of Pescara's police chief to share information and allocate resources to assist *Capitano* Gallo.

Appalled at their behaviour, Kaha gave up listening to their pointless bickering and leaned against the handrail at the edge of the marina and stared out to sea. The Austrian trawler was still partly visible but would soon disappear, and with it, any chance he had of saving Pam. The thought of her being seriously injured or even dead was inconceivable, something his mind was unwilling to accept. Boris said he saw her move – she wasn't dead – she was alive. He clung to the thread offered by Boris, it was all he had.

The question repeated itself, over and over again in his mind. *How was he going to get her back?*

After the shooting, he'd been briefly questioned by *Capitano* Gallo, but Pescara's Chief of Police showed no interest in him, stating he was nothing more than an innocent victim, an unlucky tourist involved in a robbery that went awry. Fortunately, no one stepped forward and linked him or Pam to the explosion aboard the *Mana.*

Held back by a police line, a small crowd gathered and watched with morbid curiously as the bodies of the two Austrians were carried away on stretchers from the dock to a wagon. On his left, he could make out the grey bow of the English trawler, *Bangor Castle*, and the knot of English sailors spectating from her foredeck. It gave him an idea.

After a quick glance on either side to ensure no—one was paying him any attention, he casually made his way down the marina and jogged down the dock gangway towards the English trawler. On his right, he could see the broken stump of *Mana*'s mast protruding from the water at an obscene oblique angle, he pushed aside the feeling of loss and instead focused on Pam. He gave one final look out to sea, and in the haze, he could just see the stern of small Austrian ship motoring northwards and away from Italian waters. She would soon dissolve into the greyness and disappear, along with Pam. It made him feel sick, and he couldn't sit idly by while the police argued amongst themselves and did nothing.

In the aftermath of the brief gun battle, the Italians relieved the duty *Carabiniere* tasked to watch over the English warship and had yet to have him replaced. Kaha walked unchallenged towards the *Bangor Castle* and met her commanding officer, Lieutenant Burton Sanders, at the ship's side.

"Were you involved in that skirmish, Mr Peterson?" asked Sanders as he stepped onto the dock.

"The Austrian's have taken my wife, they have her as hostage aboard that RDF trawler!"

"Dear God!" Sanders shook his head in dismay. "Then it was her, I wasn't sure. Was she shot? It looked like a bullet may have struck her."

"I, I don't know," replied Kaha slowly.

Sanders looked into Kaha's eyes. "I'm sorry." He removed a

pipe from a trouser pocket. "How can I help?"

"I need you to pursue the trawler and allow me to get aboard her."

Lieutenant Burton Sanders remained quiet. His lips compressed tightly as he considered how to reply with tact.

Kaha waited. "Well?"

"I cannot, I'm sorry, Mr Peterson, my orders are very clear. Our priority is first to remove the radio from the wreck of your boat and then extract both you and your wife to safety – in that precise order."

"But things have changed –"

"It isn't quite that simple. Yes, it is possible to go after the trawler once we have the radio, but we will not be able to catch her – "

"We are talking about my wife," interrupted Kaha, "not a damn radio, if we left now, we'd stand a better chance of catching the Austrians. Kaha's frustration was beginning to show.

Lieutenant Sanders raised the peak of his cap and scratched his brow with a finger. "Mr Peterson, the safety of your wife is of concern to me, but our objective is to secure the radio, only then can I consider pursuing the Austrian ship, but she is a newer vessel than mine and capable of travelling at a much faster speed. If it's a race, we will lose. I'm sorry, sir, those are the facts."

Kaha's eyes bored into the captain's. "In these sea conditions, the trawler won't be at full speed...."

The *Bangor Castle*'s captain didn't answer.

"Are you telling me you will not help her?"

"Mr Peterson, what I'm saying is, I cannot initiate a rescue until we have recovered the radio, then, and only then, can we begin any pursuit. But if it comes down to a contest of speed, we will lose. Do you understand this?"

"What about guns? If you get close, you could disable the Austrian ship."

"We have a 3-inch gun mounted forward, if we could get in range, we might get lucky with a shot or two to her stern," Sanders shook his head, "but we may never even get close."

Kaha held his gaze, a vein in his neck pulsed. His shoulders sagged in acceptance. "Yes, Captain, I understand," he said after a few heartbeats.

The captain began to walk alongside his ship and indicated Kaha to follow. A chief Petty Officer watched from the deck and greeted Kaha with a head nod. They walked a few steps in silence as the captain filled his pipe. Once the tobacco was tamped down, Sanders paused and turned to Kaha and spoke quietly. "Damn it, man, I'm doing you a favour, you know enough about the ships and the ocean to know this tub cannot motor quickly. Chasing that Austrian RDF trawler all over the Adriatic is a waste of time, even if we left this very minute, the *Bangor Castle* probably couldn't catch her. But I'm sure there are quicker boats here that you could use." His arm swept out across the marina.

Kaha nodded despondently.

Even with his back to the wind, Sanders successfully managed to light a match and held it to the pipe bowl as he frantically sucked. Kaha watched silently.

"Once we have the radio, we will immediately depart the Pescara Marina. However, if you find a fast boat and decide to chase the Austrians, then we will hang around, beyond the marina for forty-eight hours. We *will* wait for you to return with Mrs Peterson. I cannot travel north without an escort."

Kaha chewed his bottom lip as he considered his options. His eyes were already scanning the marina for a suitable boat. "Thank you, captain, I appreciate your willingness to help."

"If the *Bangor Castle* stood even a remote chance of catching the Austrian's then we'd already be underway." Sanders shrugged.

Kaha said nothing.

"I'm sure you will find a faster boat. And don't forget, you'll need a crew."

Kaha gave Sanders a good long hard look and decided the man was doing his job, and he was right, the *Bangor Castle* wasn't capable of catching the Austrians. His look softened. "You're correct, I do need to find a boat and a crew."

"We'll be waiting for you when you return with Mrs Peterson, sir."

They shook hands, and Kaha walked slowly down the docks searching for a fast, seaworthy boat capable of catching the Austrians.

With his pipe clamped between his teeth and hands buried deep in his pockets, Lieutenant Burton Sanders watched Kaha walk away.

Chief Petty Officer Owen stood at the rail and looked down at his captain. "What we gonna do, cap'n?'

"Send a man in civvies to watch over Mr Peterson. Keep an eye on him. I want to know what he does and if he finds a boat."

"Aye, aye, sir."

Kaha walked into the chandlery and nervously paced the floor as he waited for Luc to finish with a customer.

"I need a fast boat, Luc," said Kaha once Luc was free.

"To rescue Pam?"

"I'll buy one if I have to, and if no one helps me, then I will steal one."

"And your crew?"

"I will go to the nearest bar and hire the best men I can; at this time, I frankly don't care, Luc, but I have to do something – and soon. Every minute of delay sees the Austrians steam farther away."

Another customer entered the store, and Luc was momentarily

distracted.

"Go upstairs, I will be there in a minute to help you, my friend," said Luc over his shoulder.

After Sylvia recounted to Kaha how one of the Austrians chased them near the market and caught Pam, she insisted Zoran bathe and went to draw the bath. Boris was staring out the window.

"Did English captain offer to help?" Boris asked.

Kaha looked out across the marina to the grey bleakness beyond. The Austrian ship had disappeared. "No, he said his boat wasn't quick enough."

Boris nodded. "What you do about this?"

"Luc may know of a boat. If I no-one will help me, then I will buy or steal one. But I have to leave soon, or the Austrians will get away."

Boris rotated his injured shoulder, testing it for flexibility. "I know of such a boat."

Kaha's head shot up. "Where?"

CHAPTER TWENTY-FOUR

Turbulent white-water boiled up from the stern of the two-hundred and fourteen-foot trawler, *Trabant*, as her two, triple-expansion steam engines powered the single screw propeller pushing the ship to a ten knot cruising speed.

On leaving the waters of Pescara, the ship's captain, *Kapitänleutnant*, Mert Maas, recommended to Major Richter they steam at their maximum speed of fourteen knots. However, after fifteen minutes of unsettling vibration, and due to the excessive rolling motion, Major Richter ordered Maas to slow the *Trabant* to a more comfortable ten knots as they headed towards the Austrian port of Trieste, one–hundred and ninety nautical miles away to the north.

Brown smoke, a sure sign the *Trabant* was burning poor grade coal, belched from both her slightly raked stacks. The crew removed protective covers from their aft, quick–loading, 10.5 cm *Schnelladekanone* cannon in preparation for the anticipated arrival of the British trawler seen in Pescara that was sure to come after them. The major believed otherwise and felt he had caught the Italians and English completely unaware, and they had no ships in the area capable of overhauling them. *Kapitänleutnant*, Mert Maas, took no chances, he knew the British were a determined people and wouldn't sit back and do nothing. He briefed his crew to expect the English trawler, *Bangor Castle,* to make an attempt and sight them within the next few hours and take all necessary precautions. Even though they outgunned the English trawler and could steam faster, he was still alive today because he was a cautious man and an experienced captain. He reasoned, there may even be another British ship in the area they had not detected. He wouldn't rest until it was dark.

Below deck in the crews' mess, Richter resumed his questioning of Father Stevan Belić, and *Signora* Milani tended to his wellbeing as needed. In the last thirty minutes, the uncommunicative priest, under persistent and direct questioning, failed to provide any information and remained largely un-talkative. His newest hostage, the English woman, received a severe gash to her head from a bullet; although not life-threatening, the wound bled profusely, and Captain Maas ordered the ship's medic to treat her in a separate part of the ship.

Major Richter hadn't devoted any time to lament the loss of his two men during the brief skirmish in the marina, they were expendable and mattered not. Although he was mildly surprised at the failure of *Stabswachtmeister* Dieter Wollf to make an appearance and chastised himself for incorrectly assuming the man was a loyal and obedient soldier. With dissapointment, he delicately wiped his mouth and hands with a cloth and pushed the remains of his *Brettljause* snack away. A few pickled vegetables and sausage remained on the plate, and although tempting, both *Signora* Milani and Belić tried hard not to stare at the uneaten food. They'd not been offered the same courtesy of being fed as the major and were ravenous.

With a long, drawn-out sigh, Major Richter threw the napkin on the table, pushed his chair back and crossed his legs. He stared coldly at Belić, who sat in a chair against the bulkhead on the other side of the small space. Breaking eye contact, Richter flicked a few errant crumbs from his trousers and smiled as he looked back up at his prisoner. "We have played this game long enough, I think now is the time for you to tell me what you know, yes?"

Belić didn't respond, but *Signora* Milani felt dread and recoiled. She'd seen enough of the violent Austrian officer to know the man was a sadist, he enjoyed pain and took carnal pleasure from seeing others in agony. Richter saw her reaction.

"*Herr*, Yavuz, please take the *Signora* to a place more secluded."

The Turk, leaning against the opposite bulkhead, stepped towards the *Signora* and roughly grabbed an elbow, squeezing tightly, which caused her to cry out in pain. He pulled her to her feet and dragged her towards a storeroom. He undogged the latches with one hand, swung the heavy door open, and thrust her inside. With a clunk, the door was closed, and immediately she began banging on it in protest.

"Does the name Franz Schuhmeier mean anything to you?" asked Richter ignoring the noise from the *Signora*.

Belić didn't react and stared at the far bulkhead. His lips moved in silent prayer.

"How about Dimitar Petkov?"

Signora Milani stopped her banging and sat on the storeroom floor with her ear pressed against the door, she could hear every word with clarity.

"No?" Richter drummed his fingers on the table. "Marinos Antypas, do you remember him?" Richter's voice rose in volume, his anger evident. The files stolen from the hotel room contained all the names and details he was now trying to remember.

Father Stevan continued to recite his silent prayer, further infuriating the major.

Richter gave a nod to Mr Yavuz, who stepped towards the priest and drove a fist into his chest. Belić found his voice and screamed.

"Leave him!" yelled *Signora* Milani from the storeroom, "Can't you see he's just a priest!"

The Turk snickered.

"Shall we try another name?"

Father Stevan was doubled over and gasping for air.

"Mahmud Şevket Pasha, the Grand Vizier of the Ottoman Empire?"

In agony, Belić straightened and defiantly looked at Richter. Saliva dripped from his chin, and snot ran onto torn bloody lips.

Major Richter pulled his eyes from the priest and gave the Turk a quick look.

Mr Yavuz may not have been a large man, but he had surprising strength. He pulled his arm back, bent at the waist, then lunged, driving his arm powerfully into the midriff of the priest.

Again, Belić screamed, his cry piercing and shrill as his broken ribs scraped unnaturally against his insides - he passed out.

Signora Milan resumed banging on the door. "Stop, stop this cruelty, he is a priest!" It was too much for her, she slid to the floor, covering her ears and broke down sobbing in the confined darkened space.

The Turk grabbed Belić's chin and delivered a fierce slap to each cheek. Amidst the pain, Belić's red-rimmed eyes blinked open uncertainly. He groaned.

"You will not seek refuge in the peace of unconsciousness," reminded Richter, who leaned forward enjoying the priest's torment. "February, last year, you were in Wien and assassinated politician Franz Schuhmeier at the railway station, didn't you?"

Belić opened his mouth and again began reciting a prayer.

"Who paid you to murder *Herr* Schuhmeier? Who gave you your orders?"

Furious at the lack of response, Major Richter leapt from his seat, overturning the table and sending his plate and food scraps to the floor. He took two steps towards the priest and flung him from the chair to the deck. Belić remained unmoving. He wanted the pain to end.

Mr Yavuz checked for a pulse as Richter picked up his chair and sat down composing himself.

"Is he dead?" asked the major.

Mr Yavuz shook his head, "Not yet."

"He hasn't done those things, how could he, he's a priest," sobbed the *Signora* through the door.

Belić was lifted to his chair, and then a rope was tied around his body and then secured to pipes attached to the bulkhead so he couldn't fall.

Natalina Milani sat with her back to the door and wept quietly in the darkness. She hardly knew this man, yes, he was an enigma, a priest conflicted with his beliefs. He possessed a powerful and passionate love for his country, advocated for the oppressed, and hated seeing his people humiliated by the Austro-Hungarian invaders. So how could the Austrians mistake that for terrorism and murder?

In the weeks she had known him, he had demonstrated tenderness and an understanding of her that was surprising, and they had connected deeply on an emotional and intellectual level that left her breathless. *Was it really love? Was it possible to love someone after such a short time*? They spent countless hours talking, laughing and sharing and grew closer by the day.

He told her the claims made by Gabbi against him were false, he wasn't a killer of children. How could he? He admitted his mistakes, confessed to her his desires, and spoke candidly of intimacies. Stevan Belić had held her hands with tenderness and looked into her eyes, and professed to her the depth of his feelings. He asked her to believe him, have trust and faith, yes faith. Ironically one of his biggest doubts. Despite the temptations, they'd not been together as man and woman, and to Natalina, this was a sign of his morality and sincerity – she did trust and believe him.

He preached to her about his love of God and that his doubts were not about God but about his dedication and commitment as a clergyman to the people, his Bishop, and the Church. He'd asked her to have faith in him and each other. The warmth of his hands, the deep liquid pools of his eyes reflected the truth.

But here and now, under the control of the demented Austrian officer, Natalina knew in her heart that she accepted him, he *was* innocent. The accusations made against him by Richter were baseless and unfounded – lies. Why the major was so determined to extract a false confession from him, she didn't know, but what she felt was resolute, and it gave her strength in the face of the adversity they both faced. Stevan was nothing more than a pawn in Major Richter's game, and he was inculpable. With her sleeve, she wiped away the tears and placed her ear back against the door.

Richter continued his questioning in a conversational, almost friendly tone, his previous anger inexplicably forgotten. "Dimitar Petkov was assassinated in Sofia, Bulgaria in 1907, you were in Sofia at that time, weren't you? You killed Bulgaria's Prime Minister."

"… forgive my sins, just as You forgave Peter's denial and those who crucified You …."

Major Richter shifted in his chair, his patience was wearing thin. "Franz Schuhmeier, Dimitar Petkov, Marinos Antypas, Mahmud Şevket Pasha, the Grand Vizier of the Ottoman Empire … are there more names? More men who have died by your hand?" His voice rose in pitch, betraying his anger.

"Count not my transgressions but, rather, my tears of repentance. Remember not my iniquities …" Belićs' words were almost inaudible.

Who were these men? wondered the *Signora, their names were not totally unfamiliar.*

"Enough! Stop with the prayers, you'll have time for that later!" yelled Richter. His façade was slipping, the priest was getting to him. It was time to reassert himself. With deliberate slowness, Richter rose from his chair, licked his hands and patted his hair in place. He stepped towards the priest and turned, standing beside him with his back to the bulkhead and crouched. He reached up and tenderly stroked Belić's face with the back of his hand and smiled. With calculated precision, he moved his arm forward and then, with incredible speed, drove his elbow backwards into Belićs' chest.

Belić howled, he screamed, spittle and blood flew from his mouth where he bit through his tongue. His head lolled forward – again, he'd found sanctuary in the blackness.

Satiated, Major Richter returned to his chair and gave the Turk a subtle nod.

Natalina Milani pounded on the door, her frantic hysterical pleas ignored.

Mr Yavuz was uncomfortable, this was nothing like he'd ever previously experienced before, the level of cruelty was astounding. There were few men the Turk was frightened of, yet in this cabin aboard this ship, Mr Yavuz was terrified of Maximillian Richter. His level of sadistic brutality had no bounds. With his sleeve, he wiped the perspiration from his brow and again held the priest's chin in his hand and slapped him on each cheek. He couldn't help himself, he didn't hit the poor man as hard as last time. Belić didn't respond.

"Harder, hit him harder, *Herr* Yavuz."

Belić awoke to stinging blows and knew his injuries had worsened, just the simple natural act of breathing caused indescribable shooting pains through his chest. His breaths came in short, shallow, quick gasps.

"Are you willing to talk?" asked Major Richter in a quiet voice.

It took a moment or two for his tearful eyes to focus on the Austrian, he blinked a few times to clear his vision and looked into the lifeless pale eyes of his tormentor. He could taste blood from his tongue. He spoke a single word.

Major Maximillian Richter could see the look of defeat in the priest's eyes, he knew he'd finally broken his spirit. Now he needed to exude dominance.

"Speak louder, I can't hear you!"

"Yes. If you – promise to let – the *Signora* – go free. Release her," he gurgled

The silence in the room was oppressive, no one moved. Mr Yavuz shuddered and risked a look at the major. He was smiling.

"Of course, she will be released unharmed," lied the major.

"Nooooo!" cried Natalina.

"Give him water," ordered Richter as he leaned back against his chair.

CHAPTER TWENTY-FIVE

"I must have help, Boris, I need a crew," pleaded Kaha.

Boris looked uncomfortable and embarrassed. His crewmen wouldn't meet his eyes and turned away. "I am sorry for this, but I cannot speak their voice. This is decision they must make."

In frustration, Kaha began pacing, his knuckles showing white as he tightly clenched his fists. *What more could can I do to bring about Pam's rescue?* He spun to face Boris. "I will pay them, offer them money. How much do they want?"

Boris looked at his feet. "They do not want your money, they fear death at hands of Austrians. Do not blame them." Boris looked up and gestured towards his crew aboard the boat. "These are simple men, fishermen, they have wives and children they wish to return home to."

"But they came to help you find Zoran, did they not?"

Boris nodded. "Yes, they help me because to them, Zoran is family. These men not know you."

Kaha cursed. "Will there be people at the bars, sailors who I can hire?"

"Perhaps, yes. Will you trust them to follow orders when there is danger? Will they fight for you or run and hide?"

"Damn it!" Kaha placed his hands on either side of his head and began pacing.

Boris and Kaha stood at the dock beside the *Kralj Mora*. Boris selflessly suggested and offered that his boat could be used to pursue the fleeing Austrian trawler. Initially, Kaha scoffed at the notion, not believing the fishing boat could sail fast enough to catch them. However, Boris explained how fast his boat was, and because the wind conditions were almost perfect, they could sail at their maximum speed. The problem began when Boris explained to his crew what they were going to do. One by one, all the crew stepped forward and respectfully declined.

"I will find a crew, Boris, be ready to leave when I return."

Unhappy with his men, Boris was disappointed and spoke to them harshly and ordered them to prepare the boat and make her ready to sail. Within a short time, the 1300 square foot lateen sail was being attached to the spar and needed only to be lowered to make way. To lighten the boat, all fishing gear and unnecessary equipment were being removed and stacked on the dock, Boris wanted his boat to sail as quickly as possible.

With a practised eye, he first glanced skywards to identify cloud patterns and wind direction, then he looked beyond the marina and out to sea, assessing wave height and wind strength. Boris liked what he saw, the wind direction and strength were optimum, and he determined the conditions would hold for another twenty–four hours before the wind noticeably abated. He knew he could catch the trawler, but would the Englishman find a crew?

Thirty minutes passed when Kaha returned with only three men. Boris looked them up and down and grimaced at the thought of these sorry-looking drunks coming aboard his beloved boat.

Kaha told his new recruits to wait while he talked with the boat's skipper. "I'm sorry, this is the best I could find. They claim to be sailors."

Boris finished coiling a line and straightened, stretching his back. He looked at the three men, none looked sober, and all looked unfit and unwell, probably because they were in a bar drinking alcohol, he thought. He shook his head. "What do you think we do with them? They can hardly stand or look strong. These men are sick."

"This is it, they were all I could find."

Boris spat over the side. "Tell them to come aboard, and I will talk to them about my boat."

Ten minutes later, and feeling even less confident with his crew, Kaha decided they could wait no longer, it was time to set sail. Whether he liked it or not, these men were all he could find and would have to suffice. With all the dock lines released, the *Kralj Mora* began to inch slowly backwards. To prevent the bow from swinging out during the manoeuvre, Kaha positioned one of his new crewmen on the dock holding a bowline – standard practice when windy. The boat was almost clear of the dock when the man tripped on a dock cleat. With flailing arms and a cry, he pitched headfirst into the marina, almost hitting the bow of the boat. Kaha wanted to scream. If it weren't for the seriousness of the situation, Boris would have laughed. He did his best to hold back and wisely kept quiet.

With some fuss, the *Kralj Mora* was retied to the dock, and the man was awkwardly hauled aboard. Other than being soaked, the man appeared no worse for wear. Boris was about to give the order to cast off

"Wait!"

All heads turned to the voice. Standing on the dock was Chief Petty Officer Terrence Owen and four of his shipmates from the *Bangor Castle*.

"Going for a sail without us, are we?" growled the CPO.

Kaha was too anxious and worried about Pam to be surprised at the appearance of five English seamen, although he recognised the chief from his visit to the warship. "I'm sorry, chief, can't stop to chat, we're heading after that Austrian RDF boat!"

"A word, sir."

Kaha looked puzzled, as did Boris.

"Quickly, we don't have time," said Kaha leaping onto the dock.

"You ain't taking that miserable lot with you, are you?" said Owen, indicating the three men on the *Kralj Mora* that Kaha hired.

"What's this about, chief?"

"We're your new crew." Chief Petty Officer Owen turned his head and spoke over his shoulder, "Lads, see the gentlemen off this fine vessel."

Kaha watched open-mouthed as four Royal Navy seamen clambered aboard the fishing boat, dropped a couple of heavy canvas bags onto the deck and physically removed three protesting men. Boris, equally stunned, could only watch.

"Are you going to stand there gawking like a carp, or are we going sailing, sir?" barked Owen once the three unhappy Italian sailors stood on the dock.

"We want money," demanded their self-appointed leader.

Kaha fished in his pocket for money, handed over some lire, and scrambled aboard the *Kralj Mora.*

"Secure the lines and prepare to cast-off!" barked Owen. Boris and Kaha turned to each other and shrugged.

Near the gangway, the lone figure stood and watched as the fishing boat slowly made way. He knew where they were going, and he'd wait for their return. Enzo looked skyward, then crossed himself and closed his eyes to pray for the safe return of *Signora* Milani.

The *Kralj Mora* was heeled over in a broad reach and sailing quickly, faster than Kaha would have believed possible from a wooden boat of this unusual design. The water hissed past the wooden hull, and the rigging hummed, even Chief Petty Officer Owen seemed surprised at the turn of speed. Kaha leaned against the gunwale near the stern, and Owen scrambled along the canted deck to stand beside him.

Naturally, as sailors tend to do, both Kaha and Owen kept looking aloft at the large sail to ensure she was trimmed correctly.

"Care to explain what this is all about, chief?"

"Ease, ease! Pay attention, Price, or so help me!" yelled Owen to one of the sailors trimming the expansive sail. "The wind has shifted slightly! Keep your head up!" Owen turned back to Kaha. "It was Captain Sanders' idea, sir. He couldn't disobey his orders, but no regulations are preventing his crew from going sailing while on shore leave. He figured we would be more helpful to you than just a bunch of fishermen. No offence to the *Kralj Mora*'s master, of course."

"So, you volunteered, then?"

"Yes, kind of, sir. When the captain told me of his idea, me and the lads had a wee chat and decided we wanted to help Mrs Peterson. Those pastries she gave us were very welcome." Terrence Owen showed his teeth in a broad smile.

Kaha felt the emptiness, he missed Pam and realised again how much she meant to him. He smiled at the thought of the sailors aboard the *Bangor Castle* taking a fancy to her.

"Will we catch 'em, sir?" asked Owen after a few moments of reflective silence.

Kaha turned to Boris. "How fast do you think we are going?"

Boris was grinning, "Very fast, the *Kralj Mora* good boat, we do twelve-thirteen knots.

"We're on a broad reach, this fishing boat seems to love this wind. I think Boris is bang on," replied Chief Petty Officer Owen.

Kaha looked into the distance. "Yes, I hope so."

"What's your plan, sir?" Owen looked serious. "Damn it, Price, keep your head up, trim a little!"

CHAPTER TWENTY-SIX

Natalina felt frightened, lonely and vulnerable. It was pitch black in the cramped room, and she couldn't see anything except where a few pin-pricks of light seeped through tiny gaps around the door and frame. She sat on the deck with her knees drawn to her chin and shook her head disbelievingly at the situation she found herself in.

The accusations made against Stevan were obviously ridiculous and without merit. She tried to recall where she had heard the names of those people the Austrian had accused Stevan of killing. They were familiar, but she couldn't place them. Then she remembered a newspaper story, not that long ago, about an Austrian politician, Franz Schuhmeier, who'd been murdered outside a railway station in Wien. The reason she recalled the incident was because he'd seemed like a good man, an advocate of many worthy causes. At the time, News headlines of his murder dominated the local newspapers, and friends spoke about his horrific and needless death. But the other names the Austrian talked about meant nothing to her. She had no interest in international politics and assassinations and spared little time or thought to newspaper stories that didn't affect her personally. Perhaps the Austrian was trying to blame someone – a scapegoat. *Why*? She shrugged, it didn't matter. What was important was supporting Stevan, believing in him and ending this evil torture so they could return home.

Muted voices interrupted her musings, and she heard someone outside the door. In expectation, she rose unsteadily and waited. Eventually, the door swung open, and she stood blinking as bright light streamed in. Without a word, the Turk led her roughly by the elbow, and she was given a seat beside Stevan at the table in front of a plate of food. Slumped in a chair with his chin resting on his chest, Stevan didn't look up when she entered, but she could hear the irregular and rasping rhythm of his breathing.

With a grunt, Mr Yavuz sat on a nearby chair and watched them closely beneath unfriendly hooded eyes. The rolling motion of the ship made him feel sick. Thankfully, the Austrian major wasn't in the room.

Major Maximillian Richter stood outside, on the leeward side of the *Trabant* and enjoyed the fresh air after the stuffy confines of the crews' mess where he'd been for the last three hours. He watched the disappearing smudge of the Italian coastline as they steamed away, and he didn't miss it, he was pleased to be finally returning home to Austria. His superiors, who'd demanded so much, would be imminently delighted with the outcome of his investigation, not to mention the closure of unsolved assassinations that had plagued the *Evidenzbureau* and other European intelligence organisations for years.

A hatch opened, disturbing his reverie, and a seaman appeared. On seeing the major, he quickly about-faced and returned inside, quickly closing the heavy steel hatch behind him. Richter smiled, it felt good to be feared.

He was anxious to continue interrogating the priest and affirm what he already believed – that the priest was an extremist with radical views, a highly-skilled assassin responsible for the deaths of many dignitaries and politicians throughout Europe. Richter's pleasant mood soured as he lamented the loss of his files, the details contained in them would now be useful as he began his questioning.

He grimaced. Before he went back to the priest, he would first talk to his newest prisoner, the English woman and see what he could learn about her involvement with the priest.

Pam was lying on a cot in a cabin she thought may have been a sickbay. A kindly medic had cleaned and competently sutured her wound and completed the task by wrapping bandages around her head to protect the injury. She was in pain and anxious. When the door opened and Major Richter entered, it took all her willpower not to react in fear. The medic was cleaning his instruments and turned to face the officer.

"Leave!" ordered the major.

Leaving his instruments, the medic gave Pam a sympathetic look and stepped out of the sickbay as instructed.

Richter stood calmly with his hands clasped in front and coldly assessed her. He looked her over without embarrassment. His position of power gave him liberties that he took full advantage of and knew it reinforced his dominance that prisoners found unsettling. The bandage wrapped around her head did little to hide her beauty. There was defiance – he could see it. But she couldn't hide her fear, it made the corners of his mouth twitch. It gave him power, and power gave him pleasure.

"What do you know of the priest, what is he to you?" Richter asked after a minute or two of silence, his English accent cultured and precise.

Pam remained quiet.

"What did you do with the files you took from the hotel?"

When she didn't reply, Richter took a step forward. "Who do you work for, the British Secret Service?"

Unhappy with his questions going unanswered, Richter sat on the edge of the bed and looked at his dusty shoes. He hated to appear unkempt and slatternly. Even his trousers showed filth and looked dirty. He reached up and removed his spectacles. Sea spray coated the lenses, interfering with his vision, he breathed on them and, by using a bedsheet, obsessively polished them.

Able to see better, he leaned over and, with his left hand, grabbed her chin, twisting her head cruelly so he could look into her eyes. She struggled in vain to remove his hand.

"I will enjoy spending a little time with you."

Pam screamed, the shriek loud in the small room. Immediately the door was thrust open, and the medic appeared. Richter turned to look at the young seaman, releasing his hold on her. "Get out!" he snarled.

The medic glanced at his patient and then retreated, shutting the door as ordered.

Pam pulled her legs up and beneath her, ready to lash out and kick if needed. She was already planning how she would strike out at the major if he touched her again.

Richter stood and backed away from the bed. "I have some unfinished business to attend to, then I will return, and *you* will answer my questions." He held her gaze and saw the redness on her face where he'd grabbed her. This time she didn't turn away.

Originating from the northeast, the bora winds blew down from the Dinaric Alps of Croatia and across the Adriatic Sea and could appear at any time of the year, although mainly in the cooler months. They were gusty and cold, but to an experienced seafaring man like Boris Marković, they were predictable and frequently a nuisance. However, today he welcomed the bora winds like an old and dear friend.

They'd been sailing for three and a half hours, and Boris was constantly looking for favourable wind shifts that kept them sailing on a broad reach, their fastest point of sail. With the *Kralj Mora* heeled over and slicing through the waves, the ungainly *Falkuša* fishing boat, and her large lateen rig, raced up the Adriatic Sea. Her passengers all hunkered down on the high side of the boat, trying to remain dry and warm.

Earlier, Boris, Chief Petty Officer Owen and Kaha discussed where the Austrian trawler was headed. Boris believed they were returning to Trieste, approximately one-hundred and ninety nautical miles distant, while Owen disagreed and thought Pula, the major Austrian naval port, one–hundred and forty–five nautical miles away, was the logical destination. Kaha calculated the numbers and knew that because of a two-and-a-half-hour Austrian lead, the *Kralj Mora* had to sail very quickly to have any hope of catching the trawler, and so far, Boris was doing exactly that. However, it would be a long chase. To keep everyone's spirits up, he pointed out, if they retained their current speed, they would likely overhaul the trawler before it reached either of the Austrian ports. Both Boris and Owen agreed.

The *Kralj Mora*'s skipper took advantage of a slight change in wind direction, which allowed him to sail slightly closer to the Croatian coast, where the wind was more consistent and blowing a steady twenty knots. He knew these waters like his own backyard, and he was still confident the bora winds would last.

Kaha opened his eyes and watched Chief Petty Officer Owen talking with Boris. It seems as though both men shared a lot in common and were fast becoming good friends. Owen had been a fisherman before joining the Royal Navy, and he was about to relieve Boris at the tiller, allowing him to rest. Kaha wasn't concerned, Chief Petty Officer Owen had already shown his superb helming skills that even impressed Boris.

Earlier, Kaha spoke to each of the seamen who'd volunteered to help and warmly thanked them. They informed him that the wily Captain Sanders had suggested that Chief Petty Officer Owen take some suitable weapons from the ship's stores. Consequently, two sailors each brought aboard a large and heavy duffle bag that contained an odd assortment of weapons from hand pistols, a couple of shotguns, to a Colt–Browning M1895 machine-gun, that one of Sanders crew had liberated from an American navy ship, along with a healthy supply of ammunition. While they couldn't engage the trawler in a naval gun battle, Kaha hoped that they could pull alongside the Austrian ship and sneak aboard under cover of darkness. If they met with any opposition, as surely they must, they'd be suitably armed and hopefully, with surprise, take advantage of any resistance they'd encounter.

"You dare think to challenge me?" asked Richter.

Pam's unwavering look left an impression on the Austrian major. He took a step closer to the bed where she lay. "You have information that I need, and you will assist me." Richter reached down, and before she could react, he grabbed a handful of hair and savagely pulled her head towards him.

She cried out as the bandage wrapped around her head was pulled free. Richter held her head firmly, not caring about aggravating her injury – his eyes bored into hers.

Pam reacted on instinct and training. She already had her legs pulled back, and with no thought to consequences, she kicked out and upwards, striking the Austrian firmly on the solar plexus with her heel. Caught unaware, he collapsed on the bed gasping for air while she quickly slid away and backed into a corner of the small cabin. Blood flowed freely in rivulets from the reopened head wound and ran down her neck. She felt disoriented and nauseous and wanted to vomit. Earlier, when she explained her symptoms to the medic, he had told her she had suffered a concussion and recommended rest - no physical exertion.

Richter was trying to control his breathing, and she knew he would come after her. She didn't care; she had let him know she would fight him at every opportunity.

He stirred and slowly eased into a sitting position. His spectacles hung askew from a single ear half over his nose. Still breathing hard, he straightened his glasses and turned to face her, the look on his face surprised her, he was actually smiling. After a few heartbeats, he stood, adjusted his shirt and jacket and stepped towards her. His expression hadn't changed.

Seeing him approach, Pam reached out an arm to push him away, but he easily swatted it aside and again grabbed a handful of hair. She squirmed and fought him with what little energy she had, her hands moving quickly, trying to claw and gouge. Lacking strength and coordination, she couldn't hold him off.

With a mighty heave, he yanked hard on her hair and pulled her from the bed and flung her like a rag doll against the steel bulkhead. She collapsed, unconscious. Still breathing hard, Richter looked down at her and sneered. He'd show her.

Unsettled by what he'd witnessed in the sickbay, the medic reported what he'd seen and heard to his immediate supervisor, *Unteroffiziere* Herman Eder. Realising the implications, the Non-Commissioned—Officer dutifully reported the incident up the chain of command. Both the Medic, and *Unteroffiziere* Eder now stood uncomfortably in the stateroom of *Kapitänleutnant*, Mert Maas.

The only sound to be heard was the rhythmic tapping of *Kapitänleutnant* Maas' unlit tobacco pipe against the glass of a porthole. Both the medic and *Unteroffiziere* dared not move as they waited for their captain to speak.

Turning away from the porthole and pocketing his pipe, Maas' face looked grim. "You will do what you can for the prisoner, and it is our duty to ensure she receives the best medical care we can provide." He paused a moment and gave each man a long hard look. "And you will obey any and all legal orders from Major Richter, is that understood?"

"*Jawhol, Herr Kapitänleutnant*," replied both men in unison.

"Dismissed."

With fingers interlocked behind his back, Maas watched both young men leave his stateroom before he relaxed and slumped into a chair. He scratched his thinning scalp and wondered what to do. Maas took his orders from the *Evidenzbureau*, and as Major Richter led the code-breaking and cryptology department of the *Evidenzbureau*, then his ship, the *Trabant,* was under direct orders from the major.

While aboard a ship, a Captain's word is the law. He is the ultimate authority and is responsible for what happens under his command, even if outranked by a senior officer who happens to be aboard. There can only be one captain aboard a ship.

At risk of upsetting a volatile senior officer, Maas decided he would have a word with the major and respectfully remind him of the provisions of the Geneva Convention of 1864 contained within The Hague Convention treaties and declarations regarding the treatment of the wounded. The mistreatment of prisoners was illegal and wrong.

Stevan wouldn't eat, no matter what she said or did, he refused the food she offered, but at least he drank water. In between tortured breaths, he asked her to retrieve the old cross from his pocket. Once in his hands, he noticeable relaxed, and his breathing became more regular.

Natalina cleaned him the best she could. She wiped away the blood and dirt from his face and cared for him with tenderness. She tried to make eye contact with him as she held his hands and desperately wanted him to know she loved him. But Stevan wouldn't meet her gaze or acknowledge her, and it made her feel sad. Now more than ever, they needed each other, couldn't he see that?

She slowly raised a hand and gently touched the side of his face, then leaned forward until her mouth brushed his ear. "I love you, Stevan. I've waited a long time to meet someone like you, and now we found each other," she said in a voice little above a whisper. Her heart was thumping at her admission, and she felt her cheeks flush. "We need each other ... I need you."

Stevan didn't move, he may have been asleep.

Natalina wiped her eyes and composed herself. The outpouring of emotions caught her by surprise, she sighed, folded her arms and looked at the Turk.

"A moment of your time, *Herr* Major," asked *Kapitänleutnant*, Mert Maas.

Richter left the sickbay and was in a passageway, about to enter the crew's mess to complete his interrogation of the priest. He stopped and looked over his shoulder to see the captain. "What is it, I am busy?"

"Perhaps we should speak somewhere more private?"

"I don't have times to play games, speak now, *Kapitänleutnant*."

"Yes, of course. I am concerned for the well-being of the three prisoners. Under your direct orders, you have denied medical treatment to the male captive, and the English woman in the sickbay, she is now in a very serious condition."

Major Richter slowly turned his body and stood directly in front of the *Trabant*'s captain. They were separated by inches. "Your orders are to get this ship to Trieste as quickly as possible, not meddle in affairs that do–not–concern–you. Am I clear on this?"

"I am responsible for all people aboard this ship, and –"

"You will not interfere, Maas," hissed Richter.

Kapitänleutnant, Mert Maas was not going to back down. He stood his ground and looked up at the taller man. "The ship's medic is with the male prisoner and receiving treatment. When he has completed his prognosis, I will consult with him and determine if the prisoner can answer your questions. Until then, Major Richter, you are not permitted to visit with any of the prisoners or question them until they can respond. I've given instructions to my crew to ensure that happens. I will not have anyone tortured aboard my ship."

Richter edged closer to Maas. He craned his neck forward and glared. A hundred thoughts went through his mind, none of them had an outcome that was good for the captain. "You forget yourself, Maas, and I will do as I please. For now, I will rest for a short while before I resume my interrogation, this will allow the medic to attend to the prisoner's needs, which suits my purpose. I need him responsive. Ensure the prisoner is compliant, Maas, and I will ignore your insubordination." Richter shouldered his way past *Kapitänleutnant* Maas and strode off.

CHAPTER TWENTY-SEVEN

There was something unique about being on a sailboat at night. The darkness could be complete, like a shroud - a veil, and the feeling of isolation and loneliness could be profound. So typical of the human mind, solitude promoted thought, introspection and even fear. This was when fanciful stories of horrific sea creatures, denizens of the dark unknown depths, were imagined, told, and believed.

When there were no visible stars or moonlight, the water was black and unwelcoming. Tonight, windswept whitecaps provided a little contrast, and the feeling of dependence on the tiny boat that offered protection from the elements was heightened. The sensation of movement and noises from *Kralj Mora*'s rigging was reassuring, there was a cadence to the rise and fall of the hull as she sliced her way through the waves – it was soporific. When the rhythm was broken, it was a harsh warning that seawater would soon cascade over the hull. Everyone quickly adapted and learned to keep their heads down, it made sleeping difficult, but it was possible to doze for short periods.

As Kaha had done every few minutes for the last couple of hours, he raised his head and stared forward into the inky blackness, hoping for a glimmer of light, a pinprick on the horizon that would signal they'd finally caught the Austrian trawler. As before, he saw nothing, and again as he'd done every previous time, he wiped his eyes. Staring hard into the distance with nothing to focus on made them water.

There were other boats out, fishing boats, similar to the one they now sailed in, even some ships, big and small, were motoring to unknown ports. All the civilian craft used navigation lamps, as they did, but so far, they had not seen their quarry.

He was becoming more anxious with each passing hour. Now that he'd had time to reflect on Pam's abduction, and in the boredom of their pursuit, the idle mind tends to torment. He admitted he was more than worried, he was fearful. In understanding, Chief Petty Officer Owen already recounted to him a couple of times what he'd witnessed when he saw Pam move after she'd been shot. Kaha clung to the hope he offered. It kept him focused, as he had nothing else.

They'd been sailing for hours, and Boris, with the help of the chief, kept his small fishing boat sailing as fast as possible. A couple of the sailors from the *Bangor Castle* expressed their doubt about catching the trawler, believing they should have done so already. Chief Petty Officer Owen wasn't having any of it and ended their speculation with a quick word.

Kaha must have dozed because an excited voice jolted him awake. He turned aft to where Boris sat and could barely make out his form. As usual, Petty Officer Owen stood at his side, and they were both pointing to something in the distance.

Kaha turned to face forward, squinting into the blackness and saw nothing. "What have you seen?"

"A mast light, from a ship!" yelled the chief.

"I don't see it."

"About 5 degrees starboard of the bow."

"I can't see the bow," replied Kaha in frustration.

He heard the chief's and Boris's distinctive laugh. The three other seamen who had been napping stirred and were instantly alert. Seaman Price, who had been taking turns trimming the large lateen sail with him, pointed to the light, he saw it as well.

"Now I can see a stern light, is definitely a ship!" yelled Price.

"Just keep your bloody eyes on the sail and keep trimming!" Chief Owen testily responded. He winked at Boris, although in the darkness, it was doubtful he saw.

Kaha heard Seaman Price quietly grumble under his breath because it was too dark to see the sail and trim it properly. It made Kaha feel better because it had been difficult for him to see the sail when it had been his turn trimming.

"They on same course as us," volunteered Boris.

Kaha was hopeful. "Then whoever that ship is, we are gaining on them."

"Might be a good time to extinguish the navigation lights," suggested Chief Petty Officer Owen.

Boris and Kaha agreed.

"I'd say that ship is about two and a half miles away, that means we'll catch her in about an hour and a half," Kaha said

"We won't know if Austrian trawler until we much closer," added Boris.

"By my calculations, this is about the time we would have caught up to her," said the chief. "You lazy bums have slept long enough, get the gear checked out and moisture wiped off."

Most people aboard the *SMS Trabant* were asleep. It was agreed if they hadn't identified any pursuing vessels by now, then it was unlikely any would appear. The night-watch were routinely going about their tasks, and *Kapitänleutnant* Maas stood down all extra lookouts except one - just in case.

Seaman Karl Dosch had just come on watch and stood at the rail and yawned. This was his first assignment aboard a ship, and the novelty had yet to wear off, he felt proud that he'd been singled out as an extra lookout and took the responsibility seriously. The wind was cold and blew on the beam causing the *Trabant* to rock sideways as the waves hammered the ship's starboard side. Even though it was pitch black, he vigilantly kept an eye open for any approaching vessels. However, no one had bothered to inform Karl to pay close attention, aft, where trouble would most likely come.

It was noticeably warmer on the leeward side of the ship, and after a few minutes Seaman Dosch, found a good spot out of the wind, buried his hands deep into the pockets of his coat and stared into the darkness for anything untoward. He kept his head moving but paid little attention to the rear, preferring to look forward and out the side. Had he walked towards the stern and looked back, he would have seen the colossal sail of the *Kralj Mora* as she slowly bore down on them

Below deck, Major Richter was in his cabin and unable to sleep. He was frustrated at the attitude of *Kapitänleutnant* Maas. The incompetent man didn't realise how important this mission was, and his interference could possibly create negative consequences. The major seethed at the gall of the man – *how dare he prevent him from interrogating his prisoners.* There wasn't another person capable of completing this assignment, and Maas, a mere *Kapitänleutnant,* could ruin everything.

Richter sat up on his bunk and analysed the situation again. His affirmations were fuelling his ego. *The priest outsmarted everyone but me. I caught him, I have him, and he is my prisoner.* The major knew he was more intelligent than everyone else and wielded the authority and rank to support it – he would not allow Maas to come between him and success.

With his mind made up, he quickly dressed, left the cabin and made his way to the crew's mess. Without pause, he opened the door and stepped in and immediately saw the armed guard posted by *Kapitänleutnant* Maas. He didn't break stride and headed towards the surprised young seaman, yanked the rifle from his grasp and tossed it to the Turk, who woke from the intrusion and was rubbing sleep from his eyes when the rifle landed on his lap. Intimidated by the major, the guard chose not to respond and stared open-mouthed at the senior officer. The *Signora* was tending to the priest, freshly bandaged and laying on a cot.

"Make sure no one enters this cabin, if they try, shoot them," ordered Richter to the Turk as he dragged a chair from a table and sat down. He then turned to the guard. "Help the priest to sit up."

"Leave him alone, can't you see how hurt he is? He has done none of the things you accuse him of," said the *Signora*. "You have the wrong man."

"If you persist in interfering, I will have you thrown overboard. I'm tired of you." Major Richter gave the *Signora* a long cold, unblinking stare that left no doubt he would carry out his threat. In fact, he'd just been questioning his decision to bring her and should have thrown her overboard hours ago. "You are alive only because you are helping him – Because I allow it. Keep your mouth shut."

Signora Milani opened her mouth to speak, then thought better of it and shook her head in silent protest. As the Austrian watched intently, she turned to help the nervous guard gently assist Stevan into a sitting position.

Major Richter looked at the battered and injured body of the priest and felt no sympathy or compassion – he was incapable of sentience. The priest was nothing, just a body, a thing to inflict pain upon and control.

Yet he felt alive, his body tingled in anticipation, and he would play this out slowly – for all it was worth. He had the priest, the

English woman, and then to finish off, for dessert, he even had the *Signora*. As the French said, *Garder le meilleur pour la fin.* He could already feel his heart beginning to race, and he would save the best for last. Not for sexual satisfaction, no, carnal pleasures were base and unrefined. His tastes extended into cerebral masochistic indulgences where the senses were enhanced through visual and auditory stimulation, and if the situation permitted, he might even indulge in some self-inflicted pain. He could already imagine the coppery taste of blood on his lips.

Belić was sitting up, and his chin lolled on his chest as he waited for the Austrian to resume his torture. He saw the savage expression on the major's face, it was a feral look of hunger. He didn't care anymore, his life was over, and he knew he would die this evening. He risked a painful sideways glance at Natalina, the beautiful Natalina Milani. She was filling a glass of water from a pitcher for him. He felt pity for her.

Belić turned his attention back to the major, closed his eyes briefly, then opened them, he was resigned to his fate. "What gave me away?' he croaked.

"Stevan?" queried Natalina, unsure of what she just overheard.

Major Richter heard and said nothing, enjoying the moment.

"What – gave me away?" Belić repeated between breaths.

Natalina dropped the pitcher and glass on the deck. "What are you saying, Stevan? No, don't say that, it isn't true."

Major Richter shifted his eyes from the *Signora* to the priest's hand. He was compulsively rotating the old wooden cross, end for end, round and round. His fingers caressed the wood, rubbed smooth from use, age, and compulsiveness.

Natalina followed the Austrian's gaze, she saw the old cross and Stevan's peculiar habit. Only now the priest's words and their meaning becoming clearer. She looked up at his face, her own began to change from puzzlement to horror.

Richter's face flushed red, he felt the heat rise. Not from shame or embarrassment but from a heightened perverse pleasure. The power he wielded was euphoric, almost erotic.

Ignoring the *Signora*, Belić focused on the Austrian and waited for an answer. His breathing laboured.

Major Richter unfolded his legs and leaned forward. "Witnesses at two locations described a man, just prior to the assassination of Franz Schuhmeier at the railway station, who turned a wooden cross in his hand."

"Noooooo!" she cried, "You lie!"

Uncharacteristically, the major responded to her. "I do not lie, there are confirmed reports."

"Tell him he's wrong, Stevan. Tell him you're innocent, explain to him!" she appealed.

Belić didn't look at her, he slowly shook his head.

Major Richter laughed, but it contained no mirth. "He deceived you too."

Unwilling to accept what she was hearing, she shook her head slowly from side to side in denial. But Stevan's own words ... the Austrian's details... She bolted upright and glared at him.

"Is it true?"

The priest slowly turned his head and met her gaze. His watery eyes fixed firmly on her. He said nothing, the unspoken words an affirmation she didn't want. Without thinking, she slapped him. The crack as her hand struck his already battered face was loud. Richter laughed. The Turk looked away. The priest's head slumped on his chest. "You murdered innocent people? You lied and used me?" She looked at him in loathing, and in disgust, stomped to the farthest corner of the cabin and slumped in a chair, turning herself away and began to cry.

Savouring the moment, Richter paused briefly before continuing. "When Dimitar Petkov was murdered, there was a similar report – a man with a cross. I didn't know until later that it was you – that you were the killer. Only when it was reported to me by my staff that additional witnesses had seen a man fitting your description in Ragusa, Pescara and Chieti, who had been rotating a cross in his hands, did I put two and two together, and for a man of my talents, it was easy."

Belić nodded.

Signora Milani's head rested on the table, encircled protectively by her arms. She looked up and over towards Belic. Tears streamed down her face. "You used, deceived and took advantage of me, what an evil, despicable man you are!"

Belić knew she was correct, he didn't look or respond to her. *She didn't understand...*

"Who are you? What are you!" she cried in anger.

"He's an assassin," Richter answered.

Everyone aboard the *Kralj Mora* was tense and edgy. Three men lay across the bow of the fishing boat with weapons trained outward. Any unfortunate Austrian who appeared on the trawler's stern would be targeted and shot before they could raise the alarm. Luckily, they had seen no one as they inched ever closer. On Boris's insistence, fenders were hung over the bow to prevent damage to his boat when he made contact with the trawler, and weapons had been distributed to ensure they could defend themselves in the event they were seen.

Boris would bring the bow of his boat up the leeward side of the trawler just long enough for men to leap across. It was a dangerous and risky manoeuvre and one that could have fatal consequences if anyone misjudged their timing. The wake and propeller wash of the *Trabant* would test Boris's helming skills to keep the bow of the fishing boat steady.

Able Seaman Price had proved himself an expert sailor, and his ability would be further tested by trimming the sail just enough to slow *Kralj Mora* at exactly the right time to prevent the wooden boat from slamming into the hull of the steel ship or scraping noisily up the side. He and Boris needed to communicate and synchronise their every move with absolute precision.

Again, Chief Petty Officer Owen had proven himself more than useful. Leading Seaman, James Wright, one of the seamen he brought with them was an ERA, an Engine Room Artificer. Once aboard the trawler and the prisoners located, the chief and Wright would immediately go below and disable the engine, preventing the ship from making weigh and pursuing them after they left the Austrian trawler. Kaha and Able Seaman, Herbert Alden, would shepherd Pam, the priest and the *Signora* aboard the fishing boat as quickly as possible. As Owen reminded them all, only minimal crew would be on duty at this time of night, and they should be able to cope with any resistance as long as no alarms were raised. As Owen explained, the real danger began when the crew detected the engines had stopped. They had little time and would need to hurry.

Boris, Able Seaman Price, and Able Seaman Henning would remain onboard the fishing boat. Price and Boris would keep the *Kralj Mora* in position near the trawler's stern. While Henning in the bow would be manning a light machine gun and a rifle to provide cover fire if needed.

Austrian Seaman Karl Dosch flicked his cigarette overboard and decided he would take a stroll around the stern of the *Trabant*.

As he left the shelter of his hidey-hole and glanced casually aft, he stopped at the sight that greeted him in absolute amazement. Right before him, less than five metres away, was a wooden-hulled fishing boat flying a huge dirty sail slicing through the *Trabant*'s wake and about to nose alongside. Instinctively, he paused to watch for a few seconds before realising what was happening. He turned and began to run back down the deck and was about to raise the alarm when a well-aimed bullet fired by Able Seaman Henning entered his skull. The sound of the gunshot was lost to the wind, and it was doubtful anyone aboard the *Trabant* heard. Karl's tenure with Austria's *Kaiserliche* und *Königliche* (Imperial and Royal War Navy or KUK) was over, his life's blood flowed freely along the deck and over the side.

Kaha was crouching at the bow as the *Kralj Mora* crept closer to the Austrian ship. He was very anxious to quickly board the trawler as the body of a seaman lay across the deck, and he knew it was only a matter of time before someone came looking for him or was missed.

He would be first across, then followed by Chief Petty Officer Owen. Caught in the quarter-wave from the stern of the Austrian ship, the fishing boat seemed to lurch sideways as it approached. The gap between both boats narrowed, then opened and finally seemed to close again. Kaha climbed onto the gunwale and crouched as both vessels came together. With a mighty heave, he leapt across the gap and grabbed a stanchion, hauling himself up onto *Trabant*'s aft deck. The distance between both boats opened as the fishing boat lost speed, leaving Kaha isolated. Boris and Price tried to build speed again.

Again, the bow of the fishing boat approached, this time, Boris had Price keep their speed up until they were overlapped, then a gentle nudge on the tiller brought both boats together as Price slowed the fishing boat down to match speed. This time it worked, and Owen easily leapt across, followed by Wright and lastly, Alden, who misjudged the distance when he jumped as the gap began to open. Unable to place both feet securely on the deck, one foot slipped, and he began to topple backwards and fall between both vessels. In desperation, he managed to catch the stanchion with one hand and lay dangling over the side. Caught in the quarter-wave, the bow of the *Kralj Mora* was swinging back around towards him – he would be crushed if he didn't get out the way.

Chief Petty Officer Owen, currently straddling the safety line, reached down, grabbed Alden's wrist and, fuelled by adrenaline, hauled him out of the water seconds before both boats touched. The fenders took the brunt of the impact, and Able Seaman Alden was lucky to escape with his life.

Kaha was crouching on the deck and saw Owen haul the seaman to safety as the fishing boat dropped back to a safe distance.

Owen and Kaha dragged the dead Austrian seaman out of sight behind an aft chain locker, the smear of blood slowly being washed away by spray and wind. Kaha took a big breath and gave Chief Petty Officer Owen a nod to indicate he was ready. All four men, armed only with pistols, quietly entered the *Trabant* and began a systematic search of each cabin. Other than machinery noise, the ship was eerily silent.

The cabins and spaces in the main deck were full of technical equipment and machines, the crew spaces below were where they hoped to find the prisoners. As the ship was not operating in its capacity as a radio detection vessel, the equipment was turned off and unmanned.

Kaha and Alden silently went into each cabin while Chief Petty Officer Owen and Wright kept vigil in the passageway. In most cases, the cabins were dark, and the sound of men undisturbed in sleep was all they found. On two occasions, a light was burning in the cabin and Kaha and Alden forgoing stealth entered the room quickly and caught the Austrians unaware and unprepared. No shots were fired, and after a quick interrogation, neither prisoner could provide any helpful information. They were skilfully tied and gagged.

"Where are the prisoners?" snarled Kaha after storming into the second cabin, where a lamp shone.

Unable to understand English, the Austrians couldn't answer.

With his hands, Kaha drew the shape of a woman in the air. A universal sign men all over the world understood. The eager captive indicated he knew and nodded enthusiastically, then pointed to a cabin.

"Guards?" demanded Kaha. "How many guards?"

Unable to understand and respond, he was quickly tied and gagged. The sleepy officer stood in his underwear with a sock stuffed in his mouth, looking less than dignified, he could only stare blankly at Kaha.

The third cabin down the passageway had a small sign attached to the door that spelt '*Besatzung*'. Kaha's familiarity with German extended to three words, *Besatzung*, wasn't one of them. The sign meant nothing to the other three men, but they knew this wasn't a regular cabin.

With hand signals, Kaha indicated he wanted the more experienced chief to follow him in. Alden opened the door then stood back a step as both Kaha and Owen charged in. Kaha went left, and Owen went right, Each knew the other would cover their blind side. Caught completely by surprise, no one in the room had time to react.

Major Richter's mouth opened, but no words came out. The Turk was tired and too slow to react, by the time he began raising his rifle, Chief Petty Officer Owen drove his huge fist into the side of his head, and he collapsed in a heap to the deck. The unarmed Austrian guard, a youngish lad, no older than eighteen, immediately raised his hands.

Kaha looked around the room and saw they were in the crew's mess, where they ate. He saw the *Signora* clearly for the first time, she sat in the far corner; tears streaked her face, and she looked distressed. Another man, heavily bandaged, sat propped up on a cot, and Kaha determined he was the priest. He didn't look well, and from the sound of his breathing, had serious internal injuries. But there was no sign of Pam. He gave the Austrian major a cold hard look.

Able Seaman Wright was in the passageway and kept watch. Owen was dragging the smallish man he'd clobbered to the chair where the young Austrian sailor sat. He ordered Alden to tie both men to pipes that ran the length of the cabin by using sheets.

Kaha stepped up to Major Richter, "Where is my wife?"

The major slowly raised his head, looked at Kaha, and said nothing.

"Where is she?" hissed Kaha.

Richter's unblinking eyes were fixed on the Englishman. He remained silent.

Ignoring the stare, Kaha twisted slightly and drove a fist into the face of the Austrian officer. It was a hard blow, more than the major expected, and he fell sideways from his chair onto the deck. Kaha put a foot on his neck and pressed down. Blood trickled from the major's mouth. To Kaha, it looked like he was smiling. "I asked you, where-is-my-wife?"

The major remained tight-lipped.

Kaha removed his foot so Owen could move him.

While Alden finished securing the other two men, Owen stepped up to the major and began dragging him to another chair where the other men were. He began tying him to the pipes.

Kaha stepped up to the young Austrian guard. "Do you speak English?"

"*Englisch?*"

Kaha nodded.

"Nein."

With his hands, Kaha repeated, outlining a woman.

The young man nodded. "*Medizinisch.*"

"I think the fella means the sick berth," volunteered Owen.

"Untie him, he can show me. The rest of you stay here until I return, I will take Wright with me. Keep a close eye on that one," said Kaha pointing to Richter.

The young guard was untied from the bulkhead and now stood in front of Kaha with his hands firmly secured behind his back. Kaha gave him a push and followed him into the passageway. They were in officers territory and needed to be extra careful.

Only a few doors down, the young man indicated with his head to a door. Wright stepped up and put a hand on the Austrian's shoulder as Kaha flung the door open.

It was dark, and his eyes hadn't adjusted, he couldn't see, although he could sense the cabin was small and cramped.

"*Was zum Teufel!*" came a voice.

Kaha took a quick step and fumbled for the man who had just cursed. Using the light shining through the open door, Kaha could barely make out the shape of a person rising from a chair and from his peripheral vision, he noticed a bed against a bulkhead. He grabbed at the man, there was no room to fight or move. With a twist, he managed to spin the man around and clamped his hand over his mouth and dragged him back into the passageway. He handed the man to Wright, who stuck a pistol in his back.

"Kaha?"

He froze. *Pam?* "Take these two back to the others, I will be right there," he said to Wright as he re-entered the cabin. He saw the unmistakable outline of his wife on the cot and leaned down to hug her. "I thought you'd died," he whispered into her neck.

"And I knew you'd come," she said weakly.

"We aren't safe yet, we need to get you away from here."

Kaha tried to pull her to her feet, she teetered and wobbled. In the light from the open doorway, he saw her condition, she didn't look good. With care, Kaha helped her from the bed and slowly led her down the passageway and into the crew's mess where the others waited.

"We have to get moving," said Chief Petty Officer Owen when Kaha arrived with Pam. "And what should we do with him?" He pointed dismissively to the major.

"I think he should come with us," said Kaha after a moment."

"Very well," replied the chief.

"You are here to rescue us?" said the *Signora*. The first words she'd spoken.

The priest seemed disinterested and hadn't said a word. His breathing was torturous.

"We are, and we do need to leave now," Kaha replied. He turned to the chief. "I think we should revise the plan a little. Let me take Wright and go to the engine room, and you and Alden take Pam, the *Signora* and the priest to the stern and hide them. Leave the major and the young seaman here until Wright, and I return. If he is secure and gagged, he can't alert anyone. You'll have enough to do getting everyone aboard the *Kralj Mora* without having to worry about him. We'll pick him up on our way back and leave the lad." Owen nodded in understanding. "You'll need to be careful with the priest, he doesn't look at all well."

"Aye, aye, sir," replied the chief.

"You ready?" asked Kaha to Leading Seaman Wright.

"Aye, sir."

"My name is Kaha."

"But you're a bloody officer, though," replied Owen with a grin.

Kaha didn't reply, then turned and made brief eye contact with Pam. Their unspoken words reaffirmed their love. He held her gaze a moment, then he and Wright immediately left the cabin while Owen and Alden began assisting the priest out of the crew's mess. The *Signora* helped Pam, leaving the major and the young seaman alone.

The main berthing area for the crew aboard the *Trabant* was below deck and forward of the engine room. The upper-level cabins for officers and specialists. By Kaha's estimation, they had only been aboard the trawler for about seven minutes. It seemed a lifetime but now came the most challenging part, getting to the engine room undetected. If the engine weren't disabled, the Austrians would come after them soon as they discovered the major was captive, and the prisoners were taken.

With caution, they began to descend to the lower level, and other than the vibration and noise of the engine, they hadn't seen or heard a sound from anyone. As Owen had explained earlier, this type of ship was crewed by technical people, not frontline experienced sailors you'd find on a fighting ship. It was a small consolation.

CHAPTER TWENTY-EIGHT

Leading Seaman James Wright of Her Majesty's Royal Navy undogged the latches and swung open the heavy fire-proof door to the *Trabant*'s engine room. Immediately the clatter and din assaulted them, it was noisy and unbelievably loud. Kaha followed Wright into the space, his pistol levelled and sweeping in arcs before him. The handgun stopped its rhythmic swing and settled on the figure standing in front of a bank of gauges and dials. It was too loud to yell to the man who stood two yards away, however, yelling instructions wasn't required, the man understood his predicament and dropped the clipboard and raised his arms. With his pistol, Kaha indicated the man should lower himself to the deck.

Wright encountered another man, surprising him by tapping his pistol on his shoulder. When he turned to see who had interrupted his work, he saw the barrel of a gun pointed directly into his face. With a look of resignation and some fear, the man also raised his oil-stained hands. Wright led him to where Kaha stood, and within moments, he too felt the uncomfortable steel deck hurting his knees. Not a word was spoken.

A quick search revealed no other men were in the engineering spaces, and Wright began looking for what he needed. Kaha expected him to use a specialised tool to make some lethal adjustments to the engine to disable it. Instead, Wright turned to the bulkhead and immediately found what he sought, a fireman's axe.

Pocketing his pistol, he stepped closer to the gauges, drew the heavy axe up and behind, then powered his arms down in a mighty swing. Kaha turned to the engineers, and they looked on in horror. The sharp axe connected simultaneously with two gauges and destroyed them, knocking them from the pipe where they were once attached, steam began to leak from the ruptured pipes, and Wright swung again and again. Each time the axe connected, more steam began to leak.

Kaha and Wright had been in the engine room for less than three minutes, and already he could feel the ship beginning to slow. Wright swung again and again. He struck larger pipes, and they quickly ruptured, pumping scalding hot steam into the room.

Finding some cable, Kaha tied both Austrians to a bulkhead as Wright continued his destruction.

One pipe bigger than the others took Wright's fancy, and he swung hard, and the axe bounced from the pipe, causing only the paint to chip. Each time he swung the axe, the pipe remained undamaged. Kaha was about to tap him on the shoulder, as it was time to leave when with a concerted effort, Wright brought the axe down hard where he'd struck the pipe before. It cracked and immediately began to leak super-heated steam.

The effect was almost instantaneous, and the ship slowed further. Wright had wreaked havoc in the engine room and would take some time and skill to repair. The rolling motion of the boat seemed exaggerated as she was broadside to the swell and not making weigh, within seconds, the *Trabant* came to a completed standstill. They had succeeded in disabling the trawler, and now it was time to leave.

Both men ran from the engine room and began ascending the ladder to the accommodation deck when a figure ran past, a torn sheet trailed from his wrist. It was Richter, somehow he'd become untied and escaped. Kaha knew the capture of an Austrian military intelligence officer represented a significant coup for British intelligence and no doubt could provide a wealth of valuable information. If he hurried, he might still catch the fleeing man. An image of seeing Pam forced to go with Richter and then to watch helplessly as she slumped over after being shot in Pescara filled his mind. He saw the severely beaten priest and the fearful expression of the kidnapped *Signora*. It wasn't a decision that required much thinking about.

Kaha swung himself up and onto the passageway, and without pause, levelled his pistol, sighted and shot. The major tumbled in a heap to the deck. Kaha had no idea if he killed him, and he couldn't check, it was time to go.

In total confusion, crewmen hastily buttoning uniforms appeared from doorways. Uncertain to what was happening, they presumed Kaha was one of them, he hid his pistol. Still buttoning his trousers, an officer stumbled from a cabin, on seeing Kaha, he yelled, "*Was ist los?*"

Not understanding, Kaha presumed the man wanted to know what was happening. He pointed down the ladder and spoke one of the three German words he knew. "*Da!*"

The officer never saw the body of Richter further down the passageway as he descended the ladder, causing additional confusion as men tried to climb up.

Now, more than ever, they needed to get off this boat as fast as possible.

Leading Seaman Wright led the way, and soon they were on the main deck where the radio equipment was when the electronic sound of an alarm sounded. They hurried down the passageway.

One door previously closed was now open, as Kaha ran past, he glanced in, a man sat at a radio with a headset over his ears and was frantically speaking into a microphone. Kaha stopped.

"Go without me, I'll be right there," he shouted to Leading Seaman Wright.

Perplexed, Wright stopped and turned around. At the same time, a seaman appeared at the end of the passageway waving a rifle, and in the narrow confines of the passageway, he struggled to bring his weapon to bear. Wright watched Kaha disappear into the Radio Room cabin, and now with an unobstructed view, easily raised his pistol and squeezed the trigger. It was a good shot and struck the sailor on his chest. The impact drove the sailor back into the bulkhead, causing him to release the rifle, which clattered away, and a dark stain began spreading across his tunic. He slowly crumpled to the deck.

James Wright heard Kaha yell for him to keep going, then the door to the radio room was closed.

Inside, Kaha was frantic, he ripped the headphones from the operator, grabbed a fistful of wires and yanked hard, pulling them from the equipment they were connected to. With an experienced eye, he scanned the room, shelves, and desk. He knew what he was looking for and found it quickly.

Realising what the stranger was doing, the radio operator resisted and lunged up at Kaha, forcing him back against the door. The Austrian was big and strong and tried to get his hands around Kaha's throat. The radio room, as was every other cabin in the ship, was small and cramped, there was no room to move. Kaha was trapped by a larger and more powerful opponent. The more he struggled, the tighter the Austrian squeezed. He began to feel fingers firmly pressing against his windpipe.

He brought up a knee, the Austrian deflected it, he tried again, with the same result, and now the larger man began to apply more pressure with his hands. Kaha tried pushing and twisting, but the radio operator was strong, and in the restricted space, he couldn't use his speed or skills. It was entirely a contest of strength, and he was losing. Kaha released his grip on the man, dropped a hand low below the belt, and grabbed the Austrian's testicles. He screamed and released Kaha, preferring to defend his manhood than fight. It was all Kaha needed, he placed his hand on the forehead of the Austrian and, with all his weight, pushed. The Austrian caught unaware and still in pain, stepped back a half pace, then another, soon Kaha had momentum, and the Austrian was reeling backwards, out of balance and out of control. The back of his head slammed into a radio mounted high on a shelf, and he stopped resisting, he slid to the deck unconscious. Kaha rested his hands on his thighs as he gulped lungsful of beautiful air.

With a sense of urgency, Kaha pocketed the Austrian codebook, and opened the door, and stepped out into the passageway. All he saw were men running in different directions as they scrambled to reach their assigned stations, in the confusion, he was ignored.

Kaha made it to the exterior hatch and stepped out into the darkness. After the brightness of the lights inside, his visibility was limited. Without hesitation, he pulled the pistol from his waistband and waited near the door in case anyone followed him. Once he determined he was safe, he jogged aft to the stern of the trawler and looked for the *Kralj Mora* – she was gone.

He knew there was a valid reason, they wouldn't just leave him. He looked out beyond the stern again, saw nothing but darkness. He crouched down behind a chain locker, beside the body of the Austrian lookout, and waited.

Voices drifted down to him from forward, instructions were being issued, and from the sound of things, the Austrians weren't happy. Eventually, once order had been restored, they'd begin a systematic search of the ship – and they'd find him.

The wind still raced across the deck but because the ship wasn't under power, she was drifting, her bow began to swing head-to-wind. The angle had changed, and he reasoned that the *Kralj Mora* would approach from the starboard side. Before he could look, he heard a doorway open and more voices, this time closer. He lay down on the deck and peeked around the corner of the locker. There were three men, each armed, two with rifles and one with a pistol. Kaha slid back and checked the ammunition on his gun. He would have to shoot his way out of this.

The three sailors were cautious and approached slowly, he could hear their measured footfalls, they were only five yards away. He inched back as far as he could go and still remained out of sight when the sound of rifle fire ripped through the night. He heard a body fall. Again, another volley and another man fell. The remaining sailor fled, the sound of running feet was unmistakable.

"Kaha!" came the voice from the blackness. He heard it again. "Kaha!"

The Kralj Mora. He looked out and saw nothing, but then, from the darkness, he saw the huge lateen sail, then the hull, as the *Kralj Mora* appeared. Surprising him, the fishing boat came from the southwest. It was clever, he realised, Boris was keeping the boat out of sight from the Austrians and her forward-mounted gun for as long as possible.

The bow of the fishing boat inched ever closer, only yards away. Then the exterior door to the deck opened, and more sailors began filing out. This was it, they'd come for him with reinforcements.

Before he was spotted, Kaha climbed over the safety rail and crouched on the stern at the corner of the transom. He had only seconds before he was discovered, and the distance was still too wide to jump across safely. Above the wind, he heard a shout, they'd seen him, and he had no choice, either attempt the jump or be captured.

Kaha put all his effort into the leap, and he launched himself across the two-yard gap. The bow of the *Kralj Mora* dipped, then rose quickly to meet him as a wave passed under the hull. He bounced off the gunwale and toppled into the fishing boat, crashing heavily onto the deck. A flailing arm struck Chief Petty Officer Owen on the back of the head. Kaha didn't move, it hurt to move.

He closed his eyes in agony as Boris dropped the bow away from the Austrian ship. He heard Chief Petty Officer Owen's voice shouting at Price to trim. Gunfire from the stern told him Able Seaman Henning was keeping the Austrians heads down, and then he felt tender, familiar hands touch him. Despite the pain, he smiled.

Chief Petty Officer Owen was stomping all over the boat as Boris, tireless as ever, kept *Kralj Mora* sailing fast and heading towards the Italian coast many miles distant. The grey smear of dawn was approaching, and they had already been sailing for a few hours. Owen was perplexed. "He's gone, I tell ya, and someone must a seen something!"

At first, even Boris looked puzzled. Other than Kaha and Pam, who both suffered from serious injuries, everyone else looked around the boat. The *Signora* had not spoken much, she had remained diffident, preferring to sit away from the others, but near the priest – and that was the problem, the priest had gone. He'd vanished.

"Perhaps he decided to off his-self," said Alden.

"Why would he have done that, then, huh? We just went an rescued him, then he goes an does his-self in – not bloody likely. You young chappies think you're so smart," replied Petty Officer Owen with a measure of feigned disgust.

Boris spared another glance towards the *Signora*, she sat on the deck with her arms wrapped around her knees and stared at her feet. He knew what happened to his friend, he knew exactly what happened, his mouth tightened. Because of Stevan, he'd almost lost his son, and innocent people had nearly died. The signora raised her head, met his eyes and held his gaze. He nodded imperceptibly and she lowered her head.

Able Seaman Henning, who sat near the bow, saw it first. "I think we may have a problem, chief!" He pointed southward.

Temporarily forgetting the mystery of the disappearing priest, Chief Petty Officer Owen stood, clomped forward of the mast and stared where Henning indicated.

"And there, look!"

"I see another, yes," cried Boris pointing in another direction on the horizon.

Three ships were bearing down on them, one small ship and two larger ones. Everyone preyed they weren't Austrian's responding to the distress call made from the *Trabant*'s radio-room, but as Boris pointed out, what could they do if they were?

Owen continued to stare at the horizon. "Well, blow me down, I'd bet my first pint that the ship in the middle is the old girl herself, the *Bangor Castle*. What the dickens are they doing coming this far north?"

"They lookings for us?" said Boris. His expression softened with a grin.

"Cap'n Sanders … that cheeky bugger, he must have been in communication with the fleet the entire time," said Owen.

"Maybe they know where the priest went," suggested Leading Seaman Wright.

Boris said nothing.

EPILOGUE

London, England.

The young woman was stylish, some would say elegant, and a few men she passed on the street appreciated her refined good looks and carriage with a casual head turn and a smile. She wore her maroon dress fashionably short, which revealed a twelve-inch gap between her shoes and the hem of her dress. Choosing to forgo dated button-up boots, her new shoes were more feminine and had a high heel that added an inch or two to her height. Today was sunny and warm, and since she wasn't walking far, an overcoat wasn't required.

Her blonde hair was cut short and curled just beneath her ears, and she chose not to wear a hat. Her unblemished face revealed clear blue eyes, a delicate nose and full lips.

In contrast to her preference for tasteful accoutrements, she carried a worn leather satchel over her shoulder, marring what many men would have described as pure perfection. Further, her sense of style ended any similarity between her and other women of a similar age and God-given beauty because Miss Covington was also an expert in martial arts. She could inflict severe and permanent injury to an unwary assailant, and in her capacity as a messenger for British Intelligence, she was alert and, if need be, fully prepared to defend herself and the satchel with her life.

Miss Covington departed 'Room 40' in the Old Admiralty Building and walked briskly down Whitehall Place, where she turned right on to Whitehall Court. Without pausing, she entered number two, and escorted by an over-friendly orderly, she clip-clopped down long hallways, her maroon dress swishing in rhythm, until she reached her destination. The orderly, impressed with his dashing good looks, tried to engage Sarah Covington in conversation, and regrettably, for him, the outcome was always the same – failure.

"Miss Covington, how lovely to see you this morning," said the receptionist.

Sarah Covington looked over her shoulder at the disappearing and handsome orderly. He would eventually learn that messengers would never engage with anyone while they worked.

She turned back to the receptionist and smiled in response to the greeting, "Good Morning, Mrs Booth. Mr Sykes?"

The receptionist rose from her chair. "This way," and led Miss Covington to the office of Michael Sykes.

"What do you have for me, Sarah?" asked Sykes with a warm smile.

Miss Covington removed the satchel from her shoulder and took a seat. With the bag on her lap, she unlocked the sturdy latch and extracted a cardboard folder. Attached to the folder's exterior was a piece of paper which she unpinned and handed to him.

Without glancing at it, Sykes completed the formality and signed his name, noted the time, acknowledged receipt of the radio reports, and handed the paper back in exchange for the folder. Sarah could finally relax; her job was done.

"These new shoes are killing me, Michael," she said, rubbing her calves."

Michael risked a glance around the side of his desk.

"Do you have anything for me?" she asked, rising to her feet.

"Oh – uh, no, Sarah, that will be all. Have a good day," he replied, tearing himself away from the fantasy of Sarah Covington's much-discussed and rather long legs.

Sarah smiled, hung the satchel from her shoulder and left the office, "See you soon," she said, turning at the door and giving him a little wave.

As she returned to the Old Admiralty building where encrypted radio messages were received and decoded for Military Intelligence, Michael Sykes returned to the realities of the present. He opened the folder and began to read the communication reports.

"Yes, what is it, Marge?" answered Mansfield Smith–Cumming.

"Michael Sykes wishes a moment of your time, sir."

"Show him in, dear."

Marge opened the door, and Sykes appeared.

"How can I help you, Michael?" The director placed the document he was reading into a folder, then put it into a desk drawer. "Take a seat." Smith-Cumming waved to a chair.

"In reply to our request, we just received more details on Anchor and Chain, sir."

"From Sarah?"

Sykes inclined his head, evoking a smile from the director. Miss Covington's visits were always welcomed and were a healthy talking point with the bachelors.

"Let's hope our questions are answered, eh?"

Sykes smiled. "Anchor and Chain are now aboard a hospital ship bound for Gibraltar. Medical reports indicate that Chain suffered a fractured skull due to a beating she received from Major Maximillian Richter, which was also compounded by a gunshot wound to her head. Doctors who have looked at her don't believe there will be any lasting effects. On the other hand, Anchor suffered two broken ribs and a fractured collar bone."

"Was he shot, too?" asked the director.

"No, it seems he jumped between the Austrian RDF ship and the fishing boat, apparently the gap was too wide, and he landed awkwardly and quite heavily on the gunwale."

Smith-Cumming winced.

"The bad news is Major Richter survived, he was seen in Austria a day or so ago sporting a bandage."

"Can't win 'em all lad, better luck next time. He's a piece of work that one is."

"Anchor nearly had him... so close." Sykes shook his head. "Oh yes, the Austrian codebook is being couriered here as we speak. Room 40 will enjoy getting their hands on that, I'm sure."

"Yes, although I'm not sure how valuable it will be. On discovery that their codebook is missing, they'll change everything pretty damn quick," said Smith–Cumming, distractedly. He leaned back in his chair, deep in thought.

"Something bothering you, sir?"

"I'm still trying to understand why Major Richter had such an interest in the priest. And the only people who can answer that question with a certain degree of accuracy is Richter, the Italian woman–"

"Natalina Milani, sir," added Sykes.

Smith-Cumming nodded. " – and the priest, Belić. According to information I received, Milani isn't talking, and she refuses to discuss anything to do with him. I had Bruno Bottini, our Rome Military liaison pay her a visit and the poor man was almost beaten to death by her new husband."

"Oh dear, a sensitive topic. I hadn't heard that – uh, she married?"

Smith-Cummings raised an eyebrow. "Yes, a rush marriage, she wed a chap called Enzo. Locals say it was destined to happen. So they say, he'd been in love with her for years. I hear the woman is quite a looker."

Both men remained silent for a moment. Finally, Sykes spoke. "Any theories on what happened to the priest? His disappearance is so peculiar."

"It certainly wasn't Anchor or Chain, they were both injured. The fisherman was his friend, and he was helming the boat at the time, so it couldn't have been him. Then there are the five seamen from the *Bangor Castle*. I've had someone look into their backgrounds, and none of them had any motive or links to Serbia or Croatia."

"Then that leaves the Italian woman," suggested Sykes.

"So how did she do it without anyone seeing, Michael?

End

Author's notes

The epic and lengthy journey of writing this novel was an incredible learning experience for me. I called on the expertise of many people, all international authorities in their respective fields, and all gave me their time and patiently answered my endless questions without complaint.

The events leading to the outbreak of WWI are frequently misunderstood or simply not known. During that time, the various treaties between European countries were confusing, and I hope I have presented that information in a useful way. I have also tried to be faithful to history and detailed the murder of the Crown Prince and his wife as accurately as possible. Whether or not war would have broken out if the assassinations had not happened is open to scholarly debate. I believe war was destined, the region at that time was volatile, and any incident could have sparked an immediate response, ultimately resulting in conflict.

Although a work of fiction, this book contains some events and people who existed and were known public figures, while others are purely fictional and created by my addled and fertile mind.

Notably, the Secret Service Bureau Director, Mansfield Smith-Cumming, was a very real person. Author Ian Fleming based his James Bond character 'M' on Smith-Cumming. The letter 'M' was inspired by the director's first name, Mansfield. I chose to be as authentic as possible and retained his name and penchant for signing documents in green ink, with the letter 'C', the initial for his surname. All other Secret Service Bureau characters I wrote of in this novel are fictitious.

Kaha and Pam Peterson did not exist and are my creations. The *Mana* is based on an actual sailboat that makes her home in California, USA.

The details and background detailing the assassination of Crown Prince Archduke Franz Ferdinand of Austria and his wife, Sophie, the Duchess of Hohenberg, are based on reported historical facts, even down to the clothes they wore. I even used their actual dialogue in this story, in the sequence immediately after they were shot. When the prince was fatally wounded, his wife actually did utter, "For heaven's sake! What happened to you?" To me, her reaction seemed so stiff and formal, yet surprisingly, transcripts detail they were her exact words.

I found many written discrepancies surrounding the 1910 Graef & Stift Type Double Phaeton open tourer automobile the royal couple travelled in. Most articles I read stated the vehicle did not have a reverse gear and had to be pushed back when they stopped at the café after the driver made the wrong turn. I wasn't convinced this was accurate and, with persistence, eventually discovered the vehicle did, in fact, have the capability to drive in reverse, as I described.

The names of all members of the Black Hand organisation and what happened to them are factual. The exception was Father Stevan Belić, who did not exist. The details surrounding their political ideology and the events, as they transpired that fateful morning, are again – all based on actual recorded historical documentation, including all their weapons and the cyanide capsules.

Few maps, if any, now list the Republic of Ragusa. After WWI, Ragusa was renamed Dubrovnik, which lies in southern Croatia on the shores of the Adriatic Sea. It is doubtful a ferry travelled between Ragusa and Pescara as I described.

The *Falkuša* is a real fishing boat with an *unusual design feature* to aid fishermen with hauling their nets aboard. I used all available information to describe this remarkable boat and even double-checked the claims on its speed with naval architects. Certainly, Boris Marković, and his son Zoran, did not exist.

To advance the plot and exercise my right as a creative writer, I have taken a few liberties to alter the timeline and add embellishments, all mistakes are entirely my own.

Thank you for reading, and if you haven't yet done so, please grab a copy of my other historical fiction novels.

Paul W. Feenstra

Website www.PaulWFeenstra.com
Please leave a review and follow me on Face Book, Twitter, Instagram and Pinterest.

www.ingramcontent.com/pod-product-compliance
Lightning Source LLC
Chambersburg PA
CBHW060815120726
47909CB00006B/1928